The TRUE

Amanda Marks

Antler House
Press

First published in Great Britain in 2019 by Antler House Press

Amanda Marks has asserted her right under the Copyright, Designs and Patents Act 1988 to be identified as the author of this work.
www.amandamarks.co.uk

Cover paintings and inside drawings by Deborah Vass.

ISBN: 978-1-9161422-0-6

Antler House Press
Suffolk IP6 9JW

For Mum and Dad, who gave me a lovingly made pair of wings.
For my sister and good friends, who helped me learn to fly.
For Guy, who has thankfully shared much of the journey with me.
And for my amazing boys — always soar to the treetops.

Contents

SHE ARRIVED WITH SPRING   1

Chapter 1: FOG   16

Chapter 2: KILCAITH CASTLE   26

BIRCH   35

Chapter 3: TRUE   37

ROWAN   42

Chapter 4: THE LECTURE   44

ASH   60

Chapter 5: THE HAWK & THE HERON   62

Chapter 6: THE COVERT   73

Chapter 7: JUMPERS   86

BEECH   93

Chapter 8: HORSESHOE PRIORY   95

Chapter 9: THE EVERY TREE   111

Chapter 10: CONNECTION   122

Chapter 11: THE STRANGER   130

ALDER   146

Chapter 12: THE KING'S HEAD   148

Chapter 13: THE VALLEY   160

OAK   165

Chapter 14: SCIENTIA POTENTIA EST   167

Chapter 15: ITCH SCRATCH ITCH   176

Chapter 16: PULLING THREADS   188

WILLOW   195

Chapter 17: BABES IN THE WOOD   197

Chapter 18: CLOUDBERRY 210

Chapter 19: WANTED 224

Chapter 20: FUTURE, PAST, PRESENT 235

Chapter 21: THE PATIENT 241

SYCAMORE 245

Chapter 22: YAN, TYAN, TETHERA 247

Chapter 23: MESSAGE IN A BOTTLE 255

Chapter 24: PAPER KISSES 260

Chapter 25: LOST AND FOUND 266

Chapter 26: ROCK ART 273

Chapter 27: REVELATION 283

Chapter 28: THE RECORD PLAYER 292

Chapter 29: EN GARDE 303

Chapter 30: DAMSEL IN DISTRESS 309

Chapter 31: WAIFS AND STRAYS 316

Chapter 32: HORIZONTAL LINES 322

Chapter 33: SAMHAIN 329

YEW 337

Chapter 34: UNFINISHED BUSINESS 339

Chapter 35: A SPIDER'S WEB 346

Chapter 36: ARBOREAL SCRIBE 353

WOODLAND 362

A message from the author 365

PEOPLE & PLACES 366

ACKNOWLEDGEMENTS 368

We are woodland and we are never silent. Never.
Do you hear our voice?
Wind often makes our trees dance and shake to the rhythm of
the day, be it a gentle, leaf-ruffling breeze or an all-out branch-
cracking gale. Rain falls demurely onto our blankets of
welcoming greenery with a hushed sigh, or spitefully stabs
anything in its path in a desire to be heard. Birds sing sweet
songs from our boughs and branches, squirrels scritchety-
scratch up our trunks of wrinkly bark, and throngs of insects
hum incessantly around us.
But these sounds are not our voice.
Only a few remaining wise hearts hear our voice
— the ancient word of the forest —
and understand the true connection.
Listen.
We are a living, breathing, connected community.
We are alive.
We are life.

SHE ARRIVED WITH SPRING

Monday, May 1st, 2000

Coquetdale Wildwood Festival was getting more popular each year. This year Nick thought he'd probably taken enough orders to give him at least six months of work and you never knew what else might come of it. He wasn't a man that money held much sway over, but it was comforting to know that he had extra income to supplement his woodland coppicing.

Nick Robson was a woodsman and skilled furniture maker. He always said he could read the wood he worked with. He could look at a tree or piece of wood and see the shapes locked inside it. He worked with the organic essence of the wood to fashion uniquely beautiful tables and chairs or, occasionally, sculptures if his mood and the grain dictated. He saw it as a partnership. The trees talked to him; he listened. Of course, nothing and no-one would ever hear this big thirty-six-year-old bearded, wild-living Northumbrian woodsman expressing such un-Northern sentiments; not even the eco-warrior-hippy-dippy section at the Wildwood festival knew his real feelings about trees.

1

His granddad Archie had understood though. Nick had lived with him from the age of eight. His young, city-loving parents never seemed to have much time for him, so he'd begged Archie to let him come and live with him. Looking back, he was surprised his parents had agreed. He'd seen them quite rarely as he was growing up and now, never.

Archie had seen that, even at the tender age of eight years old, the boy had an affinity with wood that had skipped his son's generation. He'd encouraged and nurtured Nick's innate sensitivity and taught him the skills that were to make him a very special craftsmen in years to come. The pair were inseparable. Archie was full of stories and loved playing the Northumbrian pipes, and they roamed the local woods and fells together with the old woodsman constantly teaching him about the natural world all around them. When Archie died in an horrific workshop accident two years ago, it was as if Nick had lost his whole family. Archie *was* his family. He had a second-cousin he was fond of, just a few miles away, but Kate was a busy sheep farmer and they rarely got together other than meeting up at local country fairs and for the odd night in the pub.

Nick dismantled his festival tent stand and packed it all into his Land Rover pickup. Using old blankets, he carefully wrapped the oak coffee table which had been so admired over the last two days. Visitors had responded well to the waney-edged table top with its central leg in the shape of a tree trunk with branches supporting the top. He'd had twelve orders for similar tables, plus at least sixteen chairs of various sizes and styles. His oak leaf maker's mark, handed down from his granddad, was already proudly displayed in quite a few well-to-

2

do Northumbrian homes and his reputation for quality craftsmanship was starting to spread in ever-widening circles thanks to a mixture of word-of-mouth recommendations and festivals such as these.

The other godsend of this festival was how close it was to home. Half an hour's drive and he would be back in his wood at his cosy, self-built log cabin. For Nick, its secluded position in the midst of the woodland he managed and coppiced for a living completely outweighed its lack of modernities.

'Come on, Meg, let's go home. I think we've had enough of people for a while, don't you?'

His border collie jumped up into the passenger seat. Nick waved at some of his fellow stall-holder friends on the way out of the festival field and they headed home. He liked many of the other woodsmen he knew from the festival and rated some of them highly in what they did, but he had learned over the years that, at heart, he was comfortable being a loner most of the time. It was less hassle. Just him, his trees and his dog, Meg. It was enough. He was happy.

He parked up on the rough, muddy lane just below his workshop and decided to leave the unpacking until he'd got a fire going. He walked up to his cabin, Meg racing ahead of him through the birch, holly and rowan that predominated in this area of his wood. The bluebells were going to be beautiful this year. They weren't fully out yet, but already far enough on to give you that feeling of floating in a lake of blue. At the moment, though, it was the carpet of starry white stitchwort adjacent to the bluebells that drew the eye. The rowan would be coming into flower in perhaps a couple of weeks, he thought, and he could already taste the rowan jelly he'd be making in a few short months. The seasons seemed to roll by so fast once May arrived.

Meg saw her before he did and barked a short warning to Nick. She'd obviously been asleep on the wooden bench by his open-sided workshop but was startled awake by the noise.

Oh Christ, not one of the eco-warrior lot, surely? What was she doing here? This place was quite a walk from the festival. She certainly looked weird enough to be one of that crowd though, he thought, as he got closer. He noticed she was wearing a long dress and had painted her face and ... No, no, not paint.

'Bloody Nora.'

All Nick's annoyance at having his privacy invaded evaporated as he realised she was hurt. In fact, it looked like she'd been in an accident.

'Oh my God, what happened to you?' he asked, dropping his backpack and rushing towards her. She rose, looking frightened, but immediately crumpled, her legs unable to hold her up. As she sat in a heap on the ground, Nick noticed that her initial fleeting look of fear turned into an expression of resignation, as if she simply couldn't care what might happen to her.

The young woman was in her early twenties. She had almost waist-length brown hair tied back in a long, dishevelled plait. Her dress looked to Nick like a fancy dress costume for a Shakespeare play, but the front had been roughly torn down the middle, and she feebly and unsuccessfully tried to keep the sections together. But it was her face that Nick couldn't keep his eyes from. Her left eye was an angry purple and nearly closed, her lip was cut and swollen, her cheek streaked with

4

dried blood. No, this was no accident. Someone had made a real mess of her, and not too long ago.

She let Nick help her up from the ground and back onto the bench. He fetched a blanket from his workshop and gently put it around her shoulders. He asked her name and whether she needed anything, perhaps painkillers, but she didn't reply. She wasn't listening. More than pain, it was shock written large on her almost blank, battered and tear-stained features.

At first, he tried to get her to talk while he sorted the fire, but she just clutched the blanket around her, rocked slightly and stared into a nothingness some two feet in front of her. Nick had looked after enough injured animals in his time to know that it was very hard to get through to any creature in this kind of state.

Eventually, he put a mug of hot sweet tea in her hands and wordlessly encouraged her to drink. She did, registering momentary slight surprise at the taste. He also gave her a clean wad of cotton soaked in cooled boiled water with marigold tincture.

'Hold this to your face. It might help a bit.'

She half-smiled very briefly and held it to her right eye.

He took a stool nearby with his own tea. He didn't know what to say, so he said nothing. His gut feeling was that the girl didn't need any more coercion today, even verbally, so he sat, they drank, and he waited.

Another cup of sweet tea later, she put down her mug and turned fleetingly towards him.

'Thank you.'

'You're welcome. Can I ask your name?'

'Eleanor,' she said, in a flat tone, pulling the blanket further

5

round her as the evening started to get colder. Nick could see she was shivering, probably due to both the dipping temperature and her obvious trauma.

He wanted to find the right words, but where did you start?

'OK. Eleanor. Good.' He rubbed the back of his neck with his right hand and tried to decide how best to handle the situation. He decided to go for practicalities.

'Well, you've obviously been badly hurt. You need to be cared for. Is there a friend I can get in touch with for you? Can I take you to the hospital? I don't have a phone here, but there's one in the village.' He vaguely pointed in the direction of the nearest village, Mellerton, about three miles away.

Eleanor stared at the fire. Nick could see that she was in her own world and wasn't really taking anything in. He didn't want to leave her, so he decided that the best thing he could do was make her as comfortable and warm as possible for tonight and then try again tomorrow. She refused an offer to use the bed in his cabin, so he brought out an old camp bed he used to use and placed it near the fire.

'Come on, pet,' he said, as he helped her to the camp bed. 'Rest. I promise no-one will hurt you tonight. I'll stay here by the fire with you.'

She let him help her and he covered her with blankets. He stoked the fire and prepared to settle down for the night on an old armchair at the other side of the campfire from his uninvited guest. He automatically put his hand down to reach for Meg to find that his best friend and shadow had set up guard by Eleanor's bed.

Eleanor and Meg were nowhere to be seen when Nick woke

early the next morning, chilled and with a crick in his neck. He was surprised he hadn't heard her get up and leave.

'Meg!' he called, and she quickly came running over to him from the edge of the east side of the wood. Not far behind her, Eleanor also came walking out of the wood. Nick could see immediately that she had found some composure this morning. She had re-plaited her hair, washed her face and had found some way to keep her dress together. Twigs by the looks of it. He smiled inwardly at her ingenuity.

'Good morning,' he said, as she walked towards him. 'How are you feeling this morning?'

He could see her try to hold herself very straight and tall. And she was tall. About five foot ten, he guessed.

'I thank you for your kindness last night, sir. I should not have intruded on you. Please accept my apologies. I will disturb you no longer.'

She spoke calmly, but her words were overly polite, almost stilted. He noticed she had a lowland Scottish lilt. Perhaps not local then. Nick could see her struggling hard to keep control of her emotions as she spoke, but the sadness and emptiness in her face was still all-consuming.

'Nick, my name is Nick. So, can I take you somewhere you'll be looked after? Someone's bound to be searching for you.'

'No. No-one is searching. I have no-one now.'

She stopped by the campfire. The admission seemed to hit her hard and silent tears began to run down her bruised face.

'She's gone,' she said, in a strangled whisper, utter desolation flooding her features.

'Gone? Who's gone?' Nick was confused. He'd been

7

expecting her to talk about a personal attack. Was someone missing?

'Who hurt you, Eleanor? Don't you think we should get you to a doctor?'

''Tis not important. This is merely skin deep,' she said, dismissing her dramatic-looking injuries with a small flick of her hand. 'My body will mend if I let it.'

If she let it? He didn't like the sound of that.

'Where will you go?' he asked, trying another tack.

'I— I don't yet know.' She stood staring at the dregs of the fire in front of them.

Nick rubbed his rough hands through his untamed hair. What the hell was he supposed to do with her? He couldn't just let her go wandering off aimlessly by herself in that state. But this was no place for a woman, as he'd been told on more than one occasion, let alone a woman in the kind of distress she was in. And yet, she certainly wasn't quite like any woman he'd come across before.

'Well,' he ventured, 'if you're certain you don't want to go to the hospital or the police, and you don't know where you should go, why don't you stay here for a while? If you want to, that is. Though I can imagine that's the last thing you'd want to do given what you've ... well, given what's happened to you.'

Nick stopped and looked at her, wondering whether he should go on. She just stood, half looking at him, half looking through him. Turning to the fire, he squatted down and poked the dreary remnants with a stick, trying to chivvy some life into it.

'Look, I live alone here with Meg, so there's no-one to bother you,' he said, speaking into the non-existent fire. 'Maybe

8

a day or two here to gather your thoughts would be useful? I don't have much in the ways of comfort by most people's reckoning, but what I have you can share until you feel better.'

He turned and looked up at her to see if any of what he'd just said had registered.

For the first time, she stared directly at him and held his gaze. Her deep brown eyes seemed to look into his soul and he felt at once shy and curious about his silent inquisitor.

'Nick.' She said his name as if she were trying on new shoes for size. There was a long silence before she continued, speaking very slowly.

'I think you are an uncommon man, Nick. 'Tis my good fortune to find myself in your company. I have no-one to turn to. If your offer of help is genuinely meant, 'tis a kindness I accept. With gratitude.'

She smiled, then dropped her eyes back to the ashes of the fire.

Nick laughed. 'Uncommon? Hah, I think you'll find you're wrong there. I'm about as common as they come I'm afraid. But yes, of course I meant it. I'm not one for saying things I don't mean. But I have one condition. You take my bed in the cabin. I'll sleep out here in the workshop.'

Eleanor smiled and looked down at Meg, who had come to sit by her. She gave a nod of agreement to Nick.

'I accept your condition, sir. And I humbly thank you.'

'Right. Well. Ay. I mean ... that's good,' he said, again thinking what an odd, old-fashioned way of talking she had.

If he was honest, he'd not really been expecting Eleanor to stay, though he was happy enough to offer his woodland cabin as her haven for a few days. In his admittedly limited

9

experience of bringing women friends here, he'd mostly found that they quite enjoyed the "romance" of one night with intermittent electricity and no proper bathroom, but then found excuses not to stay again. He'd never yet found anyone who suited his way of life. He would have liked a partner, but he'd come to accept that his lifestyle was a bit too alternative for the women he was attracted to.

Between them, they got some breakfast together. It turned out that Eleanor knew her way around a fire, so Nick encouraged her to sort some eggs for breakfast while he did a bit of organising and tidying in his cabin. He knew that he still had a dress left by one of his very short-term girlfriends, so he dug that out. He'd been meaning to get it back to her at some point but thought the size might be about right for Eleanor. After breakfast, he showed the red cotton dress to her.

'I'm sure it's not the style you like,' he said, with a nod to her own dress, 'but I think it might fit you all right, if you'd like to try it. Perhaps it'll do til you can get yours mended?'

'I couldn't wear that. Such a beautiful bright colour and such fine fabric. No, this must be a very costly dress.'

Surprised at her reaction, he looked at the dress again in case he'd missed something obvious like a designer label.

'Oh! Well, I'm afraid my knowledge of the price of dresses isn't really up to scratch, but I'm pretty sure this is nothing particularly special. It belonged to a friend and I don't think she wants it back. Anyway,' he held the dress up against himself, 'you might as well take it. It's not really my colour or size.'

Eleanor smiled. It was the first time Nick had seen a genuine smile from her and it lit up her face — or at least half of it. She accepted the dress from him.

'So this type, this ... length of dress, these colours ... this is worn by ladies of all classes now?' she asked, as she carefully smoothed the fabric of the skirt against her leg.

That threw him. Was she playing with him or was she expecting an answer? He looked at her but found only an open questioning look.

'Er, well, I suppose this isn't exactly Yves St Laurent, but you've got to be pretty rich to get something designer, I reckon. But ay, I guess you'd say this is a pretty common style. It's not really my area of expertise, you know.'

'No, forgive me. I'm just not— not used to ... I come from quite a different type of, er, remote village. We don't have such clothes.'

Don't have such clothes. Hmm, there was no doubt she was an odd one all right, thought Nick, but he didn't want to delve into this right now. She could still be traumatised and maybe this had affected her. That gave him an idea.

'Look, if we heat some water I can rig you up a shower if you want. That might make you feel better, then you can get changed if you want to.' He clapped his hands together as he was wont to do before starting a new task. 'Does that sound like a plan?'

Eleanor agreed, though in a slightly confused manner which made Nick think she hadn't quite understood what he'd just said to her. God, maybe he really should get her to a doctor. She might have concussion or anything. Then he suddenly thought, oh Christ, she probably thinks I'm trying to get her out of her kit.

'Oh, hell,' he said, holding up his hands in the air. 'I'm really sorry, I shouldn't have suggested that. I meant nothing by

11

it, really, I don't want you to worry about me. I was just thinking you might feel better after a wash.'

'Ah, a wash. That would be most welcome. Your warm water idea sounds ... warmer than the river or the lough.' She smiled and he relaxed again knowing he hadn't upset her.

Her mention of the lough made him think that maybe she *was* local after all. The lough was a lonely stretch of water in the moorland, at the foot of the crags about a forty-minute walk away. It was a beautiful tarn frequented by teal and goosanders and surrounded by heather moorland and peat bogs, with bracken and bog myrtle, bilberry and cotton grass. Peregrine falcons and sparrowhawks loved the open skies here and Nick often went up to watch the red grouse and curlews and listen to the skylarks. He felt most at home amongst the trees, but sometimes a feeling of space and expansiveness was a welcome change.

The comforting pleasure of water flooded over her aching body. What a wonderful thing, she thought. Your own personal, warm waterfall. And he'd given her a cake of expensive-looking, sweet-smelling soap.

She still had a headache and her face was very sore, but it was her ribs that hurt most, where Richard had kicked her. The events of the previous day flooded back with horrible clarity, along with the shower of water.

It had all come to a head when their two-year-old daughter, Matty, had had a very rare tantrum. Richard had been drinking whisky steadily most of that day. Eleanor had kept out of his way, but he'd come and found her in their bedroom in mid-afternoon. Matty had been in a clingy mood all morning, so when Richard had decided that he wanted to exert his conjugal rights, the child became inconsolable at having to leave her mother's side and go with the nursemaid, Jane. Richard's self-control, negligible at the best of times, snapped. He grabbed the child from Eleanor, backhanding her across the face when she fought to keep her from him. She remembered falling, hitting her head on the table on the way down and then he'd aimed a swift kick at her prone frame, which her ribs felt the brunt of. She didn't think they were broken, but certainly badly bruised.

Matty was hysterical. Eleanor had screamed and begged Richard to leave their baby alone, but he was apoplectic, hurling insults, abuse and threats at her in a torrent of alcohol-fuelled bile.

'I should've known that the child of a witch would be an imperfect being. She has nothing of me, she's the Devil's spawn. I should have drowned her at birth,' he spat. 'And I should've killed you, not married you. Whore!' He kicked her again.

Matty screamed for her mother, who was now curled in a ball at Richard's feet, sobbing and beseeching her husband to have mercy on their child, who, she said, was simply upset.

'Upset? Upset!' The words exploded out of him. Then he stopped himself and continued in a quiet, malicious tone.

'I think, madam, you will soon know the meaning of that word.' He stormed out of the room taking the shrieking Matty with him.

The water had run out and she stood shivering under the remaining drips beneath the bucket. But now they'd found an outlet, the recent memories would not stop so easily as the flow of water.

She'd heard Matty's screams getting further and further away but, half-dazed and in great pain, she was incapable of following her daughter. Jane, who'd fled from the room when Richard began his tirade, returned to Eleanor's side. She supported Eleanor in getting over to the bed.

'Jane, you must go and see where he's taking Matty. Please,' she implored.

'I daren't. I've never seen him in such a foul temper. Forgive me, madam, but I just daren't.'

In the event, Richard had come back sooner than expected. Without Matty.

'Where is she, Richard? Please, where have you taken her?' begged Eleanor, rising from the edge of the bed.

Richard strode across the room towards her. Anger was still flaring in his eyes, but the voice was cold.

'She is gone. She will burden us no longer. Forget the child. She will not be returning.'

The anguished wail echoed through the cold stone walls of the house. It was extinguished with a fist to the side of the face, which rendered Eleanor almost insensible, and a punch to the stomach, which took most of her now unwanted breath away. Richard tore her bodice, threw her skirts up, and went through the business-like motions of raping his battered wife. All the while, though, it was his words, almost tenderly whispered in her ear, which did the most damage, hitting her like acid on her heart.

'This time we'll be certain the child is mine. With the Devil-child gone, you can stay here in the hall with me at all times. You forgo your freedom, madam, until you have borne me a healthy son to replace that— that earlier mistake.'

The sound that came from Eleanor was almost inhuman, more of a caterwaul than cry. Nick shot off his chair as if he'd been burned and rushed over to where he'd left Eleanor showering.

She was crouched on the ground, naked and wet, and now keening in a constant high pitch.

'Bloody Nora.'

He quickly grabbed the towel he'd given her and wrapped it round her. He then bent down and picked her up. He carried her to the cabin and sat on the bed with her on his knees, cradling her like a babe in arms and murmuring soothing sounds to calm the broken woman.

CHAPTER ONE

FOG

Monday, November 15th, 1723

It was early evening now. About five hours had passed. To Sam, it felt like five days.

Around three o'clock, a gang of fat grey clouds had snuffed out the untypically bright day as they barged their way over the Cheviot Hills from Scotland only to decide that they deserved a rest. They belly-flopped into Coquetdale, filling the valleys that lay between wild moorlands and sheep-scattered hills with a thick damp darkness, temporarily wiping this remote corner of Northumberland off the map.

If only his sense of foreboding could be so easily obliterated. She would be terrified. Please God, let her be found.

Fingers of fog clung to his sodden riding cloak as he walked through the front door of the White Swan. The inn's warm peaty fug was a welcome contrast to the insidious damp chill outside, but Sam Heron hardly noticed it in his eagerness for news. He had *almost* convinced himself that there would be good news by the time he reached this hub of local gossip; someone would surely have found her by now.

'Evenin' Sam,' said the landlord, with a serious nod when

he saw the tall young man coming through the doorway. 'Any luck?'

Sam dropped his hat on a table and sat down heavily on a high-backed bench. He knew he could do no more today, the blasted fog had seen to that. He'd kept looking as long as possible but it was hopeless now. For the last hour or so, he'd hardly been able to see past his horse's ears.

The landlord brought an ale over to him.

'Where've you looked?'

'Everywhere. All the places she loves. Hugo and I searched Middle Wood and down by the river all afternoon. He's gone back to the Hall by the west way to see if we missed her. There's been people looking all over. It's like the faeries took her. She's just vanished.'

Sam rubbed his hands roughly through his hair with an anguished growl before quickly downing the ale then immediately getting up to leave. He had to make his way back home to Moss Hall. His mother would be grief-stricken, but comfort and sympathy were not in his father's repertoire. Besides, it was Martha. Sir Richard had never even pretended to love his only daughter. He tolerated her. Just. Mostly.

As Sam passed the smoky peat fire, a man sitting hunched over a table staring into an ale jug mumbled at him.

'So, is it a *young* woman you've lost?'

Sam stopped. 'Aye, sir. Twenty-five years of age, wearing a green dress. Might you have seen her?'

'Might,' he said. 'All I know is I saw a group of riders heading border direction early this afternoon like. There was a young lass riding with one of the men and she was making a hell of a racket. I wouldn't wonder the fella wasn't deaf after riding with her too long.'

He cackled at the memory, then pointedly slid his empty jug in Sam's direction.

By the time Sam left the inn, only cold fury was stopping him from drowning in despair. From what the man had said, Sam was positive that he'd seen Martha and, more than that, he was as certain as he could be that the Taits had kidnapped her. The news could hardly have been worse.

Sam had never actually come face to face with the Herons' long-standing enemies from just over the border, but he was all too aware of the bitter rivalry that had been a brutal shaping force in both of these former Border Reiver families — families in the Scottish/English border regions that regularly attacked and reived from each other — for well over two centuries. His father had trained Sam to be a skilled fighter. *'Par valeur'* ('By bravery') was the family motto, and Sir Richard was determined that no son of a Heron was ever going to be bested by any of their enemies, especially the Taits.

The whole sorry saga between the Taits and the Herons began in 1598 when, after a Tait killed a son of the Heron chief on a reiving raid, the Herons kidnapped a young son of the Tait laird. This 'son-for-a-son' vengefulness had continued intermittently through the generations. Perhaps the most disturbing kidnapping had been the last one, in 1697. The victim was Sam's own mother. She was seventeen years old at the time, and the eldest daughter of the current Tait laird. It was the first time a female had been taken in the long and bloody history of the two families. Sam's father had used his considerable local influence to forcibly marry her within a day of taking her captive. This gave her family no choice but either

18

to try to kill her for acquiescing or to leave her with the Herons. She could not be taken back; her honour was now disgraced.

The shock felt by this overstepping of an unspoken and rare historic boundary between the families was palpable on both sides. After some initial intermittent blustering from the Taits, the heart seemed to go out of them and things had gone quiet between the foes for about twenty years. The Herons thought the aggressions had finally ended. They had struck the final blow. They'd won. Or so they thought, until now.

As he blindly inched his way up to Moss Hall in the fog, Sam's mind replayed the events of the morning.

He'd arrived back home with his cousin, Hugo, after delivering whisky over at Alnwick under the cover of darkness. The isolated hills of Coquetdale were a bleak place to live even by Northumbrian standards, making them the perfect hiding place for secret stills; the excisemen knew they were there but could never find them. Farming was how the land-owning Heron family mostly made their living, but they were also prolific whisky free-traders and Sam frequently ran deliveries to all parts of the county and beyond from their estate. Moss Hall had been the Heron home and stronghold for nearly three centuries. The substantial grey stone building glowered halfway up the hillside with only the bleak moors above it. Given the dangerous history of this border region, it was perhaps unsurprising that the house didn't look at all welcoming. The mean dimensions of its windows spoke of security being more important than comfort and, indeed, the house was mostly cold and dark inside. Sam's mother had always ensured that Martha's bedchamber (and his own when he was younger) had soft touches of flowers and her own beautifully-embroidered creations, but their father frowned upon frippery so only allowed trophies of stags' heads, old family portraits and displays of weaponry in the main halls.

On that fateful morning, Sam had untacked, fed and watered his horse; unlike cousin Hugo, he preferred to look after his animals himself when he could. By the time he'd finished, Martha was running out into the morning sunshine to greet him. Their father wouldn't allow his older sister the free run around the hall if they had guests — 'We don't need the world to know we have a halfwit in the house,' — but today it was just family and servants. She galloped across the yard like a beautiful leggy foal, holding up her green dress with one hand and clasping Dolly by the hair with the other.

'Sam, you're back,' she said, as she reached him. 'Hugo told me. He's in the kitchen. Where did you go?' She was full of smiles and hugged him fondly.

'Ah, there's my favourite Twiggle,' he said. 'And how are you this fine morning?'

Tall as she was, he picked her up and swung her round him; it always made her giggle. He loved to make her happy and when he succeeded, which was often, her joy was infectious. Such moments made all the more difficult times pale into insignificance. She was his big-little sister and he adored her.

'Again, again,' she said, jumping up and down. He obliged, then set her down on the worn stone mounting block.

'That's it, you've tired me out. Now, let me see,' he said, looking down at her stockinged feet, 'Don't you think you've forgotten something?'

She stuck her long legs out in front of her and wiggled her

20

toes, laughing.

'My shoes!'

'Mhm, and I think we should do something about that tatty hair, don't you, pet? Before Father sees? Where's Mama?'

The sound of footsteps on the yard cobbles made them both turn round.

'Mama is right here. I hope you're not keeping secrets from me, you two rascals.' She put her basket down next to them, took Martha's hand and squeezed and patted it lovingly.

'Sam's right, you know. You should have let Jane brush your hair this morning, so you can show the world what a pretty girl you are.'

'But she hurts, Mama,' said Martha, pulling a face. Her mother smiled and kissed her hand, then turned to Sam.

'I have to take some remedies to Elspeth Fairley over Alwinton way —'

'And half of the pantry too, by the looks of it,' he said, looking down at her basket. 'Come on then, let's get you away before Father rises. Don't concern yourself about Martha, I'll be here for her this morning.' He turned to Martha. 'It's such a lovely day, maybe we'll go to the river with the dogs later, eh, Twiggle? Why don't you go and put on some shoes and ask Jane to brush your hair?'

Martha ran back into the house and Sam carried his mother's basket to the stable where the groom was waiting with her pony. As he saw his mother off on one of her usual errands of mercy, he noticed a rider coming up towards the house from the direction of the village. They waved, and there was a glint of red hair in the morning light. Ah, Sarah. Now there was a sight to gladden a man's heart. Although she was probably coming with a delivery for his father, they usually managed to have at least some time together on such visits. He waited for her, watching as she encouraged her horse into a gallop up the last stretch.

'You'll be tiring your poor horse out, riding him like that,' he said as she reached him and grinned at her as he caught the reins to lead her into the yard. He helped her off and the groom took her mount to the stable.

'Well, I suppose I'll just have to let him rest for a while before I head back then, don't you think?' said Sarah. 'Unless you have something else I can ride?' She held his gaze with unblinking eyes and wrapped her hand around the middle finger of his left hand and squeezed.

Sam bent his head to her and whispered through the gauze of autumnal curls framing her freckled face, 'Mistress Sarah, you are a very naughty girl.'

'But as luck would have it,' she replied, 'you are a very good boy.' She looked around and, seeing no-one, reached up and kissed his cheek.

'Do you have time for a stroll up to the birches?' he asked.

It was about a ten-minute walk up to a small grove of trees. They walked hand in hand, trusting in the discretion of the hills. Neither of their fathers would look favourably on their relationship — his father wouldn't deem Sarah to be respectable enough and her father wouldn't dare anger the Heron family since much of his business depended on them — so they took what moments they could together and, for a short blissful time that morning, they ignored life's rules and restrictions, and made love under the canopy of bare winter branches before drifting into a light sleep.

Sam thought they'd just dozed for a few minutes but, when they awoke, the sun told him otherwise. They hurried back to the Hall, Sam suddenly conscious of having left Martha waiting for longer than he should; she'd probably be fretting by now. Back in the yard, he saw Sarah off with a quick, distracted wave before heading into the house to look for his sister.

He called up the stairs but got no reply so went up to her chamber. Not there. He headed for the kitchen. She loved spending time there with the cook and Jane, who often entertained her with making bread figures.

'Ah, Jane, there you are. Where's Martha?'

Jane looked confused. 'Well … I thought she was with you, sir. She said you were taking her to the river with the dogs, so I assumed …' She stopped what she was doing and wiped her hands on a cloth. 'She's probably just gone to cuddle the puppies, I reckon. I'll come and look for her with you. She can't be far, I'm sure.'

'Can't be far?' said Sam. 'You're supposed to look after her, Jane. How can you not know where she is?'

'Beg pardon, sir. I truly thought she'd gone with you. You're always so good at taking her out and … oh, I'm so sorry, really I am.' She started crying as she followed him hurriedly through the house towards the back door leading to the stableyard.

Sam stopped and turned to Jane.

'No, forgive me. It was wrong of me to blame you. It's my fault. You're right, I did say I was taking her out and I shouldn't have been so late. I'm sure you're right and she'll be with the puppies.'

But she wasn't. And she wasn't talking to the horses. And

there was no sign of her playing in the hay loft, and they couldn't see her in any of the fields closest to the hall. She was nowhere to be found.

Sam raised the alarm and soon everyone at the hall — except Sir Richard — was out searching for Martha. Since Sam had promised to take her down to the river, Hugo rode with him down to the Coquet in case she'd decided to walk there herself, unusual as that would be. They scoured the riverbanks, calling incessantly. Nothing. Then the woods. No sign of anyone.

And then the fog began to roll over the landscape, laughing at their futile searching and careless of their rising panic.

That feeling of panic had intensified for Sam earlier this evening at the White Swan, and now icy fear coursed through his veins too.

'Aaaagh!'

His anguished cry didn't penetrate far in the suffocating darkness but it spooked his horse for a moment, which stumbled on the rough ground.

'Thoughtless … selfish … irresponsible bastaaard!' He screamed again into the nothingness. He desperately wanted to hit something, someone, but he knew precisely where the responsibility lay. There was no one else to blame. He'd let Martha down and it was his fault that she'd been taken. And he now had to tell his mother the awful news that her family, the Taits, had probably kidnapped Martha.

As he got closer to Moss Hall, a light wind began to blow stirring some life into the lazy clouds. They were going to take some budging but a Northumbrian wind is relentless once it gets going, so the fog would no doubt be lifting before too long. Sam

24

prayed for a northwesterly. He was already planning the rescue party and a stiff breeze at their backs would be a blessing as they headed for Scotland over the wild moors.

He *would* be bringing his sister home.

CHAPTER TWO

KILCAITH CASTLE

Tuesday, November 16th, 1723

Even for such expert horsemen as men tended to be in these parts, the wild hills, craggy moorland and peat bogs made it too dangerous to risk a raid on a moonless winter night, so Sam had time to get a rescue party together before daybreak. He worked tirelessly all night to rally seventeen well-armed neighbours, willing tenants and friends who all gathered at Moss Hall on their small, sturdy Galloway horses. Despite Sam's protestations, Sir Richard decided to lead the party, arguing that an attack by the Taits needed swift retribution with him at the helm.

As the blackness cracked around them, it was clear that the sharp wind that sliced through the last of the night's fog had pulled a thin blanket of ice behind it. In the crystal dawn, the men rode hard and fast over the Cheviot Hills into Scotland and in a couple of hours they were closing in on Kilcaith Castle, a dilapidated-looking, crenellated stone tower house with a high-walled courtyard.

'You know the odds are not in our favour, don't you? We have no plan. We've not thought this through,' Hugo warned

Sam, in a hoarse, cross voice as the castle came into sight.

'So you want us to just leave Martha to them? Christ man, Hugo, what choice did we have?'

'I'm just saying, perhaps ... well, maybe it's not worth the risk.'

Sam simultaneously wheeled his horse round and drew his dirk and before Hugo could react he felt a blade pressing urgently into his ribs.

'It? Did you say *it,* Hugo?' Sam's voice was deliberate and quiet. 'I hope those were just unfortunately chosen words, cousin. You definitely didn't mean my sister, did you? And you most assuredly never meant to suggest that Martha is not worthy of our aid. I'm right, am I not?'

He kept his horse tight to Hugo's mare and emphasised his point through pressure to the tip of his dirk.

Hugo clouted Sam and pushed at his arm, getting a rip in his coat for his trouble.

'Give over man, Sam. You know I love Martha. But you also know as well as me that they'll be waiting for us and they have all the advantages. As soon as we get close they'll likely as not kill her anyway, if they're of a mind.'

Of course, that was true. Sam had been trying to come up with a plan all the way here but the reality of the situation was that there was little hope.

'Ay. You're right,' he replied, shortly, sheathing his dirk.

Sam knew that his father was all for a swift, brutal attack to try to hack their way through to the inside of the castle and kill as many Taits as possible. If they could rescue Martha as well, so be it, but his main focus was to teach the Taits a lesson and show no weakness. Sir Richard was convinced the old laird had lost his appetite for a fight years ago and that Martha's kidnapping was simply an opportunity on a plate which, probably, the eldest son, Angus, hadn't been able to pass up.

Sam didn't like his father's strategy, which seemed destined to be lethal to Martha whatever happened. He knew Martha was not his priority, sadly she never was, so it was up to him to rescue his sister. He'd not kept her safe. He had to find a way to bring her home to her mother.

Ah, perhaps that was the answer: his mother. He might be his father's offspring, but he was also his mother's son and she'd taught him a whole different set of strengths and skills. Could he use these to his advantage here?

Lady Heron was a healer and wise woman, with a passion for mending, calming, balancing, and seeing justice done wherever possible. She had a very strong bond with nature and in particular with trees, from which she drew strength and insight. A few years earlier, she would certainly have been taken for a witch. She'd been passing on her gifts to Sam since he was a little boy. Initially, he'd always found riding and fighting far more appealing than trying to listen to trees or learning the healing properties of plants. However, with age, his perspective had begun to change. He was, admittedly, a very skilled swordsman now and his instinct for danger combined with his agility and strength made him a man you'd only ever want on your side in a fight, but he was more than that.

His mother had planted in him the seeds of her belief that listening could be as empowering as acting, that patience could bring rewards faster than impetuousness and that the life story you live is only one of the many you could have chosen — there was always another way.

28

'A story is never finished until you can read it in the trees,' she would say. He never totally understood this, but it sounded very wise. His mother *was* wise and, in truth, Sam thought that right now, taking a leaf out of her book was his only real hope of getting Martha back. He had to talk to the Taits. If he failed, though, he would join with his father and their men and kill as many of the iniquitous bloody Taits as he could lay his sword on.

Sam could see the bloodlust in his father's eyes, despite his age, and knew that the suggestion of negotiation would get nowhere with him, but he knew how to get around this. He rode up next to his father.

'Sir, I think there is a way we could gain an advantage here and perhaps avoid putting our kin and men at too much risk, yet still save Martha and our honour. Permit me to go ahead and present myself for a duel with the laird's son. He might be persuaded to believe I had come alone. I will win, of course, take Martha back and then leave with her. If you feel it is right at that point, an attack would be less expected. Would you allow me to try?'

Sir Richard was proud of his son and confident of his abilities, so granted his wish without too much argument, as Sam had known he would.

'You have your time Samuel but take Hugo with you. God's speed.'

Of course, Sam knew that the Taits could simply decide to kill him without any discussion or duel, but he trusted that there was enough honour in this old family foe to hear him speak first, however briefly, given that it was they who had taken his sister. With just Hugo at his side, they might also be surprised at his arrival in this seemingly understated manner.

The main rescue party hid in a copse just out of sight of the castle. With outward calm, he and Hugo approached the high grey stones walls of Kilcaith at a measured trot. Within a few hundred feet of the entrance they were quickly flanked by eight Tait horsemen with twitchy broadswords. They were obviously expected.

Dismounting in the castle courtyard, Sam and Hugo were unceremoniously relieved of their weapons as they requested an audience with the laird. It was only moments before they heard a heavy door slam shut on an upper level and saw a short, stocky man coming down a flight of stone stairs that flanked the inner walls. The man was pulling along a desperate, dirty and tear-stained Martha in a tight grip by his side. She was wailing piteously.

She was alive. Thank Christ. But Sam's initial relief was instantly replaced by a murderous anger. He fought hard to quell his urge to charge immediately at the accursed man — who he assumed was the laird's son — knowing the likely outcome of such recklessness.

The man stopped at some distance from Sam and Hugo and forced Martha to her knees by his side.

'Sam, Sam.' Martha screamed and tried to wriggle out of her captor's tightening grasp. He brandished a dirk near her face, which mostly silenced her but she couldn't contain the strangled whimpers as he slowly stroked her cheek with the blade.

Sam tried to smile confidently for her. 'It's all right, Martha. Come, little one, don't cry. Be brave, sweetheart. We'll soon be going home.'

'So, you've come for the imbecile,' said the man. 'I'm quite surprised you bothered. And really, she's of little value to me so I should just give her back to you, I suppose.'

He half-pushed her towards Sam and she fell onto her hands, but he immediately pulled her back by the hair with an unpleasant smile, ignoring her piercing screams.

'But, do you know, she's quite a pretty thing. I guess she could be a pleasurable diversion from time to time. Ah but I forget, we have yet to be introduced. I am Angus Tait, laird of this castle since my father recently passed away.' He made an ironic, courtly bow, whilst keeping a firm hold on Martha. 'I believe you know my sister? She would be the mother of one or both of you, I assume. Hmmm, that makes me your uncle, does it not?'

He smiled, grotesquely, showing blackened teeth set in red gums.

The whole of Sam's being was telling him to attack the dwarfish bastard and slice his ugly head off, uncle or no. His body shook under the restraint but he forced himself to master his emotions for Martha's sake. And, in any case, the semicircle of swords around him and Hugo weren't conducive to any rash action.

He mustered all the calm control he could find and spoke to Angus Tait, the new laird of Kilcaith and, though it was hard to believe, his mother's brother.

'Sir,' he began, with a bow. 'I am Samuel Heron, son of Sir Richard and Lady Heron. This is my cousin, Hugo Heron. I fear our two families have caused each other much pain and hardship over many years. It is ... regrettable. But you and I are men of a new age. We surely don't need to follow the mistakes

31

of the past and continue with this folly? As I think you've already seen, my sister is but a child in many ways. There is no malice in her, she understands nothing of the history which brings us to this pass and, as you say,' Sam gritted his teeth to speak the next words, 'she would be of no value to you. I request, therefore, that I might return home with her.'

A heartless laugh exploded out of the laird.

'Oh, how I wish my father had been around to hear those words,' he said, making a show of wiping non-existent tears from his eyes. 'I mean, really, a Heron begging! It's too funny.'

Then his face grew quickly dark and serious as he continued.

'But my father is not here. He might have died just yesterday, but you Herons killed him years ago when you took my older sister. She might be your mother but the whore died to us twenty-six years ago.'

Sam bridled with anger and moved forward with fists clenched, but the girdle of swords drew tighter around him and Hugo. Angus sneered.

'You say we are men of a new age. I'm telling you that we live with the past every day and it's much closer than you think. Fools ignore it at their peril.'

Fighting desperately to regain his composure, Sam stepped back. He breathed hard and forced himself to bring to mind his mother's teachings. He tried again.

'I'm sorry for your loss of your sister. I would you had continued to know her as I have. She is a remarkable lady. We can neither ignore nor undo what is done, but we could change the turn of future events. We don't have to do as our forefathers did. For the love of mercy, please give Martha back to her family. If you will, I offer you myself in return for her freedom.'

Angus stood and stared at Sam for a few moments, his dirk still skimming Martha's pale wet cheek. Then he shrugged his shoulders.

'Some might say you talk fine words, young Heron, but frankly, you bore me. Return to your hovel, whoreson. The discussion is ended. Your sister stays as payment for mine.'

He lifted Martha's chin with his blade and added, 'We might just go and have some sport together this afternoon "little one". Wouldn't that be pleasant?'

The time for words had passed. This man had to die. Sam fell to the ground and upended the man nearest him, grabbing his sword as he crashed to the dirt. Hugo immediately saw what was happening and did likewise on his side. They'd used this manoeuvre together before. It was risky but unexpected, so usually gave them a few seconds head start before others realised what was happening.

At that point, all hell broke loose as an alarm was raised warning the timely approach of the Heron rescue party. Sam and Hugo were back to back now, fighting for their lives. Very quickly, some of their attackers were thinned out by the stampede of mounted Herons, but more Tait warriors were running to the aid of their clansmen.

After just a couple of minutes, Sam managed to extricate himself from the fighting and turned to look for Angus and Martha. Angus was pushing Martha at knifepoint back up the steps leading into the castle. She was crying, screaming and stumbling and looking back to the melee behind her, shouting for Sam. He dashed up the steps towards them, but Angus turned and saw him.

It actually all happened very quickly, yet it felt to Sam like the world had slowed and he could see, hear and feel each of the next few minutes with precise clarity.

Angus barked at Sam, 'No, you shall not have her.'

At that he turned and calmly and deliberately drew his dirk across Martha's throat. A necklace of bright red beads showed, startlingly, below her surprised eyes. She stood, frozen for a moment, before slumping down on to the steps like a puppet with its strings cut.

'Noooo!' Sam hurled himself forward towards her, stopping only briefly to bring his sword down, with a force driven by rage, into the belly of the laird. Angus was ill-prepared for Sam's speed of reaction and he fell back to the side wall of the castle steps clutching at his stomach. Sam dropped down to his beloved sister and cradled her fragile body tight to his own.

'Martha, no, Martha. Forgive me, Twiggle. Don't leave me. Come, mother will make you better. We'll get you home.'

It felt like an eternity that he sat on the steps rocking Martha in his arms, but it can only have been moments. Then, an excruciating, lancinating pain ripped through his side as Angus stabbed him with one last effort of will before succumbing to the inevitable.

The pain pulsated through his body, but Sam kept holding on to his sister, whispering words of comfort to her as his tears coursed down his cheeks onto hers and their mingled life bloods trickled down the stone steps.

'I'll be with you, my sweet. Stay with me. Don't cry. Don't worry, your Sam is here.'

Then he remembered no more.

BIRCH

It begins with me. I am Birch, the 'Lady of the Woods'.

I am the first. I am the fresh new start, a clean sweep. I am the settler of new lands. I show the way, prepare the ground and encourage others to join me. I love company. Woodland begins with me.

I am father and mother to my children.

I must endure, so I bend. My trunk is not too tall, and slender and flexible enough to accept the attentions of even harsh winds.

I like to think that my small, heart-shaped, serrated leaves dance attractively against the silver-white papery bark of my youth. As I grow older, I earn horizontal wrinkles which deepen into dark, handsome, arrow- or diamond-shaped decorations.

I enjoy sharing. My feathered friends of the air include greenfinches, siskins and redpolls. Sometimes woodpeckers come and live with me, and butterflies and moths visit often.

At my feet, I share nourishment with wood anemones, bluebells, wood sorrel and violets. I love their beautiful vibrancy and smiling natures. I try not to smother them with my canopy, letting light filter through to them on the forest floor.

My fungal companions — fly agaric, chanterelle and the woolly milk cap — reside close by. They accept me and help me even as I reach the end of my relatively short but good life.

I love mankind. I share my leaves with them for a tonic to cleanse and purify them internally, my oil can heal their wounds, and my bark eases their pains. Once upon a time, they used to write on the bark of my forefathers and, later, they used my bark tar oil to bind their books; I have held onto their memories for thousands of years. I can share memories with them too — if they let me, if they are True. Sharing brings community, understanding and strength. We all gain. Our lives are better.

CHAPTER THREE

TRUE

Thursday, April 26th, 1725

Sam was still and silent and had been for some time. His hands were placed either side of the trunk of the old beech tree and his forehead rested on the bark. His eyes were closed, but the upright poise of his tall, well-built frame showed him to be awake. As the light began to fade, a barn owl screeched on the edge of the woodland and a gentle breeze ruffled the tree canopy above him. But these were familiar and expected sounds, so he took no heed of them. As always, being in harmony with the trees and, through them, the wider woodland, he felt calm yet alert to his surroundings.

This was Middle Wood in Coquetdale, Northumberland, but in his mind Sam Heron was elsewhere — elsewhere and everywhere; there was no separation between himself and everything around him. He was of the world and the world was within him. It was a feeling of complete oneness, both liberating in its limitlessness and almost frightening in its vastness. It was easy to just float in this earthly aura, to let images and ideas drift in and out of his consciousness without any control from himself. At times, he was mindful of something familiar such as a landscape or an animal, but often he didn't know what was entering his awareness and he became an onlooker to unaccustomed impressions, some beautiful, some incredible and others which confused or disconcerted him.

It was a different story on days when he forced himself to concentrate. This was more difficult, but he'd been doing it from a young age and the power of control came easily to him. With focus came more command over what he chose to experience in these moments of contemplation with trees, moments which, eighteen months previously, death had almost stolen from him.

In late November 1723, Sam Heron had surprised everyone by recovering from his life-threatening injury and the ensuing fever which had racked his body for many long days. After returning to his senses, however, he discovered that, although *his* life had been spared, he'd lost all his close family on or just after that fateful day at Kilcaith Castle. Martha, oh God, Martha; the memory of her eyes looking up at him as he held her, her blood, the tears ... it was imprinted on his soul. His father had also died at the hands of the Taits that day, and later, while he was delirious with fever, his mother had mysteriously disappeared, never to be seen again.

Sam had never loved his father. Certainly, he idolised him when he was young, but he'd also feared his tempers. Since he was about twelve years old he'd hated him for his treatment of his mother and blamed him for the damage that had been done to Martha when she was just two years old (before he was born). No, he could not, in all honesty, mourn his passing.

The bond with his mother, on the other hand, was very strong and he struggled to accept it was broken, that she'd gone.

On the day his mother was last seen, the day he was closest to death, she had said she was going for help. Before she left his side, help had indeed come, in the form of her friend, Hester Sparrowhawk, a local gypsy woman and healer and mother of his best friend, Alex. Sam had been fighting the fever for five days, but on that day, he had taken a major turn for the worse. Hester arrived at the Hall to see the young man burning up and tortured with pain despite his mother's skilled attentions. The deep stab wound in his side was not healing and it seemed he did not have much longer to live.

'Hester, thank God,' said Lady Heron, as she saw her friend enter the chamber. 'Please, stay with him. Promise me you won't leave him for a moment.'

'Of course, I promise,' Hester said, gently, as she hurried over to the bed. 'But where are you going? You can't leave him now, my dear friend, you can see his time is close, can you not?'

But Lady Heron was already kissing her son tenderly on his red-hot forehead.

'Stay alive,' she whispered to him. 'I will return. Stay alive.'

She removed a leather thong from her neck. On it were two quite large, carved wooden pendants: an oak leaf and an acorn. Both the leaf and the acorn had the same mark carved on them — a long vertical line punctuated by two short horizontal lines coming off the left side. Removing the acorn, she handed it to Hester then clasped her hands around her friend's. She fought back the tears to give a message for her son, just in case.

'If I don't return —'

'Don't return! What you do mean? Please, tell me where you are going. You can't —'

'I can't let him die, Hester. This is not his time. God forgive

39

me, I never told him. I should have told him.'

'Told him what? He knows you love him.'

'I never told him about his father,' she said, mostly to herself. She squeezed Hester's hands then let them go and started walking towards the door, still muttering quietly, 'There must be something he can give me to help. I have to try.'

'He? He who?' asked Hester. 'I beg of you, tell me who you're going to see or let me go and you stay with Sam.'

Lady Heron pulled open the door and looked back at her dying son.

'If he lives … if I don't return … give him the acorn. Tell him to trust the trees of Middle Wood and to listen. Say to him: Beltane 1725. And tell him I love him.'

And then she was gone. Hester had no clue as to where she was heading. She'd never been seen since.

After all this time, Sam had to assume that either his mother had met with some accident or she'd fallen foul of one of the rogues still found in this remote border region. It was the only rational explanation. However, an unaccountable nugget of hope remained with him and stopped him from accepting the ultimate separation of death. Surely, he thought, if she were dead, he would be somehow convinced of it? He wasn't.

With Martha, on the other hand, there was, sadly, no uncertainty. He still felt her loss with his whole being, and the extreme sense of guilt that accompanied that loss held his heart in a vice-like grip. He needed to explain to his mother that he had tried to save Martha. He needed to say sorry for not bringing her back, for not keeping her safe. Martha was gone, but perhaps if he could find his mother he could tell her all this. Maybe then, she would forgive him and come home.

40

In the early days of her disappearance, Sam was sure that discovering where his mother had gone would simply be a case of finding the right tree. One of them would know. One of them would have perceived her presence all those months ago. Like him, they wouldn't forget her. The trees in this area had known her for many years and, more than that, he knew they would be happy to share their knowledge with him.

Sam knew this because, like his mother, his maternal grandmother and generations of his ancestors going back many hundreds of years, he was inextricably connected to nature through the trees. He wasn't just someone who knew about plants and animals, though he did. This was deeper. This was old knowledge, dangerous knowledge. Sam knew of no-one else who shared the skills that his mother had taught him; such things could not be discussed which is why the knowledge rarely left family lines. People would say it was witchcraft and magic. They would never understand the old ways, the old connections and the ancient word of the forest, despite it being available to all who looked for it.

There was a sign that Sam knew would identify others with the same heritage, but he'd never seen it anywhere other than on his mother's pendants, one of which, the acorn, he now wore around his own neck. The symbol — one long line with two short lines coming off the left side —represented the letter "d" in an old and little-used script called ogham. This sign and letter represented the oak. Going back to the Druids, the word for oak was *dru*. Over the years, *dru* became *true*.

Sam Heron was a rare soul. He was one of the ancient secret fellowship of the True.

He was a Tree Reader.

ROWAN

I am called by many names. My favourite is the *Lady of the Mountain*. I'm less partial to my other name, *Mountain Ash*, as I'm a cousin of the rose.

I can look after myself and make the best of whatever place I find myself in. I am one of the last on the mountain tree line, sometimes alongside the willow and downy birch. I prefer light and space to thick dark forests and I can cope with the hardships of cold. Poor soil and rocky crevices do not daunt me, partly due to my fungal friends which help my roots find water and sustenance in tough locations. I can live on the edge. I can hold strong and hold things together. I will even anchor the very ground I live in if it seems unsettled. My strong life force has earned me the name of the *Quickening Tree* and I am linked to the Celtic festival of Imbolc and the start of the year, when life begins to consider fighting back against winter and Creation stirs.

I admit I'm not very tall and I rarely live to even one hundred years, but I am tenacious and determined and I make the most of my time, spreading my seeds as far as I can. My juicy berries attract a myriad of birds and mammals, my army of seed dispersers! Mistle thrushes, waxwings, fieldfares, blackbirds ... these are just some of my feathered helpers. Four-footed creatures also fall for my ruby charms; wood mice, badgers, pine martens, dormice, red deer ... I am hard to resist. Not all my visitors are useful to me, but that is the way of the world and I will share with those who need me too — moths such as the brimstone and orange underwing enjoy my leaves, and I am home to many lichens and fungi.

Red is my colour. Yes, my May flowers are white and beloved of bees and flies, but it is my brilliant red berries of late August that I am most known for. Mankind loves my berries — a storehouse of vitamin C — for tasty jams and jellies and a tea to regulate digestion. They also know that the colour red denotes protection against enchantment and magic and, since the pentagram pattern at the base of my berries underlines my value to them in this regard, you will find me planted near their houses and they carry protective crosses made of my twigs twined with red thread.

I try hard to protect, mostly by showing that resilience and positivity can strengthen your life force and help you through difficult situations.

Innate strength offers protection.

CHAPTER FOUR

THE LECTURE

Sunday, November 23rd, 1997

For hundreds of years from the eleventh century, Durham City's castle and cathedral were the dual strongholds of the Prince-Bishops, the powerful double-edged rulers of the County of Durham. Framed by the inspired meandering of the River Wear, these twin bastions of the Crown and Christianity guarded the once-powerful, strategic and moral high ground of the north from their lofty peninsula.

At the end of the twentieth century, these impressive historic edifices still held Durham's inhabitants, pilgrims and tourists in their thrall. Their influence on both religious and earthly power in the city had, however, yielded long ago to the unstoppable force of academia. Founded by the last Prince-Bishop in 1832, Durham University was now the institution that dominated this northern city and the castle was home to one of the university colleges.

Today was a Sunday and in one of the ancient buildings flanking Palace Green, the open grassy space separating the cathedral and the castle, a lunchtime event organised by the university's History Society was taking place.

The guest speaker walked nervously into a small lecture theatre to friendly applause. This was one of their new 'wild card' talks where someone with an unusual or controversial take on a subject was invited to challenge the audience's preconceptions. They generally made good entertainment, especially in the Q&A sessions at the end. This lunchtime's offering was entitled, 'The Importance of Trees in Druid Society'.

Kate Elliott's heart was in her mouth. Not only was she one of the student organisers of the event but the speaker was a relative, albeit not a close one. Archie Robson was her second-cousin Nick's granddad, a skilled carpenter with a lifelong interest in Druids. They'd ended up talking together about his fascination with Druids at a family get-together in the first year of her history and archaeology degree. He seemed keen to share his knowledge about the history of the Druids and their connection with trees, so she thought he might fit the bill for this new series of talks. She hoped she hadn't misjudged this and that he wouldn't be an embarrassment to himself or to her. She had a real fondness for Archie even though she didn't see him that often.

The old man stood quietly in front of the gathering of expectant young people. He looked every inch the rural carpenter and rather out of place here. Nerves were certainly present as he was not used to speaking to such large groups, but there was also determination in the strong, kind face. The applause died down and he looked around slowly and silently, seemingly measuring up his audience. Kate gave him an encouraging smile, willing him not to bottle it. She'd been told that he spoke well at community events back home, but this was different. However, Archie began in the confident, calm tones of a born storyteller and she immediately breathed a sigh of relief and sat down to listen.

'I don't know about you, but when I walk into a crowded room where I don't know anyone and I don't belong, I feel a bit, well, a bit shy, I suppose. Aye, shy and perhaps a bit uncomfortable too, especially when it feels like everyone's looking at me and I don't know what I'm going to say.'

There was a soft ripple of laughter.

'Take me to any wood or forest, though, and it's a different kettle of fish; even unknown boughs of oak and branches of birch seem to offer me an open-armed invitation to stay a while and enjoy their company.'

Archie stretched his arms out wide and was smiling broadly. His audience smiled with him.

'For me, woods have always been welcoming and trees each have particular characteristics that make their community as diverse and fascinating as any group of people like yourselves. But of course, the problem for most of us is that being in the society of trees is like being the only person with sight, hearing and speech in a roomful of blind, deaf, and mute people. It's almost impossible to make any kind of meaningful connection without a specialist communication skill — speech or sign language.

'But there is no sign language for trees, and they can't communicate anyway, right?

'Well, no, that's not right. Oh, I don't mean to say there are magical walking, talking trees like you find in fantasy tales. No, lovely as that would be, we all know they're just stories. I'm talking about an actual fact. But until I share it with you, it's one that probably only a handful of people in the whole world are aware of. If that. It's quite possible that many of you simply won't believe what I'm about to tell you.'

A few people turned to neighbours with eyebrows raised and amused, quizzical expressions on their faces. Archie went on.

'It's a matter of historical record that, way back when the Romans came to the British Isles, a land then far more widely covered in forest, the incomers were aware of people known as Druids. In the early fifties BC, Caesar wrote a history of his conquest of Gaul and the Druids were mentioned in it. He understood them to be a respected and educated class with one lifetime chief, to be students of the wisdom of nature in all its forms, and to believe in the reincarnation of souls.

'We actually know very few facts about Druids as there's almost nothing written about them that can be properly corroborated. There's certainly nothing written *by* them as theirs was an oral tradition of passing on knowledge.

'They were said to be wise arbitrators and judges, they used plants for healing, and made predictions through observing the stars, birds and reputedly also through human sacrifices. One recurrent theme from the early historical writings is that Druids held all of nature, especially trees, in high esteem, with the oak being their most sacred tree and mistletoe their most sacred plant.'

Archie spent some time expanding on the various beliefs that existed concerning the ancient Druids and where these beliefs had originated, showing himself to be an erudite man on this admittedly rather hazy topic.

'Frankly, however,' he continued, 'you can either defend or

47

oppose all this supposed knowledge of Iron Age Druids depending on your opinion of the writer of the original "facts". There's no definitive proof we can turn to.

'What we think we *do* know, though, is that they were powerful people with important religious and secular roles in their society. The Romans weren't too keen on having these Druid leaders around as they tried to take over Britain, so they did everything in their power to subdue or get rid of them. They were pretty successful, as the Romans tended to be when they put their minds to something. Some Druids were given offers they couldn't refuse and decided to tow the Roman party line. Others stood up for their beliefs and positions and were killed for their stance. More of them simply went underground and continued their Druidic practices in secret. Inevitably though, under such persecution their numbers dwindled, until, by about the second century, it's thought there wasn't a single Druid left. The truth of their knowledge, skills, beliefs and traditions was lost to us.

'You might know that interest in the Druidic faith was rekindled in the sixteenth century, but the modern Druid essentially had to start from scratch and build a new system of beliefs partly based on the very few scraps of fact left from history.

'However, unbeknownst to, well, nearly everyone, there are people around today who have a direct and meaningful line back to the original Druids. The people of this line are called the True. You won't have heard of them, and even most people with True ancestry have no inkling about this link to their past.'

A general low murmur rumbled around the room and Kate's heart sank. It had all been going so well. She was worried he was going to get heckled, but Archie ignored the slight disturbance and carried on with the same calm sense of purpose. He had more to say.

'The True line came from some of the Druids who hid more or less anonymously in remote corners of Britain, especially here in the north of England, as well as in Scotland and north Wales. This group had one main goal — to keep their knowledge of trees alive.

'You could call them the original tree-huggers, but that would be to hugely underestimate their insight into trees. The True knew how to *read* trees. They could connect with the life force of a tree to read its experiences and feel the links it had with its environment. In other words, to go back to where we started, in Britain, the True effectively knew the language of the trees.'

Archie stopped. He looked almost relieved and slightly shell-shocked to have got the words out. He sat down on a tall stool next to a pedestal table and drank the water that had been left for him. The room was more or less silent bar some foot shuffling and fidgeting. The audience didn't know whether he'd finished or whether there was more. Then someone started clapping hesitantly and others joined in. Another member of the History Society committee came tentatively onto the platform next to Archie, thanked him respectfully and invited questions. A short blonde-haired girl stood up.

'Mr Robson, can I ask the question we're probably all thinking? How do you know all this? I mean about the True. You say nothing was written down and it was a long time ago, so how did you come to this theory?'

'Oh, sorry,' Archie said, in a slightly distracted tone. 'Yes, I quite forgot to say, didn't I? Well, it's more than a theory actually. The fact is that I am one of the True. I know from my ancestors.'

Well, that caused a stir! Kate couldn't quite believe what Archie had just said and neither could the rest of the audience. Some people were laughing, others were talking amongst themselves and many were just sat looking a bit bemused. Then, an older male student stood up to ask another question loudly over the rumpus. Kate knew him only by sight rather than by name — his long black hair pulled into a ponytail was quite distinctive. Everyone's attention refocused as the man spoke. There was a barely disguised sneer in his voice.

'So, you are saying you can talk to trees, Mr Robson. Fascinating, I'm sure. I can't quite imagine that myself, sorry, but even if you can, what's the point? Surely they can't have very exciting lives.'

Laughter, but then it died down as they looked to Archie for his answer.

'No,' he said, with a sad smile. 'No, Mr ...?'

'Fenwick,' replied the man. 'Silas Fenwick.'

'Well, Mr Fenwick, you'd be right for the most part, of course. And I can't *talk* to them, just read them. But —'

He looked out at the young audience, catching the eye of one after the other as he spoke.

'Just think how long many of our trees have lived. There are yews over a thousand years old, oaks well over 500 years old. Think of the changes they've seen going on around them. Think of what they know about the flora and fauna of the woodlands they've always been part of. Consider the conversations that have taken place under them or the treasures they've had hidden

50

on them for safekeeping. What about the declarations of love they've been witness to, or storms they've weathered? All this and more, and they're still here, keeping an eye on us, keeping us alive, and marking the passage of our time on earth. They are our link with what's gone before and, if you know them, they foretell what might be coming. They know when seasons are changing before we do and they can feel if an ecosystem is happy or struggling. They feed us, shelter us, clean our air, give us oxygen, heal us. Trees are barometers not only of the weather, but also of the wellbeing of our environment, and they are critical to our own health.'

Archie suddenly stood up again. His face was gravely earnest and his voice passionate.

'I don't know if I'm the only man alive who knows what I know. I hope to God I'm not. Perhaps I'm going against some unknown code of the True by telling you all this. But I feel I must do my best to let others know, so that trees don't lose their human supporters. They need our help. Ancient woodlands and forests everywhere are under attack. We must understand that the timber or the land we gain from the wanton destruction of native forests comes at a vastly higher price than most people can even dream of. Trees are quite simply vital to life.'

After a slight pause, Archie seemed to shake himself, then smiled at his bewildered, yet strangely captivated audience.

'D'you know what? If you don't believe a word of what I've said today, well, I hope you've at least had some entertainment. I've enjoyed it. But perhaps you might take away one thought with you?'

He hesitated, and looked around, obviously searching for something. Kate caught his eye and he walked over to her and, with a slight nod and a wink, took the book she was holding on her lap. Taking his place back in front of the audience, he held the book out in front of him in one hand, like an evangelical preacher brandishing a bible at his congregation of sinners.

'Books,' he said. 'Books are like trees. Not just because paper is made from wood, though it's ironic we've ended up using dead trees as our main storehouse of knowledge for hundreds of years. No, their similarity lies in the way they hold the written insights of individuals — human and plant. Some books, and indeed some trees, offer nothing of great value, but others give us life-changing information. Take the Codex Leicester; it's a book of notes and drawings by Leonardo da Vinci. Bill Gates bought it for the staggering sum of thirty million dollars a few years ago. It's a precious and priceless document. Would you destroy the wisdom contained in such an important book? Of course you wouldn't. Well, chopping down an ancient tree is akin to setting fire to such a book. Take the Ankerwycke Yew in Berkshire; it bore witness to the Magna Carta being signed beneath its aged canopy in 1215, and Henry VIII proposed to Anne Boleyn beneath its boughs in 1530. Tell me, how is this tree any less irreplaceable?'

Archie stopped and put the book on the little table.

'OK, these are extreme examples, but I'm sure each one of you can bring to mind a much lesser-known book which has affected your life in some special way. Unknown trees also have this potential. They are a living treasure. Our ancestors knew this, we need to re-learn it.'

He clasped his hands together in front of him and smiled at the once again silent audience.

'Please. Find your inner Druid. Fight for our trees. They

hold our past history and they guard our future existence.'

The weather was feeling cranky today. It had decided to throw a bit of everything into the pot. A squally wind had followed this morning's prolonged blast of icy rain but, as Kate and Archie walked down the South Bailey after the talk, there was a period of grumpy calm under the leaden sky.

They walked along silently. Kate wasn't sure how to approach Archie about what had just happened. He seemed lost in his thoughts and she noticed that he was clenching and unclenching his hands in his coat pockets.

'Let's walk down to the river, Archie. There's something I think you'd like to see.'

Kate put her arm through his and he absent-mindedly patted her chilly hand and agreed with a short nod and a half-smile.

At the end of South Bailey, the path dropped down steeply to the wooded banks of the River Wear. Here, the muddy brown waters were spanned by one of the city's five bridges. This one was Kate's favourite, Prebend's Bridge. It was built in the late eighteenth century specifically to take in the most magnificent view of the castle and cathedral. Its simple, elegant stonework held a tablet engraved with part of a poem by Sir Walter Scott.

Grey towers of Durham
Yet well I love thy mixed and massive piles
Half church of God, half castle 'gainst the Scot
And long to roam those venerable aisles
With records stored of deeds long since forgot.

'I haven't been here for years,' said Archie, leaning on the bridge and looking up at the matchless cityscape before him. 'Did you ever think how similar its location is to Horseshoe Priory up near us?'

Kate nodded with a smile. She had been a few times to the old priory near Rothbury; it, too, was almost on an island due to the river looping around it.

They both wordlessly took in the scene, each in their own private world. Kate began her unspoken ritual of trying to find the perfect word to describe the smell of the river, a smell she loved. That 'essence of damp' was redolent of all the seasons rolled into one, but this transient perfume refused to be pinned down, making it impossible to name any specific fragrance. The smell was a gypsy too. It liked to travel from its riparian confines, hitchhiking on the clothes and in the hair of anyone who came close. Kate always knew when someone had been walking by a river, be that by the Wear here in Durham or back home in Northumberland by the Coquet.

Kate was never *not* homesick for her family farmhouse, Cloudberry Farm in Coquetdale, and having Archie here was making the feeling worse. She went back home as often as she could; helped out on the hill sheep farm with her dad and brother, rode her horse and reconnected with her adored dogs. She really liked Durham City and was enjoying her history degree but, though she had some good friends, she knew she was seen as a bit of a loner and as far as men were concerned, well, none had yet passed her 'Is he worth taking to Cloudy?' test, so inevitably they didn't last too long.

'I couldn't tell him,' said Archie, suddenly, bringing Kate back to the moment. She wasn't sure if he was talking to himself or to her.

'Tell who? What?' asked Kate, confused.

'Nick,' he stated, simply and sadly.

Ah. She had, indeed, been wondering if her cousin Nick knew anything about Archie's professed ability to read trees and of being a descendant of the Druids.

'Why? I mean, why could you not tell him when you've just told a bunch of complete strangers?' she asked, genuinely curious.

'Oh, they won't believe me,' he said, dismissively. 'I'll just be some daft old git they listened to one Sunday. I just hope I got the message across about looking after our trees. That was what I really wanted to do, but I knew the Druid link would have interest and figured the outlandish truth might get their attention more than me just spouting on. I decided to risk it.'

Kate laughed. 'Ay, well, I always heard you were a good storyteller and I don't think they'll forget you or your message in a hurry! But, if it's true, which ... obviously ... it is,' she continued, with a slight questioning lilt to her voice, 'then why not tell Nick?'

Archie turned to face her. He looked disconsolate.

'You don't know how much I've always wanted to. I still do, but it's too late now. I daren't. I'm sure he'd hate me for keeping it from him all these years.'

Kate didn't know what to say, so she waited.

'You'll have heard about Gerry, Nick's dad?' Archie continued, 'Well, he never believed about the True or tree-reading. We had a huge argument about it when he was sixteen and he just upped and offed, leaving me on my own. Then, out of the blue, two years later, he came home with a girlfriend and a baby. Nick.'

Relations were still strained between father and son, much as Archie tried his hardest, but as the girlfriend had no family back up, they needed Archie's help with little Nick.

'When Nick was eight, he told his Dad he wanted to live with me. I thought Gerry and Sue would be furious but, strangely, they weren't. I couldn't understand how they could give up their gorgeous little boy so easily, but I was besotted with him and jumped at the chance to have him live with me. Only— only there was one condition,' said Archie, shutting his eyes tightly at the memory. 'I was never to mention the True or tree reading to the child.'

He then looked at her directly.

'I promised, Kate. I promised my son.'

Kate's heart went out to Archie. She'd never met Gerry, but she knew how close Archie and Nick were, even now, so keeping such an important secret from him must have been a major strain and sadness. Archie had passed on to Nick his passion for nature and his extensive knowledge about trees and woodworking, but he'd kept his word to his son and kept silent about the True.

'Perhaps ... I don't know, but perhaps it doesn't matter,' said Kate, tentatively. 'I mean, not telling Nick. Surely, the love of woodlands you've instilled in him is every bit as precious as the knowledge you *aren't* able to share with him? It comes from the same roots, literally. Trees are his life, and,' she continued, with a laugh, 'I really can't see anything making him more committed to them! You have your number one tree ambassador there. OK, so he's not aware of the full picture that you see, but perhaps the part he sees is enough. He's engaged, he's passionate, he's an out and out woodsman for God's sake

56

— a natural born tree reader, I'd say.'

Archie was looking at Kate quizzically, with his mouth partly open. Then he shook his head and laughed.

'Blimey, pet. Either this university malarkey is worth its salt after all or you've got an older soul than your face lets on.'

Kate laughed with him.

'Or maybe it's just my innate northern good sense? But hey, talking of seeing the full picture, I wanted to show you something and actually it now seems particularly apt. Come on, before it starts getting too dark.'

If you looked carefully you could see it from Prebend's Bridge, but you'd struggle to pick it out if you didn't know it was there, set as it was amongst the trees of the riverbank.

One moment, you could swear you were looking at the skeleton of a tiny, roofless church, with all that remained being twelve tall, slender wooden columns of the aisle, plus a shorter, wider column in the middle of one end. You could make out remnants of carved decorations, but the columns were all out of kilter and not at all uniform in shape or size. It didn't make sense. So you looked again. Now, the effect of a building was gone and you were sure you saw a gathering — not of people, but of trees. These trees were definite characters, with vestiges of their erstwhile magnificence shining through their rootless, barkless grey trunks. They had short stumps in place of graceful limbs, but the spirit of the elms' strength and beauty could still be sensed. You had the distinct impression that they had gathered for a purpose, though this was yet to be discovered by distant onlookers.

'Hmm, nice bit of sculpture. And what a location for it. I love it. It reminds me of the columns in the Cathedral,' said

Archie as they reached the trunks and began to walk around them.

'Yes, it's been here for about ten years. The trees were from the riverbanks here but were killed by Dutch elm disease. It's starting to decay a bit now but I still love coming here. There is more to it than meets the eye too,' said Kate, with an impish smile. 'After your talk, I realised that you really had to see this. This place is as close as most of us come to having trees talk to us. Actually, though, it's more about what we were just talking about — seeing the full picture.'

She stopped and pointed to the hefty thirteenth trunk. There was a seat carved into it, facing into the room of tree trunks.

'Just sit down there. You'll see what I mean.'

Intrigued, Archie took the seat. He looked forward for a moment, then his eyes widened with surprise.

'Hah, now *that's* clever!' said Archie, grinning widely and clapping his cold hands together.

The full picture was indeed what he was faced with. This was not just an artful huddle of tree trunks. Seen from this vantage point, the twelve elms melded together to become a canvas for an image hidden in plain sight. Archie found himself looking at the carved depiction of a room with arched windows, a panelled ceiling, tables laden with jugs and food and a bag of money.

'It represents the Last Supper,' Kate told him.

'So does that make me Jesus, sat here?'

'I guess so,' she agreed.

Archie was entranced, as she had expected. He sat, moving his body slightly to the right, then slightly to the left, to change his line of sight, and muttering to himself in delight when he realigned the picture. Eventually, he moved aside so that Kate could take up the fascinating, yet uncomfortable seat of the betrayed.

Daylight was beginning to fade, but she could still see the scene she knew almost by heart. She stared, not really looking, her head full of what-ifs and could-it-bes.

The full picture, she was thinking. It's all about perspective, isn't it? Sometimes it was easier not to look further, nor from a different angle, but to remain content with the picture you were familiar with. But sometimes having a key would open up new ways of seeing things. The key to the picture in the trees was the exact positioning of the chair. The key to a totally different way of looking at trees and nature was, if he wasn't completely mad, Archie Robson. So, right now, she was faced with a point of view she hadn't even dreamed existed, if it really did. Her mind was telling her that reading trees was a fairytale. In her heart, though, she was back in Northumberland in her favourite piece of woodland near her family farm, conversing with trees she'd known and loved all her life. Her whole being sang with excitement at the prospect. Was she brave enough to risk searching for the full picture, however weird it seemed?

Hell, yes!

She turned to her companion, who was now inspecting the carving more closely as a fine dusting of snow began to fall quietly around them.

'Archie? Can you teach *me* how to read trees?'

ASH

Look upwards. That is what I do. Not only do I grow tall, but the ends of my branches turn upwards towards the heavens. My lofty tendencies and far-reaching roots mean I am fastened to both sky and earth; I link the world above with the world below — I am the tree of connection. Above, below, past, present, life, death … to many I represent the cycles of existence so they call me the Tree of Life.

I am many and everywhere. People know me by my smooth beige-grey trunk, my sooty black winter buds on grey branches and my late-to-arrive-early-to-drop, sun-following leaves made of three to six pairs of opposite leaflets on a stalk with a single leaflet on the end. But perhaps most of all, they know my seed — one-winged keys which hang in bunches until ready to fly off.

Along with oak and beech, I am one of the woodland's tallest and oldest trees and I take my responsibility as a protector and guardian seriously. I try not to block too much sun from my smaller woodland friends or wild flowers such as violets, wild garlic and dog's mercury. Hazel trees can grow beneath my canopy and I love seeing the dormice they attract. Bullfinches eat my keys and woodpeckers, owls and nuthatches come to live with me in any holes I develop. As I grow old, stag beetles find a haven with me and I can grow a handsome coat of lichens and mosses if the air is clean.

I commonly live 250 years and can easily live for 400 years or even 1000 if I'm coppiced by man. Woodsmen value my strong, shock-absorbing timber and I am a dependable fuel, burning hot even when green, so my other name is Fraxinus, meaning firelight.

It's a shame that only very few are still aware of my healing nature and know that I can help them with detoxifying and disinfecting. We should all use each other for the good we can bring, without causing damage. Myself, I am being attacked by a new disease, but I am strong and I will learn to survive this.

I must, for I am the Tree of Life.

CHAPTER FIVE

THE HAWK & THE HERON

Thursday, April 26th, 1725

Sam found that the gossips of the wood, the middle-aged birches and beeches, usually had the most vivid hold on recent occurrences. It was easier to read the detail of each day with them than it was with more aged trees. Like people, each tree had different characteristics but whatever the species, the older the tree, the more memories they had stored away in their rings. The further back you went in time, the more tightly the rings were squeezed together, as if in a press. Peeling the layers apart took patience and skill. Sam could do it but, unless he was looking for something specific, it was far easier to skim over the years and just land on wherever his thoughts, and the tree, took him.

He read trees for different reasons. Some days he would ask for help from Nature. His mother had left behind her notebook of recipes for remedies, but not every health issue he came across could be found there, in which case he would focus the problem in his mind and ask the trees. Often an answer would come back from the forest, showing him a specific tree or a plant. It wasn't fail-safe as he wasn't a natural born healer like his mother but he did have successes.

On other days, Sam simply wanted a distraction and these were the days when he let his mind open to whatever the tree chose to show him. He'd seen the forest's fear of a huge fire one year; he'd watched a group of outlaws camp out in the wood for a long period maybe 150 years ago; and he'd seen an injured lone wolf die curled up at the foot of the ancient oak — the tree seemed fondly protective of the animal whose bones lay buried with its roots. Sam guessed that must have been at least 300 years ago. Was that Northumberland's last wolf?

Then there were the days when loneliness consumed him. Sam was lonely often but didn't wallow in self-pity — the loss of his family was of his own making. However, when he could no longer stop himself, he would go to the trees that he knew had memories of his mother and sister.

Martha's favourite was a large old beech tree with a wide canopy where no other trees or shrubs grew beneath. She used to race around the trunk, usually playing catch with her pet dog and making dens where she would play until her mother was finished collecting plants in the woodland. The tree took pleasure in her company and, watching Martha again with the beech, he felt he wasn't the only one missing her.

The tree that held his favourite memory of his mother was an oak not far from Moss Hall. It was about 200 years old. From it there were beautiful views further down into Coquetdale and you could also see across to the Harbottle Hills and the rocky summit overlooking the dale. His mother sat there sometimes, doing nothing, just sitting and watching. Sam often wondered what she was thinking of but she seemed content, even happy at those times, so that's how he preferred to see her.

After all this time, he'd had to accept defeat in finding his mother through reading the trees in Middle Wood. They'd shown him a few fleeting glimpses of her running through the wood but it always ended in confusion. She was there and then she wasn't. He'd found no trail to follow in well over a year. He knew in his heart that his search was futile. She was gone. If the trees knew her whereabouts they would have revealed it to him by now.

'So, you're still talking to trees, bonny lad? I thought you'd have grown out of that by now, Heron!'

Sam was at Martha's tree and immediately whipped around, grabbing his sword as he did so. But his agitation melted quickly into delight.

'Hawk! Gads, man, it does my heart good to see you.'

A lithe young man was leaning nonchalantly against a nearby tree watching him and absent-mindedly preening the colourful thin ribbons hanging from his shirt cuffs. Sam strode over and grabbed him in a bear hug, lifting him off the ground and swinging him round. They ended up toppling over, wrestling and thumping each other, all the while laughing like idiots.

The Hawk and the Heron. It seemed to have always been so. Sam Heron: son of a baronet and his lady — tall, well-built, well-educated, a handy swordsman since young, sheep farmer and free-trader. Alex Sparrowhawk: son of a travelling gypsy spoon maker and a minister's daughter turned palm reader and healer — average height, wiry build, a quick-witted scholar of the world, musician and sometime thief. To the outsider, it would seem there had never been a more unlikely friendship but as they were growing up, when the gypsy family were in Coquetdale over summer, the boys were inseparable.

'I hadn't heard you were back,' said Sam. 'Hester never said.'

'I just arrived today, so Mam wouldn't have known last time she saw you,' replied Alex. 'She said you might be in the wood somewhere if you weren't at the Hall. It was just a stroke of luck to come across you and you were lucky someone else didn't find you before I did. Who was watching over you in your reveries, Heron? Your horse?! I can't be with you *every* day til we're ninety you know. Come on back to the house and have some supper with us, eh? I want to know everything that's been going on.'

Hawk's family lived in a ramshackle stone bastle house on the far edge of the wood. Bastle houses were remnants of the time of the Border Reivers — not large, but tall, sturdily-built stone houses with the living quarters upstairs for safety. It was dark by the time they reached it, but next to the house the inky night was licked by the tongues of a roaring fire which seemed to dance to the sounds of merriment.

Sam could make out five people around the flames: two adults and three children. The two seated on low three-legged crackets were Hester and her husband Will. Will was playing a jig on his Northumbrian pipes to the delight of his children who were all running and jumping around the fire. When Alex's young siblings saw him riding out of the gloom with Sam, they rushed up to them both, screaming and laughing and trying to drag them over to the campfire.

'Play with Dada, Alex, go on. Please!'

So, within minutes of arriving at the Sparrowhawk

household, Sam was sitting at the campfire watching with pleasure and admiration as Alex and his father engaged in a battle of notes on their pipes. How did their fingers move so fast to produce such tunes? He'd tried and it was beyond him. Alex had showed him how to play when they were about fourteen. He could get a tune out of the instrument but only slowly, and it could hardly be called music. The father and son, on the other hand, could make the air crackle with excitement and their audiences laugh with joy or weep with melancholy. With pipes in their hands, emotions were theirs to be sculpted at will. Alex most certainly knew how to use this skill to his advantage, in all manner of circumstances. The most recent had involved the daughter of an innkeeper in a village near Alnwick about a year earlier.

'So, what's it like to be a married man, then, my friend? And where is your sweet wife?' Sam asked, as they sat alone by the fire later that night, having conversed with Will and Hester over a tasty supper of rabbit stew.

'Oh Sam, the joy of being my own man again! I love women, you know I do, and I adored Mary, really, I did. What a woman! But she changed almost as soon as we wed. I wanted to love her and be a good husband to her but much as I tried, it was never enough. She always wanted more — more clothes, more money — and when I couldn't provide fast enough, she regularly shunned my company to be with a local schoolteacher. An ugly one at that. I mean, what is a man supposed to do with such a faithless wife?'

'I wouldn't know, Hawk. You're talking to a man who spends more time with sheep and trees than women these days! But I'm truly sad to hear it. I thought you were smitten.'

'Ay, well, so did I,' said Hawk, grumpily, 'but I've left her to the schoolteacher, and good luck to him. He's welcome to my second-hand wife. I wish him joy of her. I've had my fill of married life. I'm back to bachelorhood and I vow never again to fall for the charms of a pretty woman and allow her to make a fool of me. That's an act of folly never to be repeated. So, here's to true friendship, my old mucker — a bond to be relied upon, at least if that friend is you.'

They toasted with their home-brewed beer and Sam was happy for the first time in a very long time.

By the next morning, they'd decided a fishing trip was in order. Hawk was almost as good a fisherman as his da. Sam had learned a thing or two from him over the years but preferred a more unconventional way of net fishing which Hawk disapproved of. To keep the peace though, Sam borrowed a rod from Will and they headed for the river.

They set themselves up on the banks of the Coquet at a spot where they'd had success many times in the past. Whether the peaty brown waters would relinquish a sea trout or a salmon remained to be seen, but good company, whisky and fishing was no bad way to spend a day.

'So, firstly, you'd better tell me,' said Hawk, 'have you still got that wee demon Dart in tow, or are you going to play fair today?'

Sam laughed. He'd known Hawk wouldn't be able to resist asking about Dart. Dart was his not-so-secret weapon when it came to fishing. Otters were seen as pests by nearly everyone because of the amount of fish they took from the rivers and they were invariably killed on sight by Hawk and his father.

However, about three years previously, Dart had been orphaned when very young and Sam, who had a way with animals, had found him, brought him up and trained him to use his natural skills to Sam's advantage. Dart would enthusiastically chase fish into a big net and they would share the bounty. Fishing the otter way. Sam eventually encouraged him back to the wild, but still saw him occasionally and Dart would still round up fish for him if he heard Sam calling him. He'd loved Dart but loved to see him wild and free even more.

'Actually, I haven't been down here for some time, so haven't seen him. I think your fishing prowess is safe today.'

He looked around, secretly hoping to see Dart pop up, but there was no sign of him today. It was one of those unremarkable days where nothing seemed to want to stand out or be seen. The sky was blandly grey, there was hardly a breeze to speak of, and it was neither cold nor warm. Everything was keeping a low profile, as if half expecting something to happen and not wanting to be caught up in it. Even the river was slinking along today, trying not to draw attention to itself as it went on its way — if it could have worn a cloak of fog, it would have. Across on the opposite bank, though, a couple of sizeable alders were dipping their branches into the river's velvet whisky waters, enjoying the tickling feeling as it rippled past their new leaves. You could almost hear them giggling.

'What's the plan now you're back then, Hawk?' asked Sam. 'How are you going to make your living? Just with your pipes? Do you need work?'

'Work? What, and end up talking to bloody trees like you? Bugger that for a lark, marra,' said Hawk, laughing loudly and throwing out his first line. 'No, I've discovered a great way to make money for little to no effort. I don't suppose you'll approve, but I'll tell you anyway. You know that if you join the Army, you get the King's shilling, right? Well, did you know how you can actually get a *guinea*, yes twenty-one shillings, if you're canny? A fortune! Well, perhaps not for you, but definitely for me.'

'So you've enlisted?' asked Sam, incredulously.

'Well, yes.' He paused. 'And no'. Hawk gave Sam a sideways smirk and a wink.

'Damnation, Hawk, you've taken the money and run, haven't you? They'll be after your tail forever now, you know that?' Sam was shaking his head in disbelief.

'Hypocrite,' said Hawk, throwing a clod of earth at him. 'So you're not putting yourself in the exact same situation every time you run the grey hens of whisky out from Jack's still?'

'Of course not. I have a few gaugers to draw swords with occasionally, not the whole British Army after me. Where did you sign up?'

'Well, the last time — '

'Last time?! You've done it more than once?' interrupted Sam.

'Yes, the *last* time,' continued Hawk, ignoring his friend's disapproval, 'was at Alnwick, just before I came home. That was an easy one. But the first, in Newcastle, I must admit was trickier than I expected. They got me locked up in a little cell in the garrison when I tried to flee from the recruiting sergeant. As luck would have it, though, there was a tiny trapdoor about a foot square with a drop down to a cesspit beneath.' Hawk turned to Sam with a wicked grin, 'I don't suppose the fat guard expected me to go out that way.'

Sam couldn't stop himself and the pair ended up roaring

with laughter.

'Oh, you must have stunk for a week,' said Sam, wiping tears from his eyes.

They carried on chatting and fishing, having moderate success landing a couple of salmon that they cooked up for lunch.

'So now, are you going to tell me about all the tree planting you've done since ... well, you know, recently. As a way to bring in the coins I can't really see a quick profit there!' said Hawk, as they ate.

Sam had shared much of his life with Hawk but nothing about the True. Hawk knew that Sam 'talked' to trees but he just put that down to idiosyncrasy mixed with a bit of witchcraft. His own mother, Hester, was a healer, like Sam's mother, and so with that, and being gypsy too, any involvement with nature for potions and predictions didn't seem too odd to him. However, Sam had never told Hawk about his ability to read trees and was encouraged by his mother to keep anything True-related as a secret for fear of accusations of witchcraft.

'Oh, you know, I needed to keep busy after ... after Martha and my mother. The farm's doing passably well. Sheep and horses are selling for a fair price and even with the current mania for gin, we're still making good crops of barley into pretty decent whisky, as you know.'

He held out his bottle towards Hawk and they toasted good fortune with a dram.

'I just, well, I've not really felt very much like being with people recently, so I've kept to my own company, other than trading.'

'What? Even young Sarah hasn't managed to make you

smile?' said Hawk with a nudge and a grin. 'And what about the Websters' daughter? She's been sweet on you forever. I thought you quite liked her.'

Sam tried a return smile but it wasn't convincing.

'I'm no good to anyone, Hawk. I can't even look after my own family so how can I consider a wife? No, I'm best on my own now. Anyway, I'd make very poor company for any respectable woman —'

'Who said anything about respectable?' muttered Hawk, with a raised eyebrow, as Sam continued talking.

'—and they'd rightly think me inattentive for being outdoors from morning 'til night. The walls of Moss Hall rebuke me every day. I can't stay inside for long. What good woman would understand or accept that? None that I know. The valley and the hills are my domain. I know how to care for *them* and that's what I've been doing. I work on the farm, I advise and help my tenants and workers, I breed my horses and dogs, trade whisky and I plant trees. It keeps me busy and more or less sane.'

'Oh yes, planting acres of woodland, by yourself from what I hear, yes, that's definitely the act of a sane man,' said Hawk, nodding with mock gravity. 'You've got the makings of a decent sized wood already. What will that be, maybe ten acres? You must have been planting, what? A hundred a week?'.

'Something like that,' replied Sam, with a shrug.

Hawk turned to Sam with concern.

'You know, what happened — your sister, your father, your mother — it wasn't your fault, my friend.'

'Mm,' said Sam softly. 'I was supposed to take care of her, Hawk, and I should've saved her. She relied on me and I let her down. I let them both down.'

Sam was staring out over the river but his eyes didn't see the giggling alders; he saw a knife at a pale slender throat, and a necklace of blood. The sight haunted him. The guilt tortured him.

'Hmm,' said Hawk. 'I figure I know you quite well and I don't see a man that lets people down. Far from it. In fact, I think if anyone's going to take the prize for unreliability, well, sorry but I'm top of the class!'

Sam smiled and allowed Hawk to bring him back to the moment. Shaking himself from his sombre thoughts, he also decided to share the one thing he'd discovered from the trees that had some bearing on recent events.

'Do you remember the message your mam gave me from my mother? It mentioned Beltane and 1725. And now, I've ... well, I've heard that there is something going on on the eve of Beltane in just a few days' time.'

'Heard? Heard from who? What kind of something? Where?' Hawk bombarded Sam with questions that Sam really didn't know how to answer.

In the end, without mentioning that he'd found out from reading the trees in Middle Wood, he told him that he'd discovered there was going to be some clandestine meeting on Faerie Hill at around midnight on Beltane, the 1st May.

'I really don't know what it's all about, but don't you think it's a bit of a coincidence that one of the last things my mother said was that I should look to Beltane 1725? It's so specific.'

'Hmm. Well, yes, you're not wrong there,' agreed Hawk, and he leaned back on the grass bank. 'So, it looks like the Hawk and the Heron are due an adventure. What's the plan?'

CHAPTER SIX

THE COVERT

30th April to 1st May, 1725

Hawk wouldn't take no for an answer.

'What kind of friend do you take me for? Why the hell would I let you head off alone to God knows what kind of meeting with an unknown group of people in the black of night, and at Faerie Hill of all places? And to make it worse, at Beltane, when they say the spirits are at their most troublesome. You might've gone completely mad, but I'm afraid that doesn't discharge me from looking out for you when I'm around.'

And so it was agreed. They would ride together to the Draag Stone where Hawk would wait while Sam continued to the hill for midnight. Sam wouldn't let him come any closer but said that if he wasn't back by just after sunrise, Hawk could come and look for him.

The huge, almost perfectly conical hill about two miles west of the Draag Stone was known locally as Faerie Hill. People never lingered near here because this was not thought to be the realm of mankind. The local superstitions surrounding the thickly wooded mound were as manifold as the tapestry of leaves adorning the trees, but invariably involved lights in the wood and trespassers being enticed away by sprites, never to be seen again. If naughty children of the dale could not be tamed by the belt, the threat of being left 'on the hill' was generally enough to quell most extremes of behaviour.

It struck Sam that this was a wise place for a clandestine meeting. Not only was it protected by tales of mischievous forest folk, but it was a less obvious landmark than the nearby Draag Stone.

For as long as anyone could remember, the Draag Stone had been the focus for local ceremonies, secret trysts and, as Sam and Hawk could attest, challenges for growing lads wanting to prove their mettle. The vast sandstone block stood sentinel-like in the rough boggy moorland and it pointed out towards the freezing waters of the lough which lay between it and the Harbottle Hills.

It was the focal point of the 'Call of Coquetdale', a trial which local dalesmen had used for many generations as a rite of passage to adulthood for their male offspring. It was a tough ask even for the hardy sons of this rugged corner of the kingdom and certainly not everyone took the challenge, but it was said that those who triumphed would reach their ninetieth year. Indeed, there was a surprising number of people in this valley who lived to a handsome old age and in reasonable health.

Custom dictated that you answered the Call in your fifteenth year. The path of the Call was to run five miles from Harbottle Castle out to the lough, swim across it, then climb over the Draag Stone on the way back. It sounded easy if you said it quickly, but the reality was somewhat different. Even in dry weather the moorland had treacherous bogs which some lads fell foul of before they even reached the lough. The lough itself had reeds growing on its margins which tangled legs and hindered movement, making some think they were being dragged under by unseen hands of water goblins and causing them to abandon their trial. The water of the lough was as cold and dark as death and, sadly, over the years a few of the brave souls who avoided the grasping reed fingers, succumbed instead to its chilling embrace.

Sam and Hawk had taken the Call together. They were both strong swimmers, Hawk being the faster and more agile but the heavier-built Sam having more stamina. They stuck together through the lough, urging each other on and cheating the black depths of yet more quiet companions. For them, though, it was the Draag Stone which nearly got the better of them. Climbing the thirty-foot high boulder was gruelling at the best of times, but with limbs numbed with cold in the increasingly biting wind, it was nigh on impossible. Their elation and feeling of invincibility when they reached the top was paired with a bone deep tiredness and chill, and they decided to rest for a while on their conspicuous pinnacle of success. As time ticked by, however, Sam struggled to persuade Hawk to get moving again.

'Just a little longer, Heron, then we'll go, eh?' said Hawk, sleepily. After about half an hour, Sam realised that Hawk was starting to slur his words and seemed incapable of movement. He knew he had to get him off the rock.

Sam took off his shirt and tore it in half. Grappling with the now semi-conscious Hawk, he tried to tie his cold unresisting body to his back with the cloth.

'Howay man, Hawk, give us a hand here. Just hang on to me while I get you fastened up, will you?'

Eventually, with Hawk's slim frame but nevertheless

substantial weight tied to his back and his arms dangling over his shoulders, Sam made his slow and painful way back down to moor level. What guardian angel was caring for them that day, Sam would never know. The stone claimed many patches of scraped skin from them both, a broken leg from Hawk as they fell the last few feet and, from Sam, a very deep slash on his left forearm; but they lived. The pain of the broken leg temporarily brought Hawk round somewhat at the bottom and Sam managed to splint his leg with a length of ash before staggering back with his friend to the healing care of his mother.

That was ten years ago but, as they approached the huge boulder, Sam knew that, like him, Hawk would be thinking of their adventure. They had never spoken of it since the day after the event, when Hawk had said to him, 'That's a canny long time till we're ninety, Heron. But I'll be there if you are.' They were friends for life.

Today, leaving Hawk at the Draag Stone, Sam rode slowly over the moorland towards Faerie Hill, keeping an eye out for any activity. He was aware of feeling more curious than anxious about this evening and there was a peculiar sensation he couldn't quite put his finger on. This felt somehow important, as if he was going to meet his destiny, whatever that might be.

Nothing moved in the familiar landscape, which tonight was brightly lit by a full moon in its cloudless sky. Wasn't the stillness odd if there was a meeting about to happen? Hawk had been right; he really didn't know what to expect. All he knew from the trees was that there was a gathering here tonight, possibly around midnight. How the trees knew this, he was still unsure as he'd never known them to foretell an event before, but he was as sure as he could be that this was the message they had relayed.

Coming to the edge of the wooded hill, Sam immediately began to feel more relaxed. Among trees he was amongst friends, but the question was, who else was here? He was tethering his horse to a sturdy branch when a voice came out of a stand of silver birches behind him.

'Ah, a new face! Welcome, brother.'

Sam turned to find himself faced with a short, elderly man dressed in a priest's habit, with both hands held out to him in greeting.

'Oh, no need to be concerned about me, dear fellow. A True heart is as one with the forest, is it not?' said the priest, with a broad, genuine smile.

Sam's mother had taught him those words since he was small and he knew them to be linked to the True, but it was odd hearing them from a stranger's mouth. He replied, almost without thinking, with the line that he knew followed.

'Blood and sap through trunk and limb run deep.'

'I knew it. How pleasant. Come, shall we walk up to the covert together? This will be your first meeting, I imagine. No companion or relative to introduce you? No, what a pity. Well, my name is Frayne. I would be honoured to be of assistance to you tonight, but I think you'll find it a welcoming assembly.'

The priest chatted easily as they walked through the trees up the hill towards the summit. Sam learned that Frayne was a priest from the remote Horseshoe Priory near Rothbury.

'Sadly, I am the last in that beautiful, crumbling house and my poor congregation are but few in number. So these days I seem to spend more time in the woods planting and nurturing as many trees as I can before my time comes.'

'Ah, you too. That's something we hold in common then,' replied Sam, with a laugh. 'Perhaps I should have been a priest, since it seems I now live like one.'

Frayne stopped and put a hand on Sam's arm.

'My son, to my mind, the way of the True is no lesser path. Perhaps I will be damned for my blasphemy, but I believe God is in the trees and the rest of nature as much as he is in the human heart. I serve God and the True cause with equal joy. For me, it is one and the same.'

Nearer the summit, they joined with more people heading slowly up the hill's gentle slopes. Frayne was greeted warmly by all. Sam was wondering where they had all suddenly come from, but Frayne carried on talking and walking as if this was the most natural thing to be doing at midnight on Beltane on Faerie Hill.

The hill was topped with three ancient oaks and there was a large clearing between them; it was a cathedral-like space defined by vaulted arches of living wood. Sam was met with the sight of perhaps forty people, mostly men of varied ages, and most wearing discreet travelling garb though it was obvious that there was a mixture of wealthier and poorer. Each carried a wooden staff.

'Oh, fiddlesticks!' said Frayne, as he stopped to draw breath and look up towards the small crowd. 'All this talking and I quite forgot my staff. I left it at the bottom of the hill when we met. We must find one each. Not too thick, mind you.'

They both searched for a likely-looking long branch, then Frayne took out his knife.

'I generally keep a slice of wood about the size of a gold coin with me from my staff from such nights,' he explained. 'A memento if you like. Then you need to mark the staff with your name in ogham script, so the fire recognises you if you wish to speak. You are familiar with ogham?'

Sam had loved learning this ancient gaelic script from his mother. It felt like a secret code. He had taught it to Hawk when they were young, so they had their own secret means of communication. He'd never met anyone else who knew it, though, and his mother forbade him from mentioning it.

The letters of ogham were a sequence of straight or slanted short lines drawn across or to the right or left of one longer main line. In a similar way that the word 'alphabet' came from alpha and beta, the actual ogham letters were known as the beith-luis-nin, which were the first three letters of the script. For the True, each of the twenty letters were linked to a tree or plant. Beith (b) was silver birch, Luis (l) was Rowan, and Nin (n) was ash. Sam's own name was made up of willow, pine and vine, the symbols for which he scored quickly onto this makeshift staff before taking a small slice of the staff as Frayne had suggested.

Sam and Frayne both took up a place at the fire. There was general chatter until an elegant elderly grey-haired lady stood up closer to the blaze and planted her staff firmly and purposefully on the ground before her. Conversations lulled and faces looked expectantly at her.

'My name is Sara Graham, and I am True.'

Her voice rang out in the crisp night air of the busy clearing and, as the words melted into the canopy above, she broke her slender staff in half over her knee and threw the broken pieces

79

onto the fire. It had begun.

Sara started to intone the verse that Sam knew so well and that he'd heard Frayne speak a line of already tonight. The whole gathering quickly joined in.

A True heart is as one with the forest,
Blood and sap through trunk and limb run deep.
The ancient word shall be shared with the wisest,
While other beings know naught but wakeful sleep.

Be they tethered to soil or tied to the wind,
The arboreal scribes write their stories, lest they be forgot.
A natural history by Beith, Luis and Nin,
From woodland to mankind, shared freely, with those who know not.

Endure with Oak
Accept with Elder
Connect with Ash
Balance with Alder

True connection is earthly protection
Of forests both bygone and still yet to come.

At the end of the True verse, Sara addressed the gathering.

'Welcome, my friends. Welcome to the True Covert of this day in the year of our Lord, 1725. Today is Beltane and we celebrate the start of the summer with fire and friendship. But this is a particularly special night for those of us here, since we join together only once each quarter century. Welcome to you all. And we give our respect and friendship to the spirit of woodland, our hosts who have amply provided us with warmth

80

and shelter this evening.' She bowed to the great trees watching over the meeting, as did everyone else present.

'Some faces I recognise,' Sara continued, with a smile. 'Twenty-five years changes us all on the outside, but we all know that the same light shines from older eyes. I am happy to see that our brother Frayne is still hale and hearty at his third covert,' she looked over to the priest and many people acknowledged him with cheers, 'but some faces I'd hoped to see are sadly missing. No doubt we will discover the reasons over the course of the evening. Our numbers are sadly ever in decline, something we should look to address this night. Also, on behalf of the whole covert, I am honoured to greet those joining us for the first time. We are glad of your presence with us here tonight and look forward to learning more about you.'

It transpired that Sara came from Berwick-upon-Tweed where she ran a successful cloth business. She gave general news from her area, including a report of some large woodland planting projects she'd initiated. She then ceded her place for the next speaker. Sam hadn't yet worked out what the hierarchy might be, but a bearded man stood up and walked to the same spot by the fire.

'My name is Marcus Heffer, and I am True.'

Marcus was a small man but wielded an excessively hefty-looking staff, which caused a few good-humoured laughs as he twice failed to break it. On the third attempt, though, it gave way and thus his name was added to the fire and he began to speak.

He shared news from around his home near Whinfell Forest, not far from Carlisle. As well as being a blacksmith, he was the self-styled guardian to this area of forest which included the

81

remaining ancient oak tree known as the Three Brother tree. Sadly, its two brothers were long since gone, but he reported that the last of the three was still in reasonable health for its age and had even recently attracted the attention of a writer, a man named Daniel Defoe, who intended to mention the tree in a book he was working on.

'The Brother tree is still in reasonable spirits considering his loneliness since his siblings' demise, and,' he added, almost conspiratorially, 'I can personally attest that he is able to help True travellers with links back at least 200 years.'

The news was met with a few impressed nods, but mostly a general murmuring. Sam wasn't really sure why.

And so the night went on. Each member of the covert who chose to speak added their broken staff to the fire and brought tales from their locality, including how much woodland had been planted. Slowly a picture grew of how the northern woods and their wild inhabitants were faring. The general consensus that it was better than in the last fifty years, though complacency was certainly not a feature of the conversations. The forests needed help, that was unanimously agreed.

As the hours lengthened, Sam realised that, far from being the clueless outsider he had felt himself at the start of the night, he was amongst people that he had much in common with. His mother had taught him well it seemed. When someone spoke of meditating with holly in order to focus one's energy and sense of purpose to achieve something, he understood. When a healer recommended chewing willow leaves to help reduce mouth ulcers, or ash keys for a gentle laxative effect, he recognised these as simple remedies he'd known for many years. When the advice was shared about rowan being the best tree from which to harvest a divining fork for discovering underground metals, that was new to him, and yet he could immediately grasp the truth of this given what he knew to be the traits of the rowan tree.

At some point in the proceedings, which were interspersed with breaks for general chat and some shared refreshments, Sam was invited to speak.

'My name is Samuel Heron, and I am True.'

As he threw the pieces of his staff onto the fire, he realised the truth of what he'd just said. He definitely belonged to this group of people. It was obvious to him that his mother had meant for this to happen, and he was a part of this strange congregation.

'I am new to the covert, as you will know. Since my father's demise, I head the Moss Hall estate local to here. I am a tree reader, but I know neither what is expected of me nor how I can help our purpose. However, I have been brought up to know and respect the forest and I am a farmer and trader too. I offer my services, such as they are.'

'May we ask your lineage, Sam, as Heron is not a name we've had in our recent history to my knowledge.' The question was posed by Frayne, who smiled widely at him.

'Certainly. My mother is ... was Eleanor Tait before my father married her. Perhaps that is a name you recognise?'

With that, whispering increased and looks of interest were directed more keenly at him, making him feel rather uncomfortable.

'Oh, dearest Eleanor,' said Frayne. 'I had hoped to see her here today. But I note you said "was". I'm very sorry to hear of her passing. God rest her soul. She was an extraordinary young woman. She would have only been about twenty years old at the last covert in 1700, I believe, so she died young for one of such obvious gifts of healing, did she not? Fate can seem so cruel.'

'Ay, well, to be truthful, I've not completely given up hope that she could be alive.'

Sam explained about her disappearance a year and a half earlier, but no-one could shed any light on where she might have gone.

Then, a slender, unassuming-looking man in a rough brown cloak came forward. Sam had noticed him looking at him now and then through the night, presumably interested in him as a new member of the covert.

'Perhaps ... Could she be a jumper?' he asked, quietly.

'A jumper, do you say? I'm sorry, sir, I am not familiar with the term,' replied Sam, openly.

The gathering once again lapsed into private conversations in hushed tones. There seemed to be some agitation.

'I apologise to the covert if I speak out of turn, but I think it's important. May I approach the fire?' asked the man. It was agreed and, with an almost shy smile in Sam's direction, he came forward to add his staff to the fire.

'My name is ...' The man paused for brief moment, almost as if deciding what name to give, before breaking his staff and continuing, 'Tom Baker, and I am True. I am a tree reader but, as those of you who were at the 1700 covert will hopefully already know, I am also a tree jumper. Brother Frayne, sister Sara, since you were both obviously at the 1700 gathering, might I ask, have you met me before?'

'Oh, indeed,' confirmed Frayne, enthusiastically. 'We had a most memorable meeting, and of course I remain cognisant of the gravity of your message to us all.'

Tom inclined his head in acknowledgement to Frayne, and replied politely, 'I look forward to it, sir. It's my next port of call.'

Sam was utterly baffled by the conversation and was just about to ask for an explanation when Tom continued.

He looked directly at Sam. He had one of those open, friendly faces that made you feel like you'd met him before and, if you hadn't, you'd like to.

'Mr Heron, like you and everyone else here, I can read trees. However, I can go a step further than that. Through trees it's possible to go back in time. I have come here from the year 2020.'

Sam and a few others immediately laughed out loud, but they quickly stopped. No-one else was laughing.

CHAPTER SEVEN

JUMPERS

Tuesday, May 1st, 1725

It was still pitch black, but dawn was heralded by the rich tones of the early-rising blackbirds which had just begun to sing as the fireside speeches ended. Sam hadn't really paid much heed to the speakers after Tom Baker; even Frayne's offering was more or less a blur. His mind was reeling from the world-altering news he'd heard.

It seemed that most of the covert were aware of tree jumpers. It was only news to himself and perhaps six others, who looked equally dumbfounded. Even though there was knowledge of this ability, he got the impression it was somehow frowned upon, or perhaps feared, or both, by many present. He wasn't surprised. After all, who in their right mind could even begin to get their head around travelling through time. It was absurd. No, Tom had to have been making it up. It simply couldn't be possible.

But then, how had he made that bright beam of light appear in his hand in an instant? He said he'd brought it to show doubters the truth of his claim to be from the future. Certainly, Sam had never seen the like, but maybe this was just some kind of new way of directing light from a small dark lantern, perhaps intensified by mirrors or some such thing? No, there assuredly had to be another explanation other than him coming from 300 years in the future. It could not be true, he thought to himself. The man was probably mad. And yet, he had to admit that Tom seemed very genuine and honest and not in the least bit insane. Sam had taken to him almost immediately and Frayne had nothing but good things to say about him, declaring himself fully trusting of his story. The priest said he had met Tom Baker once before, in the year 1700, so unless Frayne was complicit in a very peculiar deception, which Sam doubted, surely this had to be proof of the authenticity of Mr Baker's story that he was travelling back to each Faerie Hill covert that he could reach; proof that he was from the future.

Sam's world had just been split apart like a ripe horse chestnut. The seemingly impenetrable reality of a solid, green and spiky earth had just been wrenched asunder, offering a much more brown and slippery unreality for his consideration. His mind was flooded with questions. How had Tom got here from 2020? What role did the trees play? How could Frayne have met him already in the past, yet Tom not be aware of their meeting? Could his mother have known about tree jumping and gone back in time? Maybe he had never really come out of his fever over a year ago and this was all a ridiculous dream? What the hell was going on?!

Tom's speech by the fire hadn't answered any of these questions. It had, however, been an impassioned plea for help and his words resonated profoundly with Sam. Even given his current state of bafflement about Tom travelling through time, the message he brought had kindled a strange feeling within Sam.

For the past eighteen months, since his family were all taken from him, he had been sleepwalking through life in a state of numbness. Now, despite the bizarre nature of the current turn of events, he suddenly felt a spark which came from ... what? Annoyance? Indignation? Or even fear. Nature, and especially his precious trees, were being destroyed. Sam was a fighter. He had fought all his life to protect his mother and sister, both from his bullying father and from the harshness of life in the borders. In losing them both, he'd lost his reason for fighting for anything. Until now. Tom Baker was asking for help and his appeal for the forests was calling to him. His words were what Eleanor would have called powerful natural magic and he could feel them etched into his mind.

'My friends, as members of the True, we know that our prime purpose is to keep the forests safe, especially the ancient trees. We are their protectors and we are also guardians of all the natural world knowledge which trees have shared with us over the centuries.

'Many of you will be aware of tree jumpers such as myself, but it might still seem strange to be faced with someone from a future time. Trust me, it's just as weird for me to be visiting a time three hundred years before I was born.'

Tom half-laughed, half-grimaced, looking for a little light relief in a rather intense moment with an unsettled crowd. There were a few smiles, but most simply looked on and waited for him to continue.

'I'm here to ask for your help. Our True verse reminds us that *True connection is earthly protection of forests both bygone and still yet to come*. Well, in my time, our forests are crying

88

out for help. The world's population is about ten times what it is in your time and many people have precious little connection with the natural world. It feels like we're losing our link to the earth faster as each year goes by. Some city children don't even realise where their food comes from.'

The cloud of incomprehension and concern spread through the listeners.

'Of course, there are many people who value our natural world, but their voices cannot be heard loudly enough above the clamour of those with no interest in our forests and wild places other than for financial exploitation. In Britain we have very little ancient forest remaining and too few trees are being left to grow old for future generations. Sadly, people seem not to understand the extent of what is being lost each time an old tree is felled.

'So, I am here asking you, the True, to help your future families, your children's children and their children's children. My plea is a simple one: please, plant trees. Plant as many as you can, plant as many varieties as possible, plant them as soon as you are able and then leave them to grow old.

'Historically, the True have never written down what they know about trees and nature. I understand this was once a dangerous thing to do, but I beg for a change in this tradition now that being accused of witchcraft is no longer the threat it once was. Please, write down the things that you've learned from trees and shine a light on countryside wisdom for everyone to benefit from.

'To be blunt, if we don't help people to understand the value of the living world, then we are on course to lose it.'

As the first smudges of daybreak began to rub away at the edges of the night, the covert started to disperse. A few small groups of people, including Frayne, were standing chatting by the remains of the fire.

Sam looked around, searching for Tom, and eventually spotted his slight, cloaked figure quietly retreating downhill in the woodland.

'Mr Baker,' he called, walking briskly towards him. 'May I have a word with you before you, er, move on?'

Tom turned and waited for Sam to reach him.

'Sam. Mr Heron.' He smiled, but there were conflicting emotions of happiness and sadness etched in his face. 'I knew you would have lots of questions.'

'Indeed I do, sir. I — '

'Sam, I'm really very sorry,' interrupted Tom, 'I wish I could help you of all people, but I just daren't tell you anything. You see, I don't know how this all works or how what I say to you might affect the future. I'm just a doctor, what you would call a physician, not a time traveller really.'

'A physician perhaps, but from what you say, also a time traveller,' Sam pointed out. 'So, you were really speaking the truth?'

'I was. Certainly,' he said with earnest. 'Sam, it's so good to —' Tom stopped, and looked directly at him, then, with a slight shake of his head, took Sam's left hand in both of his own, saying, 'I promise you will find a way. You are a good man, Sam Heron. Never doubt that. And ... thank you.'

'For what?' asked Sam, perplexed, but Tom had turned and was already striding quickly away into the trees.

At that moment, Sam became aware of raised voices up at

the campfire then heard his name being shouted twice with urgency. He looked towards Tom, torn between following him and responding to the call, but knew he had to head quickly back up to the clearing.

After the intensity and extraordinary revelations of the night, it was verging on comical to see Hawk chasing Frayne and another couple of anxious-looking older men around the campfire, threatening them at sword-point.

'What have you done with him? I'm not afraid of forest faeries. Come on, give him back. Sam! Where are you? Sam!'

'Leave them be, Hawk,' said Sam, calmly, as he came towards the fire. 'I'm here and quite safe, as you can see.'

He could see a momentary look of relief on Hawk's face as he recognised Sam coming out of the semi-darkness, but then Hawk's more usual cheeky expression took over as he realised there was no danger but possible fun to be had.

'Are you sure now, Heron?' he said, with a wicked grin. 'These priest's clothes might be a ruse by the forest pixies and they could be up to no good.' He made a mock lunge towards Frayne with his sword and the three men scuttled round the fire out of his reach.

Sam laughed and went over to them. The two he didn't know rushed quickly away, then he introduced Frayne and Hawk to each other.

'This kind priest has been a generous guide to me tonight,' he said to Hawk, then turning to Frayne, added, 'I apologise for my friend. He only has my best interests at heart, but I'm sorry if he worried you.'

Frayne quickly accepted Hawk's apologies and the two were soon chatting amiably.

Sam looked back over his shoulder in the direction Tom Baker had gone and he knew he wouldn't find him now. Instead, he joined Frayne and Hawk and they began to walk together back down the wooded slopes of the opposite side of the hill. As they walked, Sam was thinking through his options. There was no doubt that Frayne was now his best chance of finding out about tree jumping. He needed to know more.

'Frayne, would you allow me to accompany you back to the priory. It is a good day's walk, the roads are still not as safe as they should be, and,' he added, looking at Frayne's small but bulging travel sack, 'you seem to have collected some extra baggage this night. I hope you'll accept.'

'With pleasure, my dear Sam, and thank you. In which case, I will say my farewells to —'

'No, no. Where he goes, I go. So you've got both of us,' said Hawk, as he mounted his horse. He held out a hand to the priest and Sam helped Frayne up behind his friend. The three set off towards Rothbury and Horseshoe Priory.

BEECH

I am mother of the woods. Some call me queen but I hope I'm never haughty. I try to show a generous spirit, sharing shelter and food with those who need it. It's true that once my leaves are full grown very little grows beneath my broad, dense canopy, but I have an understanding with wood sorrel, wood anemones and most especially bluebells, all of whom bless the forest floor with their beauty before my shadow falls. Their shining colours then give way to my bright greens which turn to burnished bronzes, bright coppers and gentle golds as the earth prepares to sleep.

At my feet a carpet of discarded leaves, prickly husks and three-sided beech masts becomes the empty dais upon which I reign for many a long year as a tall, graceful figurehead for the woodland. I live much longer as a coppiced tree or a hedge than as an undisturbed tree since my roots are shallow and — eventually, inevitably — my friend the wind and I quarrel and I am unable to stand up to the buffeting. I accept my fate with tolerance, sorry only that the badgers, mice, squirrels and birds will no longer enjoy my springtime and autumnal feasts of pollen, seeds and nuts.

Mankind connects my name with wisdom through their writings. I was the 'paper' of one of their first books, just as our king, the oak, was the ink. Together we preserved their wisdom through the written word. Beech, book — our names share the same root. I am glad of this as knowledge is important. The wisdom of our ancestors should never be overlooked; it was hard won over millennia but is easily forgotten in one careless generation.

I am mother of the woods; I teach, I nurture and I love.

CHAPTER EIGHT

HORSESHOE PRIORY

Tuesday, May 1st, 1725

The day was bright in patches, with the sun deigning to make the odd appearance through the high clouds, one moment highlighting a field of sheep with their lambs and the next picking out a ramshackle stone farmstead on the edge of the narrow floodplain.

After Rothbury, the land became more rocky and the river had gouged itself a deeper path through the countryside. Horseshoe Priory was aptly named as it sat alone on a tight loop of the river, almost on its own small island. It couldn't be seen until you descended a narrow path from the north heading through the trees towards the Coquet. Hidden as it was between wood, rock and water, only at the last moment did the warm grey limestone walls of the church show themselves to curious travellers or those in search of solace or redemption. This was no hubristic statement of God's supremacy, no edifice to overawe and control. Instead, once found, its ancient stonework offered enough grandeur to impress, sufficient size and solemnity to be taken seriously, but also enough humanity to be welcoming. Sadly though, time had been unkind to this reclusive house of worship, and it patently didn't have a wealthy family backing it with funds. It seemed that Horseshoe had been in steady decline for many years, probably since the dissolution of the monasteries by the looks of it, though perhaps the Border Reivers hadn't helped either. The church roof was a skin of serviceable but rough unmatched patches, there were whole sections of attached buildings that lay in ruins, and window glass was mostly conspicuous by its absence. Despite its sorry state though, the building still had a certain pride. Not a sinful kind of pride, of course (God forbid), but the kind that washed its face and tightened its belt, and said, 'No, perhaps I'm not looking my best, but I have a job to do and I can still do it. Let the people come.'

Sam knew where that air of cheerful dignity came from. As the three of them rode into the little peninsula, everywhere he looked he could see what he was sure was Frayne's influence. All the paths and open areas by the priory were well-kept and free of the debris from the ruins; outside of the main oak door there was a pitcher filled with bluebells; but mainly there were trees, lots of trees. Other than directly outside the church and around the buildings, trees grew everywhere. A handsome grove of about fifteen oaks had been planted maybe thirty years ago on a roughly flat plot between the priory and where the bank dropped sharply to the river. For the higher slopes behind it, in between the few much older trees, the priest had chosen a combination of mainly birch, ash and sycamore, and on the riverbanks he'd managed to establish more birch, plus alder and willow. Sam could see that he'd now begun to populate the opposite banks too.

There was a small stone house a short distance from the priory building. It was thatched and there was a neat garden in front of it. Sam knew that, in addition to vegetables, Frayne was growing all manner of herbs and medicinal flowers as he'd mentioned that he tried to use nature to heal his flock as well as offering them the word of God. Indeed, over the course of conversation on the day's ride, Sam had learned that Frayne had set up a kind of hospital where anyone in need could come and receive the good priest's ministrations from nature.

As well as his young curate and a collection of helpers who lived nearby, there were two people who were very close to Frayne: old Thomas, an ex-stonequarry worker who'd come to the priory five years ago with a crushed leg, and stayed; and Grace, a young woman that Frayne had taken in as an orphan twelve years ago when she was just nine years old. In effect, they were his family.

Thomas and Grace both appeared to greet the elderly priest. Thomas kept his distance, leaning on a wall of the priory and giving a serious nod with just the hint of a smile when Frayne looked his way. Grace, on the other hand, came rushing out of the cottage, obviously delighted and relieved to see him back safely. The sight of the two men accompanying him slowed her approach somewhat at first, but she could quickly tell that the priest was comfortable in their presence.

"You're back earlier than you thought, father. Thanks to these gentlemen, I suppose? It's getting on. Will you stay the night with us, sirs?' she asked Sam and Hawk. 'We can offer you beds in the hospital. We're not full tonight, I'm pleased to say.' She turned to Frayne. 'There is just one unfortunate patient. He annoyed the redcoats he met in Edenbury last night and ended up with a serious beating for his troubles. A friend brought him to us by cart this morning.'

Sam threw a brief, anxious glance over to Hawk — proximity to British Army redcoats would surely not be a wholly comfortable prospect for him given his recent run-ins with them — but he seemed to be taking the news with characteristic Sparrowhawk nonchalance.

'Edenbury,' said Hawk, 'a canny place to stop the night on the way to Berwick-on-Tweed barracks, I'm sure.'

Within a couple of hours of their arrival, Grace had prepared a tasty vegetable stew and there was flatbread on the table. As the weather was still fair and the nights lengthening, they all ate together outside in the last of the day's sunshine, joined by Thomas and a skinny young boy they called Midge. Midge lived a couple of miles away with his mother but came each day to help Thomas fetch and carry.

'Eat and be gone, young Midge, or your Ma will be fretting. Here, take her the rest of this loaf,' said Frayne, and put half a breadcake on the boy's lap. He gobbled down his stew and bread and scampered off home in the half light.

By the campfire later on, Hawk entertained the priory residents and neighbours with tunes on his small pipes. He was always happy to be the bearer of merriment and the centre of attention. In his left arm he held the bag with the protruding pipes, and with his right arm he pumped the bellows that gave breath to the music. The constant underlying nasal hum from the three drones were accompanied by the melody that Hawk conjured up from the eight notes of the chanter. He loved jigs and shanties, anything to get his audience clapping and dancing (and usually, though not today, parting with their money to keep him playing), but he also enjoyed making up some slower pieces, particularly when he was alone. Tonight's small group didn't get much chance to make merry, and some were taking the opportunity temporarily to dance away the cares of their hard lives. Grace was obviously rapt and itching to get on her feet.

Hawk looked over at Sam as he played and tilted his head in Grace's direction. Sam smiled. He could see the young woman struggling to keep still. He was used to it. Hawk's music always had this effect. He stood up and walked over to her.

'Might I have the pleasure of a turn around the fire with you?' He bowed courteously then held out his hand.

She hesitated only for a moment, with a brief look at Frayne. He was thoroughly enjoying himself, clapping along and, with a shooing motion, he encouraged her to get up and dance with Sam. She held out her hand and Sam pulled her up from the low cracket. With one arm, he held her gently by the waist and took her right hand in his. He looked her in the eye, saw the glint, smiled widely and they were off. They danced around the fire, soon swirling and laughing as if they'd known each other for years. Sam moved with agility and elegance. Fencing and dancing were not that different in some ways and he'd learned both from a young age. His easy, confident manner always made him a popular dance partner for the young women at gatherings wherever Hawk played. Of course, he'd also learned more formal dancing for any society occasions related to his status as the son of Sir Richard Heron, but the pleasure he felt dancing with the women at a gypsy celebration or at some local revelry was far preferable to him to the more restrained formality of a society event.

Grace's long fair hair streamed behind her as Sam twirled her around. Her pretty face was alight with happiness and

99

flushed with exertion and he was quickly taken by her infectious joy of life.

'Enough, enough!' she panted after the third tune and came to a stop, breathless. He led her back to the stool and bent to kiss her hand. Grace invited him to sit on the bench next to her. 'Perhaps a short rest, then we can go around again?'

The word hit Sam squarely in the chest and took his breath away. 'Again, again.' He couldn't stop himself seeing Martha jumping up and down with childlike excitement. His sister was never far from his mind.

'Er, no, I — I should ...' He vaguely pointed to the other side of the fire, then mumbled an inadequate, 'Forgive me,' as he walked away, feeling like a discourteous oaf and yet certain that keeping his distance from Grace was the right thing to do. With the loss of the two most precious women in his life, he'd made the decision that he couldn't take responsibility for any other. He could not bear the thought of letting down anyone else that he might grow to love. No, he would remain a bachelor, like Hawk. He'd always enjoyed the company of women, and hopefully still would, but he would give no woman cause to love him. He respected Frayne too much to even begin to get to know his adopted daughter since he feared he could fall quickly for Grace's honest charms. She deserved better.

As the evening drew on, Hawk eventually put down his pipes and the small crowd soon headed for their beds. Grace bade goodnight to Frayne, then nodded uncertainly to Sam across the fire. He smiled back and stood as she and the others left. Sam, Hawk and Frayne remained chatting by the fireplace.

'So tell me, even in these modern times, how does a man of God end up talking to trees yet not being branded a witch,

100

then?' asked Hawk, as he poked at the fire with a long stick. 'My friend here has always had a bit of witchcraft in him, so I'm not totally shocked, but a priest? That surprises me. There must be a story to tell there or I'm no gypsy.'

'Ah, so you've shared your secret with your friend,' said Frayne, looking at Sam. 'I'm pleased, you know. The bond between you is strong.'

'How could I *not* explain about the True after this morning's events?' He turned to Hawk. 'Will you forgive me for not telling you before, Hawk? I didn't want the knowledge to bring you any trouble.'

'Trouble? Me? Never in this world!' He laughed. 'My friends, I realise this is a thing far bigger than me. I'm honoured to be party to the little you've shared, but I know better than to get involved. Heron, tree reading is for you alone, but I will revel in hearing the stories you learn. Talking of which,' he said, turning back to the priest, 'come along Father Frayne, we await a fireside story of intrigue and mystery, magic and mayhem.'

Frayne began by explaining that he was born into the nobility as Thomas Forster, the youngest of three sons of Simon, Earl of Edenbury, whose seat was Edenbury Castle.

'My brothers went in for politics and the army but I was always destined for the church. I went to Cambridge to study, but left behind the love of my life, Hannah. Sadly she was but a housemaid, so not deemed worthy for someone of my birth. I'm ashamed to say that before I took my religious studies seriously... well, suffice to say, we had a child, a daughter. My family took Hannah and our newborn daughter away from me. It took me a very long time to forgive them for that.'

'I knew there'd be a woman involved somewhere down the line,' muttered Hawk, only half under his breath. Sam frowned at him.

'So, was it Hannah that was True?' asked Sam.

'Oh, no, not at all,' said Frayne. 'The connection with the True came later, once I became a deacon and then curate to a priest in Edenbury after college. He's long since dead now, God rest his soul, but he was priest, father and mentor to me, and it was *he,* Matthew, that was True.'

'Another priest. Hah! Are we to learn that *all* our clergy are witches?' said Hawk, greatly amused by this revelation.

Frayne laughed. 'You know, I think there could have been many more True priests in the past, but these days I'm afraid that those in the Church are not always there because of their strong Christian belief nor their wish to redeem or help their fellow humans, let alone protect nature. I hope this will change once again, and indeed, I was once told that, in that respect at least, the Church will improve vastly.'

Sam immediately picked up on his reference to the future.

'So did Tom Baker tell you this at a previous Covert? You got a chance to speak with him about his time?' he asked.

'Umm, no. Though you're right that I learned this at a Covert. In a way, at least. It was my first Covert. My priest, Father Matthew, was careful to combine my ongoing religious education with sharing his love of the natural world and his knowledge of the existence and importance of the True. He had no family to pass the tradition on to and I will be forever grateful that he chose me to continue his True line. I learned to read trees and began my own True journey.

'In May of the year of our Lord 1675, he sent me to my first meeting of the True. I was only twenty-six years old and I was entranced but, as you were Sam, also shocked to hear about tree jumping. I know you will want to know, but Tom Baker wasn't there. I don't know why he never made it to 1675. Perhaps he never intended to? As you found out, he doesn't remain for any length of time after a Covert and refuses to engage further than giving his message, no matter how fervently he's encouraged to do so.'

'Yes,' said Sam, 'he was unwilling to tell me anything. But in that case, how do you know about the future of the church?'

'Ah, well. He is not the only jumper I have met,' said Frayne.

'No, wait, just wait,' interrupted Hawk, who'd been getting more and more perplexed about the turn of the conversation. He held up his hands, calling a halt to the tale.

'Tree jumping? What on earth are you two blathering on about? So now we hear that not only can you talk to trees —'

'*Read* trees,' said Sam and Frayne together.

'Very well, *read* trees,' said Hawk, with an exasperated roll of the eyes. 'I think we're splitting hairs here though. So, not only can you *read* trees, you are now acting like squirrels and *jumping* between trees. To what end, though?' he asked, baffled.

Frayne looked over to Sam, trying not to laugh.

'I didn't get to that part,' said Sam, in reply to his unvoiced question. 'And anyway, I still don't really understand it well enough myself to be able to explain to Hawk.'

'None of us does to begin with. It was only jumping myself that made any of it make sense,' said Frayne.

Sam wasn't expecting that. He'd hoped that Frayne would

103

be able to shed light on tree jumping but hadn't really imagined that it would be from personal experience.

'What? You mean you're from the future too?'

'What?!' said Hawk. 'What the devil —'

'Oh, I'm not making a very good job of this story-telling am I?' said Frayne, with a chuckle. 'Now you're both confused and I've already said things that should come much later. Let me try again.'

At the Covert of May 1675, Frayne met a middle-aged man. He was dressed slightly oddly, with long trousers and a baggy woollen jumper, and he sat for most of the Covert with his back propped up against an old beech tree. A few people tried to talk to him at first but he seemed happy to be an onlooker. As the evening ended, he didn't move. The young Frayne offered help and the man had simply smiled and said, 'Hello. I'm Fred. I am a traveller in an antique land,' before falling unconscious.

'Where was he from?' asked Hawk. 'Was he from afar? A blackamoore, perhaps? I've always wanted to meet a blackamoore.'

'No, he was from even further away than Africa. I discovered a few days later that he was from Hexham —'

'Hexham? But that's just —' said Hawk, with a confused frown, and starting to point in a generally southern direction.

'Hexham, in the year of our Lord 2000,' continued Frayne. Hawk's hand dropped back down to his side and he turned, open-mouthed, to the priest. Then he started smiling and turned to Sam.

'Did you hear that, Heron? Haha, now that's a story the likes of which I never expected from a priest. You are a fabler after my own heart, good priest.' And he laughed loudly until he realised that his friend wasn't laughing with him.

'I reacted exactly the same way earlier today,' said Sam. 'I know it's hard to believe. I'm still struggling with it myself.'

'What? Well, of course it is hard to believe, you numbskull. It's a story,' said Hawk, looking at Sam incredulously. 'Wait, wait, you don't *actually* believe him, do you? Sam? Heron, please tell me you don't believe this blather.'

Sam's silence was telling.

'Oh, fire and furies! You've both been enchanted by the Faerie Hill pixies. I knew it!' He stood up and began to scrabble for his small sword which he'd put aside earlier in the evening. Sam intervened.

'Hawk, calm yourself. We're neither of us in thrall to the faeries, man. Just let Frayne finish his story, eh?'

He got a grudging nod of agreement, though noticed that Hawk kept his hand on his sword hilt.

'I quite understand your agitation, Mr Hawk, but there's truly no cause for alarm. Fred was a perfectly normal human being, just like us, but he was one of the True and he'd discovered that we have the ability to time travel through trees. It sounds to be against nature to you, I know —'

'And God, surely?!' interjected Hawk.

'— but believe me, nature itself facilitates this miracle.'

Frayne had taken Fred to Edenbury with him. There was a cave he used to play in as a child by the riverbanks near his family's castle; no-one went there so it was a secret enough hideout for a suspected time-traveller. The man was in and out of consciousness for two days before fully coming round. He was initially disorientated, forgetting where, or rather when, he was but once he remembered he calmed down and seemed content. After a couple of weeks under Frayne's care, he was much improved and he began talking.

The young priest learned that Fred had been told he had only a few weeks to live, so, with no family to worry about, he'd decided to have an adventure before he died. What better adventure than time-travelling? Fred had first learned about tree jumping in 1975 and then again at the 2000 Covert, after which, on the way home via Middle Wood, he'd made the spontaneous decision to try his luck at going back in time. He'd been advised by other True at the Covert that he had to go further back than his date of birth, but he was surprised to find himself right back in May 1675 — on the day of that year's Covert.

Over the next few weeks, a friendship grew between the seventeenth century priest and the twenty-first century traveller. They shared stories of their own times, personal intimacies, and fears and failings that neither had thought ever to share with another — their unique situation led to a deep honesty and total trust. This trust was put to the test one day when Frayne decided to ask Fred how to tree jump.

'I realised that this was my one and only chance to see my mother,' Frayne explained to Sam and Hawk. 'Yes, I know that might seem like an odd decision for a grown man, but she died when I was born. I always longed to know her. Fred was happy to help me, of course, and getting to see my mother became my overriding focus. But I admit, I didn't really think through what doing this would mean to me. Not really.'

With Fred's guidance, Frayne prepared to jump back in time. He chose a relatively young tree in case he found it difficult to control how far back in time he went, but it had to be one that was older than himself as, apparently, trees would not allow a jumper to stop in a time where they already had a presence. Then, asking for the tree's permission, he took a small section of root from the ash he'd chosen; this was to be his ticket back to the present time, his 'future wood' as Fred called it. Without it, he would be stuck in the past.

Fred had said that Frayne must simply begin to read the tree as he would normally, going back in time, season on season, year on year, but then, when he felt he was at the time he wanted to be, he had to "let go and fall in".

'I didn't really understand what I was letting go *of*,' said Frayne, 'And as for "falling in", well, I've never been a swimmer, so it all sounded very daunting yet haphazard to me. I thought there must be some specific invocation or ritual, but no.'

'Ah, but you're a man of faith,' said Sam, 'you believe the unprovable. Maybe that and your skill at tree *reading* made it easier?'

'Or maybe it was just like falling into the arms of the lovely Hannah?!' added Hawk, interested despite himself, and pretending a mock swoon before remembering he was talking to a priest and muttering an apology.

The seemingly insufficient instructions, though, turned out to be completely adequate. Frayne had trusted himself to the ash and quickly found himself at a time he knew immediately was not 1675 — for a start, his ash was very young — yet still within the grounds of Edenbury Castle.

Even dressed as the priest he now was, he suspected he'd be thrown out, or worse, if caught in the castle grounds, so he knew he had to wait for his mother to come to him. He was as nervous as a mouse but knew that she'd had a stone seat placed in the garden she loved, so positioned himself nearby, hidden by a yew hedge.

By late morning, his mother Isobel and her sister came walking through the garden.

'Oh, my heart nearly burst to see her,' related Frayne. 'She was beautiful, and barely older than myself. I was immediately a young boy, and all my childish dreams of her, all my longings for my angel-like mother (for so she had become to me as a boy), blotted out the grown man that stood there. I yearned to run to her and hold her close.'

He stopped, a clenched hand covering his heart, obviously transported back to that moment.

'But I knew our meeting could never be,' he said, with a slow distracted nod, as if still wondering what would have happened if …

'The bluebells will be so beautiful there now,' said Frayne, more to himself than his guests, then shook himself. 'Er yes, well, those were the first words I heard her say. She was talking about Horseshoe Priory. She and her sister lived close by as children and she remembered the old abandoned priory fondly. I heard her say that she always had a silly dream of living there, and she laughed at the irony of her having married into the family who owned it.' Frayne stopped again, savouring the images that were obviously still very clear in his mind's eye.

'Then, despite everything my head was telling me, I could stop myself no longer.'

'Yes!' exploded Hawk. 'I was wondering when you would grow some b—, I mean, when you might find some guts.'

Frayne laughed. 'Just you try meeting your dead mother, my son. It's not that easy.'

Frayne had plucked a few of the sparsely scattered bluebells from nearby, and he came around the hedge to greet his mother.

'She was shocked to see someone in her private garden, of course, but my priest's apparel made her less uneasy than she might have been. I introduced myself as Father Frayne, a name I'd not used until then. It means stranger as well as ash tree — it seemed apt. I said I was visiting her husband. I handed her the bluebells,' Frayne's hands reached out in front of him as he spoke, 'and I gently and all too briefly held her hand, wishing her a joyous life and assuring her of God's love. Then I left before my eyes betrayed my inner turmoil and she became concerned about my presence.

'That was it,' said Frayne, his eyes now seeing Sam and Hawk rather than his mother. 'I crept back to my ash tree. I was elated and yet all at once bone-tired. The trees had given me a gift beyond my wildest imaginings and it struck me like a hammer on an anvil. My senses were bruised and battered. A few minutes had changed my life, the whole world, my beliefs. Human existence no longer followed the rules I thought I understood.

'I knew I had to leave, but for a long long time I couldn't even make myself move. I had met my long-dead mother; a woman I had only shared the world with for a matter of minutes after my birth. It was an impossibility become reality. I was beyond happy, and yet … the laws of nature were turned on their head. I had accepted tree *reading* as easily as learning a new language; it seemed somehow right that there should be a way to converse with nature. But jumping to another time? This was very different. I went looking for my mother and I found her, but there was so much more to the experience. The reality of what I'd just done was far bigger and more earth-shattering than I could have imagined.

109

'Having eventually returned to 1675, I begged leave from Matthew and Fred, explaining briefly about the dilemma I'd been thrown into. I came here, alone, to Horseshoe Priory, a place I had never visited, but which had suddenly become immensely important to me.

'For days, I sat …' Frayne had his hands together as if in prayer, with his fingertips touching his chin and his closed eyes delegating the sense of sight to his memory. 'I sat with my mother. And I sat with the trees and the priory ruins — the True and the Church.' He dropped his hands to his lap, palms still together, and looked at them as he opened first one, then the other. 'Nature and God.'

CHAPTER NINE

THE EVERY TREE

Wednesday, May 2nd, 1725

Coming to terms with all he'd heard in the last thirty-six hours was not conducive to a peaceful mind, or sleep. Sam needed the calmness of the trees to help him try to make sense of it. About half past five in the morning, leaving Hawk still snoring in the hospital, he headed through the grove of oak trees and down to the riverbank. A narrow rope and wood bridge led him to the gentle wooded slope on the opposite side of the Coquet.

In the woodland, the ash trees had still not embraced spring and looked like tall grey ghosts stepping cautiously through a sea of cheerful bluebells. Too soon, too soon, said the ashes. But the birches, alders and hazels ignored them and offered a haze of bright, fresh green leaves to enhance the beauty of the flowers.

Last night, Frayne said that he'd eventually come to the conclusion that he couldn't choose between God and Nature. They were one and the same, he'd decided, and should be equally revered and loved. Obviously if people learned about tree reading, and certainly tree jumping, they would see it as an abomination against the laws of nature and, indeed, against

God. Heaven, Hell, the resurrection, these were all certainly difficult issues for Frayne now, given what he knew about time travel but, in essence, he believed in and loved God. He believed that God made the world, and he fundamentally rejected the idea that trees were somehow working against God's holy plan.

After sitting for some time, in solitude yet also in communion with the wood, Sam could come to no other conclusion himself. Tree jumping was certainly at odds with natural laws as he had thought he understood them, but he couldn't believe that anything offered by nature could be evil. Trees could *not* be evil.

'Good morrow,' called Frayne, as he walked up towards Sam from the riverbank. 'Grace thought she'd caught sight of you on the bridge earlier. Are you quite well, my son? What we know is a privilege and a joy but also a burden, is it not? May I sit with you?'

'It is perhaps harder for you as a man of God but, yes, it changes your world,' agreed Sam, as Frayne joined him on the dry bare ground at the foot of a large ash. 'It's certainly not a weight I'd wish on many people.'

He immediately thought of Hawk and regretted involving him, though perhaps someone who already believed in faeries wasn't too much of a concern. Sam was at least certain that the secret was safe with Hawk.

'I believe Grace has a plan for you later today, if you're willing to assist her with making some remedies,' said Frayne, then adding, 'You know, it's very possible that you turned my Gracie's head somewhat with your dancing last night.'

Sam was anxious that he might have offended Frayne. It

was the last thing he wanted to do. He tried to explain, rather clumsily, to the good priest that Grace's honour was safe with him.

'Well, of course it is,' said Frayne, surprised. 'I had no doubt.' Then he added, with a chuckle, 'It's her heart I fear for.'

'On my life, sir, I will offer nothing but friendship and what help I can give with her remedies.'

Frayne inclined his head in acknowledgment, saying, 'But you know, you rarely have control over the hearts of others, my son. Anyway, I've come to ask if you will permit me to show you something dear to my own heart?'

As they walked back over the rickety bridge to the priory, Frayne added more details to the story he'd begun the previous night.

'Did I say last night that I persuaded my brother to give me the priory and its lands soon after I went back in time and met my mother? Well, I was initially surprised when he agreed, but it meant that I could be in a place I now knew my mother loved and which I could see would be a beautiful place to live with God as well as nature. Fred came here with me because far from dying as he expected, he was getting better by the week. We began to rebuild Horseshoe together. It was a happy time.'

At the end of the hospital, Frayne had a study with one small window. When not out and about on church business, taking services, helping patients or planting trees, he would be found in here. People knew not to disturb him if he shut the thick wooden door, though that was a rare occasion. Frayne invited Sam in, then locked the door behind them.

Inside, as well as a decent-sized desk and a table full of potion bottles, paints and paintbrushes, a tall bookcase held the few precious books he owned: a Bible, a Book of Common Prayer, Pilgrim's Progress, the Compleat Angler, John Evelyn's Sylva, Nicholas Culpeper's Complete Herbal, and Gerard's Herbal among others. It was an impressive library for a country priest but then, as Sam was now aware, this priest had a rather privileged background. The shelves also displayed an assortment of oddities that Frayne must have collected over the years. A human skull looked at a small ancient stone figurine of a woman; a bowl of conkers, acorns and other nuts and seeds stood next to a small wooden cross entwined with red thread; an embroidered bluebell in a frame, probably by a child; a chunk of amber; a few ancient flint tools; and an old bird's nest lined with sheep's wool which held a large gold ring with a garnet or ruby set into it.

'Now this,' said Frayne, as he began to move a few things that were cluttered around the foot of the bookcase, 'was Fred's clever idea.' He started pushing the whole unit on one side. It was stiff, but with a few shoves it eventually slid sideways with a grumble and a creak. A low open doorway was revealed in the stonework behind. Frayne lit a candle and they both ducked through the opening. An imposing wooden strong box, reinforced with iron studs and a very sturdy lock, stood almost centrally in the small square room. The only other things in there were a wooden chair and a simple table with a five-pronged pewter candlestick, standing on a square rush mat near the far wall.

'When my brother gave me ownership of the priory, I realised that part of his reason for being unusually generous was not only to be seen to be backing the church, but also so that I could act as a trustworthy treasurer for some of his wealth.' He patted the strong box. 'Politicians can easily find themselves in hot water, so distributing money to safe places for difficult times is sensible. Sadly, he fell foul of the powers of the day and more than his wealth was taken from him; he lost his head in the year 1678. God rest his soul.'

'I'm sorry for your loss,' said Sam, genuinely. 'But I don't understand. Why would you tell me and show me this? You hardly know me. How do you know you can trust me?'

Frayne gave one of his chuckles, then reached out for one of Sam's hands and held it in both of his own.

'Of course I know you, Sam Heron. Don't tell me that after all these years of tree reading, you haven't picked up on the fact that reading your fellow humans is much easier for us than it is for most people? Perhaps at first you need contact, as with the trees, but with time and increasing skill, it's not so necessary.' He let go of Sam's hand as he turned away and moved towards the little table, saying in a matter of fact way, 'Sam, you are a good man, open and honest. You are True and I am certain I can trust you.'

Sam laughed. 'Father, believe me, I would do you no harm, but you are wrong. There is little good about me. I make money smuggling whisky, I have fought from a young age, I have killed men, and ...' He closed his eyes tightly for a couple of seconds, before opening them to continue, 'and I cannot be relied upon.'

'Hmm,' was Frayne's rather distracted reply. He had begun moving the table and chair off the reed mat which he was now pulling to another area of the floor. Sam could see that there was a trapdoor in the floorboards. More treasure?

'One day,' said Frayne, as he started to pull on an iron ring in the trapdoor, 'when Fred and I were trying to bring the priory back to life, we found an underground cave. It was just a short distance from the priory and had obviously been used but not for hundreds of years. We came across it by accident when Fred nearly disappeared down a narrow hole in its roof.' He laughed, remembering the moment. 'We later found that the original access was from the river bank, but it's long since been mostly blocked; a man can squeeze through the fallen rocks at a pinch, but it's not easy.'

With the trapdoor open, Frayne took the lit candles and began to step backwards down the narrow wooden ladder that lay beneath the door.

'Come,' he called back to Sam, as he disappeared into the gloomy depths. Sam followed, expecting to find a small empty cave with yet another strong box that he guessed contained the main treasure, as opposed to just some lesser sum that had been left as decoy in the room they'd just left.

He was wrong.

It was a surprisingly large high space and it was anything but empty. When he first reached the ground, the area around him was indeed cave-like and gloomy, but Frayne was busy lighting candles in sconces around the walls further in and the whole place began to come to life. Frayne stood beaming widely before the … the what?

While Sam was wrong that it was a secret room for the true treasure of the priory, he was right in another sense. This was a hidden chapel of True treasure; a celebration of all things linked to Nature and the True. It was completely unexpected and utterly remarkable. Sam gazed around, lost for words.

He was in a wood, an indoor wood, brought to life with a

combination of paintings and sculptures and all manner of works of art both small and large. Everywhere he looked there was natural beauty fashioned by the hand of man. It was extraordinary. The cave walls and ceiling had been painted with trees and blue sky, with grasses and wildflowers hugging the base of the trees where the depicted roots joined the cave floor and with forest animals peeping out wherever he looked. But the thing that Sam really couldn't take his eyes off was the mesmerisingly magical tree in the middle of the cave.

It was not an intact tree — they'd never have manhandled such a thing into the cave — rather it had been painstakingly crafted, piece by piece. It was about eight feet tall with a canopy spread of around six feet. The broad base, which included some above ground roots, gave the tree its balance and support, with chunky lengths of curiously gnarled wood all carefully chosen and secured into place with wooden pegs. This tapered up to the main trunk which was built of three sturdy but characterful long sections — one oak, one ash, one hawthorn — again held in position by wooden pegs and ties, and themselves being the anchor for five main branches. The branches were also differing types of wood but unlike the more roughly hewn trunk and base, they had been worked more finely. Onto them, lovingly sanded and polished twigs had been fastened either by pegs or twine.

This sculptural tree skeleton was magnificent in its own right, but it had then been adorned with a collection of diverse and exquisite works of art.

Frayne tried hard not to show pride, but his face beamed.

'Odd as it sounds,' he said, looking up at the tree, 'Fred told me that, in years to come, one of the ways we'll celebrate the feast of the nativity is by bringing fir trees into our houses and decorating them with small ornaments: the Christmas tree. So, this is our celebration of Nature. We came to call it the Every Tree.'

Sam slowly walked around the Every Tree, taking in the myriad of breathtaking creations before him. It was the foliage that struck him first. Half of the tree depicted spring and summer, with green leaves, buds and spring flowers; the other half portrayed autumn and winter, with some branches left bare and others sporting leaves of autumnal colours plus seeds, nuts and fruits. Looking closely, Sam could see that the pieces had been made of diverse materials, from wood to leather, fabrics such as linen and silk, and even shells, stones (precious and otherwise), and metals including silver and gold. A garland of finely-wrought green-painted metal ivy twined itself around the tree binding the seasons together; an elderflower of fine lace hung next to a wooden stem of pussy willow with neat rabbit fur buds; highly polished wooden conkers peeked out of spiky green casings made of pottery; beaten copper beech leaves shared a twig with a cluster of red woollen hawthorn berries; and in the highest branch there was a bouquet of mistletoe with pearl berries.

And then Sam spotted the creatures 'living' in the tree: a brightly painted kingfisher with a silver fish in his beak and, on the branch above, a blackbird enjoying a jewel-like red berry; a barn owl with glistening coal-black eyes looked serenely down from a high branch, and a cheeky red squirrel sat with a golden hazelnut in his tiny paws; butterflies and insects were dotted all over. The Every Tree was alive with likenesses of the natural world, both flora and fauna.

118

'It is beyond words,' said Sam, simply. Frayne slowly nodded his understanding.

'But you and Fred can't have made all of this, surely?'

'Oh goodness, no,' said Frayne. 'Most of the wall paintings were done by Fred, and we built the main tree together but since the year 1700 this has become the work of a community, the True community. Perhaps you noticed that some of our brothers and sisters at the Covert gave me small parcels? I brought one of them down to show you. It's from a fisherman who lives on the Yorkshire coast.' He loosened a small bundle he'd tied to his belt. A shiny black beetle about an inch and a half long, made of jet and with the True symbol on its back, emerged from its rough calico wrappings.

'I'm especially pleased with this,' said Frayne, turning it over in his hands to admire the workmanship before handing it to Sam. 'People understandably have a preference for God's prettier creatures, but I really wanted to show the full spectrum of the earth's diversity. I have the perfect spot in mind for this handsome fellow.' He pointed to an empty nook at the base of the tree.

Sam placed the little beetle in his new home then stood to take in yet more of this wondrous cave. There was so much. If Frayne had only been to two Coverts since moving to Horseshoe and starting work on this cave, he couldn't see how all of this had been achieved simply through offerings at the meetings. Frayne explained that since telling the Covert of 1700 about the cave and the Every Tree, parcels had begun to arrive, anonymously at first, and they even got True visitors — more and more as word spread. Frayne went over to a smooth rock at the foot of the tree and picked up a large leather-bound book as he chatted on.

'Some come simply to admire, others to bring something they've made, and a few come to stay and make things while they are here. Remember Marcus, the blacksmith at the Covert? He paid us a visit about twenty years ago intending just to stay a day or two before returning home, but he was so enamoured of the Every Tree and the way Fred had fashioned it that he changed his plans, befriended a smithy in Rothbury and made us that beautiful stag's head over there.' Frayne slowly flicked through the pages as Sam went over to see the stag's head.

'Early on, I started a book recording all the offerings and the True visitors we had. I paint a little, so this has become a bit of a labour of love for me. I hope you'll not think me vain, but I so adore the workmanship and our members' delight in capturing the natural world that this has become my own offering. Names and dates, messages, and even tree remedies, poetry and stories we've been sent too — it's all in here, along with drawings of each plant or creature we've been sent. I must remember to take our friend the beetle up to my study again to paint him too. He's such a fine fellow.'

Marcus's stag's head hung in front of a rowan tree painted on the cave wall. It was undoubtedly impressive. Below it, Sam noticed a circular embroidery that had been stretched over a frame roughly a foot in diameter. His eyes had almost skimmed over it as, in comparison to the stag, it didn't stand out so greatly, but there was something about it. A ring of woodland animals had been delicately and skilfully worked in bright silken threads: a russet fox jumped playfully over a mouse; there were two boxing hares; a badger had a wiggly earthworm in his mouth; a hedgehog poked his head out from a clump of grass; a chaffinch flew above a watching frog … It was joyous. In the middle of this ring there was an image of a hand holding a mound of earth with an oak sapling growing out of it and, around this, the words 'True Connection is Earthly Protection' and the date 1700.

'Oh, Heavens, how silly of me,' said Frayne when he saw Sam taking in the captivating embroidery. He came over to join Sam. 'I'm so pleased this drew you. It was one of the first pieces that came to me, in June 1700, just after the Covert. Isn't it exquisite?'

Sam agreed. 'Do you know whose work it is or was it anonymous?'

'Oh, this one I know,' said Frayne, with a fond yet sad smile on his face. He turned to Sam. 'I think we should go back up. I have things to tell you.' Then, touching the embroidered hand, he added, 'This was made by your mother.'

CHAPTER TEN

CONNECTION

Wednesday, May 2nd, 1725

Back up above ground in the study, Sam sat looking at Eleanor's embroidery on his lap. Frayne had insisted Sam take it.

'I know your mother would wish you to have it.'

The priest sat at his desk, absent-mindedly fiddling with one of the buttons on his cassock.

'The thing is,' he began, 'I can possibly … nay probably, shed light on Eleanor's whereabouts.'

'What?!' Sam's head snapped up. 'Really?'

'Yes, yes, but — but it's not going to help you, I'm sad to say,' said Frayne. 'It all comes back to Fred really, but it truly was well meant.'

Frayne explained that on 1st May 2000, Fred had travelled through the trees after the Covert and arrived in 1675. He'd brought with him a piece of wood from the year 2000 from the oak tree in Middle Wood that he'd jumped with. This *future wood*, as he called it, would guide him back through the trees whenever he wanted, to more or less the time he left (the trees weren't too precise when it came to such short lengths of time as hours). Any person who learned the True knowledge and skill could travel *back* in time, but it required future wood to travel forward in time. Fred hadn't really planned on going back to his own century — he expected to die quickly of the illness that was racking his body — but the wood was a fall-back, just in case. It was a surprise when his health unexpectedly improved and he started enjoying life in the company of his friend, the priest. Months and years passed and, though he had no intention of returning to the twenty-first century, Fred kept his future wood with him as a physical connection with his past, or future. He'd whittled it into an adjoined oak leaf and acorn.

When Frayne and Fred visited the Covert of 1700 together, they met Eleanor and her aunt. Eleanor was twenty years old and had contrived a visit to her supposedly ailing aunt (on her mother's side) in a village west of Rothbury so that they could visit the Covert together. Her mother had secretly taught Eleanor about the True, trees and herbalism all her young life — her father, the laird of Kilcaith Castle, knew nothing of the True heritage of his wife's family — and now her aunt was the only family contact she had since her kidnap and enforced marriage in 1697. Sir Richard permitted a very occasional visit and only on the agreement that she leave their daughter at Moss Hall. He was confident that Eleanor would never abandon Martha.

After Tom Baker had made his impassioned speech, Frayne and Fred overheard Eleanor and her aunt discussing how exciting it would be to see the future and wondering whether the lot of women in Tom's time was at all changed.

'Imagine, aunt, if we could be healers without the risk of being damned as witches,' Eleanor had said.

The words struck Fred deeply. He was conscious that he had it within his power to offer a different life to an obviously bright young woman. He took a leather pouch from a thong from around his neck. He held it tightly in his hands and looked at Frayne, who could see what was going through his mind. Could he really fully commit to *now*? The now of the year 1700 instead of the now 300 years hence? No way back. Ever.

'Mistress Eleanor,' he began, when there was a break in the fireside talks. 'I wonder if you would permit me to give you a small gift?' He looked at the pouch in his right hand. He smiled, at that moment certain that this was the right thing to do.

'By rights, I don't belong here. But I feel more present and alive here and now than I ever did in the place I was born.' Fred handed Eleanor the pouch with the future wood. 'If you find that this time is not your proper place, if you need to find a way to be a different *you*, if you need an escape, well, perhaps my time will be a refuge for you, as your time is for me.'

Frayne said that Fred had spent time with Eleanor over the course of the rest of the night explaining that the wood was from a large oak in Middle Wood and that he'd come from Beltane in the year 2000. He also talked her through the rudiments of tree jumping: get close to the tree the wood has come from, concentrate until you can feel the recognition spark between the wood and the tree, allow your mind to travel with the tree and then release your body to this magical force of nature.

'It's not that difficult really,' Frayne continued. 'The key is *knowing* that it's possible. The True have no special powers, just knowledge. So you see, your mother had knowledge of tree jumping and had access to the future. I'm sorry, Sam, perhaps knowing this gets you no closer to her. Indeed, I fear you could have lost her to the twenty-first century, my son, though of course there is still no guarantee this is what happened to her.'

Sam sat silently, lost in his thoughts. Could this be true? Time travel as a realistic proposition was still only just sinking in, and now he was hearing that his own mother could be living in the year 2000. But why would she go when she did, when he seemed to be dying? And why hadn't she returned, unless there was something or someone stopping her? It seemed absurd to even be contemplating all of this and yet this is exactly what he was being forced to consider — and by a priest, no less. Frayne had said that if she had jumped, she was lost to him, but Sam knew that Frayne was missing one key bit of knowledge. His hand went automatically to the wooden acorn on the leather thong around his neck.

'My mother left me this,' he said, handing over the precious memento. 'Do you think this could be part of Fred's future wood? For as long as I remember, she always had a carved acorn and a separate leaf. Perhaps she travelled with just the leaf? Would that be enough to take her to the future?'

Frayne took the wooden acorn in his rough, wrinkled hands, turning it over and over as he scrutinised it.

'Hmm,' he said, 'it's smaller than I remember, though that's probably my bad memory. And it never used to have the True sign on it, but she could have added that herself.' He handed the acorn back to Sam, who hung it back around his neck.

'I can't be certain of course, but yes, yes, this could be exactly what you say — a piece of Fred's future wood. Oh, that is so exciting,' he said, standing up then sitting down again. 'I mean, if you're right, you have the future in your hands. Or to

125

be specific, the 1st May in the year 2000. I'm sure it's enough; when I travelled I took only a small piece of wood with me.'

'So,' said Sam, holding the acorn on its familiar leather strip, 'If she's there, I might have a pathway to follow to find my mother and bring her safely home. I must —'

He was interrupted by a call from Hawk and an urgent rapping on the heavy door of the study. Frayne hurried over to the door and unlocked it. Hawk bowed politely to the priest then addressed Sam.

'We've just heard that the redcoats are coming, Sam. I can't stay around just in case … well, you know. I'm going to head up into the woods until they pass by. I don't want to be bringing any problems your way, father,' he said, turning to Frayne, 'though I'm sure there'll be no difficulties really. All just a misunderstanding, you know.'

After a short discussion, it was decided that both Hawk and Sam would keep out of the way in the woods until the redcoats left. Sam's part-time occupation as a whisky smuggler led him to prefer to keep a distance from any authorities.

'I doubt they'll stay long. They usually only want food and healing,' said Frayne. He pointed to an area of woodland east of the priory which would avoid any chance of them meeting up with the incoming soldiers.

It was a good vantage point. He could see the priory and most of the comings and goings, despite the trees, yet he knew he would be hard to spot in the woodland. He'd arrived late afternoon yesterday, walking the last couple of miles after the cart had dropped him off at a nearby farm. The light was starting to fade as he'd watched the small party at the priory cottage finishing their supper. It was hard to be sure, but he was fairly confident that the tall man sat next to the priest was the one he'd come for.

He couldn't believe his luck yesterday morning when, not far from Faerie Hill, he'd come across someone who had seen Sam Heron recently and knew him to be travelling to Horseshoe Priory with the priest that day. Two birds with one stone. This was obviously meant to be.

It had been a cold and uncomfortable night, but that wasn't important. The thrill of being here, at the right time and in the right place, and with his quarry in spitting distance, outweighed any physical discomfort. He was already awake and alert when he saw Sam come out of a low building near the priory and head over the bridge to the woodland at the other side. About two hours later, after Sam had headed back to the priory precinct with the priest, he saw a young boy walking down the path flanking the woodland where he was hiding. The boy must have walked from the neighbouring village. He kept out of sight, and soon saw the lad down by the cottage being welcomed by a pretty young woman.

Nothing much happened for the next couple of hours, just the general to-ing and fro-ing of people going about daily life. He needed to think on his feet and contrive a way to get what he wanted. As long as it caused maximum damage, preferably physical, to Sam Heron, that was fine by him. Death would be ideal, dismemberment or serious injury would be acceptable, but the minimum he would content himself with would be to cause Sam to endure a long imprisonment or transportation.

He was mulling through his options when he noticed a

flurry of activity, and Sam, the priest and another man all appeared from the low building. The priest was pointing up behind the priory to an area of thick woodland. Sam and the other, skinny chap set off quickly into the wood.

Odd. Something was definitely going on, but he couldn't fathom it. Had they wanted to leave the priory, they would have come up the pathway near him as that led up to the main road to Rothbury. Either there was something in the wood, perhaps something hidden, or maybe it was they themselves that needed to hide?

He waited and watched. Patience not rashness; the answer would be there if he looked for it.

Quite soon, the answer came marching, or rather shuffling, down the road; the army was on the way to the priory. There were only about twenty foot soldiers, so he figured this was probably a recruiting party doing the rounds of villages in the area, likely as not heading for one of the inns at Rothbury. It seemed strange that they were detouring to a priory, but the more interesting question was why Sam and the other man felt the need to avoid them — he was sure this is what he'd just witnessed. To his mind, their departure just a few minutes before the redcoats arrived was no coincidence.

So, he thought, mulling over the possibilities, why avoid soldiers? Either they're up to something dishonest here (possible, even with the church involved), or they're wanted criminals (that could easily be the case for all he knew), or maybe … maybe they were deserters? If they were chancers, and he felt sure Sam was, they could easily have taken the king's shilling then absconded, maybe even for the fun of it if they didn't need the money. It certainly wasn't a rare occurrence by all accounts. Ah yes, that definitely seemed a far more likely scenario. And the punishment for desertion? If memory served him right, a flogging was possible but branding was far more common. He would rather enjoy the thought of Sam being branded with a 'D'. What a shame they no longer branded men on the cheek though; he'd liked to have seen his pretty face scarred for life. He absentmindedly stroked the long scar on his own face, smiling thinly to himself at the image of Sam's disfigurement, and then another thought widened that mean smile into one which almost made his even features handsome, but not quite: there was always the outside chance that they'd deserted more than once, in which case his work was done for him. Sam would be shot or hanged.

So, to work. He needed to land Sam in the firm embrace of the army and, assuming all went to plan, he was then free to consider the unexpected bonus that might have just coincidentally landed in his lap: the priory treasure.

CHAPTER ELEVEN

THE STRANGER

Wednesday, May 2nd, 1725

There was nowhere they could go. With a steep drop to the river on their right and a huge sheer crag blocking their path further north, the wood that was meant to be their temporary hideout became the cage that was about to trap them.

Sam and Hawk had listened to the redcoats blundering through the woodland for the last few minutes and could now see their vivid jackets among the subtle presence of the trees. Why on earth had five soldiers decided to come up here? Had someone down in the priory said something? But who? Why? It made no sense. No one had anything to gain from turning Hawk in to the redcoats; nobody even knew of his desertion.

'Hawk, you go on and hide up where you can. They've no reason to hold me, so let them talk to me if that's what they want. I'll go with them. We'll have to hope they don't know about you being here too.' Sam wasn't too hopeful on that score, but they had little choice right now.

'Don't be daft, man, we both know it's me they'll be looking for. You go,' said Hawk, in a hoarse whisper. The soldiers were getting closer.

'Damn it, Hawk, we're *both* in the shit if you're found!' hissed Sam and gestured for him to get moving. Hawk stood for a moment, but then huffed his frustration and started walking away further into the thicker undergrowth between their current position and the crag.

Sam decided that their best defence was to try to backfoot the soldiers rather than being cornered. He strode forward with a casual confidence in the direction they were coming from; he was simply a man walking through the woods.

Two redcoats saw him heading towards them and they quickly levelled their muskets at him.

'Stand, sir!' shouted one of the soldiers, then, 'Jack, over here.' The other three soldiers quickly arrived at their side.

'Damnation, gentlemen,' said Sam, keeping his composure, and speaking in what he hoped was a tone of authority. 'You could give a man a fright turning up out of the trees like that. What's the problem?'

'Where's the other one? Where's your mate?' said one of the men, ignoring Sam's question. 'We know there's two of you.'

'You're mistaken, I'm alone,' said Sam. 'How dare you point your muskets at me. I ask again, what is the problem?'

'You'll know soon enough when we're back with the sergeant. Now where's the other rogue?'

'Rogue, is it?' said Sam, a steely calmness which gave just a hint of his annoyance. 'And what am I supposed to have done to warrant such rudeness?'

'I've told you, it's not up to me to say anything. We've just got to take you back to the priory.'

'Then I suggest we get going and sort this out with your

sergeant,' said Sam. 'You're obviously mistaking me with someone else. He won't be happy with that, and nor indeed am I.'

The soldier seemed to waver slightly in his conviction and Sam began to think that perhaps he'd get away with this tack. He was just about to force the point by starting to walk towards the soldiers in the direction of the priory when the loud crack of a snapping branch echoed through the wood.

The soldiers reacted immediately and two set off up towards the crag. It wasn't long before they returned with Hawk walking in front of them at musket-point. The looks the two friends exchanged were eloquent. '*What the hell? I had them ready to leave*' was met with '*What could I do, the bloody log just snapped.*'

Back down at the priory, the rest of the recruiting party was relaxing outside the hospital building. When Sam, Hawk and the five soldiers came into sight, one of the younger men scrambled to his feet and went inside, soon returning with an older soldier, obviously the sergeant in charge. He was a short man but very stocky, with a red scabby face that looked like it had been scoured every day of his life. Behind him, Frayne came out accompanied by another man. This man wasn't a soldier, but had the look of a merchant, perhaps. He was well but not richly dressed, had a slim frame and long black hair tied back with a ribbon. A bandage covered part of his head and one eye. A long red scar ran along his jawline on the right side of his face. He looked briefly in the direction of Sam and Hawk, then gave a short nod to the sergeant before going back inside the building.

Hawk groaned. 'Oh, perfect.' Sam shot him a look of

concern. Hawk had dejected resignation written all over his face as he stared at the sergeant who was now grinning widely as he walked towards them.

'Well, well, well, look what we've found in the woods! I always knew they were nasty evil places fit only for robbers and ne'er-do-wells. We missed you in Newcastle, you little shite, and I hear you've been a busy boy since then too.'

As he reached Hawk, he landed a hard punch to his stomach without warning. Hawk doubled up and dropped to the ground with a grunt. Sam tried to come to his defence but was immediately held back by three of the soldiers. Frayne rushed over to Hawk in his stead, remonstrating with the sergeant, Chisholm.

'Oh, a smack will be the least of Mr Sparrowfart's worries,' said Chisholm. 'The life of a two-time deserter is, well, how can I put it, uncomfortable.' Then, with an unpleasant grimace, he added, 'And short.'

He then turned to Sam, who was still firmly held between two redcoats.

'And what about your friend here?' He looked Sam up and down with disdain. 'Another filthy deserter too, I'll wager.'

'I have never joined the army and I demand to be freed,' said Sam, struggling angrily against the two men holding him.

'You could be telling the truth,' said the sergeant with disinterest. 'We'll find out when we reach Rothbury later today, but you keep bad company, that's for sure. And, of course, there is the small matter of you thrashing and robbing a gentleman of his pocket watch in the wood less than an hour ago. Hidden it in the wood for later, have you, or do you still have it on you?'

'What the hell —?' began both Sam and Hawk, but

133

Chisholm ignored their protestations and turned to the soldiers, ordering his two captives to be searched. When no watch was found, he barked that they should be bound, tightly. 'We don't want our little escape artist pulling any tricks because of a loose knot now, do we? In fact,' he added, eyeing up the oak grove, 'tie them to a tree too, until the good priest has finished patching up Jobson and Stobart.'

Hands tied behind their backs, the friends were shoved towards the nearest oak tree and lashed to one of the sturdy low boughs. Hawk was throwing every obscenity he could muster at the soldier and simultaneously trying covertly to wriggle his thin supple hands free of the ropes. However, the soldiers had taken their orders seriously; the bindings were immovable. They had no choice but to sit and await the pleasure of the sergeant.

It was less than an hour later when the redcoats began to prepare to move off again. Frayne managed to come over to Sam and Hawk under the pretence of offering them water before the journey.

'Have a care, Sam,' he said in a hushed voice, 'there's something amiss here. The stranger is called Herbert Wells and I think he means you harm. He's written an oath swearing that you robbed and beat him, even though I know you didn't. And there's another odd thing — I'm certain he inflicted the damage on himself.'

Sam was baffled. 'But I don't know the man. Well, I suppose I didn't get a good look at him, but I'm not aware of knowing him, let alone offending him.'

'Remember what I said about reading the thoughts and feelings of your fellow man?' said Frayne. 'Well, I had only a little time when tending Mr Wells's head injury but, hmm, I just don't think he belongs here. I can't be sure, but I think he could be a jumper.'

'What? One of the True? But then you can talk to him and make him understand his mistake,' said Sam, hopefully.

'I fear not,' replied Frayne. 'This man might know the trees, but his heart is certainly not True. He is ... well, it's as if he has taken the cloak of a tree reader and the trees have not yet guessed the deception.

'I don't know how to help right now, but I'll follow you to Rothbury as soon as I can. Perhaps I can learn more from Mr Wells that might help your position. And if you can get away, look to Edenbury Castle. Fred's hideout by the river is impossible to find unless you know it's there. I'll leave some food and money there for you as soon as I get a chance. There's a hiding hole at the back, with a stone in front of it. In the meantime, this might be useful.' He looked around to check no-one was watching them, before quickly putting a small sharp flint into Sam's bound hands. 'Sometimes we have to take things into our own hands,' he said, with a wink. 'God be with you both.'

The recruiting party was mustered, including the two injured men who were the cause of their detour to the priory, and the two prisoners were dragged from under the oak tree. Bound together, Sam and Hawk were positioned in the middle of the soldiers and Chisholm gave the command to start marching. As they passed Frayne's small cottage, Grace stood looking on anxiously and gave a small tentative wave. Sam replied with a smile and a short nod. Looking over to his right towards the hospital building, he noticed a pale face at one of the windows. It was Herbert Wells. He was staring directly at Sam. There was a glint in his unbandaged eye and a wide smile showed off a set of exceptionally white teeth.

He didn't like having to work on a wing and a prayer; well-laid plans were by far the better option, but he had to admit he'd derived a great deal of pleasure from seeing his spontaneous tactics succeed. He'd been assured by Sergeant Chisholm that his written avowal of the theft and beating he swore he'd endured at the hands of Sam Heron and his accomplice would be enough to see Sam suffer at least a whipping or branding, or perhaps a prison sentence or transportation. The gold coin he had pressed into his hand had made the sergeant more than willing to see 'justice' done on his behalf. Score settled. It felt good. It was unfortunate he'd had to head-butt the tree to make his story look real, it had hurt more than he expected. However, with Sam Heron out of his mind and his head beginning to clear (though a pain killer wouldn't have gone amiss), he could now turn his attention to other matters that had unexpectedly landed in his lap. The gods were definitely on his side right now. Here he was in a place he'd known about for many years and, possibly, at just the right time too. Perfect. The famous Horseshoe Priory treasure could be his.

The priest who'd dressed his head injury was still outside. The pretty girl who'd helped with the soldiers was nowhere to be seen now and there were no other patients in the little hospital. The six small wooden pallet beds lay empty. A small jug of freshly-picked bluebells sat on the long table alongside bandages, a flickering candle, an open glass jar of liquid and a bowl of water. The main door to the outside was ajar and he could hear the kerfuffle of the soldiers as they headed off. The sight of Sam and his friend bound as criminals had made him very cheerful, though he wished the proud look in Sam's eyes had been dimmed. No matter, it would be. In time.

He decided he might as well start searching where he was. There was another door at the other end of the room. It was closed, but he'd seen the priest go in and out of it a couple of times whilst he and soldiers were being treated. Probably the pharmacy, but could it be more than that? It seemed unlikely that a rural priest in charge of a ramshackle priory in the middle of nowhere would have any wealth to speak of, but stranger things had been known.

He'd started researching the Priory after coming across an article in an archived newspaper from 1794. A coin hoard had been found here that year and this had piqued his interest. He discovered that the land, indeed the priory, belonged to Thomas Forster, son of the Earl of Edenbury. Thomas was last recorded as a curate at Alnwick but seemed to have dropped off the records after about 1675. For fifty years from this same year, one Father Frayne was the priest in charge at the priory. Then, in May 1725, there was a devastating fire. He remembered reading that a building near the priory had completely collapsed, razed to the ground, though the priory itself had been relatively little affected. Could the building he was in be the place of the fire? It suddenly felt so tantalisingly close it made his spine tingle.

Thinking back to the 1794 newspaper article, he remembered that it told of the priory having been abandoned for many years, and there were rumours of ghosts and hidden

137

treasure, the usual kind of nonsense that spooky old buildings in the middle of a forest tended to provoke: a priest wandering the riverbanks beneath the priory in search of who-knows-what; a vast treasure chest stuffed with jewels and coins secreted within the woods of the little peninsula. No doubt some locals tried their luck over the years, but nothing was ever found until, in summer 1794, two gentlemen adventurers from the south heard the tales when they were in the area and decided to see what they could find. They had time on their side and set up a small camp in the priory, which was in a very sorry state by now. It was August 1794 and they struck gold, literally, on the fifteenth of that month. Having decided, on no more than a hunch, to concentrate on the small destroyed building next to the priory, now overgrown with brambles as well as being flattened, they started shifting stones and rocks and digging in the humus-rich soil. On the third morning, they found a silver coin, then another, and another, and a gold coin, and yet more gold coins. In the end the find was 50 gold coins and 114 silver coins all dating from around 1650 to 1670. The Horseshoe Priory Treasure!

Having known about the treasure for so long, to be here, with the chance that it could be right under his feet … it was more than he could have dreamed of. It had to be here. It was the 2nd of May 1725 and the building was intact, so unless the coins were going to arrive in the next few days for some reason, he was presently on top of the hoard. It was his for the finding and, with the soldiers and Sam gone, he'd seen no-one else that might be able to stop him getting what he wanted. An elderly priest, a young nurse and a small boy were no threat.

He walked over to the inner door expecting to find it locked but, surprisingly, the latch clicked and he slowly pushed open the heavy wooden door. At first glance, the room was more or less what he expected — part pharmacy, part study — with no room for a strong box or money chest, however he made a reasonably thorough search to convince himself there really was nothing here. He was about to leave when something on the bookshelf caught his attention. A gold ring with a red stone. He went over and picked it up. Ah, very nice. At a guess it was sixteenth century with what looked like a cabochon ruby. It was a man's ring. He tried it on his middle finger but it was meant for a larger hand than his.

'I see you're admiring my father's ring.'

It was the priest, standing in the doorway watching him. His voice was calm and he didn't seem annoyed about this invasion of his privacy. Clergymen, he thought, contemptuously, no sense of righteous indignation.

'Your father?' he said, taking the ring off his finger and inspecting it more closely. 'Hmm, he was a man of substance it seems, Father Frayne. The initials SF, are they his or yours?'

The priest came into the room and sat at his desk. He gestured to the other chair and Herbert Wells took a seat.

'His,' answered Frayne, briefly, with his eyes fixed on the ring, then, looking at Mr Wells, he added, 'My father was a big man in more ways than one but, sadly, a little man in the ways which mattered to me when I was young. The Lord offers us spiritual protection, but we should all be able to look to our fathers for earthly protection, don't you think that's true?'

He returned the priest's direct gaze, considering his response before replying, 'My father is a little man in all ways and I despise him for it. I take my earthly protection into my own hands and, forgive me, but I don't feel the need for spiritual protection.'

Frayne smiled kindly, yet a tinge of sadness showed in his ageing eyes.

'So, in that case, tell me, my son, what brings you to our humble house today if it is not for God's love and redemption?'

Sitting back in his chair, Herbert Wells was absent-mindedly slipping the ruby ring onto each of the fingers of his left hand one by one. When he came to his thumb, he stopped and looked down. It fitted snugly. This seemed to galvanise his thoughts. He stood up slowly and began to look carefully around the room once more. He was quite a tall man with a wiry frame. He had no bulk with which to intimidate, but unnerving people always seemed to come quite naturally to him.

'Redemption? Such an interesting word, isn't it? So inextricably entwined with sin. Do you think me a sinner Father Frayne?' he asked, not waiting for answer. 'But of course you do, we all are in the eyes of the church, are we not? Actually, though, I consider myself a kind of redeemer.'

'Indeed?' replied Frayne. 'How might that be?'

'I'm glad you asked,' he said, turning back to face Frayne. 'I … how shall I put it? I *liberate* important objects from future obscurity. History can bring us great knowledge and reward, so we should save and value what we can.'

He looked down at the ring again and slowly brought his thumb up to his chest and rubbed the stone on his jacket before admiring it once more. 'Perhaps you might approve, father. You are, after all, a purveyor of future happiness based on promises made in the distant past.'

'I'm not really sure I understand you, Mr Wells. Do you

140

mean you own a cabinet of curiosities? That would be interesting indeed,' said Frayne, conversationally,

Herbert Wells smiled. He could feel that there was a game afoot but neither of the participants knew the rules that the other was playing by. That was fine by him; he liked games and was confident of an easy victory. The odds were all on his side — the element of surprise, his age and strength, and his inside knowledge. For what he was about to retrieve, may his future make him truly thankful. Amen.

'My own interest lies in something I believe you have here at the priory, Father Frayne. Perhaps you can help me by telling me where I can find your money chest?'

'Heavens, a money chest,' chuckled Frayne. 'Have you seen the state of my church roof? If you do find one here, and it has any contents, I would be delighted, and more than happy to offer a reward for your invaluable services, Mr Wells. May I ask what has led you to believe there is any money at Horseshoe?'

'Come now, father. How long is it you've been here? Fifty years? Perhaps we could stop the pretence and, while we're at it, you could show me the meaning of those grooves in the floor there?' Mr Wells was pointing to the end of the bookcase. Frayne had not had time to replace the usefully concealing clutter that had been there before Sam arrived and the tracks of the moving shelves were visible in the wooden floor by the wall.

'Oh, most astute of you, sir, I must say. But are you really going to rob us of the few pennies we have kept aside for the church and hospital? You seem a well-educated man, surely you don't need to resort to such a shameful way to keep body and

141

soul together? God and nature's bounty provide for us all even in the most trying of times.'

'Enough,' barked Wells. He had not come for a lecture in morality from a priest. 'Nature is indeed a useful tool, but I am here for a purpose and I intend to get what I came for.'

He ripped off the bandage covering his eye, then took a moment to look over the bookcase. He then put his shoulder to the end of the bookcase and shoved. A satisfying scraping noise accompanied the movement he felt. He pushed again and again until an opening in the wall revealed a dark space behind.

'Would you oblige me by going ahead with the candles, father?'

The threat was only implied in the tone of voice, but he left Frayne in no doubt that he should comply. The priest slowly took the candlestick from his desk and led his future thief into the small secret room. He put the candlestick on the little table and stood back watching his unwelcome guest.

Herbert Wells kept his eyes fixed on the coffer, held out his right hand towards Frayne and clicked his fingers twice.

'Key.'

Silently, Frayne took hold of the keys hanging on his belt, walked over to the chest and unlocked it, before drawing back to the table and taking a seat.

Wells opened the heavy studded lid. His jaw dropped almost imperceptibly and he stared. It was here. The treasure was really here. He crouched down and started counting the coins that lay within. This wasn't right. No, there was … there was too much! It was a bigger hoard than he'd expected. Jackpot! But no, wait. Think, man, think.

He sat back on his haunches and closed his eyes, ignoring

the priest and slowly twisting the ruby ring that was still on his thumb. Then it dawned on him. Of course. Idiot. If there was no decent hoard found in 1794, there would be no newspaper report and he would never know it was here. OK, so he had to forgo the 50 gold coins and 114 silver coins he'd read about, but he could see that this would still leave him with at least the same again. Very acceptable for a couple of days work and a sore head, especially as this was an unexpected bonus on top of his main goal of causing pain and suffering to Sam Heron. What a trip. The first of many to come, he hoped.

His plan was to take the coins to a place he knew up north of Rothbury and bury them. Then, in 275 years, he could simply dig them up again — a rare Northumbrian find by a knowledgeable historian. The thought gave him a warm glow inside, and he smiled.

'You've found what you came for, my son? And are you content?' Frayne asked, watching him stash coins into his small bag.

'Indeed, father, my visit to your church has done me the power of good. I thank you for your cooperation. It was a wise decision.'

Frayne inclined his head graciously and thanked Wells for not taking all the coins but leaving a good amount for the priory.

'Perhaps I misjudged you and for that I apologise as I can see there is charity within you still.'

Wells wondered for a moment whether the body of a priest might fit into the chest, but decided against the effort and risk and merely said, 'Your father's ring, sir, I'm afraid I have in mind to —', but Frayne interrupted.

143

'Do take it as a gift from me with thanks for your forbearance, Mr Wells. Shall we go back out if you have all you came for?' He stood, picked up the candlestick, and held his arm out for Mr Wells to go first.

Herbert Wells did indeed go ahead of the priest, but he stopped at the low doorway and turned around.

'I'm afraid that I will be leaving alone, Father. Just in case you have a change of heart. I'm sure your friends will come looking for you before too long. At least one of them must be aware of your little hidey hole. Good day to you sir and thank you.'

He bowed with an exaggerated flourish and left the small room. After pushing the bookcase back over the doorway, he walked out of Frayne's office and strode quickly through the little hospital to the outer door to head north with his booty. As he did so, he didn't notice his bag lightly tapping the candle that stood next to the jar of bluebells on the table by the wall. It wobbled. It fell. Nothing happened for a moment, but then the edge of the bandages that were lying there started to smoulder. A small flame appeared. It caught and increased in intensity. Soon the glass jar exploded. Now the wooden table was alight. No-one came, so the fire quietly leapt and danced to its heart's content. It wasn't until the beds were well and truly alight that anyone noticed the riot of flames in the hospital, but by then it was too late; the heat was too intense for the small amounts of water that Grace, Thomas and others tried to fight it with. The flames licked and tickled Frayne's study door and eventually persuaded the heavy wooden door to give in and let them through. The fire loved the herbs and lotions, dried flowers, paints and potions, books and bibles in his room. It ate voraciously, gaining strength from the diet of religion and healing plants. God and Nature.

Frayne smelled the smoke when it started curling its curious wispy grey fingers under the bookcase in front of the secret door. He decided to retreat down into the cave below and wait until the danger had passed. He pulled up the hidden trapdoor, took the candlestick and descended into his True cave, shutting the entrance above him. The Every Tree was waiting for him. He felt safe. He was amongst friends. He would ascend when the time was right.

ALDER

I offer protection, support and resistance.

Water is my element. With water, I am strong in both life and death. Allow me to hug the banks of rivers, ponds and lakes and I am happy. Let my roots find their place in cool damp woodlands and I will flourish. Keep my timber wet and I will gladly support you with more than the strength of stone. When dry, I rot; when wet, I will not. River men rely on me for sluice gates and I prop up the incomparable city of Venice; I work hard for all who put their trust in me, rich or poor.

Otters favour my roots as nests; the pollen of my catkins is loved by bees; siskins, redpolls and goldfinches eat my seeds; I sustain moths, and fish enjoy my quick-rotting leaves. The very

146

earth benefits from my existence since I, more than most, improve the fertility of the soils that host me. Fair's fair, give and take. Even those that provide help in life need a firm foundation.

Not wishing to brag, I am unique; the only broad-leaf tree to produce cones. These are my female catkins turned woody over time. The passing of time is easy to see with me; past, present and future are all there on my bare winter branches — last year's black empty cones hang alongside this year's long male catkins which flirt with the small reddish oval female catkins that will become next year's cones. Along with my sticky young leaves and buds, my cones identify me.

Despite my connection with coolness, damp and water, when I burn, I burn hot, resisting my demise by flame with ferocity. Weapon forgers of the past swore by my intense fires, though ironically, they also needed me to treat their burns too. None of us is one-dimensional, we all have a different side that fewer people are aware of. Hidden depths and quiet strengths, we should never be underestimated.

CHAPTER TWELVE

THE KING'S HEAD

Wednesday, May 2nd, 1725

It was just past eight o'clock in the evening and the King's Head Inn in the centre of Rothbury was a hive of activity and a hothouse of gaiety. The two army drummers of the recruiting party were beating time to jolly tunes and shanties piped with expertise and flair by one of their prisoners. The ale was flowing, and tales of adventure and a good life with plentiful food were enchanting hard-working, pittance-earning men of the earth.

Sergeant Chisholm was confident of a successful night tonight, mostly, he had to admit, thanks to Alex Sparrowfart. He was more than happy to use anything at his disposal to get a few more takers of the king's shilling since every new man meant more money for his own purse. Mr Sparrowfart might not be long for this world, bastard deserter that he was, but he might as well be useful until it was time for the inevitable. The other man in his custody was no use at all to him, but he'd had a guinea from Mr Wells to see him into the hands of the authorities in Rothbury for his offence of robbery and assault, as asserted by the victim in writing. He would make sure this happened, but mainly because of his obvious connection with Alex Sparrowhawk, who he'd taken a very immediate and strong dislike to. Sam Heron, if that was his real name, would be handed over to the magistrate in the morning.

Sam was in a tiny corner room on the first floor of the stone-built inn. A guard stood grudgingly outside the door. The mean hearth was devoid of fire, the poky window was barred with iron, one unlit tallow candle was stuck to the three-legged wooden table, and there was a mattressless bed and one chair. Sam sat on the bare floorboards with his back to the wall, elbows resting on his bent knees and his head in his hands. He had been vaguely aware of the evening's merriment below, but mostly he was in his own world, trying to make sense of the last forty-eight hours: the True Covert, tree jumping, Tom Baker, the plight of forests, Frayne, Fred, the Every Tree, Mr Wells, the news of his mother, Hawk's dangerous situation, as well as the proximity of the past … and the future.

He'd turned twenty-four yesterday, but he felt like he'd aged by a decade. Most of mankind would live a lifetime and never know of the possibility of time travelling. Frayne was right; the knowledge weighed heavily. Somehow, though, the good priest had managed to keep his faith and principles, and indeed had found joy and contentment with this True insight, even though it could have so easily corrupted him. Sam wondered if the others he'd met at the Covert managed to live at peace with the truth they shared.

From a young age, Sam had simply accepted tree reading as a skill that he and his mother practised; a bit like any other skill, but an uncommon one that had to be kept secret. He never really felt it made him very different to other people, though. Everyone had something they were good at, like Hawk with his piping. His mother had used the ability altruistically, gleaning information from nature to heal others. He'd mostly used the gift as an escape. When he was young and his father harangued him because he'd not learned some technique of swordsmanship correctly, the trees calmed him. When he watched his father bully or beat his mother and he could do nothing to stop it, the trees soothed his anger. When he returned from risky journeys dodging or confronting excisemen to deliver whisky, the trees grounded him. The woods connected him to the land and made him feel part of a greater whole; he was just another soul walking the earth for a short time, in the company of the trees, plants, dogs, sheep, otters, badgers, owls, deer … everyone and everything just living the life they could. He knew tree reading was a rare privilege, but it also felt natural.

Tree *jumping* on the other hand, well, that changed the laws of nature and life as understood by most of mankind. He suddenly had a radically different perspective on human existence to everyone else around him. It separated him and the other True members from the rest of society in a more profound way than he'd ever thought possible.

He thought back to the previous night at the priory when he danced around the fire with Grace. He'd immediately taken to her straight-forward, practical nature and her loving temperament, and she seemed as charming as she was beautiful. He'd loved dancing with her and, from what Frayne had said, the feeling was mutual. If things had turned out differently he would have enjoyed getting to know her, but he knew it wasn't meant to be and he'd distanced himself. He'd done this partly due to his oath never to let any woman close enough to be reliant on him, but also partly due to his altered perspective on life. He held a secret so implausibly beyond reason and understanding that he could surely never expect to fully share his life with anyone — other than another True member, perhaps, but he was hardly likely to come across one of them, and probably wouldn't know if he did.

He felt lonely. Not sorry for himself, just alone.

He'd felt alone eighteen months earlier when he'd lost his family, but that was different. That was all about grief and guilt. Time mended or at least patched such emotions so that life could be lived. But now, Time itself was the problem. In theory — since he yet had to prove it to himself despite believing in Frayne and Tom Baker — he could move through trees to almost any date in history that he wished. With the aid of future wood, dates in centuries yet to come could be his tomorrow. Such concepts were almost God-like in their improbability and magnitude.

Possibilities flooded his mind, but what he really wished for was to be able to go back to the start of all this and save his sister. It wasn't to be though. Frayne had said that the trees wouldn't allow you to travel to a time when you were living, so Martha was still lost to him. His mother, however, might not be lost after all. She might be in the future, possibly the same future — 1st May 2000 — that presently hung around his neck in the form of a carved wooden acorn. There was no question, he had to try. His mother could be trapped there and in danger. He would go and bring her home. Nothing was holding him here anymore other than his friendship with Hawk, but he had his own life to live.

There was just one sticking point to his plan to try to visit the year 2000; he was currently a prisoner of the British Army in 1725, due to be handed over to the magistrate in the morning to be charged with theft and probably transported, and Hawk was to be tried and most likely executed as a two-time deserter. They needed to escape from the inn. Tonight.

There were only three ways out of the room: the small window, but the bars were solid; the door, but there was a guard outside; or the chimney, not immediately appealing.

Sam was thinking through the options when he realised that the music had stopped, in fact there was little noise downstairs at all and he could hear Hawk chatting to a soldier as they stomped up the stairs. Their conversation was easy; Hawk's music made most people warm to him, whatever the circumstances.

'He's all yours, Jed,' said the redcoat, as he handed over his charge to the soldier outside the secure room. 'Alex, that was a right good night. Sorry, about this.' He turned back down the stairs.

Jed took out his key, unlocked the door then stood back, pointing his musket at the door.

'Stay back you in there,' he called at Sam. 'In you go, Mr Piper.'

Hawk put his thumb on the latch and pushed the door. It didn't budge. He pushed again.

'No, sorry, marra, looks like I can't get in there,' said Hawk. 'Do you have another room?'

'Don't play daft buggers with me, just open it and get in.'

'I'd love to oblige, I could do with my feather bed, but it's not moving. Look, I'll hold your musket and you give it a

152

dunsh.'

The soldier was in no mood for jokes. He'd missed all the ale and tunes tonight.

'Oh, you're really funny you are. Shove over.'

The redcoat tried the latch and gave a push. No luck. Hawk stood back, leaning on the hallway wall, smirking. This had to be something Heron was up to and he knew well enough to just play along and see what happened.

'Why don't you get your mate upstairs again, Jed, and see if he can open it?' said Hawk, helpfully.

'Why don't you just shut the fuck up and push harder? Your mate must've gone to sleep behind the door I reckon. Sackless bastard.'

'Well, in that case, I'm definitely not pushing. More than my life's worth to wake him up. He's got a canny bad temper on him when he's woken up.' He leaned his head back against the wall and shut his eyes.

'Oh, for the love of —'

At that moment, a slightly muffled and eerie half whistle half screech seemed to come from the room. It wasn't Sam's best attempt at a sparrowhawk, as he was a bit out of practice.

'What the hell was that?' said Jed.

Hawk knew exactly what it was, and while he didn't know exactly what was going on, he could make a good guess. He opened his eyes and said in a loud voice, 'Well, either they've got a noisy ghost here or my friend is snoring as usual. Tell you what, sling your musket over your shoulder and let's give it one last push together, see if we can shift him. I'm not standing out here all night, despite your wonderful company.' He joined Jed in front of the door and put his hands to the door ready to shove.

153

'You do the latch. Now, on three … one, two, three.'

The redcoat flew headfirst into the room, unhindered by the previously immovable door. He was met by the awaiting arms of Sam Heron, whose firm embrace stopped Jed moving and discouraged him from shouting. Hawk came in right behind the soldier and quickly and quietly shut the door behind them.

The two friends worked fast together and, for want of rope, bound and gagged the miserable Jed with his own stock and stockings, and tied him to the window bars with his belt.

'So,' said Sam, while removing Jed's dirk and sword, 'what do you fancy, Hawk? A tight squeeze up a dirty chimney and a hop over the rooftops, or shall we use the front door and see what the redcoats have to say about that?'

'You come up with all the best plans.'

'Well sadly, this room is all out of cesspit trapdoors, otherwise I obviously know what you'd have preferred.'

Hawk laughed, but quickly clapped his hand over his mouth. 'You're right, so I guess the next dirtiest option is the chimney. Reckon we can get up it?'

'You maybe, given your eel-like build. Me, not a chance.'

'Right then, we walk out, right under the nose of the British Army. We have a musket, a sword, a dirk, a Hawk and a Heron. They don't stand a chance!'

Sam whispered slowly to the trussed-up Jed. 'We're going to be heading off now and I'd be most grateful if you'd decide not to do anything to draw attention to yourself for at least 10 minutes. Fair's fair, eh? I mean, we could have decided to quieten you permanently, couldn't we, but we're reasonable men. Are you a reasonable man, Jed?'

The dirk skimmed the redcoat's neck and he nodded

urgently.

'I'm glad to hear that as I'm going to leave my friend here just outside the door for short time while I check things out, and he can always come back in if he hears anything. Understood?'

Out on the dark landing, the pair crept to the top of the stairs. They thought they'd been cat-like in getting to this point, but just as Sam was about to start down the first stair, a door opened further down the corridor. There was no time and no place to hide. They were both about to make a noisy dash down the staircase when a high-pitched squeaky whisper made them stop.

'Is that my little chicken come to play?'

A buxom, middle-aged lady in a voluminous nightdress stuck her head and shoulders out of her bedroom door.

'Oh my, I didn't really expect you to bring a friend,' she said, as she took in the sight of Sam by Hawk's side. She looked Sam up and down. 'But I don't mind, if you don't.' She gave them both a wink that made her look like she'd just eaten something extremely unpleasant.

Sam looked back at Hawk, who had a sheepish grin on his face.

'Really?' Sam whispered. 'Little chicken?'

'She was most attentive and appreciative of my music,' said Hawk, pretending to be wounded. 'It would have been rude to ignore her, and anyway, she paid well. I'm quite surprised she's still standing though, given the amount she drank. I'll go and persuade her back into her room, otherwise we'll have the whole place waking up.'

'No,' said Sam, with a restraining hand on his arm, 'we'll both go.' He quickly quashed the surprised look on Hawk's face with the suggestion that perhaps her bedroom window might not have bars on it.

'I knew I brought you along for some reason,' said Hawk, and they both fixed wide smiles on their faces and walked purposefully towards the beckoning and rather frightening nightdress.

This was a much larger room, reasonably well-lit by candles and with a dwindling fire. There was a comfortable-looking bed which on another occasion might have seemed inviting, but right now it was mostly daubed with a surfeit of frill-covered flesh.

'She's all yours, chicken,' muttered Sam. 'Keep her busy while I check out the window.'

'Must I?' But Sam's raised eyebrows said it all, and Hawk turned on the charm as he approached the occupant of the bed. Sweet nothings flowed, syrup-like, as he desperately tried to keep the over-enthusiastic lady at a reasonable distance whilst promising intimacies that made *her* giggle and *him* slightly nauseous.

Sam quickly went behind the thick curtain to find that the window was indeed without bars and overlooked the large stable yard at the back of the inn. The only problem was the drop to the ground, and the fact that there was still light coming from a single-storey low building to the right of the stables. He'd have said it was the stable-hand's room, but he doubted they would still be awake by now. They'd have to risk it.

Hawk was offering the nightdress wine, which she knocked back with practised ease, but her exuberance was beginning to fail her.

Sam caught Hawk's attention, then started to climb out of

156

the small opening of the window. As luck would have it, the stone had not been dressed so smoothly at the back as at the front of the building so there were enough hand and footholds to get part way down the side of the building to make the fall less damaging. While he waited for Hawk, he crept over to the stables. There was a rather handsome galloway not dissimilar to his own favourite horse. He checked his feet and, as expected, found he was not shod. That was a relief, less noise. He found the bridle, but there were no saddles to be seen. Just then Hawk appeared.

'Bloody hell, don't do that to me again, Heron. She nearly smothered me when she passed out.'

'Get the gate, Hawk. We'll borrow this beauty and send him back when we're safe.'

Hawk walked over to the tall wooden gate at the back of the yard as Sam mounted the good-tempered galloway and followed behind. Hawk had managed to get the unhelpfully stiff gate part way open when the sound of metal clanging against cobbles rang through the yard. They both stopped stock still in the darkness.

'What the hell was that?' said Sam.

'Sorry, sorry,' said Hawk, and he bent down to retrieve a silver picture frame that he'd lodged in the waistband of his breeches.

'I don't believe it. What the hell are you playing at?' said Sam, forcing himself to whisper but yearning to yell.

But the clamour hadn't been missed. A voice boomed from the low building. It was unmistakably Sergeant Chisholm. Less than a minute later, he was standing in the doorway in his shirt and boots, brandishing a sword.

157

'Is that you, George? Who's there? You'd better be meant to be there or you'll be sorry.'

'Damn the man. Quick, get up behind me Hawk.' Sam held out his arm and Hawk grabbed hold and swung himself up behind Sam.

Just at that moment, Chisholm worked out who he was looking at in the blackness and, as well as shouting to his soldiers to get out there, started running out into the yard yelling, 'You bastards, don't you fucking dare run. I'll catch you and have you strung up by your balls before flaying you alive, you thieving sons of bitches.'

The gate was opened barely wide enough to pass through and the horse was so spooked with the rumpus that he was determined not to try it. Sam decided there was only one way out of this increasingly dangerous corner. He handed the reins to Hawk and jumped off, sword at the ready.

'You get out with the horse. I'll keep our man busy. Don't risk waiting for me if the soldiers come, just go.'

The apoplectic sergeant reached Sam seconds after he hit the ground, bearing down on him with a vicious slash which Sam only just had time to parry. He quickly found his balance again though and moved away from the gate to give Hawk space to escape.

The bare steel of Chisholm's sword was heated by the flame of naked anger and he attacked hard. Despite Sam's skill, only a fool would fail to take this kind of ferocity seriously — the man was out for blood. Sam also knew that he only had seconds before the other soldiers came to their sergeant's aid. He didn't want to kill the sergeant, but he had to stop him or their escape was doomed and their lives probably forfeit. He watched for the moment of yet another wild and unprotected slash, and stabbed Chisholm at the top of his sword arm near his armpit. Sam didn't wait to see what happened, but immediately fled to the gate, hearing the clang of metal on cobbles for the second time that night as Chisholm dropped his sword and yelled in pain and fury.

He'd just got to the gate when he heard the shout, 'Stop the bastard,' from the sergeant, and heavy-booted feet ran towards him.

Hawk was waiting for Sam, just about keeping control of the now highly agitated horse. He offered a hand to Sam who grabbed it to help him leap onto the horse's back, and they were off. Three half-dressed soldiers rounded the gate with muskets in hand, but they were too late. The galloway wasn't hanging around. He'd had enough of the racket and wasn't happy to have two unknown riders on his back. He shot off in a panic down the back alley behind the inn. Sam and Hawk half-wondered if Chisholm would order them shot at, but no lead came winging their way, so he must have thought better of it. At the end of the alley, they turned their stolen accomplice towards the east and headed up the dale under the cover of darkness.

CHAPTER THIRTEEN

THE VALLEY

Thursday, May 3rd, 1725

Saying goodbye to Hawk was harder than Sam expected.

During the night, after fleeing from Rothbury, they'd taken turns in walking and riding to Upper Coquetdale, keeping to the valley and to the north of the river. Eighteen months ago, when Sam had been very close to death, parts of his life had replayed in his fevered mind. Tonight, this particular valley of the shadow of death was very familiar to him, not only because he was aware he might be once again heading to his own demise, but also because he knew intimately all the landmarks hidden around them in the moonless blackness. He knew where the river looped and twisted; his mind's eye saw the heather-clad hills at either side of the valley; the sprawling dark mass over to their left was Middle Wood; Moss Hall was southwest of the wood, and Hawk's bastle house was just to the east; the ruins of Harbottle Castle sat dreaming of past days of glory; the Draag stone and the lough quietly awaited the warmth of morning; and at Faerie Hill no doubt the sprites were once again up to mischief now the visitors of the Covert had left them in peace.

As they continued westwards, the Cheviot Hills loomed and

Scotland beckoned, the valley narrowed and the hills began to close in on them. This was border terrain and they both knew it well. Hidden in the grassy folds riddled with burns and bogs, weather-beaten shepherds tended hardy flocks, whisky stills were busy, and the notorious Slymefoot pub was as remote a gathering place as you could find. From the tiny hamlet of Alwinton, the drovers' road known as Clennell Street headed up and over to Scotland. But this ancient path wasn't just for cattle; it had been used for centuries as a cross border connection for smugglers and Border Reivers and, before that, probably Roman soldiers.

It was here that the two friends had agreed to part. After a couple of hours rest, Hawk was heading off on foot for the relative safety just over the border at Kirk Yetholm where his family based themselves part of the year. Sam was ultimately headed for Middle Wood.

'Look up my old bones when you're there, Heron,' said Hawk, giving Sam a thump on the arm. 'And I expect you to share a dram with me for past times. If you get where you're going, you'll find me needing a drink after nearly 300 years in the earth.'

Sam laughed.

'I'll do that. But I'll be back before you know I've gone if all goes to plan. Together until we're ninety, we agreed. I'll get word to you when I'm back, though that could be tomorrow for all I know of this weird world.' He paused, then added seriously, 'I'll be coming back, Hawk, with or without my mother. If I don't, well, it's because I can't. Stay well and stay safe, my friend. And keep away from redcoats, you barmy bugger!'

161

'We have separate paths to travel, my friend, but whether it's in body or spirit, we will always walk them together.'

He watched as Hawk turned and started walking slowly but purposefully into the rugged hills. He didn't look back.

The sun had risen on a fairly typical Northumbrian day; the clouds couldn't be bothered to ride very high in the sky but sat morosely hugging the hilltops waiting for something better to do. No doubt the wind would come out to play later, then they could have some fun.

Sam rode to Moss Hall. It was around seven o'clock by the time he got there and, since there was no sign of any unwanted visitors, he headed to the stable yard. He quickly found Charlie, the groom, and arranged for the borrowed galloway to be fed and watered, then returned to the King's Head along with an anonymous letter that he would write, thanking the owner for the unexpected loan and apologising for any inconvenience caused. He didn't want horse theft to be added to the list of complaints levelled against Hawk.

In his chamber, he washed and dressed. He remembered Frayne saying that Fred wore long trousers when he came from the future, but he had no time to arrange this. Dark brown breeches and long boots would have to do, along with a linen shirt, waistcoat and coat. He'd take a hat and his black travelling cloak too as it made a good blanket. His favourite sword, a dirk, a flint and steel, and a pouch of gold and silver coins, and he was ready for his journey into the future. At the last moment, he added the wooden counter he'd had with him since the Covert, and his mother's embroidery.

His cousin Hugo was away, so Sam wrote him a letter

saying that he had to go off for a while and was leaving the estate in his hands. He also wrote that, should he not return within a year, Hugo should consider Moss Hall his own.

It all seemed so sudden. His preparations seemed so minimal. But this was it. He left the hall. Leaving Hawk had been hard, but this was no wrench. There was nothing there for him now.

It always seemed to come back to Middle Wood. This had been his playground with his sister when he was young, his classroom with his mother, a place for high jinks with Hawk when they were boys, his escape when he was older, and his solace for the past eighteen months. It was his place.

But today, his wood was different. Today, Middle Wood was a doorway, though he didn't know exactly what he might find on the other side of the threshold.

It was around midday. Despite the blanket of cloud, the air had that tang of a chill which can still be felt on some spring days as the last of winter's hold is loosened by the irresistible pull of the warmth of summer. He could feel the woodland revelling in its state of wakefulness. All the trees were now clothed in splendid shimmering colours of lime, citrus, moss green and glossy olive. The background of woody stems and branches, in browns ranging from chestnut to mushroom and russet, gave a sensible, structured contrast to the whimsical new leaves. Fat buds on the hawthorns promised murmurations of May blossom, and the fairy wings of the sycamore seedlings were beginning to sprout. The wood was a joyous place to be and May was always one of his favourite months.

Sam made his way to one of the oldest oaks in Middle

Wood. It had to be the one. It was a magnificent specimen even now, so in another three hundred years it would be remarkable.

It was time.

With one hand on the trunk and one clasping the charm around his neck, he started to take deeper, slower breaths. His shoulder blades relaxed down his back and his head drew upwards to that position of perfect balance on the top of his spine. He felt tall, poised, aligned and comfortable in his body. He was quickly conscious of the gentle, unhindered flow of air into his lungs, punctuated by the ever so slight hiatus after an out-breath; that all-important moment of quiet in the constant noise of living. The space. The opening. And for him ... the way in to a direct connection with nature.

OAK

I live long. I am life, strength and support.

I have sheltered royalty in my boughs and sailed the high seas for the protection of our kingdom. For many hundreds of years, documents were signed in ink from my galls, so human history, religion, music and art came alive and was shared through my existence. I am the fabric of humble dwellings and the upholder of great cathedrals. Once, I was revered simply for being myself, as well as for the mistletoe which often resides with me. I am an integral part of the story of the land I live in.

But I have had my share of hardship under the burden of humanity's reliance upon me — too many of my elders have been torn from the land. I can live for over 1000 years with good fortune, but at 150 to 200 years of age my value to man is deemed to be in my strong timber. I am felled. I fall. And much falls with me. Primroses and bluebells that once tickled my toes in spring are left without my sheltering canopy. Bats lose their roosts and birds such as pied flycatchers and marsh tits have no nesting spots. Jays, mice and squirrels miss the sustenance from my spring catkins. Deer, badgers and boar go hungry for want of my thousands of acorns. Hundreds of insect species are left homeless and cannot thrive, leading other species to starve. My leaves no longer purify the air and nor do they fall to make a rich mould at my feet for the stag beetles and fungi.

And yet, I endure, I am strong. I am father and mother to the forest; I protect, nurture and welcome. I will always strive to do so, and I will continue to hope that mankind not only uses my dead timber for their buildings, barrels and fuel, but also my living leaves, bark and acorns for food, tanning leather and for healing themselves.

So what if lightning strikes me! I rebuild. I find another way to keep going. I fight for all life.

CHAPTER FOURTEEN

SCIENTIA POTENTIA EST

November 23rd, 1997 to February 5th, 1998

When the snow started falling Silas decided enough was enough and stopped watching the old guy, Archie Robson, who'd presented the lecture today, and Kate Elliott, the girl from the university history society. He wasn't yet sure what he made of this afternoon's talk, but something was pricking at the back of his skull and that usually meant that, whatever it was, it required more attention. He'd kept his distance from the pair, of course, but it was obvious that the two knew each other reasonably well. You never knew when that information might come in handy. Scientia potentia est, he thought. Knowledge is power. Silas liked both.

As he unlocked the door and walked into the dark shop, the old-fashioned doorbell on a spring rang above him. He hated that bell, but his father wouldn't let him take it down. 'It all adds to the olde-worlde atmosphere of the place,' he'd say. 'You know how the Americans can't get enough of that.'

Fenwick's Armoury had been established in 1964 by his father, George Fenwick, based in his garage at their house in Chester-le-Street. It hadn't been a runaway success from the start but he'd worked hard at it and knew his stuff. By 1972 his parents had bought this run-down old shop on Saddler Street in Durham City and they lived in the flat above it. It was a mostly eighteenth-century building, but it had much older foundations, probably sixteenth century. They renovated what they could on a tight budget and things had taken off quite soon after they opened. Two large arched windows framed the glass door that was etched ornately with the shop name. Saddler Street was on the hill leading to the castle and cathedral, so all the shops looked slightly skew-whiff, which added to the quaintness that attracted the tourists. As tourism increased in the town, George realised that he couldn't have chosen a better place for his business. And these days, they not only got passing tourist trade, but the family was now well-known and well-respected by the university lecturers in the history department, which had in turn led to a much wider reputation for the shop and the Fenwicks' knowledge.

This shop had been Silas's world since he was at primary school. It was like living in an armoury museum. All the pieces were authentic. This was no replica tat shop; they were selling history. With a backdrop of military flags and paintings of old uniformed generals, every inch was stuffed with helmets, suits of armour, medals, guns, duelling pistols, spears and swords. When he was younger, the few of his classmates that didn't think he was creepy thought he lived in the best place ever. Sometimes, when the shop was shut, his dad even let them hold the guns and swords and they would imagine themselves heroes of the hour.

But Silas didn't think it was a game. This was proper history. It was violence. It was power. These antiques

168

demanded respect, as did he. The friends didn't last long.

Along with his parents, he'd been part of an historical re-enactment group for as long as he could remember. Moving on from simply dressing up and playing with a hoop and stick, he became a proficient archer and then, as a teenager, he joined the men of the group as a redcoat foot soldier, hefting a Brown Bess musket with a bayonet. They re-enacted battles from the times around the Jacobite rebellions to the American Wars of Independence.

Muskets, rifles and pistols were interesting, but swords were Silas's real passion. Any idiot could shoot a firearm, and even the use of old flintlocks could be grasped relatively quickly. Swords, on the other hand, they required proper skill. To have true mastery of a sword meant that the blade had to become an extension of yourself. You were the weapon. Silas felt there was honour and potential glory in fighting with swords. He had taken fencing lessons since he was eight years old, and soon invariably won all the county competitions he entered. As an adult, his first love was the sabre but he competed with the more commonly-used foil. He was fast, strong and tactically very good. Few could take him when he was on top form. Even now, as a mature part-time PhD history student of thirty-two years of age, he could still more than hold his own on the circuit and was the strongest member of Durham University's first fencing team.

Silas also had a second obsession. The buzz of finding ancient artefacts that no-one else had seen or touched for hundreds of years was an anticipated thrill he never tired of. As a metal detectorist of well over a decade now, he'd mostly had the usual disappointments of nails, horseshoes and buttons, but he also had a substantial collection of coins of various eras and denominations, and a few other interesting pieces such as a Georgian kilt pin, a lead ingot, and a Roman brooch. As with all detectorists though, he wanted the big find; a hoard of Anglo-Saxon coins, a hidden treasure box of jewellery, a ceremonial dagger ... Being a history academic, Silas knew that the value of buried treasure was not really in the monetary worth but the social significance it represented. However, since the armoury was how he and his family made their living, he was also keenly aware that history could bring substantial profit. Money meant respect and power. Silas wanted both.

He'd toyed with the idea of night-hawking at historic sites to try for the hidden cache he felt was his due after all these years of trudging the fields by himself, but other than the brooch that he knew he should have admitted to finding, he'd always kept within the law. He didn't do this because he was selfless or even particularly bothered about disturbing or stealing elements of the country's past. If he was honest with himself, and he usually was, brutally so, it was because he wanted the acclaim of the find. He wanted his peers to know that his historical knowledge and expertise was what lead to the successful discovery. He wanted the recognition and respect that would bring. The money, well, that would certainly be welcome too.

He stood in his bedroom on the top floor of the building. The small dormer window at the back looked out over the River Wear. With daylight nearly gone, the streetlights on Elvet Bridge over to his left were now shining. There was enough light for him to see the trees that lined the dark river below. Trees — ah, there was that prickle in the back of his head again.

What was it niggling him about today's ridiculous lecture? He still couldn't put his finger on it. There was far too much wittering on about trees and not enough about Druids in his view. However, maybe he'd do a little bit of digging one day and see if he could find any validation in the man's claim about an offshoot of Druids called the True. He highly doubted it. The general consensus of the students he briefly talked to at the end of the lecture was that the old boy was patently deluded, albeit entertaining.

The next few weeks turned out to be very busy in the shop, so Silas was forced to put a mental sticking plaster over the unscratchable irritant that Archie Robson had become to him. He hadn't had time to do any research as he'd hoped, but instead of just dwindling into unimportance, the 'Archie itch' had stayed with him. Three days before Christmas, walking through Durham market square, and passing the huge Christmas tree bedecked in its finery, he suddenly stopped in his tracks as if he'd walked slap-bang into a glass wall. The plaster had just been unexpectedly and unceremoniously ripped off. The momentary shock, almost pain, was intense, but Silas liked pain, it sharpened senses and made you think. Anyway, a bright new pink and shiny patch of possibilities had just been revealed to him.

He was right. The stupid old bastard was right. Trees really *were* the focus of many human rites of passage, important transactions and secret trysts. Why had it taken him so long to see the relevance of this to himself? If it really was possible to read trees, then if you found the right tree of the right age and in the right place, well, they might be able to tell you things other people could only find out by chance — if ever. Things like where people had buried treasure. He couldn't wait to get back home for some diligent deliberation. This was exciting.

Six weeks later, and nothing. Not a bloody thing. Silas had searched everything and everywhere he could think of — university libraries, museums, ancient texts — and nowhere was there even a sniff of a group called the True or of tree reading. Silas was a very good researcher and trusted in historical records. You could always find something if it was there and if you looked hard enough. He was cursing himself for the fool that he'd been taken for. Jesus, what had he been thinking, putting time and effort into such a plainly ludicrous idea? The old woodsman was obviously just some tree-hugging old hippie with a warped sense of humour who enjoyed making mugs out of university students.

However, there was still a part of him that wanted it to be true. Perhaps he should visit the old bugger and either get him to admit he was just having a bit of fun with gullible students or, at an outside chance, show him something to prove he was telling the truth. He realised, though, that he hadn't a clue where to start looking for Archie, so he'd need to find that girl from the History Society and get her to tell him. He would have preferred not to involve anyone else, but he had no other lead to go on, the man could live anywhere in the north.

Kate Elliott was sitting in her favourite coffee shop, Piper's End, under Elvet Bridge by the river. The building's characterful arched stone ceilings made a cosy daytime winter retreat, though this belied its rather gruesome history as a House of Correction from the seventeenth century. Northumbria's own traditional tartan, the ancient black and white Border plaid, was used as seat cushion fabric. The walls were hung with all manner of things traditionally Dunelmian and Northumbrian — clogs, fiddles, old sets of small pipes — and there was a shelf with a pyramid of replica tins of Mrs Clements' Durham Mustard. Scattered in and amongst the artefacts, there were some fascinating old black and white photos of Durham and the north-east and a few striking modern colour images of highlights such as Durham Cathedral, Bamburgh Castle and Lindisfarne.

Kate always tried to sit at the table by the wall on the right, which was overlooked by a print of the piper that the cafe had been named after. The man had been a famous small pipes player in the eighteenth century and came from where she lived, up near Rothbury in Northumberland. Sadly, the story was that he'd met his end here in this godforsaken Durham prison for stealing a horse in his old age. Had he always been a bad lad? She'd never know, of course, but even if he was, there was something appealingly cheeky about his face that made her think she'd have quite liked him. She sat, mismatched china teacup and saucer in hand, looking into this handsome face from the past.

'You know, they say you can still hear his ghost play some nights.'

Kate started, and spilled tea over her lap and onto her well-buttered singing hinny.

'Oh, I'm sorry,' said the man. 'I hadn't meant to startle you. You must've been in a world of your own.'

Kate was grabbing napkins to mop up the tea, but quickly looked up to see who'd addressed her.

'Oh, it's you,' she said. It wasn't said in an unfriendly manner, but neither was it a particularly welcoming response. It was that mature student who'd been at Archie's talk, the one with the ponytail who'd been very dismissive of Archie. She hadn't taken to him at the time, and this meeting hadn't exactly just endeared him to her either.

'Look, let me buy you another scone and tea, by way of an apology,' said Silas, catching the waitress's arm as she was passing. 'May I join you?'

Kate didn't really want to spend any time with this man but, since he was already pulling up a chair, it looked like she had no choice. She nodded and asked for a repeat of her previous order.

'I'm Silas. Silas Fenwick.' He held out his hand which she shook briefly. 'You might know the armoury on Saddler Street. That's our family business. You're Kate, right? I recognise you from that fascinating lecture about Druids and trees before Christmas by that speaker from ... Oh, where was it again?' He tapped his forehead with the heel of his hand.

'Northumberland,' offered Kate, vaguely. 'But I seem to remember you saying his talk was laughable.' She smiled, but the smile didn't reach her eyes. She looked at Silas. He wasn't an ugly man, in fact you could see how some women might find his even features, grey-blue eyes and long black hair quite attractive, but there was something about him that left her cold.

He attempted to pooh-pooh her comment, saying he was sure that Mr Robson had a reason for his unusual points of view but that his own interest was more in relation to his information about the Druids.

'But you think he believed what he said about

174

communicating with trees?' asked Silas.

'Oh, I think a bit of tree-hugging and meditation would do us all a power of good, don't you?'

Given that Archie had been so keen on telling people about the True, she couldn't quite put her finger on why she was now unwilling to divulge anything of the lessons and discussions she'd had with him over the Christmas holiday, but her intuition was shouting at her not to get drawn in to any association, however brief, with this man.

The tea arrived and Kate was relieved when, after a little more small talk, Silas just took a few token gulps from his cup before making his excuses and leaving her.

Walking up the stone steps to street level, Silas mentally patted himself on the back. Too easy! Okay, so she'd not been specific about where Archie lived, but he'd already found out that Kate lived near Rothbury, so it was a fair bet he wasn't too far away from there. He would make a trip this coming weekend, then that would be an end of it. The Archie itch could be suitably scratched.

CHAPTER FIFTEEN

ITCH SCRATCH ITCH

March 1998

Fenwick's Armoury always closed on a Sunday and Monday. What with taking his turn at manning the shop, and academic deadlines, it was Monday 2nd March before Silas managed to wangle borrowing his father's old dark blue Rover and head off to Northumberland to find Archie Robson. He'd tracked the old carpenter down to a place northwest of Rothbury.

He quite liked getting out into the wilds of the county. Whenever he could find a spare moment, he would throw all his metal detecting gear into the back of the car and make for one of a couple of areas near Hadrian's Wall. It was either there or a field near a ruined castle mid-way up the Devil's Causeway, an old Roman road that branched off from Dere Street just north of Corbridge and went as far as Berwick on Tweed. He'd arranged permissions from local landowners to detect at these spots. Rothbury was further north than he usually went, unless he was joining the summer dig at Bamburgh Castle, which he'd done some work at for the past couple of years. He didn't really take pleasure in the countryside per se, but he enjoyed the solitude and the potential reward. He was completely convinced that he would one day find something significant. The question was, would today be the start of his road to success?

Silas was nothing if not scrupulous in his efforts to get the best out of any situation he might benefit from. His skill as a researcher meant that, given time, he could pretty confidently pass himself off as an avid enthusiast about nearly anything. As long as people didn't know him, he could find the self-assurance and stick to the character he'd chosen to portray. He was very aware that people, especially women, didn't really take to him if he was just himself — that much had been plain since school — but he was good at acting a part if he was prepared. Today he was primed to play the role of a nature lover who'd initially not believed in the possibility of reading trees, but whose strong desire to connect with the natural world had led him to find out more. Frankly, trees bored him rigid, but he thought he'd got enough knowledge under his belt in the last month to seem plausible as a tree hugger.

As Silas drew up at the end of the long track by a hotchpotch of scruffy-looking buildings on the edge of a small wood, Archie came out of his workshop, chisel in hand. It was starting to mizzle and the wind was biting. The old man was dressed in just his shirt sleeves and some ratty old trousers mostly covered with a long leather apron. He held up a hand in greeting to his unexpected visitor.

'Morning,' said Archie, as Silas got out of the car. 'Bit of a clarty day, eh? Can I help you or are you lost?'

'No, not lost. I've just found who I'm looking for.'

Silas smiled his warmest and least supercilious smile, offered a hand to shake, and enthusiastically explained that they'd met briefly in Durham at the talk, and that Archie's message about the importance of trees had resonated with him, nature-lover that he was.

'Oh aye,' said Archie, with a serious yet noncommittal nod of the head, and waited.

Silas could immediately feel that he was going to have to work harder at this than he'd hoped. Archie was not just going to welcome him with open arms as a fellow tree-lover. Only to be expected, he thought. Maybe the old man had regrets about what he'd said in Durham last November, but whether that might be because it was true or rather because it was a pack of lies, well that was what the researcher in Silas was going to have to dig deeper to find out. Patience and focus were needed. Ask the right question and you might get a telling answer.

The tack that Silas decided to take was his least-favoured option since it was the most time-consuming, but he now knew it was the one most likely to succeed. In some ways, he couldn't quite believe he was still giving this credence, but his gut had told him to go with it and his instincts were rarely wrong.

'So, Mr Robson, I've come today to ask you about two things. I hope you might be able to help me with both, but even one would make me happy. Er, just one moment, if you don't mind.' He went back to his car and rootled around on the passenger seat for a bit of paper.

'I can't make things, you see,' he said, showing Archie the piece of paper on which he'd sketched a chest of drawers. The drawers were all different sizes, and annotations showed that this drawer should be birch, that one should be rowan, that one ash … There were thirteen drawers and thirteen different types of wood.

Archie took the rather crumpled drawing and flattened it out on a bench just inside his workshop. He found his glasses and put them on. He took his time looking over the drawing, then turned to Silas, who was waiting patiently by the workshop door.

'Hmm,' said Archie, looking over his glasses with a dubious half-frown. 'So, you know about the ogham?'

Ah, bait taken.

'Well, I wouldn't say *know*, exactly,' replied Silas, 'but I like the link between trees and the lunar cycle, or is that a bit of a modern contrivance for the True? Anyway, I really wanted to have an object that encapsulated the different trees and thought that a special piece of furniture would be ideal. I'm a collector, you see, so it would be a prized piece in its own right, but it would also house my important finds. Might you consider taking such a commission?'

Archie spoke slowly, in a measured tone that was very different from the way he'd spoken at the lecture.

'I'd be happy to do that for you,' said Archie. 'But it would take time. It won't be easy to find good timber from all these species. And it would cost, I'm afraid, but I can't rightly say how much straight off.'

'I didn't expect it to be a cheap job, Mr Robson. It's not really about the money. But I knew you were the man for the task. Shall we say £200 for an initial payment, and you let me know when you'd like some more?' Silas handed over a wad of cash and a business card from his pocket.

Archie seemed surprised and slightly confused, but he took the money and they shook hands.

'I'm delighted, really,' said Silas, 'Thank you.'

They chatted briefly about how long the work might take

and what style and size the chest should be, then Silas took his leave and started to head back to the car.

He allowed himself a brief inward smile when Archie stopped him, saying, 'You said there were two things?'

'Oh yes.' He turned back. 'Well, the other thing is perhaps more difficult, and I was unsure whether or how to ask.' He stood, feigning an effort to find the right words.

This time Archie spoke for him.

'You want to know if I really can read trees or whether I'm just an old fool?'

By the time Silas was on his way back home half an hour later, he was feeling quite smug. It had gone reasonably well. OK, Archie hadn't really told him anything new, but his story was consistent and he had in essence agreed to give him pointers to begin getting in touch with trees. Since they were in the lunar month of the ash tree, Archie had told him to meditate with ash trees until the 17th March, then change to alder on the 18th March for a month. He should then come back to inspect the chest of drawers, and perhaps discuss his success, or otherwise, with the tree meditation.

Silas had decided already that he had no choice but to try this, otherwise all his efforts so far were pointless. However, he also decided that if he ever got the impression that Archie was playing him, the old woodsman would be very sorry.

In mid-April, Silas drove back up to Rothbury to see Archie. He admired the half-completed chest of drawers, which he had to admit was an impressive work of art even in its unfinished state and handed over another £100. Archie asked him how the meditating with trees was getting on and whether he'd noticed a difference between the ash and the alder. Since he couldn't actually perceive any difference, it was impossible to feign any plausible answer other than, 'No'. Archie offered a few hints about breathing more slowly, trying different times of day, ensuring an empty mind … the type of general advice Silas assumed any meditation practitioner would offer. He tried not to show his impatience as he was sent off for another month, this time to practice with willow.

'Try meditating in the moonlight,' suggested Archie, as Silas was getting into his car. 'Willow has an affinity with the moon. And allow the trees to feel who you really are. Be open.'

Over the next month, things started to change for Silas. Firstly, he noticed that his fencing was even better than normal. His ability to focus had definitely sharpened and his already fast reactions were now quicker than ever. Then came the revelation that what he thought were daydreams while he was meditating, might, in fact, be slightly more than that.

There was an old willow that he was drawn to a few hundred yards up from Prebend's Bridge on the south side of the river. Each time he visited it, the same impression began to come into his mind. It seemed to be getting clearer each time. He felt sadness, loneliness and thought he could picture himself sitting under the willow. It was as if he was having an out of body experience. Since he didn't feel sad or lonely (these were emotions he'd banished long ago as pointless), he couldn't understand what he was seeing. On the fourth visit he realised that it wasn't himself he was seeing at all. It was a young boy. Was he looking into the past to see some unhappy child? If so, how long ago? How could he tell what any of this meant? All he knew was that he only got this image and these feelings when he meditated with this specific willow. He tried various other trees in and around Durham city, choosing ones that were away from people just in case anyone that knew him saw him and thought he'd gone crazy. To no avail.

It was another week before he was due to visit Archie again, but he was desperate to know whether this was the start of him being able to read trees. He'd figured that old trees in this busy historic city must have seen enough of interest through their lives for him to glean something, if (it was still a big if) the whole concept was true. However, he didn't class a miserable child as a success. Silas decided to give up on Durham and drove up north again to a ruined castle at Branley. Perhaps he would have better success with the trees near there.

Northumberland had more castles than any other county in England. There were well-known inhabited ones such as Bamburgh and Alnwick, and romantic ruins like Dunstanborough on the edge of the North Sea near the fishing village of Seahouses. Silas always favoured the lesser-known for his detecting, partly because he'd never get permission to detect at the famous sites, but also partly because, if there was no-one else around or showing interest in the site, the glory of any find would be solely his. He was pretty sure that he'd pinpointed places where finds were likely but perhaps not so obvious to others.

Branley Castle was small, on the edge of a tiny hamlet on the Devils Causeway. It also had an ancient church nearby which, though he hadn't yet found any recorded proof, Silas was convinced St Cuthbert would have stayed at on his travels in the county in 668AD. The whole area oozed possibilities.

Silas had relatively recently cultivated a 'friendship' with the local farmer whose fields came very close to the castle. Some large oaks, ashes and other trees dotted the hedgerows and there were a few in the middle of the field where Silas was currently searching. He headed to the oldest largest oak and settled down to try to read the tree.

'I got nothing,' he said to Archie, not hiding his exasperation when he visited him a week later. 'Over two months I've been doing this now and not a whisper, not a dicky bird.'

They were in the smaller of the two rooms of the cluttered workshop, and Archie was busying himself with jobs as he always did. He rarely looked Silas in the eye. Today he was perched on a tall stool by a roughly five by three-foot tabletop which he was sanding with fine sandpaper. The top was balanced on two trestles. There was less free space in the workshop than usual because of the table, so Silas paced up and down the narrow gap between the wall and the table, at the opposite side to where Archie was sitting.

'I thought I might be getting somewhere with that willow, but what the hell use is it to me to see some depressed child, for God's sake?'

'Hmm. And what are you expecting to find?' asked Archie, quietly, keeping up a steady rhythmic movement with the sandpaper. 'What value are the trees supposed to offer you?'

Silas could feel his frustration seeping out at the edges. This was taking too long. The tantalising taste of what he thought was a breakthrough back with the willow back in Durham had been shattered up at Branley Castle. Enough was enough. The old man must be holding out on some aspect of tree reading, unwilling to share with him.

'I expect,' he said, curtly, and stopped to face Archie, or rather the top of Archie's bent head, 'to learn something useful about things that have happened in the past. What other point is there in reading trees? I'm an historian. Past events and past lives are what I want to know about. That's what you said they could offer me. What else is there?'

Archie laughed, not unkindly, but with an edge of pity that didn't escape Silas's attention.

'Oh goodness, son, don't you see? The trees don't care about what you want to know or what you would find useful. I might have compared reading trees to reading a book, but there is no library telling you which tree knows what. You get what you get with trees. All you can do is read what they are willing or able to share.' He looked up at Silas briefly before getting back to his sanding, stroking the wood with his hands every now and then to feel whether he was getting closer to the silky-smooth finish he wanted.

'I mean, take your willow,' he continued. 'I think you were really getting somewhere there. The tree was showing you something. That's great. My instinct tells me that this willow knows you. Perhaps you didn't mean to, but maybe you did as I suggested and let the tree see some of your real self.'

He stopped sanding and looked fully at Silas. 'Think back. Could that boy have been you? Was the tree showing you the sad boy it knew years ago?'

Silas stood, silent. His face was immovable and his grey-blue eyes stared coldly down at the old carpenter. Enough.

Archie didn't notice the man's changed demeanour or he might not have spoken the next sentence.

'Do you think perhaps tree reading is not for you? It's no

184

shame. I'm sure not everyone has the right temperament for it, but there will be some that click quite quickly. I mean it didn't take … Well, I mean to say, I'm sure it never takes as long if you start younger.' He stopped, biting his lower lip.

A muscle twitched in Silas's neck. The old man had obviously been about to mention someone's name but had changed his mind and gone back to his sanding. Silas found himself almost subconsciously scanning the workshop. His eyes stopped at a long-handled broom propped up against the wall right next to him. Its well-worn soft bristles were clogged with sawdust and wood shavings. He then spoke, slowly and deliberately.

'So, you mean to have me believe that what I saw at the willow was a memory, and you've decided not to tell me the key to tree reading because…' he stopped, and swallowed, 'because you don't think it's *right* for me?'

Silas was gratified to see the look of wary concern greet him from under the wrinkled brow. He must have pitched the tone of menace about right. No more pretence, no more tree-hugger, the old carpenter would see his mistake in trying to make a fool of him. But it was too late.

Silas had never killed anyone before. He found it a distastefully mundane business. He was very aware that there was no honour in what he'd done, and he regretted that fact since he believed in honour in combat. Of course, what just happened wasn't exactly combat, but he told himself that Archie had insulted and wronged him, so reaped his just reward. Actually, given that this wasn't pre-meditated and planned out, Silas felt it couldn't have gone better in some ways.

A sweeping brush didn't really feel like a suitable weapon, but a good warrior had to use his surroundings to his advantage. Silas had quickly wielded the broom like a pike and, reaching over the table, had pushed the soft bristles hard into Archie's chest. As he hoped and expected, Archie was immediately put off balance on his stool, wobbling precariously backwards. Archie had grabbed the brush-head as a lifeline instead of the weapon that it actually was and battled hard to right himself. It was a strangely silent tussle with just the odd grunt from the woodsman. Silas played the game for a little while, just for fun, holding the shank of the broom firmly and giving just the odd push to keep Archie at the perilous angle he was in. Archie was strong, there was no doubt, but Silas knew he had him in a bad position that would be hard for him to maintain. Then Silas saw the old man's eyes. There was panic there, yes, but there was also pity. That was enough. He let go of the broom handle leaving Archie floundering backwards unable to keep himself upright any longer.

The metal hook on the wall that Archie struck behind him was a happy bonus. It meant Silas didn't have to finish him off. Death was instantaneous. Archie's head was pinioned to the oak beam, leaving him in a vaguely upright position, hanging alongside tools of his trade, a wood saw, a mallet, rasps and clamps … The look of shock on Archie's face was almost comical, but Silas respected the dead so he only smiled. A trickle of blood began to insinuate itself down the wooden beam.

So, no more itch, he thought. He'd probably got as much out of the old man as he could. He was certain Archie was giving nothing else away to him about tree reading.

Silas manhandled the fine hand-made chest of drawers into his car. He'd paid for it after all. Then, after returning the broom to its original position and wiping his fingerprints off it with a nearby dusty cloth, he left the workshop. It was a serene scene. Nothing to suggest murder. It was undoubtedly just an elderly man who had an accident when he tipped backwards off his stool. The police probably wouldn't even look any further than that. Why would they?

As Silas drove back to Durham, he was surprised to find that the itch he thought he'd just extinguished hadn't gone away after all. He was still thinking of trees and the tales they could tell him. If only. But he had nowhere to turn to now. Sure, he could practice meditating with trees alone and see if he could get any further, but he didn't rate his chances and there was no-one else to get help from.

Except … He hadn't missed Archie's unfinished sentence earlier. It dangled like a loose thread on a ragged shirt cuff. As a rule, Silas didn't like loose threads; he cut them off. This particular thread, however, might need some gentle pulling, since he had a feeling it had a name: Kate.

CHAPTER SIXTEEN

PULLING THREADS

August 1998 to September 1999

He'd found nothing in the newspapers about Archie's death. There was nothing on the news either and nobody came knocking on the armoury door. Of course they didn't.

Despite this, he left it three months before deciding to pull the 'Kate thread'. It was mid-August before he headed north again, this time to Cloudberry Farm out in the middle of nowhere in Coquetdale. In the intervening months he'd done his research on Kate Elliott and had turned up something that he was convinced backed his view that she *must* know about tree-reading.

There was an article in a recent local newspaper about the ex-Durham University history student taking on her family's hill farm tenancy on her own. A photo was taken of Kate in front of her farm sign. Silas happened to notice that the logo wasn't a cloudberry though. It was an oak leaf with a marking in the middle, and it was very similar to the logo Archie used on his furniture. From his discussions with Archie, he already knew that this mark was the letter *d* from the ogham, but he'd now discovered the link with the letter *d* and the old English word for oak — *dru*. Dru for Druids perhaps? Or maybe Dru for True? If ever a connection was shouting at him, this was it. Kate was part of all this, she had to know.

Turning up without warning at Cloudberry Farm, the welcome from Kate was as expected, surprised and a little wary.

She came out of one of the farm buildings looking hot and bothered and dressed in a very grubby set of grey baggy overalls. It was quite a change from the last time her saw her, but there was no doubting her pale, heavily-freckled face even though her long auburn hair was tied up in a kind of 1950s-style head scarf. Silas didn't like freckles as they made faces look far too untidy. He wasn't really surprised that she was living alone; she was hardly the catch of the century.

'You're a bit out of your way, aren't you?' she said, wiping her oily hands on a rag as she came towards him and recognition struck.

'Yes. Hi,' said Silas, shutting the car door. 'I was in the area looking for Archie Robson, but I gather —'

'He died in May,' said Kate, shortly.

'Yes, I've just found out. I'm sorry. An horrific accident, I gather. I don't know how close he was to you but, well, since I was up here and knew you were close by, I thought I'd come and say hi and offer my condolences.'

'Oh,' she said, seeming to soften, slightly. 'Thanks.'

He could see she didn't really want to stop and chat, but before she had a chance to say so, he said, 'You took some finding, I have to say. Your track end isn't exactly obvious even when people tell you where to look.'

'I guess not,' she said, 'But those that need to know usually find me. Well, now I've stopped, do you want a cup of tea, then?'

It wasn't the warmest invitation ever, but then he wasn't really used to those anyway.

Over tea in the farmhouse kitchen they discussed the weather and he feigned interest over her taking on the farm. She asked after his family business — he must have made an impression for her to remember — and Durham, and that brought him nicely to Archie.

'You know, I've been thinking about Archie's lecture ever since he came last November. I dismissed it as nonsense at the time —'

'Hmm, yes, I seem to remember you were quite rude to him,' said Kate, and looked at him directly, with her head on one side.

Snotty bitch, he thought, but then replied, 'Oh, I do hope not, but if I was, I apologise. I find now that I can't get what he said out of my head. I was going to ask him to tell me more about it. Perhaps you can tell me instead?'

'Me?'

'Well, I assumed that since you knew him so well, he must have told you much more detail about this tree-reading.'

When his senses were on alert, Silas could generally pick up nuances of unspoken thoughts on people's faces. Years of quickly second-guessing what his fencing opponents' next moves were going to be from their body language had definitely honed this skill. Faces were more easily readable than bodies. He watched as Kate features set themselves into lying mode.

'Not much more than he told us all at the lecture, I'm sure.'

'Oh that's a pity. You know I've tried it myself —'

'Really?' She was definitely surprised by that.

190

'Mm, haven't you? I don't seem to have the knack though.'

'Oh, shame,' she said. 'Anyway, look, I'm afraid I've got my work cut out today, so I hope you don't mind if …' She got up from the table and headed for the door.

'No, of course,' said Silas, also getting up. 'I'm sorry to trouble you, and thanks for the tea. Maybe I'll drop round again next time I'm up. I come metal detecting up this way sometimes.'

'Oh, right. Sure.'

He loved the English sense of politeness. It could usually be relied upon. He knew she wanted to say no, but she just couldn't. That was his way in. He'd just successfully invited himself to come and see her again. She could become a work in progress.

He already had it all planned out. On the next visit he would ask if he could metal detect on her land. Her farm was quite close to good historical sites, so it definitely wouldn't be a waste of time. She wouldn't say no. That would let him come more often, maybe every couple of months, and he could gain her confidence. She would probably be flattered by the attention. Anyway, he was sure that if he found something interesting — he could plant an artifact if nothing came up — the historian in her would bound to be persuaded of the sense of reading trees to discover buried treasure. *Sense!* He couldn't quite believe he was even thinking this. But he was. He was playing the long game here, he knew, but that was fine. Metal detecting was always a long game, but this might just have better odds than normal. He'd give it a year. He'd have cracked it — her — by then.

After the surprisingly hot July, the first week of August 1999 came as a shock. The thunderstorms and heavy cloud matched Silas's mood perfectly. A year. A whole bloody year had gone by. He wasn't used to failing and he didn't like it. He usually went up to Cloudberry on the first Monday of every second month, but he'd be going early this month. He'd had enough of waiting. He decided that he couldn't pussyfoot around any more, she obviously wasn't going to help him voluntarily. Not even the supposed find of the Roman brooch last month had moved her. Call herself a historian!

He knew by now that she took her lunch break about eleven thirty. In this weather, he'd be sure to find her in the kitchen.

He knocked and the door was quickly opened. She had a cup of tea in hand and the phone tucked under her chin. She'd stretched the cable to reach the door, and as she went back to the dresser where the phone was, she motioned to him to take a seat.

'Okay, so within the hour then?' she was saying. 'Thanks, I really appreciate it.' She put the phone down.

'Hi. I wasn't expecting you today. It's not exactly the weather for it, is it?'

'No,' said Silas. 'No, it's not. But I want to discuss something with you, if you have a little time. I really think we're missing a trick here with — '

'Oh crikey, Silas. Not again. I've told you, I'm not interested in finding treasure. I know that it's a big deal for you, but it's just not for me. And as for the trees helping, I'm sorry, but I can't help you with that. I don't know what you expect from me.'

'Can't or won't help?' said Silas, quietly.

'Well, *can't* obv —'

'It's just that I think you can.'

He knew that would get her hackles up and it did, but it couldn't be helped now.

'Oh, you do? And what's given you that idea all of a sudden?' asked Kate, putting her tea on the table and sitting down.

He calmly explained that he knew about the farm logo having the sign that Archie used for his furniture, and that he was now as certain as he could be that this was the sign of the True.

She laughed.

'It's just a family thing! One of our shared ancestors over a hundred years ago used it in woodworking and it's been handed down the generations on both branches on our family tree.'

'So you've got nothing to do with the True and Archie never told you anything about tree-reading?'

'No!'

'Liar!' he shouted.

'What?' She stood up quickly, the wooden chair clattering as it fell backwards onto the floor. One of her dogs that had been lying on the floor got up and started a low growl. 'How dare you! I think you should leave, Silas. Bracken, here.' The dog obediently came to her side.

He ignored her request to go.

'I have been here very early some mornings when you weren't expecting me. It seems to me you have a good conversation going with that sycamore over there.' He nodded out to the field in front of her house.

'You've been spying on me?! What the hell for? What kind of creep are you?' She reached down for the dog's head and slightly backed away.

'I just want to know what you know. Is that such a big deal? I know you know, I just don't understand why you refuse to tell me. Why is that, Kate?'

She screamed at him, now holding the dog's collar as the dog snarled at him.

'Get out! I wouldn't tell you if you were the last man alive. You're a manipulative user and I'm glad the trees won't talk to you.' She stopped and breathed — regretting what she'd just said, he wondered? Then with a quiet anger, she said, 'Now get out of here before I set the dog on you.'

The dog he could probably cope with, but she was on guard now and she was strong. Even then he might have given it a go, but her earlier phone call stopped him. 'Within the hour,' she'd said. No, he'd have to leave this. He'd handled it badly and luck wasn't on his side. He said no more but got up and left.

She yelled after him, 'And don't come back or I'll call the police.'

WILLOW

Be open to your emotions. Spend some time with me and I will help you to understand yourself better.

My way is surrender, change and movement — resistance is not for me. Does that make me weak? Not in the slightest, despite me being mostly linked to the feminine side of life. I bend. My flexible branches and stems are pliable; I can survive in diverse terrain and climates. You might know the beautiful white, furry catkins of my pussy willow species and think me soft and frivolous. That would be a mistake, I am tough and adaptable.

From living shelters to wicker baskets and fishing nets, I

provide for mankind. I can lead them to water if they dowse with my twigs, and I make good charcoal to warm them.

Tenacity is my middle name. Try as you might to contain my roots, I will find a way to spread in search of stability and moisture. Hack at my limbs and I will grow more. I come back fighting after injury, perhaps this is how humans know they can use my leaves to staunch bleeding or my bark to relieve pain. While I live, I am vital, I grow, I renew.

I have an affinity with the moon, that sphere of magical brightness, and in the past I was known as the tree of dreams and enchantment. I like that. Dreams and imagination create scope for wider horizons and positive growth and can help us trust our intuition.

I wish you sweet dreams.

CHAPTER SEVENTEEN

BABES IN THE WOOD

May 3rd, 1725 to September 4th, 2000

In the middle of Middle Wood, Sam allowed his breathing to quieten and deepen as he had done hundreds of times before. His heartbeat calmed in response, and his blood flow slowed. He could sense the welcome change in his perceptions. Time was strolling rather than rushing by, and his awareness of all things around him grew keener. He could feel, even hear, the sap enthusiastically rising and spreading through the old oak. He felt himself becoming part of the tree and, by extension, part of the whole wood. He breathed in the woodland.

Blood. Sap. Sap. Blood.

Whispers of wind rustled through boughs grown heavy with leaf. There was the buzz of myriad insects. Fungi crept through the ground littered with decaying leaves that were being slowly hidden by the fresh new grasses. Giggles of bluebells burst through in the patches of dappled woodland light. He could feel the trees' pleasure in the springtime. He sensed the beginnings of new growth; another layer of wood to be added to the expanding girth of the trunk. Another ring of life to be read by those who knew how.

Sam prayed that tree jumping would be as easy as Frayne had seemed to suggest.

'You've known trees all your life,' Frayne had said. 'It's just a slight shift from what you already know. And you need to be prepared to let yourself go. Trust the trees to take you where you need to be.'

'And how do I know where I need to be?' he'd asked.

'Only the acorn talisman knows that!' Frayne had replied with a chuckle. 'What an adventure.'

But adventures are not always comfortable. It was like being forced to walk along an unfamiliar and rocky mountain ridge with sheer drops on either side, blindfolded, and with your hands tied behind your back. He had no choice but to move forward but was in constant fear of losing his footing and falling over the edge. Going back wasn't an option. The journey had begun. He could feel a strong pulling sensation he'd never felt before. His natural reaction was to fight against it, to draw back. It felt dangerous. But he remembered Frayne's words. He let go and fell in.

The pitch blackness was initially frightening and disorientating, and his mind felt rather foggy. He tried to make himself calmly think through any facts he could grasp about his situation. He was alive (seemingly), it was night-time (presumably), it was windier and colder than it had been (definitely), and he was still in a wood by a large old oak tree. He pressed his hands harder against the gnarled and fissured bark of the tree, but he found he couldn't read the tree as his mind was rather too befuddled to focus properly. Instead, as his eyes grew accustomed to the dark, he stepped back to take in what he could see and feel of

198

the magnificent oak he was standing next to. Was this really the same tree but nearly three hundred years older? Yes, he thought, after walking around its expanded girth, he knew this tree or, at least, he knew its younger self. It really had worked. He'd miraculously jumped through time. Hah! He was in the future!

There was just one thing confusing him: it didn't smell like spring. He'd expected it to be May, but this felt more like summer or perhaps early autumn. Frayne had definitely said that Fred, the tree jumper he assumed his mother had obtained the wood from, jumped on 1st May 2000, immediately after leaving the Covert. So how could this be a different date? According to the priest, trees were unlikely to lead a tree jumper to the exact minute or even hour that future wood was taken from them, but he never mentioned them being months awry. His wood must have come from someone else.

Despite the confusion over the date, Sam decided to take the precaution of moving away from the oak in case Fred or some other tree jumper was nearby. A meeting might complicate matters. He walked for about five minutes, then tried to make himself comfortable for the night by a beech tree. Wrapping his cloak tightly around himself, his mind was filled with thoughts of how and where he was going to begin to look for his mother, especially as he was now unsure he was in the right time — season or year. As he drifted into an uneasy sleep, he thought of Hawk and wished he could have shared this journey with him.

The wind whipping through the leaves muffled the sound of the footsteps until they were almost upon him. However, the owner of the feet was seemingly the more shocked of the two of them, and a short high-pitched scream pierced the agitation of the trees.

The moon had risen since Sam had fallen asleep so, snapping open his eyes, he could make out the short, skinny figure of a young boy standing stock still about ten feet from him. He held one of the same kind of lanterns that Tom Baker had shown them at the Covert. The boy quickly bent to pick up a nearby fallen branch and held it in both shaking hands. The light fell to the ground and went out.

'Who are you? What are you doing in my wood?'

It was a very young voice and, while it was gripped with undoubted anxiety, there was also a note of belligerence in there which made Sam smile inwardly.

'Please forgive me, I hadn't realised the wood was your property. My apologies for trespassing, young sir.'

Sam sat himself upright leaning against the beech with his knees pulled up in front of him.

'Stay back you, you ... whoever you are,' said the boy, in strangled tones, as he brandished the branch towards Sam.

Sam held up his hands in a gesture of peace and smiled.

'It seems rather late to be checking on your wood. Is there a problem?'

'No. Yes. I mean ...'

The conflicting emotions in the boy were easily read in his shaky voice. Should he trust or should he run? But he stood his ground, slowly waving his branch to and fro as if it were a heavy broadsword.

'Well, I find myself lost in your magnificent wood. I had hoped to shelter the night here. Would that be permissible, given that it is your wood, after all?'

'Lost? So you're not some weird paedo or anything like that? Linda says I mustn't trust strange men.'

'Well, I admit that it's possible I'm strange, I might even be weird, and I was a man last time I looked,' Sam glanced down at his crotch in a mock questioning manner, then grimaced at the boy, eyebrows raised. 'But as for being a peedo, that I couldn't tell you as I don't know what that is.'

The boy's branch stopped moving and sagged a little in his grip.

'You don't know what a paedo is?' he said, incredulously. 'Everyone at school knows that. And they're on telly. They're bad men.'

'Ah, bad men. No, in that case,' said Sam, 'I'm pleased to say I'm not one of them. I am not without faults, but I hope I'm not a bad man.'

He remained sitting, not wanting to frighten the boy with any sudden movement, but held out his hand. 'My name is Sam. Might I know the name of the keeper of the wood?'

The boy kept his distance and looked at Sam without speaking for a moment, then threw down his log. He'd obviously reached a decision. Trust.

'You definitely speak weird,' he said. 'I'm Joe.' He came and shook Sam's outstretched hand. 'But it's not really my wood. I just come here a lot. I like trees and I have a den here. It's just over there. I— I came to sleep here tonight.'

'Well, sometimes a man needs his freedom, does he not? Are you sure your mother — Linda was it? — won't be anxious for your safety?'

'Oh, Linda's not my real mam. Anyway, she won't notice,' said Joe. 'And she'll be pleased I've gone. She doesn't even like me. She said I'm a bag-of-bloody-trouble-they-don't-need'. He emphasised each word with a nod of his head, then stopped for a moment before continuing.

'None of 'em like me. I don't belong there, so I left. I'm going to live in the forest and look after myself til I can get to Newcastle. I've brought some tins of beans and some cheese, bread and some other stuff from the house. I'll be fine, j—just fine. I'm ten now.'

'Oh, I'm certain you will be more than fine. You're a capable-looking lad. I guess you're good with a slingshot and perhaps a fair hand at fishing? And you'll know how to make a fire, won't you?'

'Um, well, yes ... I can.' He looked pensive for a moment, then asked, 'Can you?'

'Yes, I learned when I was a young boy. They can be tricky sometimes though, don't you think?'

'Yes,' agreed Joe, seriously. 'Maybe you could show me how you do your fires?'

Sam smiled widely. 'I'd be happy to, of course. In fact why don't I make a fire for us both since we're sharing the forest tonight? If that's acceptable to you, young Joe? Shall we gather some sticks and get that going?'

The wind started to abate as they searched for twigs and logs. Sam found some old dry leaves and grass and got out his flint and steel.

'Oh cool,' said Joe, beaming. 'Just like Ray Mears uses on telly. I've only got matches. How do you make it work?'

Sam was initially surprised but reminded himself quickly that he had to be ready for a lot of new things that he didn't know about. Goodness knows what had changed, for good or ill. He was certainly already struggling with a few of Joe's words: peedo, tins, telly, matches. This was going to be more difficult than he'd expected.

When they had a good fire going, Joe, who'd rattled and hit his light until it magically started working again, rummaged in his pack and handed Sam a sealed metal cylinder with patterned paper around the body.

'Here, but I forgot a tin opener,' the boy said. 'Don't suppose you've got one?'

'Well, no. What is this? Will a dirk do the job?' asked Sam, very slowly uncovering his hidden knife, in case the lad got frightened.

'Mega cool,' cried Joe, who seemed oddly impressed. He'd obviously decided that Sam was no threat to him. 'It's a tin of beans. Do you like beans? I do. Can you open them, then?'

Sam looked at the tin, passing it from hand to hand to try and work out what he should be doing with it. It had no opening or lid that he could see to prise open, so he went to plunge his dirk into the centre of the tin.

'Stop. What are you doing? Don't you know how to open a tin? The beans will go everywhere.'

And so, ten-year-old Joe patiently explained to twenty-four-year-old Sam how to open a tin of beans. Sam was amazed to find that there really were beans in this canister, in a sweet sauce, though how they'd been sealed in was a mystery.

For want of a pan they stuck the tin on the fire, and sat chatting on a long log as they stirred the beans with a stick.

Sam listened as Joe explained that he'd been taken into care from Newcastle when he was six years old and that he now lived with a family nearby.

'Mam was poorly, see. So she had to have lots of medicines to make her better. This man brought them for her. She called

203

him Uncle Micky, but I don't think he was a real uncle and I didn't like him and the medicines only seemed to make her worse. She really needed me to look after her. She gave me money to go to the shop and buy food sometimes. Sometimes she came with me, and she bought me some sweets once. She's lovely.'

Joe smiled at the memory.

'I tried hard, really I did, but,' he stopped and looked up at Sam, his eyes seemed to beg for understanding and forgiveness, 'but I didn't do a very good job. So then these social workers came and took me away from her. I told them I couldn't go cos I had to care for her, but they made me leave her. I — I still don't know what happened to her, if she's okay, and if she got someone else to look after her. And ... ' a single tear welled over the rim of his right eye and trickled down his cheek, 'I can't remember her now. I used to remember her face, but I couldn't keep her in my head and I don't have a picture of her. I wish I had a photo of her. I don't know how to find her now.' He screwed up his features, wiped away the tear with the back of his hand, then continued, 'But I'm going to try. I'm sure she'll still need me. Uncle Micky won't be looking after her well enough. I have to go back.'

Sam was silent. He'd understood the gist of Joe's story if not all the detail. He wondered what this *photo* was that Joe wanted so badly — a likeness, perhaps? Occasional sparks flew up from the burning logs and smoke rose up into the sheltering tree canopy above. The firelight made Joe's face glow with warmth, but his little body was huddled and scrunched as he sat there staring, now wordlessly, into the fire.

'Are you cold, Joe?' asked Sam, taking off his cloak to wrap around the boy.

Without lifting his head, and in a small, quiet voice, Joe replied, 'I'm cold right through to my heart.'

Just before dawn, with Joe's tiny frame still in a dormant bundle near their makeshift fireplace, Sam headed some distance from their small camp to find out what the trees could tell him about his surroundings. He'd known Middle Wood all his life but he was aware that this was not *his* Middle Wood. He needed to get his bearings.

He chose an elegant ash tree of about 200 years of age. Its mostly smooth grey trunk was clothed in velvety moss up to three feet from the woodland floor. It was hard to grasp that this impressive specimen was probably not even a sapling in his time. Yesterday.

Sam's mind had cleared and calmed after a night's rest, and the tree willingly shared its experiences with him. It had not had an eventful life so far, but it oozed contentment with its woodland companions and neighbours, with whom it had shared sunny days and extremes of weather, from odd periods of drought to more frequent harsh winters. Within the last twenty years, Sam was aware of the tree counting a human male amongst its frequent visitors and friends. He could also read that Joe had been coming to the wood for at least two years now. The ash loved Joe's childish happy spirit and the woodland watched over the boy whenever he came. The most recent memories Sam could make out included a recent female presence. Was it too much to hope that this might be his mother? Probably. The wood must surely get lots of visitors. The essence he felt certainly had something of Eleanor's signature about it, but it was just too recent for the tree to have fully committed this to its woody heart so he simply couldn't tell. This meant that he was none the wiser as far as his mother was concerned, however at least he could be pretty sure that nothing dramatic or violent had been happening here. It all seemed quite safe.

Sam returned to the little campfire by sunrise. Joe was just waking up. He looked rather forlorn and his teeth were chattering.

'Don't you think you should go home now, Joe? To get some warmer clothes at least, and maybe a tin opener?'

'No chance,' said Joe, now jumping up and down to get warm. 'For one, I'll be in for a major telling off, for two, they won't let me out by myself again for ages, like last time, and for three, then I'll never get to Newcastle, will I?' He counted the points out on his fingers and spoke the words as if describing the obvious to a simpleton. 'So I'll come with you,' he finished, decisively.

'With me? But I don't really know where I'm going. At least not yet.'

'Well then, you need me!' Joe said, triumphantly. 'I know where I am, pretty much. So where do you want to go?'

'I— er, well, truth to tell I'm not very sure. I'm also looking for someone and I'm not exactly from around here, so I don't really know where to begin.'

'OK. So, who are you looking for?' asked Joe, in a business-like manner. 'Maybe I know them?'

Sam smiled ruefully. It suddenly seemed such a strange thing to be telling a child, especially one in Joe's shoes. 'My mother has gone missing. I'm looking for my mother.'

'Hah, so we're both looking for our mams! That's funny. Oh', he added with a hiccup, 'and sad. But maybe I can help you and then you can help me? We're mates, right?' Joe looked up at him with expectant, puppy dog eyes and his head tilted to one side.

Sam thought about his rather unique predicament. He was here in Middle Wood, a place he'd known since childhood, but which didn't bear much resemblance to the place he knew intimately. He was definitely in another time. He'd asked Joe the date last night and he'd said it was early September in the year 2000, just before school starts. If Frayne was right and Eleanor had jumped to 1st May 2000 with Fred's future wood, she'd either have been here for about 4 months or ... or ... Oh, there was no point speculating, if she was still alive she could be anywhere and anytime. He'd have a look around locally and see if he could find anyone who might have seen his mother, then jump back home to a time he understood, either with or without her.

He was not feeling very hopeful. He had no idea about the way people in this time spoke, acted, dressed, ate ... anything. He was a babe in the woods. So what the hell was he going to do? He was an idiot. He hadn't really looked any further ahead than the getting here, though planning a trip into the future was not something he could imagine would have been too easy even if he had given it some thought.

He looked down at his eager little friend. Perhaps a child's view of this new world was not such a stupid idea. He could ask questions an adult might think odd, and perhaps slowly find his feet. If he couldn't find his own mother perhaps he could find Joe's. That surely had to be easier.

207

'Master Joe,' he said, putting out his hand, 'it would be an honour to have your company and I swear to do all I am able to help you find your mother.'

'It's a deal!' said Joe, with gusto and a manly handshake. A huge toothy grin split his face. 'So where shall we go first? Have you got any money?'

'Er, no. Not exactly.' He thought about the gold and silver coins in his pocket but decided this was probably not the right time to get them out.

'No money, no ride,' chimed Joe. The fair had been in the village for Easter and he'd heard this more than once. Sam, however, took a completely different meaning from this statement.

'No, I guess you don't have a horse. Perhaps we'll have to temporarily borrow one instead?'

'You want to go horse riding?' Joe was confused.

'I, well, I guess you don't really want to walk all the way to wherever were going? You *can* ride?'

'I can ride a bus!' said Joe, brightly. 'Let's go into the village and see when Rob's bus is coming past today. He sometimes lets me on for free. He might let you on too.'

'Rob's what?' asked Sam.

'Bus,' repeated Joe, before rattling on with more thoughts. 'Maybe Rob's seen your mam on the bus? Or we could make like a Wanted poster for her, like on the cowboy films, but only if you can remember her face. I know, we could go and see my friend Kate. She's Rob's friend too. She's a really nice lady, you'd like her. She's got lovely dogs and puppies, and a warm kitchen, and she's got paper and felt pens. She's a farmer.' He stopped to draw breath.

Sam's head was reeling with trying to make sense of the influx of new words and Joe's effusiveness. A bus was obviously some kind of carriage or cart. Fine. The rest would have to wait. A local farmer's wife with dogs? That couldn't be too overwhelming, could it?

'Lead on, my friend.'

CHAPTER EIGHTEEN

CLOUDBERRY

Monday, September 4th, 2000

Kate Elliott cantered her handsome grey Irish draught mare, Mellow, along the ridge of the Harbottle Hills, stopping, breathless and happy, by five lonesome wind-blasted pines she called the Old Timers. She smiled as she looked down at the green valley which, today, was pretending to be an innocent picture postcard view of a rural idyll in the very early September sunshine. The purple of the rugged heather-clad hills eventually gave way to what looked, from this distance, like neatly mowed fields bounded by stone walls. The fells were dotted with the fleecy smudges of feisty flocks of sheep. Angular blocks of dark green commercial pine forest made a patchwork effect on the wider landscape, but her eyes were always drawn to her favourite piece of broadleaf woodland, the mottled green blanket of Heron Wood with its impressive old oaks and elegant beeches which was far over to her right, this side of Middle Wood. Below her, straight ahead, near the silver thread of the Coquet River which wound through the valley, was Cloudberry Farmhouse. Cloudy. It was a small but perfectly formed grey stone farmhouse with a slate roof, nestled between low hills with pasture down to the river's edge. Home.

Looking down from here onto her farm and the lands she cared for always gave her a sense of perspective that she found reinvigorating and freeing. The day to day business of running a farm single-handedly, even a farm as small her 400 acres, was hard work to say the least. It was more of a struggle than she was ever willing to admit to. She had about 60 acres of decent in-bye land, but the rest was hills and fells. From up here it never seemed quite so daunting. Hers was just a tiny portion of a vast landscape. Sometimes she needed to step back to remember that, and to remind herself that she *could* do it and she wasn't crazy to have taken it on.

There was no denying it had been a complete shock when, the day after her father's funeral in June two years ago, her older brother had told her he wasn't going to stay on. It was taken as read that Ed would assume the running of the farm when their Dad was no longer up to it. He always worked alongside Dad. Sheep farming was what he knew. He was good at it. Yes, she adored the farm too and had worked just as hard as he had in previous years, but *he* was the farmer, for God's sake, not her.

'What do you mean you're not staying?' she'd said, not really believing what she'd just heard. Then wearily, 'Don't be stupid Ed. It's really not the time to start playing games.'

'Kate, look, I know, I— I should maybe have warned you before. I should have said something to Dad maybe. But I just couldn't. I couldn't break his heart. You'd gone off to your university. It was just me and him. There was never a good time, never a proper moment or the right words. I mean, how do you tell your ever-so-northern, salt of the earth father that

211

instead of keeping up the family farming tradition, his only son would rather go and cook fancy-bloody-pants-meals-for-folk-that-wouldn't-know-a-good-home-cooked-meal-if-it-bit-'em.'

Kate laughed. She could hear her dad saying that as he occasionally came across one of the many cookery shows on the television. Ed was right, of course, he would have been mortified.

'Are you serious Eddie? Really? You want to be a chef? But, where the bloody hell did that come from? It's not like you ever did much of the cooking when I was at home. I've only been away three years, and even then not all the time. How did I miss this? Why didn't you tell me?'

Shifting old Bracken, the border collie, out of his favourite spot, Ed slumped down into the grubby kitchen armchair by the coal-fired aga. His head was in his big rough hands and Kate could see this was no easy thing for him to speak about.

'Well, I guess your leaving was kind of the start of it really. I soon got sick of the same old meals we ended up eating. You know I like my food K,' he said, almost imploring her to understand. 'Anyway, so I started looking at Mum's old cookbooks and then watching Gary Rhodes and those other blokes, and that Masterchef. The top chefs are nearly all men, did you know that? And, well, I got better. And I got to really enjoy it. Dad never said anything, but I started serving up some different meals and he seemed to just accept it. Odd, now I look back, I suppose. When you came back,' he said, smirking, 'well, I piked out, kept quiet and just let you do the cooking or made the bog standard fare you knew I could. Sorry sis. I'm a coward, aren't I?'

'Yes, you bloody well are!' she yelled, and threw a tea

towel at him, but smiled as he caught it. 'So, can you really cook then?'

'I'll cook for you tonight and you can judge for yourself.' He grinned. 'Honest Kate, I just feel in my bones that this is something I could be really good at. A bit like you with the dogs and horses. You know you can always get animals to do anything for you. And the love of it always shows in your face. Well, when I cook something good, I guess I feel like you look when the dogs do as you've told them. It's a thrill, it's a challenge, and I want more of it. I want to be really good at it Kate. And, well, I think I can be. I'd told myself it wasn't possible, that it wasn't for me, but now Dad's gone...'

Kate had always known that the farm couldn't support two families, and she figured Ed would eventually choose some girl from local farming stock to marry and they'd settle here. So she had bowed out and, instead, followed her second passion and enrolled in a history and archaeology degree course at Durham University. It wasn't too far away, so she could come back to the farm easily if needed, on holidays and even on weekends. She really didn't want to be far away from Coquetdale. Its hotchpotch landscape of wild fells and tamed fields was part of who she was. It framed her life. She'd always assumed Ed felt the same. But it now seemed that Ed's mind was made up and he was off to London to learn the culinary arts.

'I feel so bad to be letting you down Kate. I know this place means everything to you. Losing it will be a massive wrench. It means the world to me too. It's our home. But I just feel that "life's too short" thing banging away at my head. If I don't do it now, I'll never do it. If I've got it wrong I'll be up shit creek without a paddle of course, but, well, I need to try. All or nothing. I was thinking to maybe get a manager in for a few months, you know, to give me a bit of time to see if I'm an idiot or not, and then, well, then I'll have to tell Bruce we're giving up the tenancy.'

At first the words hadn't really sunk in. It was bad enough to hear that her dear Eddie was leaving her, but the realisation that this might mean losing the home they'd known all their lives, even back when their mother was alive, was a shock too far. And all this after they'd just buried their father. It felt like someone had taken a fork and scrambled her brain.

Kate had headed for the stables. The comforting presence of her horse always calmed her. She tacked up Melly and went off up the hills. They'd ridden most of the remote Border trails together since her dad had bought Mellow for her when she was fifteen years old. He was dependable and brave and she was an almost fearless rider. She loved their shared border adventures. The height and space of the moors and hills gave her room to breathe and feel life's expanse and limitlessness.

Of course, none of this was expected or planned for. This was not the way life was supposed to go. She was supposed to continue with her history degree, then become an archaeologist and settle in the area as an expert in the castles, bastles and general heritage of Coquetdale. Or at least, that was her plan. And it had seemed like such a good plan, albeit perhaps a little hopeful in terms of the prospects of finding such a position.

In the end, though, as she'd sat astride Melly, watching the light fade on that cold grey June afternoon in 1998, it had come down to one simple question. Could she bear to lose all this — the farm, the sheep, the dogs, Mellow... her life? Emphatically and unequivocally, the answer was no. After that, it was just a question of working out how she could keep it.

'Now look who's talking nonsense!' said Ed, when she returned later that day to tell him what she'd decided. 'I mean how the hell do you think you're going to cope with this whole farm by yourself? Come on Kate, get real. We've got to be sensible about this. I mean I get that you're upset but we should probably let the dust settle before we decide anything.'

'Oh, so it's OK for big brother to make a momentous, life-changing decision the day after we bury Dad, but I'm not grown up or sensible enough?' she countered gently, with her head to one side and eyebrows raised.

'I hate it when you do that,' muttered Ed.

'Do what?'

'That oh-so-reasonable, I'm-a-thoughtful-academic look.'

'Sorry, but Ed, I can't give up Cloudy. The thought makes me queasy. It's my rock. It's Mum, it's Dad, it's us'. She stopped, unsure how to make him understand.

'Look, I know a *thing* shouldn't be that important, but this is more than that. It's what helps me be who I am. All my security is here. When I go away, I'm confident because I know Cloudy is still here for me. When I'm in a city, I can still breathe because I know the freedom of the hills is still all around this place. When I'm in a crowd, I imagine the trees of Heron Wood and I can be calm. I belong here. I can't believe you don't feel the same.'

Silence. Then she added, 'But you can bloody well drop your pinny and chef's hat and get back here to help with lambing in Spring.'

Of course, that hadn't been the end of the discussion by a long chalk, but their dad always said that Kate had inherited her mother's stubbornness, and that, when she was set on something, her mind was as unmovable and mysterious as the Draag Stone.

So, here she was, mistress of all she surveyed, or at least that small, beautiful slice of Northumberland at her feet. It was just her, Mellow her horse, Bracken and four other border collies (currently with five young rascally pups she was training), various farm cats, a beaten-up but invaluable Land Rover 90 pickup, a God-send of a quad bike, assorted farm machinery, and her hefted flock of Cheviot sheep - 150 breeding ewes and, at the moment, their 245 lambs. The farm was too remote for any mains services, including electricity, so she also had a substantial but temperamental generator called Frankly III. When she was young, she'd once heard her father yelling at their much older generator, ending with, 'Frankly if you don't stop sulking and get your arse in gear right now, you're off to the knacker's yard'. A hefty final steel-capped kick followed, and life surprisingly returned to the old machine. It was called Frankly ever after.

Stirring from her reverie of events over two years ago, Kate rode back down to the farmhouse. It was a Monday morning so Robbie should be coming in for an early cuppa and a chat on the way to pick up his first passengers over in Alwinton.

Robbie was Kate's oldest and dearest friend. They'd been at school together from age five and they'd been best friends ever since. When they were nine years old they'd solemnly promised their everlasting friendship at the Draag Stone, with blood from pricked fingers to bind their oath. When they were thirteen, Kate had taken on the school bully, Janice Armstrong, when she decided to start calling Rob 'gay boy Roberta'. Of course, Janice had been right as it turned out, but that didn't stop her from being a complete bitch, and she thoroughly deserved the bloody nose and split lip Kate had given her. It was worth every minute of the detention and the bruised hand.

Rob was now a mechanic and, much more importantly to him, the stalwart, part-time independent bus driver keeping people in rural Northumbrian villages around Coquetdale connected with the 'big' town of Alnwick twice a week and the city of Newcastle once a week. Larger bus firms had given up on these non-commercial rural routes that made no money. Rob had a passion for old vehicles and, with the help of his dad, had bought and lovingly restored an early 1950s Guy Arab III single decker bus he found in a scrapyard in Hexham some years ago. He was now a lifeline for folk with no cars, a source of much-attended gossip and local news, and an accepted fount of knowledge on anything from diets to holidays or the best places to buy anything you might need. He supplemented his income with summer bus explorations of the area for tourists. These were hugely popular and highly rated, in large part due to his entertaining commentary about Northumbrian history and local characters past and present. He also offered 'Guy' out for weddings and other events. Everyone knew and loved "wor Rob".

Rob was just pulling Guy into the farmyard when Kate reached the stables. It looked like he had someone with him. That wasn't unusual in itself, but he rarely brought them round to the farm. People often took advantage of Rob's good nature to cadge a lift even when he wasn't officially working. She knew he never minded. He often picked up lost hikers and other waifs and strays, and they left his bus feeling they had a new best mate.

'Morning Katie!' Rob shouted cheerily from the window. 'Any chance of a cuppa for me and Joe and our new friend?'

Ah, Joe. That explained at least part of it.

'I'll just sort Melly and I'll be in in a minute. Stick the kettle on, eh?'

When she got into the kitchen she found Joe playing with one of the puppies she'd brought into the house yesterday because he wasn't looking too happy. He looked just fine now.

Rob was in fusspot mode, offering tea to a rather dour, wary-looking chap sat in the armchair by the Aga, wrapped in a cloak. Where on earth had Rob found this unlikely-looking specimen?

'Kate, Kate, this is my friend Sam.' Joe rushed over to Kate and gave her a big hug. 'He's looking for his Mam, like me, and I'm going to help him. And he's going to help me find my Mam. Isn't that good Kate? So we need some paper and felt tip pens please so we can make a poster.'

'Woah, slow down soldier. Nice to see you too, but does Linda know you're here?' The suddenly-drooping head and shoulders said it all. 'Hmm, thought not. Well, we'll see about that in a moment, but meantime, have you had breakfast? No? Well, go and get some bread and jam from the pantry, and take the puppy outside to play. I'll make you some hot chocolate in just a bit.'

As she turned away from Joe, she caught Rob motioning towards the door with his head, so Kate followed him outside, pulling the door closed behind them.

'Oh my lord, Kate, he's gorgeous!' he whispered, barely

containing his excitement. This was not like Rob; he was exceptionally picky. 'Well, if you look past the startled rabbit look he's currently wearing. Have you seen those chestnut eyes? And how many men do you know that can wear long hair in a ponytail and still manage to look cool? And that body... and in those boots! He obviously works out and looks after himself.'

Kate laughed. 'I haven't heard you talk like this about anybody since that Ryan last year. Calm down before you burst.' She fanned him in the mock-swoon he was acting out. 'Who is he? Where did you find him?'

'I've no idea who he is. All I know is that he's called Sam. I found Joe at the bus stop in Mellerton as I was passing — I assume he's run away from Linda again — and Sam was with him. Joe seems completely taken with him, but of course Joe likes nearly everyone.'

Look who's talking, thought Kate.

'He seemed a little bit anxious when he got on the bus. And apparently he's got no money. He's never said a word yet. Joe's been gabbling on all the way here, as he does.'

Then Rob stopped himself.

'Oh— Oh, no, Katie, I've just thought, maybe he's not all there, maybe he can't talk. Or— Oh God, what if he's a wrong'un and what if— Jesus, do you think Joe's alright? He said they spent the night together in Middle Wood.'

'Stop, Robbie, stop,' she countered calmly, with a gentle hand on his arm. She was used to his flow of unsieved thoughts and could see him moving from excitement to concern in a couple of sentences.

'Look, we'll just go back into the kitchen and find out about him. Don't panic. Joe looked completely normal and fine. If we're not happy we can call the police, can't we?' A now anxious Rob nodded his agreement.

The man was looking less grey about the gills now. He'd taken off his cloak and, as they came back in, he stood and politely bowed to them. Yes, he actually bowed. Well, that was odd. And what the hell was he wearing? His clothes were straight out of the eighteenth century. She should know, she'd studied the era for long enough.

The stranger spoke to Rob first.

'Sir, I thank you for the bus ride. It was… it was very fast …and smooth, very smooth.' Rob beamed.

He then turned to look at Kate, but almost immediately dropped his eyes shyly to the floor as he spoke to her.

'Madam, I apologise for intruding on you in this way, it was not my intention, but, well, Joe was insistent that we visit you.'

'Er, Sam, wasn't it?' said Kate. 'I'm Kate. It's no intrusion. Joe is a special friend of ours, and his friends are welcome. But would you mind me asking how you know our Joe?' She sat down at the end of the big scrubbed pine kitchen table and gestured for him to take a seat too. Rob put the kettle back on the Aga to heat up again.

Sam, who, she noted, had quickly recovered from his shyness and fixed his brown eyes on her as he spoke, explained briefly about their meeting the previous night, then added, 'He is a fine young man with a strong character. We talked and kept each other company in the wood. I didn't feel I could leave him alone. He told me he wants to search for his mother. He is surprisingly persuasive for one so young so I offered to help in any way I could, though to be frank, I'm not sure where to start.

It's a long time since I lived here.'

'Ah, so you're originally from the dale? I've never noticed you before. And I'm pretty sure Rob would have mentioned you if he'd bumped into you before.' Kate raised an eyebrow in the direction of Rob who returned a look of mock indignation as he poured tea from the large brown pot with a cracked lid.

'So, Sam, have you come back for some local eighteenth century re-enactment event that I've missed?' she continued, in her usual direct manner and with an obvious look at his attire.

'Kate, really! Maybe Sam just likes to dress in a... in an individual way,' interrupted Rob, as he put three mugs of tea on the table and pulled up a chair for himself opposite their visitor. 'I remember wishing I'd been around for the New Romantics era myself — baggy shirts, tight trousers, you know, all very Adam and the Ant — and besides, it suits him.' Rob had patently quickly recovered from his fleeting concerns about Sam. 'Is that it? Bit of a new romantic?' he asked, 'Or have you been to a fancy dress stag party and they left you in the wood... tied up?'

Kate rolled her eyes and Rob hid his face in his large mug which made his glasses steam up. As he wiped them on his shirt, he said, 'I met a man in Alnwick once who was dressed as a fairy, wings and everything, and had been left in a bus stop overnight. No money, no identity on him, nothing. He didn't have a clue how he got to Alnwick, he was from Newcastle! I drove him to the police station, poor chap. Decent legs I seem to remember.'

He and Kate laughed. Sam's mouth fell very slightly open.

'Oh, bloomin' heck. Look at the time already,' said Rob, suddenly in a flap. 'I've got to get off or my passengers will wonder where I've got to. I'll leave you to talk about Joe with Kate if that's OK with you, Sam, unless you'd like me to drop you somewhere else? Or I can always come and pick you up later... you know, if you're stuck.' He lingered, half hopefully.

'Er, no. I'd be pleased to stay and help any way I can with Joe, of course. I made a promise to him. I have nowhere in particular to get to today, but perhaps, er, Kate and her husband, might not want—'

'Husband!' interrupted Rob, laughing with pretend shock. 'Oh, you'll pay for that!'

Kate glared at him. 'It's fine,' she said, shortly. 'Sam doesn't know me.'

She still hadn't quite got the measure of her strange visitor, and he hadn't yet explained why he was dressed in period costume, but, while she wasn't used to entertaining random wanderers, like Joe, she didn't feel any threat.

'You'd better get off, Robbie, or Mrs Franklin will have your guts for garters if you're much later. We'll be fine. I'll call Linda now so she can come and get Joe. See you next Monday if not before.'

Sam Heron sat at a kitchen table in a farmhouse called Cloudberry. It was in the valley where he was born, Coquetdale, possibly somewhere slightly north west of his own Moss Hall yet a long way from all he knew. The farmer was apparently an unmarried woman, young, very attractive, and wearing unseemly breeches that were so tight as to leave nothing to the imagination (where *was* one supposed to look?) but which neither Rob nor Joe had seemed surprised at. He was drinking tea, an expensive luxury in his time, but he didn't know if this

222

meant Kate was rich or tea was now affordable. He'd travelled here in a coach without horses on a road as smooth as the finest paved pathways and at a speed that defied comprehension. Yes, he really was in the future.

However, this was not the date he'd been expecting. Yesterday was Thursday, May 3rd, 1725. Today, according to Joe his ten-year old guide, was Monday, September 4th, 2000. So, this was the right *year*, but not the right month. Frayne said it would be May 1st 2000 if Eleanor's wooden acorn had come from his friend Fred. Either Frayne was wrong about the date Fred came from — unlikely — or his mother's acorn came from another, unknown source — surely equally unlikely? Either way, he had no clue whether his mother was here at all and, if she was, where he should start looking for her.

Right now, the important thing was for him to find his feet as quickly as possible in this strange new world. Then he could help Joe as he'd promised, before heading back to Middle Wood and starting his search. He prayed he'd be jumping back with Eleanor before too long, but his gut told him this was a lost cause and that he'd be returning alone. He decided he would say as little as possible whilst learning as much as he could about life in this century. Perhaps he could offer his services here at Cloudberry for a few days; he could think of worse places to learn than at the feet of farmer Kate.

CHAPTER NINETEEN

WANTED

Monday, September 4th, 2000

Sam had seen Martha talking to her 'secret' friend many times but, as he watched Kate having a one-sided conversation with an object she held in her hand, he knew this was very different, despite not understanding how. He tried hard not to gawp.

'I'm making Joe some hot chocolate,' said Kate, when she finished. 'Would you like some too?' She bent down to open a low white cupboard from where she took a glass bottle of milk.

Oh good god, don't look, he thought, as he took in Kate's long slender legs and— Christ, what an arse. It looked like the blue fabric of her breeches had been painted on, and he couldn't see any buttons. How the hell would she get them off?

'Er, no, no thank you.' He stood up and forced himself to look out of the window, wishing she'd sit down again.

Thankfully, Joe then bounced into the house with his arms full of paper and pens that he dumped on the table. He'd been outside playing with the puppy and drawing what he'd told Sam would be a *Wanted* poster.

'Does your mam wear glasses, Sam? I can add some if she does,' said Joe, rifling through his pens to find a black one. He smoothed out a piece of paper so Kate and Sam could admire his artwork.

The word *Wanted* was neatly written above a bright pink round face with smiling red lips, blue eyes and long straight black hair. Beneath were the words, '*Sams mam*'.

'Eyeglasses?' said Sam. 'No, she doesn't. Joe, this is excellent. You're a talented lad and I'm sure this will be a great help in finding my mother.

'Good work, Leonardo,' said Kate, ruffling Joe's hair fondly.

'We can ask Rob to stick it up in his bus, can't we Kate?' he said, beaming. 'And I can make more for the bus stop and things. So can we try and find *my* mam now?' he added, looking up at his new friend.

Kate stepped in. She broke the bad news to Joe that his foster mum, Linda, was already on her way to pick him up and take him back home. The new school term was starting tomorrow.

'But… but… but Sam said…' Joe's face went quickly puce. He didn't cry, but angry tears sprang to his eyes. 'But… he was going to… he's going to try and help me find my mam. He said so. Didn't you, Sam? No. That's not fair.' He grabbed the Wanted poster, scrunched it up and threw it across the kitchen. Then he turned and started lashing out at Kate. 'I won't. I don't want to go back. You can't make me.'

Sam crouched down to Joe's level and gently but firmly held the boy's arms by his side to stop him hitting Kate, then turned him round and looked him straight in the eye.

'Joe, I won't go back on my promise,' he said, calmly, 'but I need a little time to work out how I can help you. Will you go

225

home with Linda so I know where you are? Will you do that for me, so I can do my best for you?'

The taut little body slowly began to relax as the anger abated and he eventually huffily agreed, as long as Kate would let him come back to stay and play with the puppies at the weekend.

'You're very good with Joe,' said Kate, after the little boy left with Linda about half an hour later. 'Do you have young children?'

'Er, no. I have… I had a sister.'

'Oh, I'm sorry,' said Kate. 'I shouldn't have pried. Look, I need to get on with my sheep, and —'

Sam saw his chance. 'Could I perhaps be of use to you? I know a bit about sheep. I— I was brought up on a farm.'

'Really? Hmm, well, an extra pair of hands would be useful today, I'll admit. This morning hasn't quite panned out as I'd planned so I'm a bit behind. Maybe …'

She began clearing the mugs, plates and teapot into the sink. Sam looked on and waited.

'Ok,' said Kate, suddenly turning around with hands on her hips and looking him up and down. 'I'll pay you for a day's work, but —'

'I'm not asking for —'

'And I don't ask for favours,' she said, stopping his argument with a firm gesture of the hand. 'Either I pay you or you don't work.'

Sam nodded. 'Very well, thank you.'

'Great. But perhaps let me lend you some more suitable clothes? I reckon my brother's stuff should more or less fit you.'

226

Meeting outside in the yard after they'd both changed into work clothes, Sam was relieved to see that Kate was wearing less revealing, baggy trousers. She gave him some uncomfortable stiff boots she called wellies, then they set off over the field in front of the house. By now it was a reasonably bright day and the valley looked as beautiful to Sam as it always did. It might be the year 2000, and there were obvious differences, but it was still his dale.

'So, the Kelso ram sales are on next Friday,' Kate explained as they walked through the field. 'Have you been before?'

'Um, no,' said Sam.

'But I expect you've heard of them if you know about sheep,' Kate continued. 'They're my best bet for getting a good price for my rams. I've got twenty to sell this year.' Two of her dogs ran ahead of them. 'Most of them should do okay, but I've one fella that's my main hope of a big price and another that should do pretty well, as long as the other farmers at the show don't take against me.' Kate stopped walking and looked at Sam. 'I'm a bit of an anomaly, you see. Women shouldn't be running a hill farm alone apparently.'

'Is that right?' said Sam, trying not to sound as if he agreed. He found it hard to get his mind around a woman running a farm without male help. She must surely struggle, so he'd do what he could to help her.

'Oh, it's no big deal. Actually, most of the farmers are very decent and I've known them all my life. They don't care as long as I do a good job, which I do! It's just the odd misogynist that has a problem, and unfortunately I came up against one of them at last year's sales.'

In a field bounded by neat dry stone walls, a small flock of sheep was grazing contentedly. Kate opened a gate on a metal pen in one corner by a stone barn.

'We'll get them in here to work on. All my gear's in the shed. Bracken, come bye.'

One of her border collies immediately shot off across the field and giving the sheep a wide berth. Sam was then treated to an incredible display of skill — from both Kate and Bracken — as the sheep were herded expertly into the pen. Kate swung the gate closed with a smile and bent down to make a fuss of her little helper. 'Good lad, Bracken. He's a bit of a special boy, this one,' she said to Sam. 'We've even won a few competitions together, haven't we lad?'

'I'm lost for words,' said Sam. 'I've never seen anyone with so much control over their dogs. That was, well, astounding.' He'd always had dogs, many of whom he'd trained very well, but he had never seen such an expert partnership in shepherding. It reminded him of how he fished with Dart, his otter. 'And *you* trained Bracken to do this?'

'Who else?' said Kate. 'Yes, I've trained quite a lot of dogs in my time. I couldn't run the farm without them and I make some much-needed extra income from selling trained dogs. Right, let's start with that one over there.'

Kate pointed to a hefty ram that was staring imperiously at them. There was the hint of a smile on Kate's face as she leaned back against the gate and said, 'Fancy trying first? That's Nero.'

The grass was still a bit wet and the ground was soft from the recent rain. Sam headed confidently towards the ram, ewes scattering before him. He got within grabbing distance and launched himself at the animal, grabbing at the dirty fleece but

228

quickly finding himself eating mud.

'Agh, you little bugg—.' He stopped himself, got up and tried again, not looking at Kate. He was ready for him this time and held on tightly as the ram fought against being caught.

'Oh, well done,' said Kate. 'He doesn't like strangers. Sorry that was unfair of me.' She walked over to Sam, then bent down and started scratching Nero's head. The ram put his head to one side. 'You can let go now,' she said, and sure enough the feisty ram stayed put as meek as a lamb. 'I brought this one up from a newborn, you see. I'm not selling him, but I'll show him.'

The whole day was taken up with the sheep; checking teeth, trimming feet, treating sores, washing fleece and doing a bit of hand-clipping. Kate was very particular about the shape she was looking for. Sam couldn't see the point but kept quiet and did as he was asked.

By the end of the afternoon, Sam was in awe of this woman who dressed like a man and, though she didn't have the strength of a man, was tough and stubborn and had the skill and sensitivity of some of the best shepherds he'd ever worked with. Sure, he'd done a large share of the hard, physical work, but that wasn't because Kate was incapable, rather because he'd insisted. Moreover, it had been fun. This had surprised him. With the sheep as their shared focus, they'd laughed and joked when each had inevitably fallen on their backside or been head-butted by an intolerant ram. Despite many strange things that Sam wasn't used to — clippers, ways of treating injuries, fabrics — spending time with Kate was somehow easy. And it wasn't like being with any other woman he'd known, it was more like being with Hawk.

By the time they were cleaning up, the weather was turning

again. It was about six o'clock and a curtain of dense black cloud had been drawn across the hills calling an end to the day. There was no rain yet though, and the last remaining shafts of light lit up a small flock of black-headed gulls as they danced in their expansive stage of sky.

Sam and Kate suddenly each realised the other was watching, mesmerised, in the midst of washing their wellies.

Later that evening they relaxed in Kate's sitting room after sharing a pre-prepared slow-cooked hotpot from the bottom oven of the Aga. *Fingal's Cave* by Mendelssohn, one of her dad's favourites, was playing on her old-fashioned record player.

She wasn't used to sharing Cloudy with anyone except her family, but she had to admit it had been a good day. They'd worked well together. Sam obviously knew his stuff about sheep even though he seemed unsure of a few things she took for granted, like the drugs she'd administered. He was quiet but good company. Right now, she noticed he was sitting with his glass of red wine in hand seemingly struck dumb by the music, though moving his head very slightly to the rhythms. He'd given her a real shock when she put the record on earlier, as he'd shot off his chair, looking around in alarm. She didn't know what that was all about, but he'd calmed down quickly. He could be a bit twitchy.

Kate savoured a mouthful of merlot, curled her feet up by her bottom and looked thoughtfully into the log fire. For once it wasn't smoking and it was toasty warm within its rather limited sphere of influence. It might only be September but the temperature had dropped tonight and the wind whistled through the draughty old farmhouse. One of her cats, Hodgson, came and inveigled his way onto her lap. She tickled him gently, waiting for the creaky-squeaky purr to begin rumbling through his little body. He always sounded as if he needed oiling.

The music stopped and Kate could almost swear that Sam was about to clap but changed his mind. Instead he asked her a question.

'Kate, do you know where I could start to search for Joe's mother? Might Linda know?'

'Hmm, no, I'm afraid not. As far as we know, no-one knows where she is now, or even if she's alive. Drugs, you know. It's all very sad. I really don't know what will happen to poor Joe. He's never really taken to Linda's family and it's getting worse as he gets older. They're looking for another foster family for him currently — not that he knows that, by the way.'

'Can't he live with you?' asked Sam. 'He seems to love being here with you.'

'Oh, you don't beat around the bush, do you? Make a girl feel bad, why don't you?'

'I'm sorry. Really. I didn't mean —' said Sam quickly. 'I just thought —'

'Yes, I know. Believe me, I've thought about it too, and I've lost sleep over it, but I just can't. I'm here alone. I have a farm to run all by myself. I can't look after a child too, much as I don't want to lose him from my life. He's a handful, but he's a gorgeous boy and I do love him.'

'Well, in that case' said Sam, 'I'll just have to find another way to keep my promise.'

He took a piece of paper out of his pocket. It was Joe's crumpled Wanted poster that he'd smoothed out and kept.

'He told me he can't remember his mother's face anymore. I *might* be able to help with that.' He stared at the poster, lost in his thoughts again.

'And what about *your* mother?' said Kate, after a few minutes. 'Was Joe right that you're looking for your mam too? Is she missing?'

'Um, well, it's a bit of a long story,' he said, then went quiet again. He definitely wasn't a man who was uncomfortable with silences. She waited, strangely relaxed in the company of her gentle, uninvited guest. Eventually he spoke again.

'She disappeared a few years ago around Middle Wood. I've searched before, but thought it was time to look again. That's what I was doing when I met Joe.'

'Oh, sorry. I gather you had no luck. I guess she could be anywhere by now if it was a while ago.'

'Mhm.'

He obviously didn't want to speak about it, so Kate decided to leave it. It was none of her business, and anyway, she could see he was tired.

She wasn't keen on offering Sam her spare room — she really didn't know him from Adam — but said she would give him a camp bed in the barn. He seemed happy enough with that.

Settled in the barn with the dogs, Sam decided against the small rickety camp bed and leaned back on a bed of hay with the pillow and pile of blankets Kate had given him. He'd wrapped his own clothes, dirk and coins in a bundle with his cloak. The only other things he'd brought with him from home were his sword that he'd hidden in Middle Wood when he arrived, the wooden counter, and his mother's embroidery from Horseshoe

232

Priory. As he took stock of his first full day in the future, it was this last precious item, as well as Joe's Wanted poster, that he reached for to look at by the light of Kate's miraculous torch.

The year 2000 had turned out to be fairly normal and shockingly incomprehensible in roughly equal measure. Coquetdale was still fundamentally unchanged, even though the enclosed fields were a surprise. Sheep were still farmed. People looked the same despite their clothing being odd and, if Kate was anything to go by, the fact that women dressed more like men. Rob's bus was terrifying, but the farmhouse was structurally no different to what he was used to, though inside he'd come across many things that he found hard to believe or understand: candle-less light that came on by touching a patch on a wall; an object that allowed Kate to speak to Linda without her presence; luxurious and comfortable furniture; beautiful music with no musicians in sight... the list was never-ending.

Was Kate a rich woman who just chose to labour alone? Was she unusual for women in this time? Certainly he'd never met her like before. She was obviously well-educated, very confident, hugely capable, a skilled farmer, and her own mistress. Had he not also found her to be friendly (though a little wary) and undeniably attractive, he'd have thought her formidable.

She was obviously happy living alone with just her dogs for company and he could sense she was ambivalent about having him around. He would see how the land lay tomorrow, but another day or two here to find his feet would be useful if Kate would let him stay and help on the farm. Anyway, there was little Joe to think about too. He couldn't let him down. Looking at the Wanted poster had given him the start of an idea: Frayne had said that reading humans became easier once you knew how to read trees. It seemed to him that the process of travelling through the oak tree had intensified his awareness of everything around him. Was it just that it was all so new and different, or was it something more? Time would tell.

He folded up Joe's poster of Eleanor. Sam was not a religious man, but prayer had always been part of his life even if he wasn't sure who or what he was praying to. Tonight, as the rain hammered down outside, he prayed for Eleanor.

'If she is here, in this time, may the trees have led her to as good a soul as Kate. Let her not be alone and frightened. I am here, mother, and if you are too, I promise I will find you.'

CHAPTER TWENTY

FUTURE, PAST, PRESENT

Monday, September 4th, 2000

Time. We travel from the past, to the present, to the future. Ever onward. Ever changing. Another sunrise, another moonrise, another day lost to history, another day yet to give up its secrets.

Lady Eleanor Heron was one of the few people on earth who understood that this linear view of time is flawed. She knew that the present is all we have. The past and the future are just different presents — a present memory and a present hope — and both are equally out of our grasp. It is our experiences in the moment which hold meaning for us and make us who we are. Life is about the now. Whoever we are, we are now. We are the figure standing with arms raised in welcome of the morning drenched with cherry-blossom pink. We are the rain- and wind-lashed soul fighting in a muddy field alongside comrades. We are the moment we see our newborn child, and the day the accident happens. We are the joy of singing or dancing, the laughter of shared silliness, and the anger of injustice. We are the confused, misunderstood teenager with a knife in his hand, and the tired grandmother staring with awe at the star-filled night sky. We are the first time he says, 'I love you', and the last time she says, 'Goodbye'.

Through the miracle of the trees and the future wood given to her by a man at the Covert , Eleanor had first jumped to the future — to May 1st 2000 — as a distraught twenty-year-old on the dreadful day in 1700 when she thought her husband, Richard, had killed their two-year old daughter Martha, her poor little Matty. That 'future' had then become her past when, after 4 months with Nick Robson, she felt compelled to return to her own time. She thanked God she had returned as she discovered that Matty was alive though irrevocably damaged by her husband's abuse. Now, twenty-three years later, she had tree-jumped to the future a second time in the hope of saving her dying son, Sam. This was now her present once again. It was the night she left Nick and now, it was the night she was returning to him.

A few minutes, twenty-three years, or 277 years. It depended on your point of view as to how long it was since she last felt the rain drip through the canopy of Middle Wood on the day of 4th September 2000, but to Eleanor it felt like an eternity. She was not the same Eleanor who previously walked on this woodland floor. She was no longer a young woman escaping a tyrannical husband-cum-apparent-child-murderer by travelling to a future time she knew nothing about. She was now forty-three years old, much wiser, a more skilled healer, and had brought up two children in a forced, loveless marriage she had endured through necessity. She was also a woman who, in the space of one day on 16th November 1723, had discovered that her daughter had been murdered by her estranged brother at Kilcaith Castle; her husband had been killed in an armed skirmish; and that her son had a sustained a serious stab wound that he seemed likely to die from.

Critically, on this second visit to the future Eleanor knew where, when and why she was coming, and who she was looking for.

Using the *future wood* she'd harvested from the oak tree on the night she left Nick Robson — this very evening, as far as he would be concerned — she had come back to Nick for the medicines she hoped might save Sam. But there was a problem.

She found herself oddly disorientated in Middle Wood and didn't know which way to go to get to the cabin. She naturally turned to the trees to find the right path. They would quickly show her the way.

Except they didn't. A tendril of anxiety began to creep, ivy-like, up her body. She couldn't connect to the trees. She couldn't read them. Something wasn't right.

She tried again, this time touching them physically as well as through her mind. No response. The ivy wound its way higher.

Had she broached some tree jumping limit? Had something changed this time? She hadn't been separated from the trees since her mother taught her to read them when she was a little girl. The creeping anxiety thickened.

This shouldn't be.

She tried again, and again, her panic rising with each failed attempt. The ivy fingers climbed higher, searching for her heart.

This couldn't be.

She tried different trees. Surely a curious birch would let her in? No. The ash, tree of guidance and connection, she would not block her out, would she? She would.

No, this ... must ... not ... be.

237

The ivy wrapped itself around her heart and squeezed. Her anguished scream echoed in the living silence of the night, but the life she knew was all around her was not acknowledging her. The wood was no longer a friendly haven with open doors welcoming her into the natural world. This was a coffin. Cold. Black. Unspeaking.

Then a voice did reach her, but it was a very dark voice and one she didn't want to hear, even though she knew that she herself had conjured it. It smothered her like an insidious fog. Despite her best efforts to fight against it and her adamant refusal to listen, the words were forced into her ears, stuffed into her head, crammed into her whole body.

You can not get back to him. You can not get back to him. You can not get back to him. He will die.

'Saaaaam,' she yelled, and started to run.

She ran and ran, unseeing, until two astonishingly bright white lights raced towards her. She stopped and faced them. She knew this was the end and she embraced it. Life no longer had any meaning.

She was just standing there in the middle of the road. It was still raining and the night was thick black, so he didn't see her until his headlights illuminated her frozen figure. He was perilously close to hitting her but managed to screech to a halt a few feet before her. Or at least, he thought he had.

She dropped like a rag doll onto the road, disappearing into the pool of darkness in front of his bonnet. Arms locked straight on the steering wheel and feet pressed desperately onto the brake and clutch, he sat motionless for a few moments, gathering his wits after the shock of what just happened.

He was not a man who enjoyed the countryside. Why on earth his mother had decided to move to the wilds of Northumberland in her dotage, he would never understand. He couldn't wait to get back home to his flat in Newcastle, and he was cross that he'd had to set off so late. And now here he was, in the pitch darkness, surrounded by pine forest which scared him silly even in the daytime and, what's worse, he had to get out of the car. He wasn't even totally certain that he hadn't just imagined the woman. Perhaps she was some ghostly apparition from the ruined castle he'd passed not long since? The area certainly felt spooky enough for that to be possible. I mean, she wasn't there now, not that he could see. Still, he knew he had to get out and check. Keeping the engine running and the headlights on, he got out and peered tentatively around the front of the car.

She was real enough. But she also looked very dead. What the hell was he supposed to do now? He'd watched enough TV programmes to know that you should check someone's pulse, so he tried that. OK so she was alive, and probably just fainted. He couldn't bring her round though, despite the hand-patting and arm-jiggling. The car hadn't hit her, had it? He couldn't see any blood. But what if it was just a small bump and he'd knocked her out? It wasn't his fault. She was just standing there. But would they take his word for that, with his record? Oh God, he could see it all. She'd die and he'd be had up for manslaughter. No, he'd have to leave her. She wasn't his problem. He started to get back into the driver's seat.

But he couldn't. He wasn't really a bad man, and certainly no killer. Maybe she would come round eventually. He decided to take her to the big hospital in Newcastle and just drop her off and leave. They couldn't ask any awkward questions if he scarpered and no-one could link her to him or to where he found her. That way he'd be kept in the clear, but he'd have done the right thing. He congratulated himself for a good plan well thought out. Sorted. He picked her limp body off the floor, manhandled her into the back seat and set off on the forty-minute drive back to the city.

CHAPTER TWENTY-ONE

THE PATIENT

Monday, September 11th, 2000

The nameless patient in Room 7c had been in a coma for a week. She'd been dropped off at Newcastle Royal Infirmary late one night, but the driver hadn't stayed to identify either themselves or the woman. They had nothing to go on to explain either who she was or where she'd come from. The police had ongoing appeals out about her, of course, but no-one had claimed her yet.

As for why she was in a coma, it seemed she'd had a brain seizure, probably from a bang on the head. All they could do now was treat her immediate physical needs and hope and wait for her to wake up.

On the morning of the seventh day, a nurse had just finished checking on the patient, when a programme came on the radio they'd put next to the bed. It was a Radio Four nature programme about how to identify birds from their songs. The leisurely mellow, yet joyous sounds of a blackbird were followed by the flat, soft whistles of the bullfinch, and the rich babbling of swallows. By the time the soothing, rhythmic song of the wood pigeon could be heard, with a background of rustling trees and other birdsong, patient 7c began to stir.

It was the first time that the neurologist, Dr Frances Armstrong, had personally come across a coma patient waking with a confused belief of who they were. Of course, she'd read about such things; people waking up speaking only a foreign language or being able to play a musical instrument they'd never had any skill in previously, or believing they were a teenager when, in fact, they were forty-five years old and a father of two. Such events were well-documented, if rare. While obviously very disturbing for the patient, there was no doubt it made for interesting work. Frances was intrigued.

Patient 7c was initially calm on waking, but soon extremely agitated, not to say terrified, about where she was. She'd tried to tear out the tubes and monitors attached to her and had to be restrained and mildly sedated. This was not too unusual. What was unusual, though, was that later, after having given her name as Eleanor, she was asked if she knew the date. 'November 1723' was the rather unexpected answer. Frances probed a little further without showing her surprise.

'And the monarch on the throne is...?'

'King George,' came the sleepy, yet unhesitating reply.

'OK. And where do you live Eleanor?'

'Moss Hall.'

All the nursing staff knew Moss Hall. It was one of the Newcastle council estates with the worst reputation for various forms of anti-social behaviour and the hospital was no stranger to Moss Hall inhabitants. A link to the troublesome elements in Moss Hall could possibly account for the fact that no-one had registered Eleanor as missing. And yet, the woman was in obvious good health, had no track marks pointing to her being a drug user, and other than the bruise on her head, had no physical injuries consistent with recent abuse. They knew she'd had various bones fractures and breaks in the past — ribs, left arm, and she had a scar on her right hand that looked very much like a knife had gone right through — but these were all old. There were no fresh injuries.

That night, back at home in the rural outskirts of the city, Frances was sharing her day over a glass of red wine and an oven-ready lasagna from Tesco's with her husband, Greg, a history lecturer at Durham University.

'So she thinks she was born in 1680 and that it's now 1723. Which, of course, means that King George I is on the throne. Only she didn't call him George the first, presumably because she doesn't know there's been six of them!'

'Wow, someone's done their homework,' said Greg, laughing. 'I thought you didn't like history.'

'Oh, hah bloody hah. I did know we've had six Georges, as it happens. But I'll admit I didn't know that the date of 1723 tallied with George I. Anyway I checked and she's right. Oh, and she called her husband Richard, and there's someone called Sam, but we haven't worked out who he is yet. God, this lasagna's dreadful.' She pushed her plate away and sat back with her wine.

'Anyway, there is something wrong with Sam and she's worried about him. She kept saying she can't help him and that he's going to die. So ideally we need to work out whether this guy Sam really is in danger somewhere.'

Greg finished his own lasagna and started to polish off hers.

'You know there might be an anomaly there. Moss Hall

243

Estate probably won't have existed in 1723,' he said, facetiously.

'Quite,' said Frances, ignoring the sarcasm. 'We were trying to get to the bottom of it all to give the police as much information as we could, but we were getting a very mixed picture from her. At the same time as confidently saying she was from the early eighteenth century, she mentioned car lights and penicillin. Anyway, we're keeping her mildly sedated currently. I guess we'll see what tomorrow brings.'

'Well, it's all very fascinating,' said Greg. 'Would it help if I checked on whether there was an actual Moss Hall and a Richard in the area around in 1723? It's always possible that the estate was named after a long-lost stately home, and maybe she's interested in history and has just got her wires crossed for the moment.'

'Yeah, no harm in looking I suppose.'

'I'll ask one of my ex-students to have a hunt around. Silas, you know, the mature student I've mentioned before, he's like a dog with a bone with mysteries. It's not exactly his area, but it's right up his street.'

SYCAMORE

I am the traveller, the incomer, settling my roots in these welcoming isles over five hundred years before the second millennium.

In far off lands in ages past, I was revered as a connection between the world of the living and the dead — a symbol of peace for the soul.

But you know me now. In my prime, I am the tall, handsome tree with a lush canopy of five-lobed leaves and a mottled, peeling bark of greens, creams and pinkish-greys. In autumn, my winged seeds are the food of birds and small mammals and the helicopters of laughing children. I give my pollen and nectar freely and copiously, but I am yet to tempt many cautious insects. Honeybees love me, though!

I love woodlands and hedgerows, but I am not precious about where I live. I will take wind-ravaged hillsides and exposed coasts; I can settle in cities, abandoned industrial land, and on salt-sprayed roadsides. Wherever I go I offer protection — against wind, sun and air pollution — and a habitat for invertebrates like ladybirds. I do my bit. I've worked hard to belong and to find a place in your heart. No, I'm not native, but I'm home.

CHAPTER TWENTY-TWO

YAN, TYAN, TETHERA

Tuesday, September 5th, 2000

Kate stood looking out of her kitchen window with a mug of tea in her hands. On the edge of her low-lying in-bye lands, just before the fells took over the tough job of covering the hills with heather and bracken, crowberry and bilberry, she had her very own Sycamore Gap. Its namesake was the much-photographed spot on Hadrian's Wall, famed for its starring role in the film *Robin Hood, Prince of Thieves* which Kate couldn't help loving. Ok, so *her* gap wasn't quite so dramatic as *the* gap, and her stone wall was less epic Roman edifice and more Humpty Dumpty's rickety perch, but she still loved it and at this time in the early morning, on clear days, her tree was always the focus of the first rays of light.

Today, there was an additional element to her familiar view. Her uninvited guest, Sam, was standing there, leaning with his left shoulder on the sycamore, wrapped in his woollen cloak and looking out towards the hills. Being so early, she hadn't expected him to be up yet, so the sight came as a bit of a shock — in more ways than one.

'Dad!'

With a lump in her throat, she pressed a hot hand to the cold glass of the windowpane which quickly misted up obscuring the poignant image that had immediately brought her father back to her. He had frequently taken up that exact same position as he surveyed their farmland and the dale each morning. It had always been as if he'd belonged to the landscape.

As the glass cleared, the short-lived stab of longing melted away. Kate stared out at Sam, half-expecting to feel cheated or angry, but she didn't. Oddly, instead of Sam feeling like an intruder, he seemed to fit. This was *her* Cloudy, *her* little piece of Coquetdale, yet Sam slotted in as if he'd been a missing jigsaw puzzle piece.

This is stupid, she thought. She hardly knew the man and yet had invited him in, strange as he was, and was now becoming used to his presence more quickly than she ought. This is not how it normally went with the men in her life. Not that she had many men in her life, and not that he *was* a man in her life, she told herself quickly, but still, what was it about him?

She decided to let the dogs out and take a flask of tea up to Sam. Maybe he'd had a sleepless cold night? In hindsight, she felt a bit guilty about not giving him a proper bed. He seemed to be a bit of a lost soul and, while he was undoubtedly odd, she couldn't see him as an axe-murderer or anything like that. She already trusted him more than that creep Silas Fenwick who still came and pestered her, unannounced, on occasion. She'd never really worked out whether Silas just fancied her or wanted something from her. She suspected the latter as he'd made so many barely disguised hints about tree reading to find buried treasure. It was all about money to him, not about the trees. God

248

knows why he'd had such a change of heart about the possibility of tree reading being true since Archie's talk at uni nearly three years ago, but anyway, there was no way she was letting on that Archie had taught her this lost skill before he died. It felt like such a precious, almost sacred gift that she'd been given and however judgemental she was being, she believed that to use it simply to make yourself rich was all wrong. So, Silas would have to do without the help of the trees and do his own digging into the past. As far as she was concerned the best place for him was at arm's length.

'So, you've met the Lord of the Marches, our guardian and protector?' said Kate, as she reached Sam and the sycamore.

He turned but didn't really seem to focus on her. His face was solemn, and he had a distant look in his eyes as if he wasn't quite in the moment.

'He is a well-loved tree,' he said softly, adding, 'I'm very sorry about your father.'

'Wh— what? You knew my father?'

At her reaction, Sam quickly snapped out of the rather vague state he'd been in.

'No, no, sorry. I didn't. I— I heard that he was a good man and is greatly missed. Perhaps Rob said something?'

'Hmm, maybe,' said Kate, frowning slightly, but then brushed it off. If Sam really had been brought up in the area, she guessed he could even have come across her father at some point.

'I still miss him, and Mum, terribly at times. But my brother Eddie comes back to the farm when he gets a break at the restaurant. And this old boy is one of the family too,' she said, patting the trunk of the sycamore fondly. 'He's quite a character, you know. And such a good listener — I tell him everything.' She laughed, conscious that her words were closer to the truth than he'd ever imagine. 'And now you think I'm mad!'

'No,' said Sam, not looking at her. 'I don't.'

Kate wondered how he could make three simple words seem so full meaning. It wasn't flippant, he meant it. He was almost too serious.

She poured the tea into the melamine mugs she'd brought and they sat down on Sam's cloak at the foot of Lord March and drank silently for a while, watching the day brighten. The tops of the moors still had a purple hue even though the heather was starting to die back now; the morning sun added warmth and a last touch of vibrancy to the fading blooms. The sound of a skylark came and went on the breeze. Kate couldn't see it but knew that each sweet note would be broadcast once the tiny bird had launched itself vertically into the air.

Then, finishing the dregs of her tea, Kate got up in a suddenly business-like manner.

'Right,' she said, 'Well, this won't get the chores done. So, Sam, are you off to search for your mam now? Or would you perhaps be interested in, say, a week or so's work on the farm with me? Maybe til the Kelso sales a week on Friday? I can give you board and lodging in the house, but I can't pay much on top of that I'm afraid.'

As the unplanned words came tumbling out of her mouth, she was at once surprised and pleased with herself. She tried to sound indifferent as to what his decision would be but she found herself hoping he would stay.

She offered a hand to help pull him to his feet.

'If you can stay, I'm sure Joe would be pleased to see you when he comes next.'

As Sam looked up at Kate's proffered hand, relief swept through him. He'd feared his careless comment about her father could have made her suspicious of him. He needed to be more careful about what he said. The truth was that he felt at ease in Kate's presence and, on top of that, the short time he'd had with the sycamore had given him some insight into both her family and the farm as well as Kate herself. This was a happy place.

He reached up to take Kate's hand. Perhaps it should have felt wrong, but it didn't. Accepting help from this woman from the future somehow felt oddly comfortable.

'Kate,' he said, having quickly learned yesterday that she would accept no formal address from him, 'it would be my privilege to help.'

'Ah, great,' she said, and Sam thought she seemed genuinely pleased. 'Shall we get started?'

Kate's plan for the next few days was to bring her flock down from the fells to the in-bye land near the farmhouse. A couple of weeks ago she'd taken this season's lambs off their mothers and brought them down, and now it was the turn of her breeding ewes. They, too, would need dosing with wormer, vaccinating, their feet would need checking and they'd just get a general health check and tidy up before she let them have a few weeks in-bye to fatten up a bit before tupping by the end of October. Flushing the ewes, it was called, but she never liked that term. She just thought of it as a bit of 'me' time for her girls — a few weeks of good grass and no annoying lambs or needy rams.

'I only have one quad,' said Kate, when they reached the

main barn. 'You take that and I'll ride Melly.'

'Er, I prefer to walk if it's all right with you. I don't, I mean I can't …' he nodded towards the quad bike.

'Oh. Really? You don't drive?' She didn't remember ever meeting a farmer's lad that couldn't drive. Everyone brought up on a farm could usually drive by the age of ten, if not earlier. 'Not even a tractor?'

'No. Sadly not.'

'Right.' Well, that stymied her, but if he was going to help she had to get him up the hills. Walking would take all day. Reluctantly, she asked, 'Do you ride, maybe?'

'Of course.'

'OK, well, let me introduce you to Mellow, then. She's not used to anyone else riding her though, and she's quite feisty, so … are you quite a confident rider?'

'Quite.' He smiled, obviously finding her question amusing, but then seemed to check himself and added, 'You need not be concerned, Kate. I'm a confident rider.'

She took him over to the stable block to introduce him to Melly and he went straight over to the grey mare.

'She's a beauty. And in such fine fettle.' He went into the stable, talking softly to Melly, stroking her gently and keeping his hand on her at all times while he checked her over.

Kate could immediately tell that this was a man who did indeed know horses. She brought the tack over to him. 'I'll leave you two to get to know each other while I get some sandwiches and refuel the quad. See you in the yard. Don't worry, she's used to the bike.'

As they headed off up to the hills, Kate soon discovered that Sam was one of the best and most natural horsemen she'd ever seen. Her beloved Melly rode like a dream with him on her back. She was almost jealous yet found herself getting pleasure from the bond that quickly built between Sam and her horse. A few hours later, between the two of them and her immaculately-trained border collies, they'd found and herded a good number of her flock. Pausing to take stock before they turned for home, Kate turned off the quad engine.

'What do you think we've got, then? I reckon 129.'

'I made it 124. I'll count again.' He started counting under his breath, but Kate could just hear him. 'Yan, tyan, tethera, methera, pimp, sethera, lethera, hovera, dovera, dik, yanadik, tyanadik, tetheradik, metheradik, bumfit—' Kate couldn't help it and burst out laughing. He stopped, wondering what was so funny.

'Sorry, sorry,' she said. 'I've just never heard anyone use that old counting system before and it's just hit my funny bone. My father told me about it, but you really know it! Bumfit?! Really? What number is that?'

'Oh, it's fifteen. The numbers go up to twenty, then you start again. I've never really thought about the words separately before.' He laughed. 'An old shepherd I knew taught me to count sheep that way. I guess it's a bit old-fashioned now?'

'You could say,' said Kate. 'I reckon shepherds must have used that 300 years ago or more.'

'Yes,' agreed Sam, 'At least 300 years.'

'It sounds like gobbledygook, though, doesn't it? Will you teach me? I'd love to give the old farmers at the autumn show a surprise!'

'Gobbledygook! Now who's talking nonsense!' said Sam.

Their shared laughter seemed to set the tone for the next ten days. They worked hard together but there was always time to see the funny side of life or to appreciate the beauty that surrounded them. Kate loved her work but she had to admit that she couldn't remember the last time she'd been so happy. Sam was unlike anyone she'd ever met before. She knew almost nothing about him as he gave very little away, but he seemed to want to know everything about her and her life and, for the first time with a stranger, it seemed easy and right to tell him.

For Sam, taking in so many new things whilst trying not to seem either surprised or stupid was far more tiring than the physical work. It meant that although he and Kate enjoyed each other's company, he was often quiet and he usually retired early to the barn. He wouldn't accept a bed in the farmhouse — it just didn't seem right. Although she was always friendly and happy, he was sure Kate must think him a boring stupid clod of a man. He, on the other hand, was totally entranced by this incredible woman whose life he'd accidentally barged into.

CHAPTER TWENTY-THREE

MESSAGE IN A BOTTLE

Thursday, 14th September, 2000

Being with Kate was a kind of sweet torture.

At first, he'd stayed at Cloudy because he didn't know what else to do or how to go about finding Eleanor, or even how to live life in the future. After ten days, though, he had to admit that he was staying because he couldn't bear the idea of leaving. But he *had* to leave, he knew that. This wasn't his time. He couldn't just stay. Could he? No, of course not. He lived in 1725. What did he know about cars and electricity, wormers and vaccinations, record players and fridges? Okay, he now knew these things existed and could see them for the miraculous inventions they were, but he still didn't *understand* them and would never be able to ask. He was a fish out of water, and though the air was delicious, he couldn't live without considering each intake of breath and each spoken word that might betray him as someone who didn't belong, who had no right to be there.

Every day he was with Kate it became harder to pull back, to keep from touching her hair, her hand, her face … her lips. He knew her intimately, from a distance. At night, in his barn, the separation felt like a gulf, but it was hardest to bear when they worked together and their hands touched.

Tomorrow was the Kelso ram sales. He'd promised to stay and help her until then but wouldn't go with her to Kelso as she'd already arranged help from a local farmer. Joe was visiting on Saturday, so he decided that that would be his last day. He would try to keep his promise to Joe that day — he had a plan — and then leave on Sunday morning. The decision was made.

Knowing what he now knew about the number of people in this world and the speed of travel, he could see no way of finding his mother in this time even if she *was* here. He'd spent the previous Sunday scouring Middle Wood, but other than coming across a very bad-tempered woodsman who said he'd seen no-one and rudely asked him to leave, there was no sign of her. The trees had no clue to offer him, he had nowhere to turn. So he would go back to his own time, his own life. It was the right thing to do.

'Fancy a picnic lunch in the woods?' asked Kate. They'd spent the morning putting the finishing touches to the rams that were going up for sale tomorrow. 'Thanks to you we're all ready for tomorrow, and since this is your last day on the farm …'

They decided on Heron Wood. It was Kate's favourite bit of woodland in the area. They piled the dogs and a quickly cobbled-together picnic into the Land Rover. It was a mellow day which seemed to suit the mood. Summer was coming to an end, but the wood was still protected from the harshness of winter by the intervening glories of autumn — a time for the trees to wash their arboreal laundry and prepare for a rest.

256

'It seems apt, coming to Heron Wood, doesn't it?' said Kate. 'I've never asked before 'cos I know Heron isn't an uncommon name round here, but any connection with your family?'

'None that I know of,' said Sam, smiling inside at the ridiculousness of the situation. He'd planted most of these oaks and beeches himself, on his own land, within the past year. Now look at them. They'd been left alone for 275 years and turned into a beautiful old wood full of life. What a privilege it was to see this. Tom Baker had been right to beg the Covert to plant trees. The potential would never be fully realised in the lifetime of the planter, but what a legacy to leave for the future. He thought this might just be the best thing he would ever do in his life. Heron Wood! He wondered who'd named it.

After walking through the wood with the dogs, they sat on the thick low-hanging branch of a particularly beautiful old oak to eat their picnic. Shafts of sunlight filtered through the canopy of green now tinged with golds and apricots. Sam took out his dirk and started to whittle a knobbly piece of oak he'd found. Kate sat watching her dogs play as she slowly drank her tea.

'You know, I'll miss you,' said Kate, not looking at him. 'It's been … well, it's been great having the help and the company.'

Sam didn't reply. Then after a few minutes, without lifting his eyes from his carving, he asked, 'Have you heard of John Donne? He's the fellow who reckoned that no man is an island.'

She laughed. 'Well, yes, I have heard of him, but what has that—'

'I think he was right, we *are* all connected, and I believe it's the same for trees and wildlife, and yet …'

He looked over to Kate, weighing up whether or not he should continue. He desperately wanted to say something to her before he left, but it was so difficult. He wanted to say it, to tell her, but he couldn't. He couldn't let himself.

'Sometimes,' he continued, 'I think the truth is that we're more like tiny islands adrift in a very large sea.'

'Hmm,' said Kate, then they sat quietly for a while longer, lost in their own thoughts, Sam whittling away and Kate watching her dogs.

'I have a thought for you,' said Sam. 'To stop the islands drifting, I mean.' Oh god, how ridiculous this sounded, but he'd started now. 'I think it's up to each of us to connect our personal islands. We build bridges, we throw ropes, or even just shout VERY LOUDLY'. He bellowed the last two words up into the trees, then turned back to her, smiling, his chestnut eyes glinting in the sun. 'Anything to make the connection, you see? It just relies on someone grabbing the other end of the rope or answering your call. And once you start, well, then you realise how many other islands you can reach by taking that first step.'

'A network of islands,' said Kate. 'Yes, just like the internet everyone is starting to use more and more now.'

'The inter...? Er, yes,' he muttered, not having a clue what she was talking about. Again.

Seeming to randomly change the subject, he asked, 'Did you know that Queen Elizabeth had an official position of Uncorker of Ocean Bottles? You could face the death penalty if you opened one without his permission. But luckily that was then, so you should be safe with this.'

He opened his hand and held out the results of his whittling to her.

About five centimetres tall, it was a rough but perfect little replica of a bottle, complete with a lip around the top, a dimpled bottom, and a label where he'd carved *K*.

'A message in a bottle. From my island to yours.'

CHAPTER TWENTY-FOUR

PAPER KISSES

Saturday, September 16th, 2000

Kate got back late on Friday from the ram sales. It had been a success and she was happy but exhausted. Sam was still up reading a book in the kitchen. He rarely stayed up late, so despite him saying that he'd lost track of time because it was a good story, she had a hunch that he was waiting up for her. No-one had done that for her since her mam died.

On Saturday morning, an excited Joe was dropped off at Cloudy by Linda, along with an unexpected overnight bag. He'd not been able to come last weekend as he had a cold. Sam took him off to the barn to see the puppies.

'Sorry Kate, but can you have him for the night? Please?' pleaded Linda. With a nod in the direction of the barn, she added, 'He's done our heads in all this week saying that Sam is going to find his mam. He shouldn't have done that, Kate. It's not fair on the lad.'

'Oh God, I'm sorry Linda. I really don't think he meant any harm, but yes, of course. I'm sure you need a break and I'll do what I can to help Sam make it right.' As she was saying that, though, she knew she really didn't have a clue how she'd do that. 'I'll bring him home after Sunday lunch. OK?'

When she got a chance to speak privately to Sam later in the day, she broached the subject of Linda's displeasure about his promise to Joe and the problems it had caused. He took it seriously but seemed quite unperturbed about it, explaining that he had a plan, one that wasn't foolproof, but that he would try very hard to make work. He wouldn't tell her any more other than that they needed to keep Joe up quite late tonight as he needed the boy to be sleepy.

In the middle of the large kitchen table, creaky-squeaky purring emanated from a large tray of recently harvested onions; Hodgson had found his bed for the night.

The lateness of the hour, a milky hot chocolate, and the comforting warmth of the Aga in the kitchen dimly lit with candles, were together inducing sleepiness in Joe's small body. He sat on Sam's knee, facing one of the long sides of the table. In front of them, a large piece of plain paper was challenging them with its blankness.

'Right, Joe, I'm going to hold the pencil and you put your hand on top of mine.'

Joe's skinny fingers held on to the back of Sam's large hand.

'Now we'll both shut our eyes and keep still, and I want you to think about your mam.'

'But I told you, I don't remember her,' whined Joe.

'I know, but trust me. Just start telling me anything you remember from when you were at home with her,' Sam said, in a calm, encouraging tone.

Intrigued, Kate looked on from the chair at the end of the

261

table, a glass of red wine in hand. She listened as, after a sigh suggesting this-will-be-pointless-don't-say-I-didn't-tell-you, Joe started talking.

He told Sam of their small flat up lots of flights of steps and their tiny bedroom with the one bed they shared. There was a bread bin he could reach if he stood on a chair and sometimes it even had bread in it. He still liked dry bread; it was comforting. He remembered Uncle Micky coming round with medicine for his mam, and her being poorly and sleeping a lot on the sofa. He remembered playing quietly by himself near her, just in case she woke up and needed him. His voice was flat whilst relating all this, but then, suddenly, he brightened as something came to him.

'Ooh, the musical dancer box. I remember that,' he said. 'I loved the dancer, she was like an angel. And Mam liked her too. We liked watching the ballet dancer going round and round to the music.'

Joe was quiet for a moment but he twitched, his pale fingers moving slightly on top of Sam's hand.

'She had a soft face when she looked at the dancer,' he continued, with a dreamy quality to his voice, and Kate could see his eyelids getting heavier. 'Her hair was long and silky.' He stopped in his reverie.

'She sounds very pretty, your mam,' said Sam, almost in a whisper. He kept completely still. 'Just keep thinking about her now. You don't have to say anything if you don't want to, just keep her face in your mind.'

With closed eyes and slow, regular breathing, Sam's hand now started guiding the pencil over the paper. Joe's hand stayed firmly clasped to Sam's. The movements were hesitant at first

262

— a short horizontal line here, a gentle curve there — but they quickly became more fluent and confident. Before long, the two hands were dancing in tandem across the page, almost joyously, as if freed from the control of their owners and wanting to make their mark before their independence was noticed and curtailed.

Kate knew it couldn't be happening, but it was as if Sam was seeing Joe's memories and translating them into lines and shapes. She could hear Joe occasionally making little sounds to himself, but he was mostly silent now and his eyes were closed, though he wasn't asleep. Sam kept up a constant scribbling and shading with the pencil, at times answering some of Joe's murmurs with small, meaningless sounds of his own.

Kate felt like a voyeur watching a very private scene and she didn't dare move a muscle in case they noticed her and she broke the spell they seemed to be under. In the diffuse light of the cosy kitchen, it was as if the two people in front of her had become one. There was something very intense, yet totally tranquil about the moment. She was entranced and deeply moved, seeing the impossible happen in front of her eyes. Unbidden and unstopped, silent tears rolled down her cheeks as she watched the pencil caress the emerging face of a young woman.

After a few minutes, Sam stopped drawing, put down the pencil and gently released Joe's grip from his hand. He smiled briefly at Kate.

Joe roused from his meditative state, opened his eyes and, after looking around the room and over at Kate, turned to the sketch on the table. For a couple of long minutes, he said nothing. He just looked. There was no frown, no smile. Kate and Sam waited with bated breath.

Eventually Joe took in a big, staggered breath, then let it

263

out, slowly.

'You found her,' he said, softly and seriously, with a slight wobble in his voice. 'You really found her for me.' His eyes never left the drawing. 'It's ... it's my mam'. He reached out and tenderly stroked the cold paper cheek that was once alive to his warm, childish kisses.

'I thought I lost her.'

'She was with you all the time, Joe,' said Sam. 'She never left you. Nobody can take her memory from you.'

Kate returned to the kitchen having taken Joe up to bed, the drawing of his mother firmly clenched in his little fists. Sam was still in the same chair. She sat down at the end of the table again.

'That was … what *was* that?'

Sam looked up. Oh, how desperately he wanted to explain everything to her; to tell her that this was the first time he'd done that, to tell her of the hurt he'd felt in Joe's mind, to tell her that life was so much more than she knew, to tell her … to tell her that he loved her.

Instead, he kept to the plan he'd made. He had to.

'It was nothing,' he said, coolly. 'I just had to make it seem magical to him so that he could believe the drawing really was his mother. It was a risk, I know. I was banking on him not remembering her in detail. I just made her look pretty, I hope, with long silky hair.'

Kate released a long breath, then laughed.

'Oh crikey, never mind Joe, you had *me* all the way! That was amazing. You are a dark horse, Mr Heron, and you never fail to surprise me.'

She picked up the wine bottle, poured him a glass, and went

264

to sit on the chair next to him. And then she did something he'd been praying for ever since he met her: she leaned across and kissed him softly on the lips. A tingle shivered through his body. He stood up slowly, bringing her up with him and cradling her closer, his mouth never leaving hers, and the length of their bodies touching.

The lateness of the hour, the glasses of red wine, the last few days of constant proximity, the loneliness, the shared interests, and the comforting warmth of the Aga in the kitchen dimly lit with candles ...

Sam breathed her in, literally; he gently took her breath away. Then he gave it back and shared his with her. In. Out. Out. In. Sam. Kate. Kate, Sam. Never before had he felt so close to anyone. He was intoxicated by her. It was like being part of her, similar to being part of the trees when he read them, except he wasn't reading Kate, he was breathing her.

They pulled away from each other, breathless, smiling and happy.

'You know, you don't *have* to go back to the barn tonight,' said Kate, touching his cheek.

It was like she'd flicked some kind of switch on him. He suddenly pulled back, looking almost scared of her.

'I— no, I—' His eyes were still entrapped by hers, but he forced himself to look away and started moving towards the door.

'I'm really sorry, I can't. I ...' He opened the door, looking bereft. 'I'm sorry, Kate.' He looked away and went out into the black of night.

CHAPTER TWENTY-FIVE

LOST AND FOUND

Saturday, September 16th, 2000

It seemed that the mystery woman in Newcastle Royal Infirmary was going to remain a mystery for a little longer. Silas was happy to help his old lecturer (you never knew when the contact could be useful for business), but he'd had no luck in finding anything that could help with the woman's identification.

Moss Hall Estate in Newcastle had, in fact, been preceded by a big house of the same name, but that was built in the 1830s and demolished in the 1950s. No house, no Richard, no Eleanor. Oddly, in the course of researching Moss Hall, he had come across an old house near Rothbury of that name. It belonged to the Heron family for many generations but was abandoned in the mid-1700s and scavenged for stone for local houses. The family just seemed to have disappeared and the precise site of the old house was now unknown. Silas knew the Heron name to be one of the graynes of the region, as the surnames of Border Reivers had once been known. No point going down that avenue though, as it obviously had no bearing on this unknown woman.

The Newcastle police had decided to allow the local paper

to run an article about the mystery woman in the Saturday edition this weekend. They had nothing to lose. The lady was recovering surprisingly quickly, but she'd stopped talking to anyone and just sat staring out of the window. Someone must know her though. The hospital needed her bed.

'When you said you were in the sticks, you really meant it, didn't you?' said the man, as he got out of his new Mercedes estate which now looked like it had just finished a rally. He anxiously inspected the paintwork through the grime.

Nick Robson laughed. 'Well, I did warn you. I seem to remember you wanting a bit of a trip out to the country to get away from Newcastle. I expect it'll wash,' he said, nodding at the filthy car that had just negotiated the mud tracks up to his cabin.

The man had come to collect one of Nick's bespoke oak side tables as a present for his wife. Nick went to fetch it.

'Oh, she'll love it,' he said, suitably delighted with the piece when he saw it. He opened the car boot, where he'd laid a newspaper on the pristine carpeting. Nick smiled, wondering why he thought a finely made table meant for a sitting room would make his car boot grubby.

He was lifting the table in when something caught his eye and stopped him in his tracks. Eleanor's face was staring up at him from the pages of the newspaper. He nearly dropped the table but managed to set it down before extracting the newspaper page.

'How old is this paper?' he asked, his heart in his mouth.

'I just picked it up this morning,' he replied, looking at the picture Nick was staring at. 'Someone you know?'

'Er, maybe,' he replied, distracted by reading the short

267

article. *Woman probably suffering from amnesia... thought to be in her late thirties... recent head trauma... anyone knowing the identity of the woman please contact Newcastle police...*

Nick couldn't get away quick enough. It was a bad photo of Eleanor in the article — it made her look older than she was — however, there was no doubt that that was Eleanor. It was nearly two weeks since she had disappeared. He thought he'd lost her, he thought she'd left him after their four blissfully happy months together. He'd been so shell-shocked by her loss that he'd struggled to function properly recently.

He saw his customer away, then grabbed his keys and a blanket and pillow and set off to Newcastle Infirmary. She had to be there. Eleanor. Oh my god, what happened? Why did he never think to check hospitals just in case? He'd been so selfishly wallowing in his own misery at being left that he'd never even thought she might have been hurt. Idiot. But why Newcastle? Thoughts and questions flew around his head, but then one answer made him go cold. Maybe she'd gone back to her husband and maybe, well, he was almost certain that she'd been raped before, so he didn't put it past the bastard to batter her if she'd gone back to him after such a long time away. He'd heard that some women feel weirdly attached to their abusers, but he just never thought that his Eleanor ...

For three days after she turned up out of the blue back on 1st May, Eleanor had said very little and slept a great deal. Nick brought her food but she ate almost nothing. Perhaps his cooking was worse than he thought? He tried to make conversation but, though she listened, she rarely made any comments, and gave mostly monosyllabic answers to his questions. True to his word, however, he expected nothing from her and just gave her space to recover.

On the fourth day, he had some work in a nearby village. He was loathe to leave her but he had to go. Half-expecting that she might take the opportunity to leave quietly whilst he was gone, he said goodbye.

'See you later this afternoon?' She just smiled and he resigned himself to returning to an empty cabin. Shame. Even though she said next to nothing, he'd quite liked her company.

It was almost seven o'clock when he got back home after the job and he was very surprised to find that not only was there a campfire burning, but there was a pan of nettle and wild garlic soup ready for him, along with freshly baked flatbreads. A jug of bluebells adorned his work bench that was nearest the fire and there was an old kilner jar stuffed with what, on closer inspection, turned out to be young birch leaves steeped in oil.

'The birch oil will be ready in a few weeks. It'll help with your aches and pains,' she said, by way of explanation. 'If you have some beeswax I could make you a comfrey salve tomorrow if you like.'

They never discussed her staying on, but the days rolled by amicably and, with each new dawn, Eleanor's injuries improved, she seemed happier and talked more. She even began to smile. She had a beautiful smile.

She said very little about her life other than that she was married and that she had just lost her young child. From little things that she did and said from early on, Nick reckoned that her husband was a physical and emotional bully. She showed no wish to return to him. He was also almost certain that they lived in some weird, remote cult or something, probably up in the

269

remote Cheviots, and certainly somewhere with no facilities and very little contact with the modern world. He'd heard about such places but had found it hard to believe that they really shunned modern amenities to the extent they seemed to if Eleanor was anything to go by. She had no clue about some of the simplest things and was almost childlike in her amazement about many things he showed her, even electric lights. She loved the radio — but only Radio 4 as very little music was to her taste; she thought zips were laugh-out-loud funny; tinned foods were a revelation to her, and oh my goodness how she loved chocolate. Her pleasure in all these things and more that she'd obviously never known was joyous to watch.

She devoured books of any genre. Being an avid reader himself, Nick had collected a decent library over the years, from books about trees, mechanics and first aid, to novels and travelogues. Books became a source of shared interest and discussion, and he found her to be an intelligent and wise soul, despite her youthfulness. But that wasn't all. What she didn't know about trees, plants and wildlife wasn't worth knowing. It was as if she was part of the forest.

Of course, he knew Eleanor belonged somewhere else and with someone else, but when, after a couple of weeks, she showed no sign of wanting to leave him, he began to realise that he was praying she wouldn't go. Every time he had to leave the wood he was overjoyed when she was still there on his return.

And then there was the night, towards the end of May, that they no longer went their separate ways as evening turned to night.

Being thirty-six, Nick knew people would think she was too young for him — she said she was twenty — so partly because of that, and partly due to her strange naivety about modern life, they kept themselves to themselves in his woodland hideaway, sharing work and play. He didn't even tell his cousin, Kate. The summer blossomed, the wood was bursting with life and, well, Nick hadn't meant to fall in love with her, he simply had no choice. By mid-summer, he simply could not imagine life without her.

He thought she was happy too, but if he was honest with himself, he'd had a feeling around the end of August that she was starting to pull away from him. Then, when he and Meg had found her wandering in the wood late in the evening of 3rd September, his gut was telling him that she was trying to leave. He wished he'd been brave enough to face her with his fears, but the next day they'd had such a perfect day together, gathering early conkers, making blackberry pie, and laughing — there was always lots of laughter with her. He just hoped he'd been wrong. The following day, however, he'd awoken feeling groggy about five o'clock, and she was gone. There was no point looking. He knew.

Kicking himself that he had just accepted her disappearance and not searched for her, Nick knew that he now needed to get to Eleanor before her husband Richard did. He prayed he wasn't too late. The newspaper had said head trauma. Was it an accident or had the bastard beaten her up again? Obviously it must be severe if she had amnesia.

Of course, he should have known it wouldn't be as simple as walking into the hospital and walking out with her. Even though he knew her name, there were a lot of questions and suspicious looks before the hospital and the police eventually accepted his assertions that she lived with him and would be pleased to see him. He'd crossed his fingers at the latter.

He looked through the half-glass door into her room. She had her back to him and was staring out of the window. She didn't turn when he opened the door.

'Eleanor.'

Her head moved, but still she didn't turn.

'Eleanor, it's me. Nick.'

This time she turned, slowly, as if unsure that the words she'd heard were real.

It was definitely Eleanor, but she'd changed. The photo in the newspaper hadn't lied. She looked, well, older. Much older. About his own age, actually. The newspaper had guessed her age at late thirties and he could see why. He hesitated on the threshold and looked again. Could he have made a mistake? Might this be Eleanor's mother perhaps? And yet she was *so* like Eleanor; a very handsome woman and with the same eyes. He stared without moving closer. The eyes; those were Eleanor's eyes. He closed the door behind him. Could a head trauma have such an effect? Could it dramatically age a person? What other answer was there? He smiled at her but didn't move forward to her just yet. If it was her, she would know him, wouldn't she?

She stared at him. Then tears started pouring silently down her face. She smiled.

'Hello, Nick.'

He rushed over to her and wrapped his arms around her. He didn't understand what was going on, but explanations would have to wait. It *was* Eleanor. He knew it. She was no longer lost. He'd found her and he wouldn't be letting her go.

CHAPTER TWENTY-SIX

ROCK ART

Sunday, September 17th, 2000

Eleanor was physically on the mend, but the hospital was still concerned about her mental health. However, she was adamant that she wanted to leave with Nick, so they had discharged her into his care.

She'd said very little yesterday, both in the car journey from hospital back to Middle Wood and that evening. Nick had made a point of saying that she didn't have to talk if she didn't want to. He just wanted to get her home and look after her. The last two weeks had felt like years of separation. It had been almost unbearable to him, and the helplessness he felt in not knowing how or where to find her had left him hardly able to function. He'd known grief when Archie died, but this was somehow different, more debilitating. He'd started daring to hope for a future with this special woman. The hope had walked out of his life.

There were so many unanswered questions for Nick, but he didn't dare ask anything just yet as Dr Armstrong had explained to him that her brain had taken a battering and her grasp on reality had been shaken. She would need time to recover fully.

No-one had been able to answer his question about her having visibly aged, coming up with vague answers reminding him of the stress her body had been under. It was confusing and extremely odd, but would it stop him loving her? Not a chance. He even found an extra beauty in her more mature features, which seemed to more suitably reflect her wise nature.

After a quiet breakfast on Sunday morning, Eleanor persuaded Nick to go for a walk with her, despite his reservations about her being well enough.

They walked side by side. Occasionally, their hands briefly touched and they each drew quickly away, intensely conscious of the connection which neither knew how to deal with just then.

Nick could see that she was finding the walk tiring. Normally she'd happily walk for hours with him through the heather-clad hills. He offered to take her back home, but she wanted to continue.

'It seems so long since I felt the wind on my face.'

The wind was obliging, though thankfully it was now a considerate, if brisk, breeze, rather than the non-stop, get-out-of-my-way-or-be-sorry freight train of a wind that the day had begun with.

She looked up towards the craggy tops of the Harbottle Hills where a prominent flat rock jutted out over the dale below. Nick followed her gaze.

'Well, see how you're feeling,' he said, 'but if you think you can go further I can show you something I found last week just up there.'

He pointed more-or-less in the direction her sight was already fixed upon.

She smiled very briefly, then turned to look at him. Despite the obvious changes to her face, her eyes were no different. He had no guard against her piercing gaze; he always felt that her eyes saw straight through to his soul.

'I'd like to see what you've found,' she said. 'I'll make it up there, perhaps just not at my usual pace.'

They continued walking slowly up to the flat rock, taking a break whenever Eleanor needed one. At one point, she stumbled as her foot sank into a bog and Nick caught her arm to stop her falling. They were a bit more relaxed with each other after that, and so for the last steep section to the top, Nick was able to help pull her up to their goal.

The large, flat, weathered rock they'd reached offered a stunning 360-degree view, half onto fells behind them and half onto the dale down below. The long ridge of crags they were on dropped quite sharply down to the valley. Here, the River Coquet snaked along in a distinctly un-Roman manner. It had all the time in the world and was determined to enjoy the journey. The narrow floodplain framing its twisty brown waters was a lush green in comparison to the faded purples and russets of the fells the couple were looking down from. Grey dry-stone walls marshalled and dissected the acquiescent lands of the green valley bottom. The walls mostly only went so high as the start of the fells, apart from the odd over-zealous one that seemed determined to restrain even the messy exuberance of the hilltops.

'I've always loved this spot,' said Eleanor, as she stood drinking in the sweet air and the intoxicating beauty all around them. 'It's an age since I've been here.'

'You never mentioned coming up here,' Nick said, as he sat down.

'I— I don't think I did when I was, er, staying with you,' she replied. 'It was somewhere I visited ... another time. But I knew you came.'

Nick watched her, thinking she looked rather like a figurehead at the prow of a ship with the breeze blowing her long, loose hair around her head but with her focus resolutely forward-facing.

'So, tell me, then,' she said, as she sat down next to Nick and began to deftly plait her errant locks. 'What did you find up here?'

'Ay, right. Well, I've been up here many times over the years, but the day you disappeared, I walked up here to try to—' He stopped. 'Oh, I don't know really, but it's a good place for helping you put things into perspective.'

Was it perspective he'd been looking for up here that day, the day she left him? No. He'd been looking for a place to vent his anger; to scream and shout his pain away, and to watch it carried off by the oblivious winds.

No-one had got so close to him before. Before Eleanor he'd given up on the thought of finding someone to share his life with and had come to terms with living alone. Given his chosen lifestyle, that was obviously meant to be his lot and he'd accepted it.

And then she came, unbidden, and she fitted. She was strong-willed; she wasn't needy, well, not after getting over the immediacy of her ordeal; and she was as much a part of the wood as he was, if not more so. It was just so right. Yes, she was odd, but she was his kind of odd.

That morning, numb with the realisation of his loss, he'd started walking, heading through Middle Wood with Meg at his heels. The contentment that normally wrapped itself around him like a blanket here couldn't touch him. He needed height and air, he needed space to cope with the unexpected enormity of this feeling of rejection.

When he first reached top flat rocks, he just stood and looked down onto his valley, hoping to feel better. But it wasn't high enough or far enough away to escape the cloud of sadness that had settled on him. He yelled his frustration onto the lands below and viciously kicked at stones and rocks nearby. Meg looked on, bemused and concerned. The anger quite quickly blew away, though, and Nick sat down on the rock feeling empty.

It was then that he noticed what looked like marks in the rock where he'd displaced some loose stone. This area of Northumberland was known for its neolithic rock art but he'd not noticed any up here before. Glad of a distraction, he cleared away the loose rock to see whether it was just natural striations that had caught his attention, or something more. It was definitely something more, but it certainly wasn't Neolithic.

Carved neatly into the rock was a message from the past. It had been eroded over time but was still clear enough to make out.

N
The love we will share,
was forever in my heart.
F

'You don't know how much I wanted that F to be an E that day,' said Nick, as he cleared away the debris to show Eleanor the message of love he'd found in the stone.

'Even though it was obviously carved a long time ago, and the person writing it had an even worse grasp of English than me, the fact that it was written to N ... well, I'll admit to a few tears when I saw it. Strangely, I didn't feel quite so alone. Stupid, I know.' He brushed off remaining bits of mud and moss and studied the carving again. They were both silent for a few minutes before Eleanor spoke.

'It is an E,' she said, with a quiet, matter of fact tone, as she stood behind him.

'No, definitely an F. Believe me, I looked hard!' said Nick, with a short laugh. 'Look, there's no trace of a horizontal line at the bottom.'

Eleanor walked over to the edge of the crag again, and stared out across the dale, breathing slowly and deeply. Then she turned back to Nick.

'Nick, it's an E. I know it's an E because,' she paused, and drew in another deep breath before continuing, 'because I carved it. For you.'

Nick frowned briefly, then laughed. 'Oh, good one. Nice bit of distressing and antiquating. Circa 1800 I would say at a guess. Is that about right?'

'Spring of 1704,' said Eleanor, looking at him with a face so earnest that he was really thrown for a moment.

He quickly recovered though and got to his feet and went over to her. Putting his arm around her shoulders, he explained that the doctors had said that the odd flashback to her previous confusion was possible. It was probably the exertion that had troubled her. They would get back home and she would soon be fine again.

'No!'

She shrugged away from his well-meaning embrace. Her vehement response was accompanied by tears beginning to trickle down her face, but she wiped them away impatiently before facing him.

'Nick, I need to tell you the truth. I always wanted to, but— I didn't dare, before. I feared, I still fear, that you will think me mad. But I'm not deluded, and I'm not ill. I'm of sound mind, it's just that... it's just ...I just don't belong here. At least, not now.'

Nick hadn't a clue what she was talking about but agreed to sit and to listen. Eleanor began.

How do you react when someone tells you, in all seriousness, that they were born over 300 years ago in 1680? What are you supposed to say when they explain that it's possible to time travel through trees, and mean it? What's the proper response when the reason you're given for someone seeming older than they did twelve days ago is that they have been living in the early eighteenth century — for twenty-three years?

Despite what seemed to him to be an outlandish account of fairytale and foolishness brought on by a brain injury, Nick sat, didn't interrupt, and just listened to her. He knew she was looking for him to believe her, but he was sure that all she was reading on his face was perplexity, disbelief and concern. He couldn't help it.

'You think I'm a witch and a mad woman, don't you?' she said. 'But look at me, I'm different, I'm older. You can see that, I know you can.'

She was sitting upright, staring straight ahead. She was calm and seemingly unemotional now. The only thing that betrayed her inner turmoil was her right hand. Her middle finger rubbed incessantly against her thumb.

Nick knew that this small movement meant she was hurting. He'd seen her do this many times during the first few weeks she was with him. He reached over and gently held her hand.

'It'll be all right, Ellie.' He spoke softly. 'I don't think you're mad. You've just been through a trauma. It's affected your mind and your body. Perhaps it was too soon to bring you out of hospital. As for being a witch, well,' he turned her hand over and opened her fingers, 'anyone with half the skills you hold in the palms of your hands must surely have a bit of witch in them?' He smiled at her. 'I have never seen your equal for understanding the natural world. If you are a witch, so be it. You are a beautiful witch.'

She didn't respond and seemed lost in her thoughts. Nick decided to risk asking the question he'd been longing and fearing to know the answer to for twelve long days. He didn't want to pressurise her, but he needed to know.

'Did you go back? To him? To your husband?'

She nodded. He squeezed her hand involuntarily at this, then let go.

'Why?'

She turned to him.

'I didn't dare risk staying away any longer. This was not my time. I had to get back before it was obvious. It could have been his.'

'What wasn't your time? Before what was obvious?'

Thoroughly confused, he was totally unprepared for her answer.

'I was with child, Nick. It could have been Richard's. I was not your wife — you wouldn't have wanted a baby, possibly of another man. I had to go back.'

He made a brief sound of pain and covered his face with his hands. After a couple of minutes, he asked, 'And is it? Is it Richard's child? Do you know?'

'When he was born on 1st May, I knew he couldn't be Richard's,' she said, looking down at the ground.

Nick paled. He wasn't hearing the details, just the revelation that he might have a child.

'I'm going to be a father?' he said, half under his breath. He sounded bemused.

Suddenly, he got up and began pacing around the rock, his hands ruffling his hair. Then he stopped and turned to Eleanor.

'I'm to have a son?'

'Well, yes, you have, or rather you *had* a son. He became a fine man. A man to be proud of.'

She then tried to explain again that he was born in May 1701, so obviously he was well and truly — Well, it was a very long time ago.

'Oh no,' he said, shaking his head vehemently. 'No, Ellie, please don't do this to me. You're ill. We need to get you home, maybe back to hospital. I shouldn't have taken you out. Your mind hasn't had time to mend properly. We have to look after you. The last two weeks, they've, well, they've taken their toll on your mind and body. Oh my God, Ellie, we're going to have a baby.' He went over to her and picked her up and hugged her, momentarily forgetting the last couple of weeks. He was ecstatic.

She was devastated. This wasn't working out as she'd hoped. And now she was hurting him even more. It had to stop.

'Nick, listen to me.' He quickly put her down. 'I think the doctors told you everything about my health. Did they tell you I am with child?'

Nick had to admit that they hadn't.

'So, you're not pregnant?' he asked, seeming almost numb with confusion.

'No,' she replied, as gently as she could.

'I don't understand. Ellie, I just don't understand what's going on,' he said, the pain obvious in his voice.

'I know,' she said, sadly. 'Maybe we should go back to the cabin.'

If she couldn't get Nick to believe her, she knew she couldn't stay. They'd walked up to the hills with hearts full of hope. They both returned with a debilitating weight of sadness.

CHAPTER TWENTY-SEVEN

REVELATION

Sunday, September 17th, 2000

On the Sunday morning, Sam woke with a heavy heart. After spurning Kate last night, he knew he couldn't even say goodbye to her. She wouldn't want to see him.

It was shortly after sunrise and, knowing how early Kate (and Joe) awoke, he'd already dressed in the modern clothes he'd been given. He'd bundled up his own clothes along with the embroidery, his money and the wooden counter he always kept with him, and he was ready to set off. His short dirk was in his boot, as always.

He said goodbye to the dogs and opened the barn door onto a day that matched his mood — desolate. A steady Northumbrian drizzle was knocked sideways by a blustering northern wind. He pulled his cloak tighter around him and stepped out.

He'd gone no further than a few steps when he heard a high-pitched voice call his name. It was Joe. He was running quickly towards Sam, still dressed in his red and blue pyjamas and Spiderman slippers. He ran straight into Sam's legs, grabbed his hand and started pulling him towards the house.

'Sam, Sam. You have to come quickly. There's a man shouting at Kate. He's frightening her. Please come, please. Quickly.' He was shivering in the cold wet wind, so Sam wrapped him in his cloak.

'Who is the man, Joe? Do you know him?'

'No, I've not seen him. But please, you have to hurry. They're in the kitchen. I climbed out of the living room window. Come *on* Sam,' he appealed, trying to pull Sam towards the house.

'No Joe, you stay here. Get into the barn and look after the dogs for me, will you? I promise I will go and help Kate. It's probably nothing and they will have made friends again by now. Don't worry but stay here until I come back for you.'

Sam ran up to the big house but standing outside the kitchen door, dirk in hand, he heard no raised voices. Joe must have been mistaken but he really had to check she was safe now before he left. He put his knife back in his boot. It looked like he would have to say goodbye to her after all. He opened the kitchen door.

The sight he was met with threw him for a moment. Kate was backed into the corner between the Aga and the kitchen sink. She had a poker in her hand and was obviously frightened. A tall man with long black hair was calmly perched on the edge of the kitchen table between her and the door. Not only was the scenario odd in itself, but the other thing that really made Sam look twice was the man himself. Apart from the lack of a scarred face, he was the very spit of Herbert Wells that he'd come up against just two weeks (or over two centuries) ago in Horseshoe Priory.

It took Sam a moment to tell himself that this couldn't be

the man, he would be long dead. He must be a current relative with a striking resemblance. But then he remembered Frayne's suspicions that Mr Wells might be a tree jumper.

In the short time that this was going through Sam's head, Kate called Sam's name and made a bolt towards him. She didn't make it.

Kate was strong, but she was no match for the man's surprising speed and strength. He grabbed her with his left hand, knocking the poker out of her hand which went skidding across the floor, and pulled her back to the Aga. He then produced a hidden knife which he held unwaveringly at her throat.

'Er no, I don't think so,' he said to her, sharply, 'I'm not finished yet.'

Sam had immediately reached down for his dirk but couldn't risk a move on the man with Kate in such a precarious position. Memories of Martha at Kilcaith Castle flooded back to him. This was not going to happen again. This man would have to give her up or die.

The intruder looked directly at Sam but spoke to Kate.

'So, who is your knight-in-shining-armour then, Kate? How very chivalrous — so in keeping with our shared historical interests, don't you think? But is he a *true* friend, I wonder?'

Lonely.

The emphasis on the word *True* cut through the fog of uncertainty and immediately confirmed to Sam that this man had a connection with the True, though, as with Frayne's feeling about Herbert Wells, he knew there was something not quite right here. He was no friendly associate of the ancient altruistic membership.

At the same time, the link the man has just intimated between Kate and the True … that was unexpected.

'He's nothing to do with this, for God's sake. He works on the farm,' Kate was saying.

'Ah, but sadly he now *is* something to do with this, isn't he? And he seems to be a prepared sort by the looks of that knife. That's not exactly standard farm issue, I'm guessing. That's a very fine old bog oak handled dagger. What's your name, farm boy?'

Arrogant.

Tight-lipped, but in complete and calm control, Sam offered a polite formal introduction.

'My name, sir, is Samuel Heron of Moss Hall. And may I know which scum of the earth I might be addressing, and what problem you have with my friend Kate?'

The man laughed. 'Oh, I love it. That's really not what I was expecting from a farm hand. How delightfully formal,' and then he added, with a frown, 'and rude of you. Now, put down your handsome knife. Please.' The man pressed the knife more firmly into Kate's neck. Sam did as he was asked.

Vindictive.

'Since we are being so formal, *my* name, *sir*,' he said with a small, ironic bow of the head, 'is Silas Fenwick. I'm not a violent man, Mr Heron. However, I do like to get my own way. My mother tells me it has always been a failure of mine. She's wrong, of course. Failure is not something I do very well.'

Relentless.

Kate wriggled under his restraint but succeeded only in having her neck nicked by the knife. She stopped struggling. Sam paled inwardly when he saw a bead of bright red blood

286

bloom and begin to trickle down her slender neck.

'Please, Kate, do try to calm yourself whilst Mr Heron and I have a sensible chat. I'm sorry to say that I've had no joy from you, so perhaps your friend here can help me, before I lose my temper and do something we will both regret.

Unpitying.

'As I was about to say, your friend Kate here has some information I need, that's all. However, she is rather unwilling to share. Seems a bit mean, doesn't it? So, perhaps you can help me instead? There's recently been a big discovery of old treasure near Alnwick and I feel slightly aggrieved that it was not me that found it. I think I would have if she'd been more forthcoming.'

'Silas, I told you, he knows nothing of —' began Kate, but Sam interrupted.

'What would you like to know, Mr Fenwick?'

Now that Sam was almost certain Kate knew about the True, he had nothing to lose by telling this man he was part of the True fellowship. After all, Silas Fenwick was most likely about to die.

'Hm, now that's far more amenable. It's quite simple, Mr Heron, I'd like to know about trees. Presuming you have a similarly true understanding of them as your friend Kate, that is?'

There was the word again. He'd not been mistaken.

'The answer is yes,' replied Sam. 'If, by that, you mean to know whether I am a member of the ancient order of the True.'

Kate's jaw fell open, and Silas, who obviously hadn't for a moment believed that this unexpected visitor would have any connection with the True, seemed to almost drop his guard for a moment.

'I see. Unexpected … and enlightening, I must admit. And, well, perhaps you *can* help then. No point beating about the bush, I would simply like to know if you would be willing to share with me the knowledge of how to read trees?'

Covetous.

Ah, so that was it. The man knew about the possibility of tree reading in theory but hadn't mastered it in practice. Interesting.

'Well,' said Sam, sensing the hidden desperation behind the question, 'I'm sure you can see the problem with that request.'

He looked at Kate, who had fixed him with wide unblinking eyes.

'Mhm, mhm, I see your point,' replied Silas.

'I'm glad you see my point,' said Sam, with a smile that was not reflected in the rest of his face, 'as you *will* be paying for the blood you've already spilled, and if you draw even one more drop, I promise faithfully that you will die where you stand. I suggest you let her go.'

'Oh, come now, please don't insult me with threats you can't follow through with,' said Silas, with a barely disguised sneer. 'Let's be realistic, shall we? There's really no need for unpleasantness. If you agree to help me with what I want, I will let her go. Unharmed, on my honour.' He slightly inclined his head, alluding to the bow he would have made had he not been indisposed.

Cruel.

'Honour? My word, so you hold a lady hostage with a knife and yet believe you are an honourable man? How the world has changed,' said Sam. Then, fixing Silas with an unwavering stare, added slowly, 'I do not see an honourable man. I see a

288

coward.'

The sneer left Silas's face as the insult punched him in the guts. Sam could feel the man's dawning realisation that he had to change his tactics if he was to come away from this encounter with anything he wanted. He waited for a response.

'Looking at it from my point of view,' Silas said, 'I'm sure you'll see that, once I let her go, I no longer have any leverage to persuade you to assist me. However,' he shifted his attention to Kate, 'I really never had any intention of hurting you. I'm sorry, this has gone too far, I can see that now. Perhaps we could start again?'

He took the blade slowly away from Kate's neck and released his grip on her. As she pulled away and fled towards Sam, Sam quickly retrieved his own knife from the floor and motioned Kate to go behind him.

Silas slowly and deliberately put away his knife, then showed himself to be unarmed.

'Look, no harm done.' He pulled out one of the kitchen table chairs and sat down. 'Could we not just sit calmly and discuss the incredible link we all have? Really, Kate, isn't this what Archie wanted? For people to join together to help the True cause?'

Manipulative.

'No harm?! You are a *maniac*,' Kate screamed at him from by Sam's side. 'For all I know you would have killed me if Sam hadn't turned up. And don't you *dare* bring Archie into this. You were plain rude to him after his lecture. I don't know what changed your mind and brought you to my door, but you're not welcome. You never have been. And what would you know or care about the True cause?'

Ever since he walked into the kitchen, Sam had been focused on Silas Fenwick. His senses were on high alert and he'd found himself becoming acutely aware of this man. Frayne had been right. He was somehow reading this man's heart, soul, mind — he wasn't sure which. He couldn't read detail, as he had with Joe last night. Perhaps he needed a physical connection for that? It was more like just getting a strong impression of someone, but more intensely.

Sam didn't like what he sensed. He was sure that Silas had no qualms about the possibility of killing Kate, and he had the impression that killing was not new to him. This man was determined to get exactly what he wanted, no matter what. He was dangerous. He was specifically dangerous to Kate. It was obvious that once Sam left for his own time, he could not protect her, so he would have to take Silas Fenwick out of Kate's life. Did people still fight in this time? He'd have to find out.

'I'm sure you won't be surprised to hear that I am not well-disposed to sharing any knowledge of any kind with you, Mr Fenwick. However, I'm also conscious of the fact that you are probably not a man to walk away from something you've set your mind to — at least without some encouragement.'

Silas laughed and leaned back on his chair. 'Encouragement! Oh please, do explain what *encouragement* you have in mind.'

'A duel,' said Sam, to the surprise of Silas and the horror of Kate. 'You think you are an honourable man — prove it. I challenge you to a duel by small sword, always assuming you have any skill with a sword?'

'Some, as it happens,' said Silas, confidently relishing the prospect just handed to him.

'I believe I did warn you that you would have to pay for Kate's blood. I will have satisfaction for your treatment of her. If I win, you will leave her alone ever more.'

'And if you lose?'

'Then I will give you what you ask for — I will show you how to read trees.'

'What are you thinking?! You're both mad,' said Kate. 'You can't be serious. This isn't the seventeenth century, you know. Sam, you can't do this, Silas is a county champion fencer. He could hurt you. Silas, you know this is unfair. He didn't know about your skill with swords.'

They both ignored her.

'Tomorrow, by the big sycamore, at dawn, no seconds, no rules?' suggested Sam.

'To first blood?' asked Silas.

'I think you and I both know that would never do,' replied Sam.

Silas stood up and walked towards Sam. They shook hands. He then made for the door and, with a short nod, Sam stepped back and let him go.

CHAPTER TWENTY-EIGHT

THE RECORD PLAYER

Sunday, September 17th, 2000

Closing the kitchen door behind their unwanted visitor, Sam quickly turned and walked over to Kate. Not waiting for her permission, he enfolded her tightly in his arms. They clung together, his tension and her fear slowly subsiding until they both felt a level of composure beginning to return.

'Thank you,' said Kate, pulling away gently. 'I don't know what to say. You were— I think he's mad. I think you saved my life.'

'Who is he?' asked Sam, guiding Kate to a kitchen chair, then heading to the Aga to stick the kettle on. Kate always wanted tea.

Kate explained how she knew Silas from university, about Archie's lecture, and how he'd pestered her on and off for a year then tried to threaten her into telling him about tree-reading when he'd cottoned onto her farm logo being the True symbol.

'I've never felt comfortable around him, but I felt even less comfortable saying no to him visiting. And in any case, he never really gave me an option. He just came. I knew he wanted to know about reading trees, but I just didn't want to let him know that Archie had taught me, even though he obviously suspected. Perhaps I've been stupidly stubborn, but it seemed wrong to me that Silas should be part of such a wonderfully magical thing. He doesn't care about trees or nature, he only cares about himself — and weapons and metal detecting.'

'So, I'm not mistaken,' said Sam, incredulous that he'd not seen the farm sign she was talking about, 'You *are* one of the True?'

'Well, I don't know that I'd say that. Archie certainly was, and his father was my great-grandfather, but the connection with the True seems to have been kept on his side of the family and lost on mine. By rights, my second-cousin Nick should have carried on the tradition and knowledge from Archie, his grandad, but, well, sadly, it wasn't to be.'

'But you *can* read trees?' Sam persisted.

'Yes,' said Kate, with a smile. 'And I still can't quite believe it. Archie was teaching me, but then he died in May two years ago. I've been practising by myself ever since. It's a joy,' then added, 'Isn't it?'

'It is. The connection with nature, it's ... it would be hard to live without it now.'

'I'm just so shocked,' Kate continued. 'I can't get my head around the fact that you're one of the True. Really, I never even suspected. I mean, I suppose I just assumed that there were none left. Archie didn't know anyone else. And yet ... here you are.'

She frowned, as thoughts obviously began racing round her head.

'Why *are* you here? Is this more than a coincidence? I mean, did you know Archie? This seems very odd, now I think about it. Did you come here for a reason?'

Sam sat, hands clasped together, trying to decide what he could tell her, how far he should go in his explanations. Kate being one of the True changed everything for him, but just because she knew about tree reading didn't mean she knew about tree jumping. After all, it was still new to *him* and he'd been reading trees all his life.

Then he remembered something and shot up and headed towards the door.

'Joe! I forgot about Joe. He's in the barn. It was him that came to get me this morning. He'll be worried sick.'

In fact, Joe had snuggled up with the puppies for warmth and comfort and was now dozing happily amongst his furry friends. Sam carried him back to the house, where, after being assured that the man had gone and Kate was all right, he went to get himself dressed.

Kate and Sam wanted to talk but it was tricky until they could take young Joe home after the Sunday lunch. On top of that, Sam told her that he had to get back to Middle Wood to retrieve his sword before tomorrow morning.

'What?! You can't be serious — on both counts! I mean, what the hell are you doing with a sword hidden up in Middle Wood? And secondly, you're not *really* thinking of going ahead with the idea of a duel, are you? Please tell me you're joking.'

'It was agreed,' said Sam, simply. 'You needn't worry. I can handle a sword, Kate.'

'Handle a sword!' she screamed. 'You don't seem to understand, Silas is a county fencing champion. He's one of the best in the country, or so he tells me.' She walked over to where Sam was looking through a pile of picture books that Joe had brought down. She took his hand in hers and looked him directly in the eyes. 'Sam, you can't do this for me. He could kill you. Seriously. I— I couldn't bear that.'

'Oh?' said Sam, hardly daring to hope her comment meant what he thought. 'And why might that be, Mistress Kate?'

'Well,' she replied, pulling her hand away slowly. 'There would be *such* a mess and I really am busy enough, you know.' She hit out at him playfully with the dish cloth she was holding, but he caught her hand, pulled her towards him and kissed her tenderly.

'Sam loves Ka-ate. Sam loves Ka-ate,' sang Joe, as he came in the kitchen and saw them. He put another couple of books on the pile Sam had been looking at, and added, 'Kate, please can I read Eddie's Doctor Who annuals again? I'll be careful with them, honest.'

What with trying to catch up with morning tasks on the farm, cooking and eating lunch, and keeping Joe busy, the morning sped by. Kate had no choice but to take Sam over to Middle Wood after dropping off Joe at Linda's, otherwise she knew he would just have walked.

'My cousin Nick, the one I was telling you about, lives on the eastern edge of this wood,' she said as they drove closer. 'It's a shame, I don't really see him much. He's older than me so we never really spent much time together even though we live pretty close. He's a really good guy though; a woodsman, a bit of a loner. I think you'd like him.'

'Hmm, I think I might have met him last weekend,' said Sam. 'He wasn't feeling very friendly that day.'

They parked the Land Rover and set off walking through the ancient wood that they both knew so well in their own ways.

295

On the way here, Sam had been trying to decide what to tell Kate. He could just share the love of being a tree reader with her and leave it there. She would be happy with that, he was sure. But actually, the more he thought about it, the more he realised that *he* wouldn't be content with that. Now he knew she could read trees, it changed everything for him. There was hope. Before this revelation, he knew the chasm between them was just too great to negotiate; he couldn't have stayed with her. Now though, now he could fight — literally — to stay with this extraordinary woman that he loved with more intensity than he could ever have imagined loving anyone. For her, he'd fight to the death if needed, to prove that he could protect her. So it had to be all or nothing. He would share everything and hope she could somehow accept the impossible.

Kate thought he was taking her to find his sword, but he suggested showing her Joe's den as they passed. The weather was still intermittently squally, even though it wasn't as cold as this morning. They both squeezed inside the tent of branches and twigs, and Kate laughed at the empty baked bean tin and biscuit wrapper there. She thought Sam had just brought her here to show her the den, but then Sam took her hand as they sat, and started talking to her, seriously — about her record player.

She tried not to show her bemusement as he began, as she'd become used to his oddly random trains of thought. A bit like with Robbie, they usually ended up somewhere, you just needed to give it time.

'It's a bit like your record player, don't you think? Tree reading, I mean. You put that needle on a groove and the needle reads the music in the record. I don't really understand how the

296

record turns or how the sounds get there, but they are there and you can hear them if you put the needle in the right place.'

'Yes, you're right. I don't know why that hadn't struck me before,' she said, laughing at the effective comparison.

'You said to me earlier that tree reading is magical,' Sam continued. 'It is. Life is more surprisingly wondrous than most people can imagine. My mother taught me to read trees from a young age. I've done it all my life and experienced some incredible insights into the natural world and its interaction with humanity. But the True are few. I have no clue how many remain these days and you and I both know that our knowledge would be ridiculed by most people.'

'That's for sure,' said Kate. 'No-one would believe us if we told them. Archie tried and they all thought it was a laughable hoax — except Silas, it seems.'

'But you believed. Why?'

'Why? Well, I suppose because I wanted it to be true. The chance to talk to trees I've loved all my life, how could I not want that to be possible? And I liked Archie. I guess that was another reason. He made it seem real, like it should be the most natural thing in the world to do.'

Sam brought her hand up to his lips and kissed her fingers.

'You are the most incredible woman I've ever met, Kate Elliott. I want to tell you something and right now I'm praying that you like me even just a little bit as much as you liked Archie.'

Kate looked at him quizzically as Sam took out a small flat object from his pocket. He unfolded a fabric covering and inside was an embroidery. He flattened it out as well as he could on his knee.

'Goodness, that is beautiful,' said Kate. 'You didn't …?

Sam laughed. 'No, not me! My mother.'

'Oh, it's gorgeous, and it's got the True symbol. And the words?' She read them out loud: '*True Connection is Earthly Protection*'.

'Archie never mentioned the True verse to you?'

'No. Is it more than this short sentence then?'

Sam recited the verse for her.

'Wow, this gets more and more interesting. And why does it have the date 1700 on it? Is that significant for the True?'

'Er, no,' said Sam, taking in a deep breath. 'It's the date she embroidered it.'

Kate didn't know whether to be perplexed or amused. She plumped for both at the same time.

'Um, right. Well, I'm sure there's something I should understand in what you've just said, but I'm afraid I don't. What do you mean?'

'I mean for you to know the truth, Kate. I need you to believe the impossible, just like you did when Archie told you that he could read trees. The truth is that my mother, Eleanor, was born in 1680 and I was born here in Coquetdale in 1701.'

Kate laughed. 'Right, OK. If you say so. And what does that really mean? Does the True have a different calendar system?'

'Please Kate, please just listen to me with the same open heart and mind that you use to read the trees.' He squeezed her hand and began to explain once more. Kate, now sensing this was important to him, however mad it seemed, listened.

'The day before I met you, I was still living in the year 1725. Remember my clothes that you found so odd? They were my own clothes from that year. My sword we've come for? It was made in 1713 and was a present from my father, Sir Richard Heron of Moss Hall. I don't know if the house still stands today. The reason I seem so ignorant to you about so many things? I have no understanding of such modern objects as cars and record players — they are like magic to me.

'Kate, much to my own amazement, believe me, I travelled to this time through the trees.'

Kate's eyes widened at that but she still said nothing, just looked at him.

'I can only try to explain it by going back to your record player. Somewhere, sometime, musicians are playing instruments to make those sounds. They are not in your sitting room (believe me, I looked!), and they didn't make that music on the day you're playing the record. They are elsewhere and in another time. Imagine if you could travel there, through the record, and actually be at that concert as it was happening. Tree *jumping*, the name the True give to travelling through time via trees, is a lot like that. You just have to think of your mind as the needle, the tree rings as the groove, and the stories of the trees — history — as the music.

'Think about what it feels like to read a tree, Kate. You are almost part of the tree, aren't you? Well, if you let your mind go, you can fall into the time that you're reading. It's a bit frightening, I admit, and I really don't know how it happens, no more than I understand how the musicians come to be captured in a black plate, but can you perhaps see that this is just a small stretch further than the reality of reading trees? Magical, yes, but not impossible.'

He stopped and waited.

Kate was at a loss as to what to think. It was an immense

concept. Her mind, though, was ignoring the big picture as being too difficult for the moment and going for the nitty gritty. She sat quietly, thinking through what Sam had said, before replying.

'Ok, say I believe you — which I don't know yet — what you've said doesn't explain how you've moved from the past to the future. How can I read the future of a tree? There are no tree rings formed for the future.'

'No, you're right,' said Sam. 'Jumping to the future is a bit more difficult than moving back in some ways.'

He explained the idea of future wood as well as he could and told Kate about his mother's disappearance and her oak pendant.

'I thought I knew where she got the future wood from and so I was expecting to jump to May 1st. I've no idea how she came by future wood from September 3rd, the day I arrived. Perhaps *she* jumped to May using Fred's wood and the future wood she left for me was from someone else. I just don't know.'

'So, let me get this straight. Your forty-three-year old mother, Eleanor, who you haven't seen for almost two years and who you suspected must be dead (but now you're not sure) *might* have been here in 2000 since May 1st, but she might not. She might not have come here at all. You simply don't know, but that's why you're here. Oh, and she probably travelled through time through the trees to get here from 1723 when she thought you were about to die after a sword injury.'

'Mhm, that's about right,' said Sam. 'I know, it all sounds preposterous. Ah, but wait. I can prove one bit.' He started to pull at his shirt and lifted it to show her the ugly scar on his side.

300

'This is what nearly killed me. It probably should have.'

Kate reached over and tenderly touched the raised flesh. That had been a significant wound.

She sat back, the middle finger of her left hand unconsciously tracing the contour of her lips. Sam knew she did this when she was thinking things through.

'And you really haven't a clue where to look for her?' she said, eventually.

'No.'

'Oh, my God, if she's here she must be terrified,' said Kate, not really realising at first what this sympathetic thought meant. Sam, however, didn't miss it.

'You— you believe me?'

Kate looked at him and thought about the peculiar situation she was in. She was in a child's woodland den on a mizzly September afternoon in Middle Wood with a man who had turned up out of nowhere. She had now found out that he could read trees and, more than that, swore he was a time traveller. Things couldn't really have been stranger.

Except, they could. The weirdest thing of all was something that she could no longer ignore; she was falling in love with this man.

She could hear Joe's voice in her head (Kate loves Sa-am) and she started laughing. The laughter filled her head, her lungs and her heart, and spilled over as tears in her eyes. She could see that Sam was unsure as to whether this was good or bad, but she couldn't help that right now. Right now, she just had to laugh. It wasn't long before Sam succumbed to the infection and started laughing along with her. They cried with laughter at the sight of each other and it was a good few minutes before

301

either of them could speak.

In the end, still slightly breathless, Kate answered Sam's question.

'When we first came in here, you said that you were praying that I liked you even a little bit as much as I liked Archie.' She reached over and touched his cheek. 'Mr Heron, I think you should know that I liked Archie very much. But you … I'm afraid I think I *love* you.'

CHAPTER TWENTY-NINE

EN GARDE

Monday, September 18th, 2000

Kate had reluctantly agreed that, if Silas turned up, she would stay in the farmhouse during the duel. Sam had argued that any swordsman worth his salt would use whatever was around to gain an advantage. It wasn't safe for her to be near them. She still didn't really believe this could be happening, but Sam had retrieved his sword from Middle Wood and was more than willing to take on Silas despite her warnings.

They had talked and talked last night, learning a little about each other's lives, though Sam did most of the talking in the end, since, whilst she believed him in her heart, Kate still couldn't quite make her head accept his assertion of being from 1725. The historian in her had so many questions, but she forced these aside, choosing instead to find out about Sam's personal life. Who was this man that she'd taken to her heart and accepted at Cloudy so readily? In the end they parted around midnight, Sam going back to the barn despite Kate's invitation for him to stay. This time, though, it didn't feel like a rejection. They both knew they needed some time alone to let the revelations of the day sink in.

Kate was at the kitchen sink well before the sun rose, mug of tea in hand. Sycamore Gap was still shrouded in darkness. She paced the kitchen, praying Silas wouldn't turn up. There were bandages and medical supplies on the kitchen table. It's all she could think of to prepare. There was no-one she could get help from. She couldn't call the police without getting Sam in trouble too, her brother was too far away, Nick didn't have a phone, and Robbie would be no help at all.

At twenty past six she heard a car. Christ, he'd really come. She kept her eyes directed at the Lord of the March.

It was a still day and as the blackness began to lift from Cloudberry Farm, she could see that a light mist hung in patches in the valley. It was the kind that would probably burn off quickly to leave a pleasant day. But this was not a pleasant day.

In the twilight she spotted Silas's grey shadowy figure approaching the foot of the tree. He was carrying a long hold-all which he placed on the ground before walking around the tree and checking out the scene of action. He then took out his sword and began to practice squatting and lunging. Kate's heart sank. He was taking this seriously.

As the first diffuse ray of sunlight struck the very top of the sycamore, she saw Sam walk slowly across the field. He was wrapped in his big cloak and didn't appear to be carrying anything. Perhaps he'd seen sense and was going to stop this?

The morning rays slowly crept a little further down the tree canopy and the day's new sky began to offer an unsuitably beautiful canvas of pinks and oranges streaked with high-flying grey clouds.

She watched as the two men met, shook hands and spoke for a moment, then parted. But this wasn't an agreement to stop the duel. After a few steps, Sam took off his cloak and she could see that he had dressed in his own clothes and leather boots. His sword was at his side. He was a similar height to Silas but a heavier build. He turned to face Silas, who stood ready, and drew his sword. The stage was set. The sun's rays now seemed to be moving more quickly down the sycamore. Almost there. And… lights! Action.

Kate's mouth went dry as the first bright sound of steel on steel sliced its way across the field to the farmhouse.

Silas had adopted a classic fencing pose, side on to Sam, with his left arm elegantly raised behind him and knees bent. He was sure he looked every inch the expert that he was, especially when compared with Sam, who had simply raised his right sword arm in readiness, but otherwise seemed unprepared and unfocused.

Silas lightly grazed down the side of Sam's blade before making his first testing lunge towards him. This was going to be so easy! Poor fool. What a mistake to call him out in this way. Of all the people he could have picked, Sam ended up with the county fencing champion. He almost felt sorry for him. He didn't know where he'd learned to fence, but if he'd been any good Silas was pretty sure he would have come up against him by now. He parried a pathetically slow attack and offered a riposte to make the farm boy jump. Farm boy *did* jump, and faster than Silas had expected, so that he quickly found himself parrying a very creditable lunge. They circled each other, beating each other's blades before Sam again attacked with a speed that shocked Silas into congratulating himself less and concentrating more. That was fine by him. He preferred a

305

worthy opponent as it brought the best out in him. Perhaps this would be a good fight instead of the boring walkover he imagined. Silas began to focus more, and within the next minute he'd drawn first blood—a slash on Sam's left upper arm. Ah, that felt good. This was becoming a proper duel; a real sword fight with a real purpose. Club fencing was going to seem very tame after this.

The next few minutes were physically and mentally intense as the pair attacked and counter-attacked. This was longer by far than any club fight and, fit as he was, Silas was starting to tire. He decided it was time to stop playing and to finish it. He upped the ferocity of his attack, looking for a strike that would force Sam to cede. He didn't find it. Instead he found that every time he redoubled his efforts, Sam was right there with him. It was then that an amount of panic started to set in. It was as if Sam was just waiting. Here he was, throwing everything he had at this nobody, but he wasn't falling.

And then he felt it. Sam's blade sliced through the skin on his jawline. His left hand automatically reached up to his face which he could feel was slippery with blood. All remaining fencing etiquette went out of the window. He was now fighting for his life, or rather for the death of Sam Heron. So what if that meant he lost his potential tree reading teacher, with him out of the way he would force Kate to play ball. This man had lived long enough.

As soon as Sam saw his blade open Silas's face, he immediately knew that this man was Herbert Wells. How he got to 1725 if he couldn't even read trees, he had no clue, but this was most definitely who he was fighting. Of course, Silas didn't know they'd met before. It hadn't happened for him yet. And perhaps it didn't have to, thought Sam. This man was trouble and would certainly be better off dead. He had to admit that he'd fought well, but he was no warrior and he had him back-footed now. It would be a simple enough matter to finish it. The world didn't need men like Silas 'Herbert Wells' Fenwick.

Neither of them heard Kate. They were engrossed in each other and the fight.

She had ear defenders on and, about twenty feet away from them, she fired her shot gun into the air.

'Stop it. Stop. Now,' she yelled. 'You're going to kill each other.'

It had the desired effect.

She levelled the gun at Silas.

'Drop the sword.' Then looking over at Sam, said, 'And you, Sam. Christ Almighty, look at the state of you both. That's enough. Now, you,' waving her gun at Silas, 'pick up your gear and walk in front of me. Sam, with me.'

Both men were tired and bleeding. They walked slowly back to the farmhouse kitchen, where Kate gave the gun to Sam and told him to keep it trained on Silas while she did what she could for his face. Silas silently let her tend him and took the painkillers she offered him. When she was finished, he got up and made for the door, but turned on the threshold.

'You've made a mistake in making me an enemy. Believe me, you will both wish you'd helped me. And I *will* find out about Moss Hall. Funny, but the connection didn't strike me until this morning. Missing one of your little group, are you? Well, I know where she is and I'm sure the poor deluded soul would love a friendly visitor.'

307

With that, he left the kitchen.

'What the heck was *that* all about?' said Kate. 'Moss Hall, isn't that where you said you live … lived? Is it still standing? And what little group and missing person is he talking about?'

'I don't know, but— Kate, what if he's found my mother? Who else could it be with a connection to Moss Hall? And he called her deluded. She certainly could seem that way in this time. Damn the man, it's got to be Eleanor. He knows where she is.'

CHAPTER THIRTY

DAMSEL IN DISTRESS

Monday, September 18th, 2000

'What in God's earth has been going on here?' asked Robbie when he came into the kitchen ten minutes later on his early Monday morning visit. Kate had just started to clear up the piles of bloody swabs and cotton wool.

Robbie dropped his newspaper and a loaf of fresh bread onto the other end of the kitchen table to the carnage.

'Are you hurt? You don't seem —'

Then he noticed Sam's shirt on the floor, drenched in blood.

'Oh, hell's bells, where's Sam?'

'He's fine, we're both fine. Don't panic, I haven't murdered him. He's upstairs putting on some clean clothes.'

'What the heck's happened, Katie?'

'If I told you, you wouldn't believe me.'

'Ooh, that sounds interesting. I'll put the kettle on while you finish getting rid of the evidence!'

'If I tell you though, Robbie, this has to go *no* further. Agreed? This most definitely can *not* be one of your stories to entertain the bus passengers.' She added, 'I'm serious.' when she saw the shocked, butter-wouldn't-melt-in-his-mouth look on his face. 'It could get Sam into a lot of trouble.'

Sam came back into the kitchen as Robbie was putting three mugs of strong tea onto the newly washed and disinfected table.

'Morning, wounded soldier. I'm just about to hear the tale of you saving the day when Kate was attacked by armed robbers or some such drama,' said Robbie, smiling widely at Sam. 'Here, pass over that loaf and I'll make some toast for you both too.'

Sam picked up the bread off the newspaper— and immediately froze.

'Any time you like,' said Robbie at the other side of the table with his hand out waiting for the bread. 'Sam?'

Kate heard the concern in Robbie's voice and turned to see Sam, the blood drained from his face, staring wordlessly down at the table.

'Jesus, are you alright? Perhaps it's delayed shock?'

She made him sit down before noticing that his eyes were glued to the newspaper. Looking at it, she saw the photo of a woman and the headline, "Do you know this woman?"

'That's not—?'

'It's my mother. It's Eleanor,' said Sam. 'What does this mean? What's amnesia? Is she in a gaol?'

Kate explained that the short piece meant that the woman was probably in hospital having suffered a head injury, and that she didn't know who she was.

'This must be what Silas was talking about. Though it doesn't mention Moss Hall. Are you sure it's her?'

'Yes,' said Sam. 'The likeness is uncanny.'

Kate smiled. She would have to explain about photographs.

'Would someone *please* tell me what's going on?' said

Robbie, straining to get a look at the picture in the paper.

'Christ, I have to go,' said Sam, suddenly getting up. 'Silas said he was going to visit her. What if he kidnaps her? If she doesn't know who she is, he might persuade her she knows him. Kate, I have to get to Newcastle. Can I take Melly?'

'Melly? No, of course not. I'll drive you there, you twerp. Don't worry, we'll go now and find her and bring her back here.'

'Stop!' said Robbie. 'I'm here too you know. Will someone please tell me what all this is about. Why is your mother in Newcastle with amnesia and what has Silas Fenwick got to do with this? He *is* that weirdo you hate, isn't he?'

'Robbie, I'm sorry, but we just don't have time to explain it all now. We have to get to Newcastle as fast as we can and bring this lady, Sam's mother, back here. Silas and Sam fought a duel and we think Silas means Eleanor harm, even though he possibly doesn't know she is his mother.'

'Oh, my days, it's like being in the middle of a soap opera. That was complete gibberish and I haven't a clue what you're talking about, but there's no way you're leaving me behind. Anyway, you can't put a woman with a head injury into your two-seater bone-rattler of a Land Rover. You'll kill her. I'll take you in Guy. My passengers will have to do without me today. I'll make it up to them.'

Sam and Kate looked at him but didn't move immediately.

'Well, come on then,' chivvied Robbie. 'We have to go and save a damsel in distress. Oh God, how exciting!'

On the way, Kate explained to Robbie about Silas threatening her and Sam saving her, and about the duel. It all seemed so improbable now she was relating it. She also told him about Sam being a tree reader since she'd confided in him about this part of her life, but she chose not to go into the time travelling. There were some things you couldn't share even with best friends without them thinking you'd completely flipped.

As the traffic increased as they got closer to the city it struck Kate that Sam would never have seen so many vehicles. She also knew that he didn't like speed and Robbie was gunning it as fast as he dared.

'How do all these cars not crash into each other going so fast?' asked Sam, in a low voice so that Robbie wouldn't hear.

'There's a lot I need to explain to you, but it's probably not the time or place. I promise I will though.'

Just then, they slowed to pay for the Tyne Tunnel.

'OK,' Kate said, 'don't panic, but we're going in a tunnel under the Tyne. It's quite safe though.'

'Under? Under the Tyne? God help us.' He clung onto the bench seat as they headed into the Tunnel, but she could see him relax his hold after a couple of minutes.

'No water,' he said. 'None.'

Kate laughed. 'No, we tend to prefer tunnels without water!'

The city itself shocked Sam even more. The high-rise blocks and the sheer number of people milling around the streets had him gaping open-mouthed out of the windows. His questions came thick and fast and Kate answered what she could, but so much was beyond his comprehension. It would take time.

Having parked up in the hospital car park, Robbie locked the bus and the three of them started walking towards the main entrance. Sam twice walked in front of moving cars, before Kate grabbed his hand on the pretence, for Robbie's sake, of acknowledging his anxiety.

At the reception, Kate explained who they were looking for. They were asked to take a seat in the waiting area. Sam was silent and awe-struck. She squeezed his hand.

'Don't worry, it's not as scary a place as it looks. They do some incredible work in hospitals now.' She knew that early eighteenth-century hospitals could be quite frightening places.

Eventually, a young man came over to them and took Sam and Kate to a small meeting room.

'So, you're looking for the amnesia patient who was in the newspaper on Saturday?' said the young man, putting a sheaf of papers on the desk and sitting down. 'Do sit down. And may I ask how you think you know her?'

'She's my mother,' replied Sam. 'I would like to see her.'

'Ah, so you can tell me her name?'

'Yes. Eleanor Heron.'

'OK, and your name please, sir?'

'Samuel Heron.'

'Mhm.' The man scribbled on one of the sheets. 'And does your mother live with you?'

'What? Er, no. She, er, she went missing some time ago and I've been looking for her.' Kate could see Sam getting frustrated.

'I see.' More scribbling.

'Look,' said Kate. 'Can you at least tell us that she's all right?'

'Well, when I last saw her, she was doing reasonably well, considering. However,' he put his pen down and looked at them both, 'I'm afraid you've had a wasted journey. Someone has already been to collect her.'

Sam jumped up off the chair.

'What? Who? Who took her?'

'I'm afraid I'm not able to give you that information, sir.'

'Not able—' said Sam. His fear tipped over into anger with this news and he took a step towards the man.

Kate grabbed his hand to stop him going any further.

'Sam, it's not his fault. They're not allowed to.' Then she asked, 'Can you tell us *when* this was? Please? It's important. Was it just recently?'

The man looked warily at Sam. 'I— er, well I guess it doesn't hurt you knowing. It was a couple of days ago, I think. Yes, Saturday. The same day that the notice was put in the paper.'

'Saturday.' That surprised them both, but at least it seemed unlikely that Silas had anything to do with it which was a huge relief.

'May I ask, was it a woman that took her?' asked Kate.

'Er, no,' said the man. 'I probably shouldn't say, but, well, by the looks of you,' he nodded at Sam, 'I'd say you need to look to your father.'

'My father is dead,' said Sam, coldly. 'I ask you, sir, please tell me what you know. She is my mother and obviously ill. She knows no-one round here, so who have you sent her off with?' Sam's tone was not exactly threatening, but the man had begun looking at the door every few seconds.

'Ok, look, I'll give you a name, but nothing, and I mean *nothing* more. Then you need to leave.' He rustled through a couple of the top papers.

'Nick Robson. Perhaps he is a relative?'

'Nick!' said Kate. 'What? Nick Robson, six-foot tall, well-built with a full beard?'

314

'Yes, yes,' said the man as he headed for the door. 'Like I said, with a striking resemblance to yourself, sir. Now, if you'll excuse me.' He shot out of the door, obviously relieved to be out of potential striking distance of Sam.

Kate looked at Sam. She hadn't seen it before, but oddly, the man was right. Stick a beard on Sam and he would be the spit of Nick. How strange. But if it *was* her cousin Nick, how the hell did he know Eleanor?

'But then I suppose when you think about it,' Kate said, 'he lives right in Middle Wood, so if that's where she came to when she ... you know, well, she could easily have come across Nick.'

They walked back to reception.

'Would your cousin not have mentioned befriending someone if they'd been here since May?' asked Sam, once Kate had explained to Robbie about their wasted journey.

'Well, now that I think about it, I've seen even less of him than usual over summer, but that doesn't necessarily mean anything. He's probably just been busy. Nick's a caring sort, though, so he could easily have helped out Eleanor.'

'Oh yes, he's a lovely bear of a man,' said Robbie. 'She's fallen on her feet if she's with him.'

Nick didn't possess a phone, so the only thing to do now was to drive back to Coquetdale and head for Nick's cabin in Middle Wood, praying that Eleanor was with him.

CHAPTER THIRTY-ONE

WAIFS AND STRAYS

Monday, September 18th, 2000

Passing through Mellerton village on the way from Newcastle to Middle Wood, Robbie stopped the bus near a police car that was parked outside the primary school.

Winding his window down he called out, 'Everything all right there, George?' Robbie knew all the local policemen. He pretty well knew everyone in the dale.

'Wotcha, Rob. One of the young lads has gone missing. We're just about to start searching for him. Little Joe. You know him, don't you? Any ideas where he might have gone? It's not the first time, of course.'

'Oh, hell. Not again. We're just headed for Middle Wood. He likes it there, so we'll keep a look out for him. I'll let you know if we find him.'

'Ta mate.'

Robbie parked up near one of the entrance paths to the wood and he, Kate and Sam detoured to check Joe's den before heading to Nick's place. Sure enough, hiding in his nest of branches with a blanket wrapped round him, a very miserable Joe was sitting with one of the *Doctor Who* annuals that he'd accidentally-on-purpose forgotten to ask Kate if he could borrow.

'So, did you remember the tin opener this time?' said Sam, as he bent his head to look inside the den.

'Sam!'

'Come on out, lad. Kate and Robbie are here too.'

Tears welled up as Joe put his book into his small backpack, and he started crying as he crawled out of the den. Kate kneeled down and hugged him tightly. Sobs racked his little body.

'It's OK, Joe. We're here.'

'I want to go home, Kate. I want to go home, but I don't know who that is.' He buried his face in her hair and clung on.

'Who?' said Kate. 'You mean "where", sweetheart. I know.' But Joe shook his head. Kate looked up at Sam. She didn't have to say anything, Sam knew what she was thinking.

'Tell you what, Joe,' said Robbie, 'why don't you come back down to the village with me and we'll go and get some cake in Mrs Johnson's. Sam and Kate are going to see Nick in the forest cabin. They can come and see us there when they're done.'

'No,' said Joe, wiping his runny nose with the back of his sleeve. 'You'll take me back to Linda's. She'll be cross with me again. Can't I stay with you, Kate? Please. I'll stay with Sam in the barn so I'm not a bother. Honest. Pleeease, Kate. I'll be really good.'

'Oh, you're not a bother. Never.' She hugged him to her again. His hurt showed on her face.

In the end, it was agreed that Robbie would go back and let the police know that Joe was safe, and Sam and Kate would take him back to Linda's after seeing Nick and see if maybe he could stay a few nights at Cloudy. Robbie and Kate knew that this latest escape would have been a final straw for Linda. Social services would have to be brought in now to urgently try to re-home Joe — not an easy prospect for a ten-year old. Despite some forced jollity to try and cheer Joe up, it was an anxious and sombre little party that parted ways on the woodland path.

It had been a very stressful day yesterday, but Nick wouldn't hear of Eleanor leaving his cabin. He was convinced she was still suffering from the head injury she'd had and he wanted to keep her safe and look after her. She would recover. He would help her. She would feel better in the wood among the trees. She always did.

She was sleeping a lot and didn't wake up until around eleven o'clock. He brought her a breakfast of blackberries with some hazelnuts he'd foraged for that morning, topped with some of his homemade yoghurt and honey from his own bees.

Nick had decided to ignore the strained emotions between them and concentrate on just getting Eleanor healthy and happy again. He made her laugh telling her about Meg's recent antics in trying to catch a red squirrel that tormented her daily. He told her of the barn owl they both loved watching and how she'd at last taken to one of the boxes they'd put up for her on the edge of the woodland a few weeks ago. He brought her a book to read, one he didn't think he'd given to her before but couldn't think why since he loved it as a boy: James Herriot's *All Creatures Great and Small*. He was certain she would like that.

He didn't know what she was thinking as she wasn't

318

speaking much, but when she came outside after breakfast and sat by the fire with the book while he was carving, he felt a bit calmer and more hopeful that she might settle with him again. It was very early days though. He knew that.

It was rare that anyone visited the cabin, but a few stray hikers did sometimes come through his plot. He usually tried to be as helpful as possible, but today he really didn't feel sociable and couldn't stop his irritation bubbling up to the surface when he saw two adults and a child heading through the clearing in his direction. Was it really that difficult to read footpath signs?

It was only when he was sure they were coming directly towards him that he stopped working to concentrate on them and realised that the woman was his cousin, Kate. Oh, bloody Nora, how did he explain Eleanor to her? He'd never mentioned her all summer, but it was too late to ask Eleanor to go in the cabin. He really liked Kate, but they were both so busy that he rarely saw her. She was a good sort, though, and actually, now he thought about it, perhaps this was a good thing. Eleanor would like Kate, and maybe a female friend would help.

He recognised the young boy too. He was often around the wood, though always ran away when Nick spotted him. Nick knew he had a little den. He was doing no harm, just enjoying the wood like he'd done himself when he was a boy. The man with them was a stranger to Nick, though he had a feeling that perhaps it was the chap that came round about a week ago looking for someone. Being so soon after Eleanor had left him, he'd not really taken much notice of him and had probably been quite rude to him now he thought about it. Nick hoped it wasn't a good friend of Kate's that he'd upset.

Eleanor was engrossed in her book and unaware of their

319

visitors until Nick called a greeting to them then turned to her and said, 'It's my cousin, Kate. You remember the sheep farmer I told you about? You OK with this?' Eleanor nodded, so he went over to welcome them.

With his back to her, he didn't see Eleanor's face as, over the next minute, her emotions changed from shy curiosity at the chance of meeting one of Nick's relatives, to confusion, and then shock.

'Kate, how lovely! To what do I owe this rare pleasure?' He gave her a big hug. 'And who've you brought along with you? I know you, young man, don't I?' he said, ruffling Joe's hair. 'You like the wood almost as much as me, don't you?' He laughed as Joe smiled but half-hid behind Kate.

'This is Joe, Nick,' said Kate. 'And this—'

She turned to introduce Sam but stopped. Sam was transfixed on the woman at the fireplace behind Nick. Kate turned to look at her. A handsome woman was sitting by the fire, book in her lap, staring at them open-mouthed as if they'd just walked out of Joe's *Doctor Who* annual.

'Is that her?' she asked Sam.

He nodded, not taking his eyes off her, but not moving either.

Nick turned to see Eleanor still sitting there, but her hand was now clasped over her mouth and tears ran down her face. She looked frightened.

'Er, this might take some explaining,' Kate was saying to Nick, but he wasn't listening. The heat of fury had immediately filled his head, and without a moment's consideration, he turned back towards Sam and landed a right fist onto his jaw. Sam wasn't prepared for it and staggered backwards under the blow.

Joe screamed and clung on to Kate, who was so shocked she said nothing.

'You bastard,' Nick shouted. 'You bloody well leave her alone. She's not coming back to you, you hear. You've done enough damage.' As Sam righted himself, Nick was preparing to throw another punch. But then Eleanor rushed over to his side.

'Nick, Nick, stop,' she said, touching his arm. 'It's not him. It's not Richard.'

Through the roar of anger raging in his head, he wasn't sure he heard her right at first, but he stopped and looked at her.

'What? Oh God, really? Not your husband?'

She was looking at Sam and now he could see that it wasn't fear in her eyes.

Eleanor then looked up at him.

'Nick, this is Sam.'

CHAPTER THIRTY-TWO

HORIZONTAL LINES

Monday, September 18th, 2000

The spell of disbelief that had rooted Sam to the spot when he first saw Eleanor by the campfire broke when he heard her voice. Ignoring Nick, he rushed forward and threw his arms around her. He held her tightly, unashamed tears of joy and relief running down his face. She was alive, she was here — against all the odds she was here, now. He'd found her. He stopped hugging her to look at her face and wiped her happy tears away from her cheeks with his hand before checking her up and down.

'You are not hurt, mother? You are well?'

'Quite well, Sam,' she replied, smiling, at which point Sam picked her up and swung her around him as he used to with Martha. They were both laughing as he carefully put her back on her feet, but then that little lost voice rang in his head, 'Again, again.' Sam's thoughts quickly turned to what he'd needed to say to Eleanor for over eighteen months. It could wait not a moment longer. He held both her hands together in his and bowed his head.

'I'm so sorry. I tried so hard to save her, but it's my fault she was taken from you. I should have died, not her. I will regret it always.' He brought their clasped hands up to his forehead for a moment. 'Can you ever forgive me?'

Eleanor gently released her hands from his and lifted Sam's face with a touch under his chin.

'I have nothing to forgive, Sam. I know you did all you could. Her death was not your fault, it was the doing of a very bitter man who I once called brother but never loved. Your efforts to save her nearly cost you your life, I was convinced they would, which is why—' She stopped, looking briefly round at the bemused faces surrounding them. 'But there is time for stories and explanations later. You're here, thanks be to God. By some miracle you made it.' She looked at him. 'And you look so… so healthy and strong … so alive!'

Sam suddenly remembered they had an audience. He turned to Kate and Joe who were both standing grinning at him.

'Kate, Joe, may I introduce Eleanor Heron, my mother.' Joe dropped Kate's hand and went and wrapped his arms around Eleanor's waist.

'Hello, Sam's mam. I've been helping Sam to find you. I drew a picture and everything.'

Eleanor was initially surprised at finding an unknown child attached to her, but quickly bent down to Joe. 'Have you indeed?! Then you're a very fine gentleman, Joe. Thank you.'

Sam could sense that Kate was holding herself back from a more effusive welcome as she shook hands with Eleanor. She was the only other one here who could even begin to see the magnitude of this meeting, or at least he assumed she was. Did Nick know, he wondered? Had he perhaps taken in Eleanor as Kate had taken him in? He'd made no mention of Eleanor when

Sam had come to the wood to ask about her a week or so ago. He wasn't even sure the man remembered him from that short meeting. Sam waited for a formal introduction to the man who'd just floored him so powerfully and unexpectedly a few minutes earlier, but rather than introducing him, Eleanor spoke directly to him, very gently, almost as if speaking to a frightened child. She touched his hand and said, 'Nick, will you—'

'No,' he said, shortly, shaking his head and looking at Eleanor as if he was scared. 'No, I can't, I— Sorry.' And with that he turned away abruptly and began to walk towards the trees without looking back.

Eleanor was choking back tears. Sam could see that she'd perhaps half-expected that reaction but it obviously still hurt her.

'Leave him to me,' Kate said to Sam. 'Can I leave Joe with you?' Eleanor automatically held out her hand for the little boy and Joe went straight to her. Looking at Eleanor, Kate asked, 'Does he know anything? I mean about …'

'Kate knows, mother,' explained Sam. 'Not the detail, but the essence.'

'Oh. You are True?'

'Well, no, not exactly,' said Kate, 'but close.' She smiled at Sam. 'And getting closer.'

'Oh, that's so wonderful. I tried so hard to explain to Nick, but he can't accept it. How could you? It's impossible. And it's more difficult than you know.' She bent her head, then looked up at Sam.

'Sam, this is not the first time I've been here. I mean, I came before you were born. Oh, I have so much to explain and apologise for.'

324

'You? Apologise!' said Sam, 'You've done nothing. What could you possibly need to apologise for?'

'You remember me telling you of the day your— er, the day Richard took Matty from me when she was but two years old?'

'Yes, you thought he'd killed her.'

'Mhm. Well, when I still believed that to be true I ran away and I came here. God forgive me, I stayed with Nick for four months. I might never have returned to my rightful time, except that — oh, please don't hate me Sam — except that I was with child... with you.'

'With me? But—' A frown furrowed Sam's brow as the unexpected news began to bounce around his head like a trapped animal.

'I loved Nick, Sam, but I didn't belong here. I was so scared. Scared to leave, scared to stay, scared that I shouldn't be here in the first place, that it was against God's will — that it was wrong. Going back seemed the right thing, the only thing, to do with a baby due.'

'What?' said Kate, shocked. 'You mean—'

Eleanor nodded slowly. 'Sam, I'm so sorry I never told you. I meant to. So many times I began, but couldn't face the possibility of you hating me. But you must know now. Your father— Richard was not your father. Nick is your father. Your life began here, in this time. I have told Nick of this, but don't think badly of him, please. Think how hard this is for him. To him, I left him one night about two weeks ago as a twenty-year-old and he thinks I had an accident and have been in hospital ever since. Whereas actually ...' She stopped talking as she looked briefly down at Joe.

Sam was speechless. He'd known there was much to

discuss, but this was completely unforeseen. He stared open-mouthed at Eleanor.

'Look,' said Kate, 'you two stay here and talk. I'll find Nick. He has a heritage he knows nothing about. It's about time he was told.' Kate squeezed Sam's arm briefly, then set off in the direction Nick had gone.

Sam, Eleanor and Joe walked back to the campfire in silence and when Eleanor sat, Sam knelt before her.

'We will talk later,' he said, quietly, 'but I want you to know this: if this man gave you four months of happiness and love, then he is already a man I respect. You said to me that I do not need your forgiveness for Martha. You need my forgiveness even less. I am born of love; that is a gift I never thought to own. If Nick can accept me, then I will welcome him as the father I never knew. You endured twenty-three years with a man you hated in order to give Martha and myself a life. You are more remarkable than I ever knew.'

Eleanor stared down at her son, tears flowing down her cheeks, her hands pressed together prayer-like in front of her lips. She nodded and gave a half-smile of relief.

'Don't cry any more,' said Joe seeing Eleanor's fresh-flowing tears. 'Look, I'll read you a story to make you happy again.'

'Hah.' Eleanor half-laughed and half-sobbed, then brushed tears away and concentrated on Joe. Sam sat down next to them.

'So, what's the story about then, Joe?' asked Eleanor.

'Oh, it's the best,' he enthused. 'It's about a doctor that has a sonic screwdriver and a tardis. And he's called The Doctor and he's a time lord and he travels through time and— Didn't

326

you watch Doctor Who on telly when you were a little girl? It's not on now, but there's lots of repeats of the old ones. I like the ones with Tom Baker in best. He's my favourite doctor cos he's got this really long scarf.'

Tom Baker! Despite all the emotions and revelations of the last few minutes, the name hit Sam like a whip lash. Tom Baker. He stared at Joe for a moment, trying to think back to what he knew about *his* Tom Baker, the tree jumper at the Covert. For a start, Sam had been almost certain that Tom Baker hadn't been his real name as he'd obviously hesitated before deciding on what to call himself. He'd said he was a doctor and had come from 2020, and Sam had guessed him to be around thirty years old. Could Joe be the future Tom Baker? Joe was ten years old now, so he would be thirty in 2020. Sam tried to scrutinize Joe's face, looking for any resemblance to the man he'd met at the Covert. He couldn't see it, but with this love of Doctor Who and Tom Baker, and now the connection (albeit very new) with himself, it *had* to be Joe, didn't it? Sam laughed at the wonderful absurdity of the situation.

Eleanor was laughing too. 'No,' she said, 'I'm afraid I missed that when I was a little girl.'

'Look, here's a picture of the tardis.' Joe opened the annual to show her. A sheet of paper fell out and Eleanor picked it up.

'And who is this attractive lady?'

'Oh, that's my mam,' said Joe, reverently, and carefully taking the picture from Eleanor, he smoothed it out on his leg.

'Sam drew her for me. I can remember her now. Linda says I can't go back to my mam though. I need another mam. I'd like a pretty one, like you.'

Nick and Kate walked back to the cabin together almost two hours later. They seemed quite serious, but Kate gave Sam a small smile as they approached the fire. Eleanor stood up — it seemed important to do so, as if a sentence was about to be passed and due reverence had to be shown to the moment.

Nick was obviously very nervous. He went straight to Eleanor, picked up her left hand and held it, keeping his eyes fixed on her fingers. He stayed like that for a moment before looking at her. No one spoke as he drank in the face of this woman that he obviously loved so much.

'So,' he said, at last. 'So you said there was another horizontal line on that F in the rock carving you made?'

Eleanor threw her hands around his neck and kissed his cheeks.

'Yes, oh yes,' she cried. He hugged her tightly, beaming, and for the second time that day, she was lifted off the ground and swung around.

Then Nick gently put her down and turned to Sam.

'I— I don't know what to say,' he said, shyly. 'Kate tells me you're a fine man. Eleanor tried to tell me that too, but I— I mean how could I know. I have a son. *You* are my *son*!'

He ruffled his hands through his hair, then, as if deciding to do something very quickly so it wouldn't hurt, strode the two paces over to Sam and clutched him in a bear hug. If he was expecting rejection, he didn't get it. The two bewildered grown men, barely twelve years difference in age, held on to each other for just a short time, but it was enough wordlessly to say what was needed: I'm willing to get to know and love you. I accept that we belong to each other. Time cannot and must not divide us. We are family.

CHAPTER THIRTY-THREE

SAMHAIN

Wednesday, September 20th to October 31st, 2000

Sam was sitting on the low stone wall by the sycamore tree, two dogs at his feet, waiting for Kate to return from taking Joe to school. The essentially unchanged lands of Coquetdale were an anchor for him in the uncertain waters he was currently navigating.

Two days had passed since Monday's extraordinary revelations, but no-one had been able to persuade Joe to go back to Linda's house. Instead, Kate and Sam had taken him back to Cloudy, where his social worker visited the next day. Sam had kept out of the way so as not to complicate matters. Any 'So who are you?' questions would have been awkward to deal with, whereas Kate had already been police-checked to allow Joe to stay overnight with her. The question of identity — his and Eleanor's — was obviously going to be an issue, but that was for another day.

Sam turned towards the house when the dogs shot off to greet the returning Land Rover. He saw Kate looking over at the Lord of the Marches and waving as she started walking over the field towards him, her dogs either side of her. Having already done a morning's work, she was wearing her baggy work overalls and had her hair tied up in a scarf. Sam smiled, thinking that in his time Kate would have been seen as an unseemly-dressed peasant in such clothes, but class, clothes and occupation meant nothing to him. This woman was extraordinary.

When she reached him, she kissed him and put her arms around his waist.

'Was he fine with going to school?' Sam asked.

'Oh yes, he's happy now he knows he's not going back to Linda's. Poor Linda. She tried so hard for him but he just never took to the family. It's sad all round.'

'But do you think he understands he's not allowed to stay with you?'

'Well, he says he does, but I have a feeling that he might just be ignoring that for the timebeing. I think we'll be in for a storm when they come to move him.'

Sam could feel the pain she was trying to hide. It wasn't only Joe that was in for a rough time. Yesterday, Kate had begged the social worker to let her keep Joe, but she'd been told that as a single woman working the long hours she does on the farm, she wouldn't be acceptable.

'Anyway, I had a thought,' said Kate. 'How about I drop by Nick's when I pick up Joe this afternoon and invite him and Eleanor for tea tomorrow? You've not really had a chance to talk since you found your mam ... and your father!'

'Well, good luck getting Eleanor in a vehicle!'

'Oh, she'll do it for you. Hell, she's done a lot more than get in a car for you, she travelled nearly three hundred years away to save you. That's devotion!'

Eleanor did make it and Sam was relieved to see her much improved. Not only had she regained some strength thanks to Nick's unwavering care and attention, but the weight of worry and fear had been lifted and it showed in her face, which was radiant and relaxed despite the car journey. Sam had never seen her looking so happy. The constant underlying anxiety that she'd tried to hide from him all his life had gone. And more than that, when they arrived she quickly whispered to him, 'I've got them back. I can read the trees again.' Sam knew that the belief she'd lost her connection to nature had been almost impossible for her to bear, so this gift was worth more than all the treasures in the world — after family.

'I've been so anxious about poor Joe,' Eleanor said as they sat in the garden. 'He was so upset. Is he still very sad?'

'Oh, he's fine when he's with Kate,' Sam said, looking over to where Joe had gone off to play with the dogs. 'He adores her,' he added, with a brief look at Kate, 'and I can see why. But he really took to you too, you know. He keeps wanting to know all about where you've been and why I'm not coming to live with you now I've found you!'

As he was laughing with the others at this child's view of the world, a thought suddenly struck him: Nick, his mother and Joe. Of course! They would make a lovely family. Was it too early to suggest something so potentially life-changing? Surely anyone who had been through what his mother and Nick had recently experienced could cope with major life changes, and as for Joe, Sam had no doubt that he'd be delighted. But would it be possible? The problem of Eleanor's identity might scupper as such plans, but it might be worth trying.

'He's very easy to love, you know,' Sam began, tentatively.

'He reminds me so much of you when you were that age' said Eleanor.

'Really?' said Nick, turning to watch Joe.

'Oh, certainly. That feistiness coupled with an endearing sweetness.' Kate grinned and pinched Sam's leg. 'And look at him with the dogs,' Eleanor continued. 'You always had a way with dogs, Sam, didn't you?'

'So, what's going to happen to him?' asked Nick.

'Well, I heard this morning that the social services have found a foster family for him,' said Kate, 'He's due to move to them on the weekend. I'll miss him so much. I'm dreading him leaving but the family are only in Rothbury and it's already been agreed that he can come and stay with us sometimes after a bit of settling in time. What he really needs, though, is a long-term foster family or, even better, someone to adopt him. It's so difficult to find anyone to take on an older child, though.'

'Would—'

'Could—'

Both Sam and Nick began to speak at once. Sam gestured for Nick to speak first, happy to have a little more time to think how to put his suggestion.

'Would they let us look after him, do you think? If he'd take us.' Nick was asking Kate, but he was looking at Eleanor.

Eleanor wasn't the only person surprised by this question but she was the only one to jump off her seat with her hands covering her mouth as a high-pitched squeal emerged before she could stop it.

'Oh, blessed birches! Do you mean it? Nick, could we? Would you?'

'Would you like to?'

'Like to? I'd love to. Oh, Nick, we could love him so well, couldn't we? Together.' Tears started pouring down her face and she gripped the hand that he held out to her.

Within a month, Nick had passed the required background checks and the couple were naively hopeful that Nick could adopt Joe without bringing Eleanor into the official process. However, the first meeting with the adoption service made it clear that Eleanor's presence in Nick's life made that plan impossible. Nobody was able to tell them how a woman with amnesia and no memory of anything beyond knowing Nick since May 1st, 2000 — the only story that seemed vaguely plausible — could prove her identity to the satisfaction of the authorities and the adoption agency.

But, on 31st October, a glimmer of hope sparkled. Despite everyone hoping that Joe might settle even for a short while, he was already causing problems with the new foster family. He'd given them a week's grace then he'd begun to run away. He'd turned up at Nick and Eleanor's three times, twice having 'borrowed' the foster father's bike and cycled all the way from Rothbury to Middle Wood (which was much closer than Cloudberry Farm), and the third time having walked, since the bike had been locked up. It wasn't the foster mum who came to pick him up this last time, it was his social worker. Three hours later, she left. Without Joe.

Later that evening, Sam and Kate arrived at the woodland cabin. They'd all been invited to celebrate Joe being allowed to stay for the night. The social worker had promised nothing but she'd suggested more discussions in the days to come. It seemed that the chance of finding Joe somewhere he really might settle could, in the end, work a little bit of magic.

'Sam! Kate!' Joe ran towards them as they walked into the clearing that was lit by the fire and the friendly twinkle of lamps in the nearby trees. 'She let me stay 'cos I told her I would only live here or at Cloudy.'

Sam laughed. 'You're a man who knows his mind, young Joe. That's excellent news. Nick and Eleanor will be very pleased to have you here.'

'They are,' said Joe. 'I told Jenny, that's my social worker, that I'd worked it all out and that if she lets me stay here with Nick and Eleanor I promise not to run away again.' He took their hands and led them back to the campfire.

Hot mulled cider in hand, each of the small party gathered around the fire and Eleanor coughed before asking to say a few words.

'Today is All Hallow's Eve or Samhain. People think that, being the start of winter, Samhain is all about death, but I would say it is *partly* about death,' then, directing her words at Joe, she added with a wink, 'but that doesn't make it frightening. Sometimes death is just about the end of one cycle and the beginning of another. So, we're here to celebrate transformation and a new period of life. And today we have particularly special news.'

Eleanor and Nick joined hands and then held their hands out to Joe as Sam and Kate looked on with fire-warmed faces.

'Today, this young man asked us if we would be his new Ma and Da.'

Joe jumped up and down shouting, 'Yes, yes, yes.' There

were smiles all round, though Sam could feel a slight shiver of anxiety run through Kate.

'Joe, we can never take the place of your mam, nor would we want to, but we would be honoured to be your parents if we're permitted. We will do all we can do make it happen, but there's still a long way to go and we can't promise you, you understand that?'

'I've going to have the prettiest mam and the strongest dad,' he yelled. Then, bounding over to see Sam, he added, 'and the best ever big brother.' Sam picked him up and turned him upside down to his utter delight. Eventually righted, he went and hugged Kate too, pulling Kate down so he could whisper, not very quietly, in her ear.

'I know who home is now.' As he left her, his cheeks were wet with her tears.

Once Joe had calmed down, Eleanor began to speak at the fireside once more.

'Samhain is the start of winter and darkness after a period of light and fruitfulness. It's like the moment you drift off to sleep, knowing that the sleep you'll have will leave you refreshed and ready for life again. We all need rest. The earth and all of nature needs it too.

'At this point of moving from waking to sleep, light to darkness or, if you prefer, life to death, we are in a twilight zone where the everyday normalities of life are no longer at the forefront of our mind and we have space and time for those who have gone before us — our ancestors. It doesn't matter if they left us yesterday or many years ago; they are always with us. So, while we never forget them, tonight more than any other night, we remember them and cherish them.'

She saluted the flames with her cup of cider.

'I remember my darling daughter, Matty, and my mother.' She drank, then, after a moment's reflection, looked to Nick.

'I drink to Archie — more of a father than a grandfather to me. I miss you Archie.' He looked down at Joe. 'Do you want to say anything Joe?'

'Can't,' he said, shaking his head.

Kate drank to her parents and then it was Sam's turn.

'To Matty — I'm sorry Twiggle. I love you always. To Frayne — thank you, and may God be with you. And to Hawk — here's to you, my dear friend.' He took a mouthful of whisky which he sprayed onto the fire for Hawk as he'd promised to do 275 years ago. A pang of guilt twinged as he thought of his friend and their pact to be there for each other until they reached ninety years old. He couldn't have been further away if he'd tried.

YEW

Old bones of departed souls sleep by grey stones steeped in hope, cradled by the understanding touch of an ancient life.

I am that ancient life. I am yew.

For the two thousand or more years before the church came to stand beside me, mankind looked to me to protect them from harmful spirits and give them faith in resurrection. To this day, in me they see that life can persevere against the challenges of time.

I rarely grow very tall, but I am firmly rooted in life and my girth grows strong and broad with age. To remain vital I can lose my early growth and become hollow, but this doesn't mean I lose my heart — transformation is the way I bend against the buffeting of strong winds and cope with the trials of passing years. I can reincarnate. I can go on. And on. Indefinitely.

I knew your ancestors. They lie with me. They are safe. I will know you too. I will cherish you in death. In life, however, you should treat me with care. I am toxic — my flat needle-like leaves (tolerated only by the caterpillar of the satin beauty moth), my scaly papery bark, my hard close-grained wood appreciated by musical instrument and weapon makers, and especially my black seed held in a ruby red berry cup — all are poisonous. The red fruit of our females is the only part of me that is not deadly. Blackbirds, thrushes, greenfinches are all very aware of this, as are squirrels and dormice. What an autumnal feast I offer these knowing creatures.

The wisdom of the animal kingdom is passed down through the generations. I, on the other hand, have learned from the air and the earth, from the rain and the sun, from night and day, summer and winter. Come, sit with me, and let me tell you tales of ages past.

CHAPTER THIRTY-FOUR

UNFINISHED BUSINESS

Friday, November 3rd, 2000

It's funny how even the simplest things in life are imbued with different shades of meaning when you've been brought up nearly three hundred years apart. But Kate and Sam loved learning and teaching each other about their hopes and dreams, expectations and understanding of life. To Sam's never-ending surprise, Kate already knew huge amounts about the era he grew up in, but that didn't stop her asking every question under the sun. In turn, Kate took great delight in introducing Sam to all aspects of twenty-first century living, from the mundane to the seemingly magical. It would take time for him to feel at home in this century, perhaps it might never fully happen, but there were plenty of reasons why he'd made the decision to stay; mainly Kate, of course, but also Eleanor, and, unexpectedly, Nick.

It was just past dawn and Sam was awake, thinking yet again about the incredible turn his life had taken. Kate lay in his arms. The long slender legs that he'd tried so hard not to stare at when he first arrived at Cloudberry were now entwined with his. For him, time was no longer playing by generally-accepted rules, but despite this, it was hard to believe that it was just a few weeks since he'd jumped into the future and, accidentally, into Kate's life. What had begun with the sharing of hard work on the farm had changed into friendship and trust of the kind he'd never experienced with a woman before. And now, she was quite simply everything to him. He loved her beyond doubt or understanding.

Could you fall in love in such a short space of time? So much had happened to him in the last eight weeks that he had, at first, questioned whether his feelings were simply due to the extraordinary circumstances he found himself in. But he knew that wasn't the case. Kate was meant for him, and him alone; he was certain of it. Her soul spoke to him, sang to him. He was so alive to her presence that he swore he could sometimes see her bright spirit smiling, laughing and dancing around her. And the joy of it was that her spirit was smiling at *him*. The connection between them was at a level neither could really fathom as it had not happened to either of them before. But it was undeniable. He'd travelled through time itself to find the love of his life and, now he'd found her, he could not and would not let time separate them again. Ever.

'You know, really, you should be ashamed of yourself,' Sam said. 'I mean, you've just made love to a man who's old enough to be your great, great grandfather!'

'And the rest! And you're on your bike as soon as you start looking your age, I can tell you now.'

Kate screamed as he began tickling her mercilessly.

Kate had known for a few weeks that she would have to broach the subject of Sam's friend, Hawk. She knew that his friend and the piper who was the namesake of her favourite coffee shop in Durham were one and the same person. With a name like Sparrowhawk, there wasn't much room for mistaken identity. Should she tell Sam, given the piper's tragic ending? In the end, she felt she had to. She couldn't keep such a secret from him.

Kate persuaded Sam to take a day trip to Durham with her so she could show him her old haunts. She would let him see the picture in the cafe and, assuming it really was Hawk, explain what was known of his friend's life and death. Today was the day.

She knew that going to Durham was a bit of a risk given that Silas Fenwick lived there — they would have to walk right past his armoury — but she couldn't avoid Durham for the rest of her life, and anyway, what were the chances of bumping into him or of him seeing them pass his shop?

They went first to the Piper's End cafe. She was in luck; her old table by the wall was free, alongside the picture that was the reason for the visit. She ordered tea. Appropriately, the music of Kathryn Tickell was playing in the background.

Kate's heart was racing as she motioned Sam towards the little table. He didn't notice the image at first, but then as they sat down, his eyes caught the picture. He did a classic double take, then stared with his mouth open.

'I've always loved this picture,' she said. 'I assume from your face that this *is* your friend, Hawk? I'm sorry for the shock, but I had to be sure first, I mean, before I tell you what I know about him.'

Sam's eyes were fixed on the framed print of his friend.

'I don't understand,' he said. 'Yes, that's Hawk. But why? Why is his likeness on the wall here? Are the people here family?'

Kate laughed. 'I doubt it. The thing is, well, I can tell you quite a bit about your friend. Alex Sparrowhawk became very well known in the north. He was quite famous, or perhaps infamous would be a better word.'

'Hawk! What for? Was it his piping? It must be.'

This was going to be difficult.

'Well, yes. He was mostly known for making a lot of people very happy with his music. He looks like such a character,' she said, aware that she was putting off the moment. 'I wish I'd known him and heard him play. Was he really as good a piper as the history books say?'

Sam smiled. 'He's brilliant. I've never seen anyone's fingers fly so fast, and...' He stopped. 'Infamous, you said. Infamous how? Oh God, what's he done?'

'Are you sure you want to know?'

'What happened to him, Kate?' asked Sam, obviously fearing the worst.

She explained that he'd lived to a good age, into his late seventies if reports were correct, but that he'd probably died here in the building they were currently in.

'This was a house of correction. I'm afraid he stole a horse when he was in his mid-seventies and was brought here. Sadly that's the last we know of him. The records were lost, but it's thought that he never made it out of here alive. I'm so sorry, Sam. No one knows where he was buried.'

Sam was silent for a few minutes. Kate waited for the reaction.

'I wasn't there for him,' he said, quietly, after a short while. 'I've let him down. We always watched out for each other. He should've lived till he was ninety. That was the deal. But I broke it, Kate. I wasn't there.'

Sam stared at the picture of his dearest friend that he'd left behind just a few short weeks ago, age twenty-four.

Kate reached across the table and held his hands in hers. But Sam stood up abruptly. She'd never seen his face looking so severe and cold since her brush with Silas in the farmhouse kitchen. She rose.

'I'm so sorry, Sam. I shouldn't have told you. Oh, I'm an idiot. Will you forgive me? Please.'

'I have unfinished business, Kate,' he said, in a quiet, restrained voice, still staring at Hawk.

'Wh— what? What do you mean?'

Sam turned and started walking out of the cafe. Kate grabbed her things and rushed after him, distraught at the turn events had just taken.

Sam was heading towards Prebend's Bridge along the river pathway. The River Wear was flowing with silent determination, its high waters swelled by recent rains. Kate hurried to catch up with Sam. He grabbed her hand when she arrived at his side and held it tight as he rushed her along the riverbank, passing lunchtime strollers and dog walkers. When there was no-one else around, he veered off the path into the trees, pulling her with him. He pushed her against the trunk of a large beech tree, still without saying a word. Tears began pouring down Kate's face. She'd ruined everything. She'd hurt him and he was going to leave her and go back to his time. He'd obviously just realised that he shouldn't be here, with her.

'Sam, please, I'm —'

He stopped her words with a kiss. But this was not a tender

343

kiss; he kissed her as if he'd not seen her for a lifetime, or as if he might never see her again.

She clung on to him, sobbing.

'I'm sorry, Sam. Please, please don't go.'

'I have to. I'm not going to let anyone else down.'

He looked down at her, lifting her face up towards him. But she pulled away and turned to face the tree, putting her forehead against its trunk.

'You're going to leave me and go back, aren't you? Back to Hawk and— oh God, I've spoiled everything by telling you about your friend. I'm a bloody fool.' She kicked the tree.

'Leave? Leave *you*?' He sounded surprised.

He gently turned her round to face him. He was smiling, and she could see that the flare of anger that had just consumed him was gone.

'Kate, you and I are meant to be together. Time itself couldn't keep us apart, could it? Leave you? No, my little shepherdess, I'm afraid you're stuck with me for a lifetime.'

He brushed away the tears from her face, then held her close.

'Really?' she snuffled, 'So, what did you mean, then, about unfinished business? What business?'

'Silas Fenwick,' he said. 'The man is dangerous, Kate. You're not safe with him around. He might have gone away for now, but I'm certain he won't forget his humiliation. He has a black heart.'

'But there's nothing you can do, Sam. What are you planning — to walk up and kill the man? This isn't 1725. You will end up in prison for murder.'

'No, I won't kill him, even though I think I should. I just

344

want him far enough away from you that he is no threat to you anymore. It struck me back in the cafe when you told me about Hawk. I've failed too many people Kate. I know I'm not Hawk's keeper, and perhaps I couldn't have helped even if I was with him, but I could have tried. But I swear this: I will not fail *you*. We have to get rid of Silas, and I think I know how to.'

He reached into his trouser pocket and pulled out the gold guinea and the wooden coin that she knew he always kept with him. She assumed it was a link to the past life he was as yet unwilling to let go.

'Now is a good time, don't you think?' he said. 'It's the only time we really have. So, where is this armoury of his?'

CHAPTER THIRTY-FIVE

A SPIDER'S WEB

Friday, November 3rd, 2000

Durham was busy, as always, with a melee of university students, local people and tourists. Sam and Kate walked hand in hand up Saddler Street, the cobbled road that led up to the castle and cathedral. Fenwick's Armoury was about halfway up the hill. The windows were so stuffed with swords, rifles, helmets and other paraphernalia linked to warfare and ceremony that it was unlikely anyone inside could see out.

'Are you sure?' said Kate, as they lingered suspiciously on the other side of the narrow street.

'It's the only way,' Sam replied. 'I can't think of anything else — if you won't let me kill the bastard, that is. We've just got to hope he believes what I tell him, but let's face it, it's rather a large leap of faith and he doesn't trust us. It might well be a waste of time.'

Kate nodded. They had been waiting for a moment when there was no-one else in the shop and, just then, a stocky man came out looking very pleased with himself and carrying a helmet-shaped package. That was it. Fenwick's was empty.

She felt as if they were about to walk into a shop-sized

spider's web and that Silas would be sat inside waiting to pounce. The old-fashioned doorbell jangled their entrance. Kate had noticed the 'Open' sign from outside and turned it over as she shut the door. They could do without an audience.

There was so much clutter everywhere that they didn't see him at first. He was sitting at a small desk at the back of the shop watching them.

'Well, that's unexpected,' he said, coldly, not getting up, but pointedly moving a long-bladed dagger that was on his desk to within easier reach.

Sam noticed that the slash on his face had healed but left a significant fresh red scar along his jawbone; just like the scar on the face of Herbert Wells.

That stiffened his resolve. He'd have to make this good. The man would obviously reach the past, he'd seen him there with his own eyes after all, but Sam wanted to ensure that he didn't come back from the past, so *he* wanted to be the one to plan Silas's time travelling. If they could ensure he was stuck in 1725, he couldn't be a threat to Kate.

'So, have you come for a re-match, Mr Heron? If you have, I do hope you'll control your little bitch this time so she doesn't spoil our fun. I'd like to repay you for your kindness in providing me with an excellent conversation starter with the ladies.' He was stroking his scar with his thumb.

Sam bridled inwardly at the insult to Kate, but let it pass.

'I'm sure I'd enjoy that as much as you, but sadly, I'm told that duelling is frowned upon these days as ungentlemanly. Forgive me for not realising that. However, I do feel that you and I didn't get to finish our … discussion the last time we met, and I'd like to set that straight today, if that is acceptable to you.'

347

'I hardly think you've anything worthwhile to say to me. So, what is it you want from me? I have business to attend to.'

'Yes, quite right,' said Sam, 'Straight to the point. Well, to be blunt, and I do hope you take this the right way, I want to be sure that you never go anywhere near Kate ever again. I don't feel that I had a chance to make that clear at our parting the other week.'

Silas laughed. 'Hah, so you've come to threaten me to stay away. Is that it? Oh, I'm flattered that you are concerned about me. Though, of course, you should be. I must admit that I do tend to hold grudges. Perhaps you guessed that? It's very bad of me, I know, but I'm afraid I can't help it.'

He leaned back on his chair, obviously pleased to hear that he'd at least made them squirm with discomfort.

'So, surprise me, what do you have in mind this time, Mr Heron? I do so enjoy our little games.'

Sam walked purposefully towards Silas, who put his hand on the nearby dagger. Sam looked him in the eye and placed the gold coin onto the desk.

'Hmm.' Silas picked it up to inspect it. 'A William III guinea, 1695. Very nice condition indeed. Probably worth … oh, let's say £800 between friends.' He placed the coin back on the desk. 'But honestly, you don't really think you're going to buy me off with one gold coin, do you? Surely you know me better than that, eh Kate?' He looked around Sam at Kate, who was staying in the background at Sam's request. 'You and I both know that one coin doesn't make the kind of history we're interested in, now does it?'

'No, you're right again,' said Sam. 'My mistake.' He took back the guinea and dropped it in his pocket, swapping it for the wooden coin. He placed this on the desk.

'This, however, is *exactly* the kind of history that you're interested in. And this is what I'm willing to offer you in exchange for your agreement, on your honour, that you will *never* seek to hurt Kate again, nor come anywhere near her.'

Silas picked it up and turned it over and over in his hands, looking for telltale marks to explain what it was meant to be. Then he threw it back towards Sam.

'So, I suppose you're going to tell me that this counter is more than a slice of wood and worth a small fortune?' He sneered at them. 'It's not even old wood.'

'No.'

'No?'

'No, I'm not going to tell you that. For the third time today, you're right. But only partially this time. This is indeed a slice of wood. Oak to be precise.' Sam picked it up and inspected it as he held it between his thumb and forefinger.

'But I know that this wooden coin has far more value to you than my golden guinea,' he looked up at Silas, 'because this is your link to the past.'

Sam let the words sink in without saying anything. He could see that Silas wasn't sure if he was being played for a fool. He sat eyeing up Sam, trying to decide what to make of him and his wooden counter. Sam continued.

'You already know that we are part of a group of people who can read trees, the True. You've had some success with reading, I'm sure, but it's not easy, is it? Well, with this, everything becomes clearer. This offers you a direct connection to an oak tree on the east side of Faerie Hill in Coquetdale— a key, if you like. If you meditate near the tree with this in your hand, it will let you in. Do it once and you'll understand how to read trees. The trees themselves are your best teacher.'

Sam put the counter back on the desk. The two men looked at each other, both trying to decide what was going through the head of the other, but one had a hidden upper hand in this regard; Sam could read him almost like a book.

Silas reached forward and picked up the counter once again.

'Why? Why give this to me now?'

'A fair question,' said Sam. 'Kate tells me that your passion lies in history and treasure hunting. My passion is for Kate. I'd rather give you what you want if it means I can ensure her safety. I believe you are not a man to let things lie. I admit that I would happily have sliced your unfeeling heart out of your body at our last meeting, indeed I would have preferred that, but sadly that was not to be. Kate won't allow it. This is my backup plan for protecting my own.'

He could feel the acceptance beginning to seep through the man; the rising excitement at what Sam might be offering him — a key to reading trees, a key to his longed-for treasure hoards.

Sam was fairly sure he'd succeeded so far. Now for the more difficult part. He had to get Silas to believe that he could go back in time. He knew himself that just reading trees wouldn't give you the insight to this possibility. Time travel is not something you'd even consider unless you were told about it. You don't look for things that don't exist.

'Before I have your answer, though,' Sam continued, 'I'm going to share something else with you. This is part of the True legacy that I believe you're unaware of. You said this wooden counter is not old. You're wrong. It's about 300 years old. I'm

350

sure you remember the small sword I fought you with, and my dirk you commented on? And when we duelled, do you remember mocking me about the period clothes I wore? And the gold coin I just showed you …' He took it out of his pocket again and laid it on the desk. 'Well, they all have something in common with that piece of wood. They're all roughly the same age, or older.' He paused for a moment. 'As am I. I was born in 1701.'

Sam stood and waited as Silas looked at him stony faced. No emotion registered on his face, but Sam could feel anger start to rise from him like invisible steam. He couldn't lose him now. He forged ahead.

'Kate told me that you are a skilled researcher, and by now you will have looked into Moss Hall. I mistakenly mentioned the name of my home to you and you connected this with Eleanor, the lady in hospital. Am I right?'

'Moss Hall in Coquetdale no longer exists,' he barked. 'One Samuel Heron, son of Sir Richard Heron, lived there, as did an Eleanor and others. They all died in the early eighteenth century. But you obviously know all this. So what? Is this the link back to the True, and you take names of past members?'

Sam could see that Silas couldn't help but be interested.

'No, sir, we didn't take the names of those people, Eleanor and I *are* those people.

Kate and Sam were in the armoury for well over an hour. In the end, they were fairly sure that Silas had believed all they said, albeit with the natural reticence that was to be expected until it was proven to him through personal experience. Certainly they had departed without the wooden coin *and* the gold one too, since Silas wasn't going to let that one pass.

'It's funny how we can believe the most extraordinary things if we really want to, isn't it?' Kate observed, as they headed back to the Land Rover.

'So, do you think it'll work? Will he be able to get back to 1st May 1725 through that wood?'

'I don't know why it wouldn't work. He obviously has the rudiments of tree reading, he's just not very good at it. The counter should take him to near the time I took that branch from the oak tree. I suppose that since I didn't see him at the Covert that night, it's possible the jumping might have knocked him out for a while. It seems to affect everyone differently. Frayne's friend, Fred, apparently moved in and out of consciousness for a good few hours. And, as you know, the last time mother tried it, her mind shut down for days. It's not without risks.'

'So, we just have to hope he doesn't somehow come across another tree jumping member of the True before he takes the plunge, so that he never finds out about the need for future wood to get back home.'

'That's the plan,' replied Sam. 'Then you won't have to worry about him again. He'll soon be long dead.'

CHAPTER THIRTY-SIX

ARBOREAL SCRIBE

Friday, November 3rd, 2000

On the way home from Durham, just before they reached Rothbury, Sam noticed a sign for Horseshoe Priory. He'd mentioned Frayne fondly to Kate when he explained how he'd learned about tree jumping and about meeting Silas in his guise as Herbert Wells. He'd told her about Frayne trying to help him and Alex when they were arrested, and he'd described the Every Tree in great detail, much to her delight.

'I'm sure the old place will be a complete ruin by now, but it's such a beautiful position and the woodlands around it should be stunning after all this time. Could we take a quick look?'

'Oh, of course, you won't know, will you?' said Kate, turning down the track towards the priory.

'I won't know what?'

'You'll see!'

Parking the car, they set off on foot down a steep path flanked by woodland with jagged rocks to their left. Kate was obviously relishing the surprise that Sam had in store, and her face was aglow with almost childlike pleasure.

They turned the last corner and looked down towards the river as it negotiated the tight bends along this section of its course. Horseshoe Priory stood waiting for them, but this was most certainly not the derelict ruin that Sam had expected. Tender loving care, great skill, and no doubt a lot of money, had brought the old building back to life. No longer did it have to apologise for its dirty face, someone had taken a cloth to it and no mistake. It sat majestically yet quietly amongst the trees without making a fuss about its makeover, knowing that it was amongst beauty of a mature, natural and lasting kind.

'I can hardly believe it. It's like a new building. Frayne would be so happy to see this. And his trees … he planted most of these by himself. Isn't it magnificent woodland?' Sam looked around the picturesque site, drinking it in and struggling to match it with what he'd seen just a few weeks earlier.

'Yes, it's a gorgeous spot. I used to come here quite often when I was at Durham. You pass right by on the way to Cloudy, as you can see. The building was apparently left derelict after there was a fire in one of the smaller buildings in the early eighteenth century. I can't remember what happened to it after that, but then in the mid-nineteenth century the owners decided to renovate it. It's beautiful, isn't it? English Heritage owns it now, so it's run by a charity.'

'Frayne would have approved.'

Sam looked around for the little hospital, but there was no sign of it. Kate suggested they ask one of the volunteer guides in the priory building.

'Ah no, you'll not find that. They reckon that's where the fire started back in May 1725, so the building was completely destroyed. Of course, the famous priory treasure was found in

354

the ruins of that section. The building was just over there.' He pointed to a large area of grass just before the now mature oak grove that Sam remembered so well.

'Given the stash of gold and silver coins, it's thought there was a benefactor behind the priory, but after the fire he disappeared, as did the priest in charge, Father Frayne. Perhaps they were caught in the blaze. You know, they do say that there is the ghost of a priest in black robes that wanders through the woods and along the riverbanks. But I've never seen him.'

Sam went suddenly cold.

'May, you say. Do you know the exact date of the fire?'

The volunteer seemed pleased to be able to show off the knowledge he had about the place.

'Oh aye. May 2nd 1725, according to the records.'

The blood drained from Sam's face. He rushed outside. Kate thanked the guide, then quickly followed after him. She saw Sam striding over to the oak grove and went to sit by him on a low branch.

'Oh my God, Kate. What have I done?'

'I— I don't know, Sam. What have you done? What's happened?'

'I think I've just sent Frayne to his death.'

He explained that May 2nd was the date he last saw Frayne, and that he'd left him in the company of Herbert Wells. Silas.

'He has to have set the fire, Kate. It's too much of a coincidence. I've as good as killed Frayne myself by sending Silas back to that date.'

He took hold of Kate's right hand and held it to his face, then kissed her palm.

'I am frightened,' he said, his eyes closed tightly, as if he

355

was in pain.

'Frightened of what? Sam, what's wrong?'

'I'm frightened that I love you too much. I seem to lose the things I care for. I don't want to lose you.'

'You won't lose me, Sam. Why would you lose me? There's no one else I want to share my life with. You are mine and I'm not letting you go. We agreed, didn't we? We travel through life together from now on.'

She held his hand in both of hers.

He turned to look at her.

'And if I have to travel back in time? Kate, I fear I can't live at peace with myself knowing what I know. In sending Silas to the past, I've more than likely just caused the death of Frayne, a man I respect and to whom I owe so much.'

'Ah.'

They sat together silently for some time.

Then Kate turned to Sam. There was a confidence and a calmness about her demeanour. She smiled at this man of hers, and make no mistake, he *was* hers. This mixed up human being who was as comfortable in a sword fight as he was caring for a child — he was hers. This handsome, 299-year-old son of a Northumbrian baronet. This shepherd to whom horses and dogs gave their unquestioning trust. This brother/son/cousin/friend who would risk life and limb for those dear to him. This man who hated cars, loved tinned beans, and made her laugh. This special soul who could read trees and who loved her … he was hers. And she was not going to lose him.

'Right, you need to think back,' she said. 'Just because there was a fire doesn't mean that he died in it. We can try and trace him through the records. I'm good at that. Think. Did he make mention of any place that was important to him or that he had links with?'

'No, his life was here, he— Ah! Of course. You're right,' he jumped up. 'Come on. Can we go to Edenbury?'

'Sure, why? What do you expect to find there after all this time?'

'Frayne had a secret cave near the castle that he grew up in. He told me how to find it in case I ever needed somewhere to hide. It's where he hid Fred.'

It was only about a thirty-minute drive to Edenbury. The village was yet another settlement located on a horseshoe bend of the Coquet River, and the ruined castle on a rocky outcrop dominated the skyline here. Kate and Sam walked down to the riverside path until they were almost directly beneath the castle.

'It should be here somewhere,' said Sam, scouring the bramble-covered banks.

'Mmm, looks to me like his secret cave isn't so secret any more.' She pointed to a trail leading up from the river just ahead of them.

Sure enough, the cave had been found and obviously quite well used, probably because it was very dry. It had a faint whiff of urine and the earth floor had been flattened by years of curious visitors. Kate was certain that, after three hundred years, the chance of anything being left undisturbed was negligible but she didn't want to say so just yet.

'A secret hole at the back, you say.'

'Yes, that's what he said. But look, there are quite a few holes but none with anything inside.' They both walked up and down the back of the cave, but after a couple of minutes, Sam started to walk out.

'This is hopeless,' he said. 'If he did get here and leave anything, it's gone.'

But the historian and archaeologist in Kate wouldn't let her give up with such a peremptory search. If they'd come all this way, they might as well do the job properly. She started feeling at the back wall and pushing bits of rock. After a few minutes, in a tight dark corner, a very rough piece of rock gave way *very* slightly under her touch. She pushed again. It moved a tiny amount.

'Sam.' She called him back in to help her.

'It might be nothing, but—'

With some more pushing and wiggling, fine loose earth finally shifted enough for the rock to move significantly. Sam then managed to pull at it, and they both held their breath as it was encouraged out of its resting place.

It was too dark to see inside, so Sam put his arm into the void to feel if there was anything inside.

His fingers touched something flat and dusty. He grasped the edge. It felt like a book, a large wrapped book. He pulled the parcel out into the gloomy light of the cave.

'Oh my god. Oh my god,' Kate repeated, barely containing her excitement. 'Is it from him? From Frayne?'

Sam unwrapped the sacking to reveal a leather-bound book. He blew the dust off it. He'd seen this before. It was Frayne's Book of the True that he kept by the Every Tree. For a three-hundred-year-old book, it was in remarkable condition. Yes, it was dirty, but it was intact.

Sam squatted down and opened the book on his knees. Kate gasped. A beautiful painting of a kingfisher shone from the page on the right, its colours still vivid. On the left-hand side a verse had been neatly written in old-fashioned script. It was a thing of beauty.

'Frayne made this,' said Sam. He was oddly proud. 'He did all the paintings, drawings and words. It's a history of the True from about 1700 to 1725. I think the last thing was a bullrush made out of cuddy's beads.' He carefully turned to the last page. But the bullrush wasn't the last painting. The last painting was a jet black beetle — not as fine a work as the previous paintings, but by a skilled hand.

'Oh, Kate, look.' Knowing the significance of the painting, Sam's face was bright with relief and happiness. 'I wonder ...' he said. 'Take the book a moment, will you?' He stood up and put his hand in the hole again. Feeling around, he came across a small rough parcel.

Kate was reading the words to the left of the beetle painting, but looked up when he showed her the contents of the dirty bundle: a small jet beetle and a golden acorn borrowed from a hungry red squirrel on the Every Tree.

'They're beautiful,' said Kate, in awe of what they'd found. 'But I think you should read the last page, Sam. It's for you.' She passed the book back, and they both sat and read the words handed down by a friend from three hundred years ago.

Sam,
It is a fortnight since our auspicious meeting. I felt an immediate kinship with you, as if you were my own son. Forgive an old man's unseemly words. I write from my heart near the end of my time.

We knew each other for a mere breath of time, but every

359

breath can change the world.

I pray to God and the trees that you are reunited with dearest Eleanor. Send to her the blessings of the forest from the old priest she once briefly knew.

If you have visited the Priory, you will know that my circumstances have changed. There was a fire. I was underground for four days, kept company in the darkness by the Every Tree and its inhabitants. Each day I worked at the blocked riverside entrance until I managed to squeeze myself from the earth. A rebirth, though it cost my old body dear.

Was I wrong to let Grace and Thomas remain with their current grief of my passing rather than watch me die once more? I pray not.

So, I came here, to see out my final days in the place I was born, the place I nurtured Fred and saw my mother, and the place that only one other soul knew about. You.

If you read this in our present time, mourn me not. I am content with the trees. You, and God, will find me by the sign of the True and the cross on an ancient ash with a split crown, downriver from here. "Blood and sap through trunk and limb run deep." I was Frayne (ash) in life and now I will be ash in death. It is fitting.

If, perchance, you read this in Fred's time, then mine are ancient words. Share them with the wisest.

This book tells of our heritage. It is your heritage. It is the heritage of us all. "Arboreal scribes write their stories, lest they be forgot." Perhaps, in fellowship with the trees, I was an arboreal scribe for a short time.

Sam, you are a True heart. I pass this book to you.

I urge you to be the ink of nature. Protect what we have and what they know.

   True connection is earthly protection
   Of forests both bygone and still yet to come.

Goodbye, my young friend.
Live with love.
Frayne

WOODLAND

Whatever our age, we are ancient. We've lived, we've learned, we've shared, we've died. It's the way things should be. It's the natural way.

We, trees, are fundamental. We, woodlands, are elemental.

We are breath. We filter and humidify. We orchestrate clouds and rain. We tether the soil.

We are food and medicine. We are shade and shelter. We are warmth. We are recreation and relaxation.

We are timekeepers and celebrations.

We are home.

We are life.

A message from the author

I'd like to thank you for buying my debut novel. I do hope you liked the story. If you did, it would be a great help to me if you would consider recommending it and especially reviewing it online.

Also, I have a personal website where I post articles and images as inspiration takes me. It is also where I will notify readers of any future books I write, and you will find some suggestions for discussion points for book clubs there too. Do get in touch by visiting me at :

www.amandamarks.co.uk

I'm also on social media (Facebook and Instagram) at:
@AndNatureWrote

Thank you very much for choosing to read 'The True'.

Amanda

PEOPLE & PLACES

Born and brought up in Durham, I love Great Britain's northern reaches, especially the wilder regions such as Northumberland. So it seemed natural to set my story in a remote area of the north as well as my native city. Much of the landscape in the book is real, though I admit to taking liberties with names, details and distances.

PEOPLE

The True, sadly, do not exist, but I'm sure there's room for such a fellowship of tree-lovers! Perhaps time travel through the trees might be off the agenda, but I'm always up for talking to a birch or learning from an oak, and keen on anything that encourages more people to care for our trees.

The Border Reivers really did exist. They were part of a fascinating piece of history in the Anglo-Scottish borders from about the late 13th century to the late 17th century. The word 'reiver' is from old English and means to pillage or rob and that is exactly what happened in those times in this lawless part of the British Isles. The 'graynes' or names of Border Reiver families live on, so today Armstrongs, Elliotts, Herons, Grahams and many more families from that region know that they come from a reiving heritage.

The character of Alex Sparrowhawk is strongly influenced by a famous/infamous Northumbrian piper called James Allan (living around 1734-1810, records vary), whose life story I was fascinated by after reading about it in an old biography.

All other characters in *The True* are fictional and any resemblance to actual people, living or dead, is coincidental.

PLACES

In Northumberland, Coquetdale (not pronounced like croquet, but more like 'coke-et') is a real dale, with the lovely Rothbury being its 'capital' or main market town. And there really is a Draag (or Drake) stone which, for many generations, was thought to cure ailments of children who were passed over its bulk. The views from here are spectacular and include the lonely lough that I mention in the 'Call of Coquetdale' (fiction) which Sam and Hawk endured.

Horseshoe Priory is fictional, though I had Brinkburn Priory near Pauperhaugh firmly in mind when writing about it. Likewise, people in the know might recognise Edenbury Castle being borrowed from Warkworth. Kilcaith and Branley castles are pure fiction and there is no Faerie Hill.

In Durham, the Piper's End café doesn't exist, though the building does and it was indeed the city's house of correction, where James Allan died after being imprisoned for stealing a horse. Fenwick's Armoury is also make-believe, though if you go up Saddler Street which leads to Durham Cathedral and Castle you will see on old shop with windows similar to those I describe. The tree sculpture on the banks of the River Wear (pronounced 'we're' not 'ware') did once exist and is something I remember fondly, though it was removed in 2001. It was made from diseased elm trees which were skilfully fashioned by artist Colin Willbourn and entitled *The Last Supper*.

ACKNOWLEDGEMENTS

I have been blessed to have lived all my life with and around people who believe that anything is possible if you put your mind to it and that, if you're doing no harm, you should have a go at everything you want to. We're all capable of far more than we think. My parents, Brian and Valerie, instilled in me a quiet belief that, whilst I might not be great at everything I put my hand to, I could probably do well enough at the things I *really* wanted to. I believe that is one of the most important gifts you can give a child. Thank you, Dad, for being the best (and my number one fan of *The True*!), and thank you Mum – though you left us years ago, you're still with me always.

Despite the old saying that we all have a book inside of us, I never imagined that I could write a novel. One day in 2013, I decided to give it a try. I had only one nugget of inspiration about a link with trees, but no story. I started writing anyway. At this point, it was a dear friend who gave me the encouragement to keep going. Without Karen Coe, I would probably have given up after the first few chapters since I struggled to believe my writing had any worth. Thank you, Karen, I wouldn't have done it without you.

Other friends and family have also given me much encouragement, often just by being there with a word at the right time in the right place. Thank you to Mo Hewitt, Jill Lound, Alison Hyde, Kecia Harris, Francesca Gilpin, Tim Leffman, Tim Butterworth, Chris Coe and Chris MacDougall.

My sister, Sam, is not a big reader, but she is always there and always willing the best for me and all the family. I gave her one small part of a chapter to read one day and she said, 'I feel like crying.' I figured that meant I'd got something right. Thanks Sam.

I'm no sheep farmer, so trying to make Kate's life as a lone hill sheep farmer seem real proved tricky. Until, that was, I spoke to old family friends, Dorothy and Ian Hedley – retired sheep farmers from Durham. Ian patiently talked me through the ins and outs of sheep farming in the hills. It was an intense ninety-minute learning curve for me, and Ian was hugely amused by all my questions. What a great conversation! Thanks so much, Ian. I hope I've used the information you gave me well, and I won't have any sheep farmers out there laughing their socks off at my descriptions.

When I finished my second draft (thanks to Sophie Playle for some helpful editing advice), I asked a group of friends to beta-read the book for me. It's a hard thing to ask as it requires honesty in the feedback given. They did a wonderful job for me, giving me heaps of their time and lots of suggestions, criticisms and encouragement. A huge thank you to: Karen Coe, Guy Marks, Brian & Maureen Hewitt, Ben Box, Sarah Cameron, Fran Speight, Geoff and Maggie Peck, Catherine Beaumont, Jane Hall and David Peek.

I want to acknowledge a writer called David 'Dippie' Dixon. He wrote a book called 'Upper Coquetdale, Northumberland: Its History, Traditions, Folk-Lore and Scenery' in 1903. This gave me lots of good information about the history of the area.

I also thank Joseph Crawhall (1821-1896), author of 'The History of James Allan the celebrated Northumbrian Piper.' I loved the story of James Allan's life, and my character Alex Sparrowhawk, whilst not intended to offer a factual representation of James Allan, was strongly influenced by what I read in this old manuscript.

We all know that phrase about not judging a book by its cover, but we also all know that we do exactly that. I talked to Deborah Vass – a local ex-English teacher turned nature artist – who offered to read *The True* then, to my delight, said she'd be keen to do the cover for me and also some drawings for my tree chapters. I couldn't have been happier as I knew I was in good hands. She'd never done a book cover previously, so was out of her comfort zone, but just look at the end result! Deborah, to say you've done me proud is an understatement. I adore the cover and the drawings, and they make a huge difference to the book. Thank you.

[Please visit Deborah's website at: **www.deborahvass.com**]

Last but not least, thank you to my family. To my husband, Guy, for unfailing support even when I ignored him night after night as I tried to get yet another few hundred words written before bedtime. Thank you for all the checking and rechecking and words of encouragement. I chose well. And to my boys, Dan and Luke. As I write, they've yet to read *The True* but that didn't stop them helping me by buying pens, 'Go Away, I'm Writing' signs, notebooks and other things to keep me going, as well as pulling their weight on cooking too. My thanks and love to all my boys.

One final thought: If this novel is enjoyed for a few hours, I'm very happy. If it encourages a few people to look at trees a bit more carefully, I'm even happier.

To learn more about trees, I recommend checking out charities such as Woodland Trust and the World Land Trust.